NECESSARY EVIL

PRAISE FOR THE MILKWEED NOVELS

'A major talent ... I can't wait to see more'
George R. R. Martin

'Eloquent and utterly compelling'
Kirkus Reviews

'This is some of the best – and most exciting –
alternate history I've read. Bravo'
Cory Doctorow

'Remarkable ... confident and thrilling'
SFX Magazine

'Magic and mad science mix in this entertaining
alternate history of WWII ... A striking first novel'
Locus

'A damned entertaining novel ... receives
my highest recommendations'
SFFWorld

By Ian Tregillis

The Milkweed Triptych

Bitter Seeds

The Coldest War

Necessary Evil

THE MILKWEED TRIPTYCH: BOOK THREE

NECESSARY EVIL

IAN TREGILLIS

www.orbitbooks.net

ORBIT

First published in Great Britain in 2013 by Orbit

Copyright © 2013 by Ian Tregillis

Excerpt from *Hounded* by Kevin Hearne
Copyright © 2011 by Kevin Hearne

The moral right of the author has been asserted.

A CIP catalogue record for this book
is available from the British Library.

ISBN 978-0-356-50171-0

Typeset in Baskerville by M Rules
Printed and bound in Great Britain by
Clays Ltd, St Ives plc

Papers used by Orbit are from well-managed forests
and other responsible sources.

MIX
Paper from
responsible sources
FSC
www.fsc.org   FSC® C104740

Orbit
An imprint of
Little, Brown Book Group
100 Victoria Embankment
London EC4Y 0DY

An Hachette UK Company
www.hachette.co.uk

www.orbitbooks.net

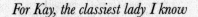

For Kay, the classiest lady I know

This life as you now live it and have lived it, you will have to live once more.

FRIEDRICH NIETZSCHE

Oh God! Oh God! That it were possible / To undo things done; to call back yesterday.

THOMAS HEYWOOD

PROLOGUE

She is five years old when the poor farmer sells her to the mad doctor.

It is autumn, damp and cold. Hunger twists her stomach into a knot. She kneels in a smear of oak leaves, holding a terrier by the hind legs while her brother tries to wrestle the soup bone from its mouth. The bone is a treasure, glistening with flecks of precious marrow. The dog growls and whimpers; they do not hear the wagon approach.

The farmer asks if they are hungry. He says he knows somebody who can feed them, if they're willing to take a ride in his cart.

They are. The dog keeps the bone.

She huddles in the hay of the farmer's wagon. Brother holds her, tries to fend off the seeping cold. Another boy rides with them. His chest gurgles when he coughs.

They arrive at a farm. The field behind the house is studded with little mounds of black earth. Here and there, ravens pick at the mounds. They pull at tattered cloth, tug on scraps of skin.

A doctor inspects the children. She realizes he will feed them if he likes what he sees. But he hates weakness.

She watches the coughing boy. Illness has made him weak. And she is so very hungry.

She trips him. The doctor sees his weakness and it disgusts

him. Soon there is another mound behind the farmhouse. And there is more food for her.

She considers doing the same to the boy called brother. Perhaps she could know the comfort of a full belly. But brother wants to help her. And she might want other things after the hunger has passed.

Brother lives.

It is winter, long and dark.

The doctor is a sick man, driven to madness by the weight of his genius. And he is looking for something. He purchases children in order to remake them. He hurts them, cuts them, in his desperate search for something greater.

The days are full of scalpels, needles, shackles, drills, wires. The stench of hot bone dust, the metallic tang of blood, the sting of ozone. The nights are full of whimpering, crying, moaning. Torments pile up like snowflakes. So do the bodies behind the farmhouse.

Brother tries to protect her. He is punished.

But she survives. Sometimes the pain is pleasant; when it isn't, she retreats to the dark place in her mind.

Brother survives, too. She is glad. He is useful.

The doctor operates on her, over and over again. But no matter how many times he opens her skull, no matter how often he studies her brain to awaken a dormant potential that only he believes is real, he never notices that she is different. He does not see that she is like him.

In the meantime, she discovers the joy of poetry. The pleasure of arranging dried wildflowers. She collects sunrises and sunsets.

She grows. So does brother. Taller. Stronger. Wiser. And they are joined by others – a rare few who endure years of the doctor's scrutiny. She and brother differ from the others. Their skin is darker, like tea-stained cotton, and their eyes like shadows, while the others have light skin and colorful eyes. But she and brother survive, and so the doctor keeps them.

One day, deep in that long winter, the doctor sees his first success. His tinkering unleashes that elusive thing he calls the Will to Power. But it consumes the boy upon whom he is working. The screams shatter windows and crumble bricks in those few moments between transcendence and death.

The doctor, vindicated by this fleeting triumph, redoubles his efforts. He drills wires through their skulls, embeds electrodes in their minds. Electricity, he decides, is key to unleashing the Will to Power. When it does not work he opens their skulls and tries again. And again. The doctor is a patient man.

Sometimes the pain is so great that the oubliette in her mind is scarcely deep enough to keep her safe. Some of the others break; they become imbeciles, or mutes. Those who do not break are warped. The doctor is their father; they strive to please him. They think they can. But she knows better. They don't understand the doctor as she does.

The doctor connects their altered minds to batteries. And, one by one, the survivors become more than human. They fly. They burn. They move things with their minds.

Yet she is a puzzle the doctor cannot crack. He takes her into the laboratory again and again. But nothing works. She is unchanged by the surgeries. Until one morning.

When she wakes, her mind is ablaze.

She is wracked by apparitions. Assaulted with visions of unknown places and people. Brilliant, luminous, the images streak through her mind like falling stars flaring across the heavenly vault of her consciousness. The heat of their passage rakes her body with fever.

The light show etches patterns inside her eyelids. A shifting, rippling cobweb of fire and shadow enfolds her mind. It hurts. She flails. Tries to tear free of the web. But she cannot separate herself from the luminous tapestry any more than the sea can divest itself of wet. It is a part of her.

She fumbles for something constant. Through sheer willpower she forces her mind to focus, to pluck a single image from the chaos before the cascade drives her mad.

Everything changes.

The web shimmers, ripples, reconfigures itself. A new sequence of visions assaults her senses. She sees them, feels them, smells and tastes and hears them.

The earth, swallowing brother.

The doctor, wearing a military uniform.

War.

Oblivion, vast and cold and deeper than the dark place in her own mind.

She passes out.

When next she wakes, she is sprawled on the stone floor of her cell. Brother kneels over her. He cradles the back of her head, strong fingers running through the stubble of her shaven skull. His fingertips come back glistening red. His eyes widen. Brother tells her not to move, takes the pillow from her cot, slides it beneath her head.

Trembling and cold, she watches it all through the shimmering curtain, past pulsing strands of silver, gold, and shadow. The images wash over her again.

Brother standing . . . rushing into the corridor . . . bowling over one of the others in his haste to summon the doctor . . . angry words ... the corridor erupting in flames ... she is trapped her skin bubbling blackening shriveling in the inferno heat twisting her body ripping the breath from her lungs before she can scream the agony oh god the agony she is burningtodeathohgod-OHGOD—

Brother runs for the door.

She is going to dieohgodtheagonyohgod—

She cries out. He pauses in the doorway.

The shimmering cobwebs flicker, blink, reconfigure themselves again.

The future changes. There is no fire.

It is springtime, bright and colorful.

Her Will to Power has manifested, and it is glorious.

The cascade of experiences still assaults her like a rushing cataract, still threatens to sweep her away to permanent madness. A lesser person would embrace insanity for succor and refuge. But not her. She understands now.

The scenes she experiences are snippets of her own future. One of her possible futures. One of an infinity.

The Götterelektron flows up her wires, enters her mind, hits the loom of her Willenskräfte and explodes into a trillion gossamer threads of possibility. A tapestry of potential time lines fans out before her. Countless golden strands, each future path branching into uncountable variations, and innumerable variations on those variations, on and on and on and on. Each choice she makes nudges the world from one set of paths to another.

She is a prophet, an oracle, a seer. She is nothing less than a vessel of Fate.

The web of possible futures is infinitely wide and grows wider the further she looks. It takes strength of mind and will to plumb the depths, to explore the far fringes of possibility. There is a horizon that limits her omniscience, a boundary built from her own weakness.

In the first fragile hours of her new ability, she can't peer ahead any further than a few moments. Brother runs for the doctor, she dies in fire; he stays, she lives.

With practice, she pushes the horizon back several hours. Tell brother she is hungry: he comes back with stew, bread, and cherry strudel. Wait an hour, then tell him: there is no strudel left. Wait two hours, then tell him she is ravenous: the doctor catches him breaking curfew, punishes him with a night and a day in the coffin box; brother rips off his fingernails trying to claw out.

With several days' practice, she can follow the time lines almost a week into the future. Steal a knife from the kitchen, stab brother in the neck: whole branches of the infinite web disappear and are replaced with others that begin with a shallow grave and a sack of quicklime.

The process is beautiful. Mesmerizing. She watches it again and again.

She learns to focus her will like a scalpel, learns to prune the decision tree, learns to slice away the gossamer tangle of unwanted possibilities.

The further she pushes the horizon, the more powerful she becomes. Yet there are still things she cannot do, events she cannot bring to fruition. She cannot make it snow in June. She cannot make brother fall in love in the next two days. Nothing she does will cause the doctor to tumble down the farmhouse stairs and break his neck in the next six hours. But push the horizon back, and possibilities open up. Why hurry? In three days' time the skies will open with a torrential downpour. The doctor will wear galoshes. He will leave them outside his door on the third floor of the farmhouse lest he track mud inside. He oversees the daily training exercises from his parlor window. She distracts one of the others with a well-timed wink; he loses his concentration and destroys delicate equipment in an explosion of Willenskräfte. The doctor flies into a rage. Throws the door open. Does not see the galoshes. Lands at the bottom of the stairs with splinters of vertebrae poking through his lifeless neck.

She can kill the doctor with a single wink. One pebble starts a landslide; a single snowflake begets an avalanche.

But she is comfortable here. The doctor's death would change the farm, compromise her comforts. The doctor lives a bit longer: she has decided his fate.

She has cast off the winter cocoon of her childhood to stretch her wings in the sun.

She is a butterfly, leaving hurricanes in her wake.

It is summertime, hot and green and glorious.

Her ability is extensive, flexible. Full of subtleties. She can make anybody do practically anything, if only she's willing to search the web of future time lines long and hard enough. Willing to practice countless variations on a brief conversation, or a momentary interaction. Infinity always includes a time line that spools out according to her whims.

The doctor fails to comprehend the extent of his creation. She revels in paradox.

She pushes the horizon back years. And when her power grows sufficiently grand, she does what any self-respecting demigoddess would do: she divines her own fate. Fates.

Alas. She is not a true goddess; she won't live forever. But surely, with the proper choices at the appropriate junctures, she will live a very long time. She plunges ahead, looking for the day her body finally succumbs to age. Is she ninety years old? A full century?

Along the way, she sees other things looming. All time lines show the world soon engulfed in war. It doesn't worry her. Finding a comfortable path through the wartime years is trivial.

She explores the most promising potentialities first. She plumbs the future, and looks deeper still, until the branching and rebranching of parallel time lines has woven the threads of possibility into the finest fur . . .

. . . and discovers something watching her.

Something that lurks in the gaps *between* the time lines.

An interstitial horror, prowling the places where nothing should exist. Titanic. Malevolent.

It notices her. And it is angry.

Winter again. Nothing but ice and shadow.

Nightmares torment her for weeks. It takes longer than that before she recovers the courage to explore the deep future again. And when she does, she encounters that same wall of suffocating malice, that same sense of something vast and ancient watching her from outside the time lines.

Every exploration of the future – discarding, as always, the branches that end prematurely when she is shot, strangled, struck by lightning – ends with her tumbling into that abyss. Ends with a darkness so complete that even her fearless heart quails before it.

Again and again and again and again she tries. But there is no avoiding this destiny. She learns what she can.

The demons are called Eidolons. They are everywhere, everywhen. They are the mortar between the bricks of the universe. They are beings of sheer volition, and they despise humanity.

Despise the stain, the corruption, humanity leaves upon the otherwise perfect cosmos. For humans are nothing but a pointless accident of space and time – minuscule, meaningless – forever shackled by their spatial and temporal limitations, yet somehow sentient and possessing a limited form of free will. Nothing could be more offensive to the Eidolons. And thus they seek to eradicate the insult.

But the Eidolons' vastness is their weakness; humanity's salvation is its insignificance on the boundless scale of the cosmos. All of human existence rests on a problem of demarcation. This is a precarious balance, stable only as long as the Eidolons never truly perceive humanity.

But they will. For there are warlocks in the world. Men who commune with the Eidolons. Men willing to improve the Eidolons' perception of humanity in exchange for fantastical, impossible feats. For the demons are not bound by the laws of nature.

The horrors the warlocks will unleash are a consequence of the looming war. Even she cannot avert it. It is far too large, and coming far too soon. The world committed itself to this path before she was handed the reins.

In many time lines, the end comes during the war itself. There are other future paths, more complicated and less likely scenarios, where the Eidolons consume the world years after the war has ended. Perhaps even decades. But even at the fringes of possibility, on the most convoluted and unlikely time lines she can discern, everything ends in darkness. Everything ends with the Eidolons.

She ends with the Eidolons.

In every single time line.

*

The seasons turn. She struggles to find meaning in the face of her own doom. Slides into nihilism. Brother doesn't understand. He can't. Her concerns extend far beyond mortal comprehension.

What point is there of being a demigoddess if she can't change the things that matter? Can't alter her own fate?

She whiles away the months with desultory explorations of the future. Like brother, many of the same people reappear in her investigations, their fates braided with hers across a multiplicity of futures. But one man piques her interest. In some time lines, their interaction lasts for no more than a few moments. But that is immaterial: she sees him again and again and again.

His name is Raybould Marsh. He is strong. Courageous. Beautiful. Burdened with anger. Not as clever as she, but that is no sin.

Clearly, they are meant to be together. Why else would this magnificent stranger appear in so many of her futures?

She experiences something new: it begins as a lump in her throat, turns into a wonderful ache in her chest, becomes butterflies in her belly, and spreads down her spine to create a warmth between her legs.

She plays at seduction. Explores the futures in which she snares his heart. He is a prickly man, and difficult at times. But love is just another emotion, and she can make anybody do virtually anything – feel almost anything – given enough time and patience. And there are time lines where he succumbs to her charms. Difficult to access, and rare, but they do exist.

On lonely nights she pleasures herself while watching him sleep. It is one such night, spent imagining his calloused hands on her naked body, when she discovers that Raybould Marsh can be something more than her lover.

He can be her savior. He can save her from the Eidolons.

What would Raybould do in the face of inescapable doom? Every time line ends with the Eidolons. But he would see it differently: every *preexisting* time line ends thus.

So why not build a *new* time line? From scratch?

She sits bolt upright, the first tremors of orgasm forgotten.

Springtime again. The butterfly stretches her wings.

Outwitting the Eidolons is a superb challenge. The only challenge worthy of her attentions. It becomes her sole focus for years on end: mastering manipulations; piercing the dark heart of the knottiest paradoxes; culling insights from obscure potential futures; skirting her own death at the hands of enraged allies and determined enemies; weaving cause and effect across decades.

She inspects every detail, for she must leave nothing to chance. The plan must unfold over so many years that the tiniest crosscurrents will grow into cyclones capable of unraveling the slender thread of her machinations.

It is a Herculean undertaking. But she succeeds.

It will start with a man named Krasnopolsky.

Soon, the doctor will use the civil war in Spain as a field test for his children's abilities, thus proving to his benefactors that he can make real their dreams of conquest. The triumphant feats of Willenskräfte will be filmed for further study. Krasnopolsky will be one of the cameramen. He will witness unnatural things. Things that disturb him.

It will be easy for her to nudge Krasnopolsky's disquiet into thoughts of defection. The British will send a spy to collect him. A spy named Raybould Marsh.

He and she will first glimpse each other at the port in Barcelona. She will set the hook with a wink.

And thus, after the war begins, Raybould will return to the Continent, seeking information about the doctor's farm. She will let him capture her.

He will bring her to England, where he and his colleagues will show her to an Eidolon. The Eidolons will see Raybould, too, and sense what she intends for him. He will catch their interest. And that moment will become her anchor, the graft point from which the new time line will grow. But there will be so much more to do.

With her guidance, brother will rescue her. She will become the most valuable advisor to the highest echelons of the military. She will guide them through the annihilation of Britain's army on the beaches of Dunkirk; direct the systematic destruction of Britain's air defenses. Her Willenskräfte will become a scalpel, cutting away all hope.

Raybould, meanwhile, will attempt to raise a family. It hurts to think of him with another woman. But it's a necessary part of the plan. And his misguided infatuation with the freckled whore won't last forever. He is meant for one woman and nobody else: she is the woman who sees through time, and he the man who will transcend it.

She will orchestrate a bombing raid that kills Raybould's infant daughter. He will go mad with sorrow. Grief will make him careless. He will spearhead a surprise attack on the farm. The British will use the Eidolons to transport soldiers to Germany. It is a very clever idea. But she will thwart the British, to lay the groundwork for a desperate withdrawal. The Eidolons will claim Raybould's next child for themselves before letting the few survivors make a panicked retreat to England.

Britain's survival will require drastic action. Raybould's compatriots will break the Wehrmacht with supernatural winter and lure the Red Army to finish the job. Their ploy will succeed. But in spite of Raybould's efforts to prevent it, the farm will fall to the Soviets. The Soviets will claim the doctor's work for themselves.

Including her. And brother.

Events will coast without her adjustments for over twenty years. The British Empire and the Soviet Union will settle into a precarious stalemate. Eidolons on one side, the doctor's research on the other. But when the time is right, she and brother will escape. And their return to England will lure Raybould out of retirement.

He will be a different man by then. Bowed, but not yet broken. The strain of living with a child twisted by the Eidolons will have destroyed his marriage. But he endures because Britain is free; he endures because he believes his sacrifices are meaningful.

By then, the Soviets will have improved the doctor's technology. But Raybould's attempt to eliminate the Soviet Willenskräfte army will fail, and he will be grievously injured (not killed, of course; she will never allow that). His beloved Britain will fall under withering attack.

Then, and only then, will Raybould be in the proper emotional state for what she needs.

Lost in despair and rage, he will unleash the Eidolons. But the demons will inhabit his empty son and use human eyes to see humanity in full. Raybould's anguish will become the thing that hurls their time line into the malevolent abyss.

But. She will have long since set her anchor in the past, long ago laid the bait to lure Raybould back. And in the final moments of that world, when he finally comprehends her plan, he will step forward to save her.

He won't understand he's doing it for her. He'll think he's seizing a second chance to save his infant daughter.

But all that matters is he relents and allows the last of the warlocks to send him into the past. He will arrive at the anchor point, and create a new time line.

One in which she isn't consumed by the Eidolons.

Saving herself means stitching new threads into the tapestry of possible futures. It means breaking Raybould Marsh, the man she loves, and forging his sorrow into a tool for destroying the world.

It means tempting him with the one thing he desires above all else. It means luring him into the past.

It works.

ONE

I crouched in the painful embrace of a hawthorn hedge, the screams of a dying world still echoing in my ears.

Hot sweat tickled my scalp. But I shivered from chills, nausea, and the lingering touch of the Eidolons. I hadn't realized just how ill I felt until those demons took me apart and reassembled me twenty-three years in the past.

I was a time traveler. A refugee from the world's end. The sole survivor of a cataclysm that I had caused.

The western sky blushed orange and pink beyond a swath of royal parkland. The last traces of gloaming silhouetted lampposts in St. James'. All dark, all unlit. The only other light came from a narrow gap in the opaque curtain covering the window overhead; a shaft of pale light speared through the shadows above my hiding spot. London itself was a hulking presence sensed but unseen in the night. The Admiralty building loomed behind me, cloaked in blackout. I could smell the dampness from a recent rainstorm and woody sap from where I'd cracked a few hawthorn branches in my hasty exit through the window.

Everything was silent but for the occasional distant hum of a car along Whitehall.

The darkness lent an unexpected familiarity to this place and time. Like encountering an old lover after leaving her behind long ago, and discovering she hadn't changed a jot.

This was the spring of 1940. Those early days of the Second World War, before France had fallen and we'd lost an army on the beaches of Dunkirk. Before the first dominoes had toppled in that long chain of events culminating decades later in a demonic apocalypse.

My job was to break that chain. Somehow.

The suffocating weight of that task left me breathless. I couldn't take in the sheer enormity of it all without becoming dizzy. A spasm cramped my gut.

I took a steadying breath and tried to ground myself in the here and now. In a previous life I had been a gardener, and so I concentrated on my immediate surroundings.

Long thin shoots poked randomly from the top of the unkempt hedge. They broke the clean, level lines of the shrubbery. The slender branches had just begun to swell with white May blossoms, and my shivering caused green thorns to skitter against the window glass of the Admiralty. Thorns like those had pierced my shirt when I leaped from the window. They raked my skin from waist to armpit.

It was probably a quickset hedge, a century old or more. But now there was a war on, and people had more pressing concerns than keeping the hedges tidy.

That simple observation, more than anything else, even more than the blackout, forced me to accept the reality of it all. Will had done it. He'd sent me back.

Picture this, if you will: A man, not quite fifty-three years old, a bit heavier than he ought to be, plagued with a bad knee and a worse temper, his face and voice ruined by fire. Make him nauseated, feverish, alone. Now watch his back bend, his shoulders slump with despair, as he grapples with the enormity of his impossible task.

That was me.

Footsteps rattled floorboards inside the Admiralty, approaching the window where I'd made my escape. I retreated deeper into the hawthorn, clamping my jaw as thorns pierced me in a dozen new places. I put the cold, unyielding stone of the Admiralty building at my back and tried not to breathe. My muscles ached with the effort not to tremble lest somebody heard the bramble rattling against the windowsill. My stomach gurgled.

Somebody fixed the blackout curtains. Darkness engulfed me.

And then a woman's voice floated through the shadows. She had to be standing in the room where I'd landed, just a few feet from where I now hunched in the cold and dark. What she said was muffled by the window and the curtains, but I could still make it out. I think she intended that.

'Ah.'

I knew that voice. Another spasm twisted my gut.

A man said, gruffly, 'What?'

Of course, I recognized *his* voice as well. But I wasn't ready to think about that yet.

'It worked,' said the woman.

God as my witness, I could hear the corner of her mouth curling up as she said it. Only two words, but more than enough to send another volley of chills rattling through me.

Gretel. The clairvoyant who manipulated the world for decades – and killed my daughter and destroyed my marriage – in her paradoxical bid to elude the Eidolons on the last day of history. I and the people I cared for had been nothing more than unwitting pieces in Gretel's long, elaborate chess game. As had Great Britain itself, and the Third Reich, and the Soviet Union. Puppets all. I trembled again, this time with rage.

It worked.

Yes, it had. She'd tricked me into unleashing the Eidolons. And then, as the world had ended around us, she'd dangled an irresistible carrot before me: the chance to save my dead daughter. Because she knew Agnes was the only lure strong enough to yank me out of my apathy; by that point, I didn't much care the world was ending.

And now she knew I was here. Knew that she'd won.

Or had she?

For *my* Gretel, my bête noire – the Gretel who instigated the bombing raid that killed Agnes; the Gretel whose specter had haunted every day of my life in the decades since war's end – had perished along with everybody else when the Eidolons ended the world. But, of course, she didn't care. For though she was mad, she wielded the power of the gods. Thus her long game amounted to nothing more than a convoluted self-sacrifice. A feint at the Eidolons, a bit of supernatural sleight of hand, so that another version of herself could thrive. So that a different Gretel, the Gretel of this new splinter time line, could live free of the Eidolons.

What a privileged perspective I enjoyed. A sickening thing, this insider's view of her cold-blooded machinations. Revolting, the extent of that madwoman's psychosis. Terrifying.

I doubled over and retched while the footsteps receded and *he* took the prisoner back to her cell. I knew he was doing that because I had been there.

I am *there. Right now. But so is* he.

Was this me, shivering and sweating and bleeding in the darkness? Or was I that other person, safe and warm inside the Admiralty? I had his memories, but he didn't share mine. Didn't share my wounds. Didn't share my disfigurement, didn't feel the constant pain in my throat. He hadn't endured two failed attempts to start a family.

Tears squeezed through the corners of my clenched eyelids when I thought of family. My darling daughter, Agnes, dead so young. My son, John, a soulless vessel carved by the Eidolons to facilitate the eradication of humanity. And my wife, Liv, with her freckles, cutting wit, and poisonous resentment.

A new realization hit me in the gut so sharply that it threatened to loose my watery bowels. This was 1940. None of that had happened yet. Liv still loved *him*. Loved him in a way that had long since withered and died for me. Loved him in a way he didn't deserve. It wasn't fair. I hated him for it.

But the seed of an idea lodged in the fertile soil at the back of my mind. I couldn't dislodge it. Nor did I want to.

I waited until I was certain Gretel and her escort had gone downstairs and nobody inside would hear me shaking the hedge. An owl hooted in St. James' while I extricated myself from the hawthorn. Several minutes of cursing earned my freedom along with a bevy of fresh scratches. They bled freely as I staggered across Horse Guards to the park.

Footing was precarious; many of the city's parks had been turned over to gardening and home defense. I took a tumble in a trench that had probably been dug for the sake of filling sandbags.

My head throbbed in time with the pulse of sweat down my temples. Another wave of nausea rippled through me. The watery churning lent an urgency to my wanderings. But I knew the park had no public loo. Not in 1940. And I couldn't spare the time to find one.

As I squatted in the mud beside the lake, it occurred to me that I'd once seen this shoreline studded with tents. A staging area. That memory dredged up others in its wake, most particularly of a strange and frightening encounter. But my thoughts skittered away again; I was reluctant to dwell on that, though I couldn't put my finger on why.

My relief was short-lived. I had just pulled up my trousers when a light shone in my face. The mild throbbing in my temples flared into a mature headache.

'Oy now, what are you about?'

Oh, dear God, no. Not now.

I couldn't see for the light in my eyes. Something pale fluttered in the shadows outside the torchlight. Possibly a handkerchief. A second voice with a plugged nose said, 'Christ. I think he shitted in the lake.'

'I'm ill,' I mumbled. Each word a fire in my throat.

The full extent of the humiliation slowly dawned on me, easily the worst in all my miserable life. The possibility Gretel knew about this made it even worse. At that moment I didn't care about saving the world. I wanted it all to go away.

'Maybe so,' said the second voice, 'but the royal parks aren't your personal toilet. That's rotten disgusting.'

The first man tipped his electric torch so that it wasn't aimed directly into my eyes. I made out the glint of a badge and the silhouette of a bobby's helmet.

'I'd like to see your identity card, sir.'

And that's when I realized I was in trouble. The dread lay so heavy upon me I thought I might sink into the mud.

HMG had issued ID cards to all its citizens at the start of the war, back in 1939. We'd carried them until the early 50s, when the wretched National Registration program was finally scrapped.

But none of that mattered. Because today, in 1940, in wartime, I was required by law to produce my ID card for the coppers. I was required by law to never venture outside the house without the card on my person. But ID cards had been far from my mind as the Eidolons devoured the world.

I started to shiver again. 'Lost it,' I rasped.

'Is that so? How'd you lose it, then?'

I couldn't tell the copper that I tossed it during a bout of spring cleaning ten or twelve years ago. But the second copper sensed my hesitation before I could concoct a plausible lie.

'I won't ask again. Where's your identity card, sir?'

'I . . . I haven't got it.'

'Right,' he said. 'You do know we could haul you in for that? And for *that*.' He gesturing at the lakeshore with his truncheon. 'Bloody public indecency, that is.'

'Francis,' said the first copper. 'C'mere a sec. You,' he said, pointing to me, 'stay put.'

I'd been hauled in by the coppers enough times to recognize when a difference of opinion was brewing. I eavesdropped and considered making a run for it. The still night air carried their whispered conversation to me. I had to strain to hear it over the lapping of the lake, but I knew they were arguing.

'We're taking him in,' said Francis, still holding the handkerchief over his nose.

'He needs a hospital,' said the other copper.

'You can't be serious.'

'You can tell the poor old duffer is confused. Look at his eyes. Probably half senile. Could be somebody's da.'

'Maybe that's what the Jerries want us to think.'

'Look at his scars. He's seen some action. Bet he fought in the Great War.'

'Maybe he fought for the Boche.'

'Being a bit extreme, aren't you?'

'No. You're being a bit lazy.'

'Let me try to sort the poor fellow out, what?'

They returned. I hadn't moved. I knew I was in no state to make a proper fugitive. They'd catch me, and that would spike my mission before it ever started.

In my younger days I might have considered taking them both by surprise. And on a very lucky day I might have succeeded. But I was older and wiser now, which is to say slower, so I knew it would take but one well-placed truncheon to make an even bigger hash of things.

The first copper took the lead again, and that gave me hope. 'What's your name, sir?'

His speculation about me being a vet of the Great War gave me an idea. I said, 'John Stephenson, officer.'

'Where do you live, Mr. Stephenson?'

'St. Pancras.' I gave him the old man's address. Still knew it by heart; I'd been married there.

'Haven't you got any ID on you? A billfold, perhaps?'

The sense of dread lifted, leaving behind a damp layer of sweat. I tried not to let my relief show. I'd been through this with the coppers enough times to know when I was off the hook. They might haul me to a hospital, but that wasn't a problem. Any hospital was a damn sight better than jail.

'Yeah,' I told him. 'I've got a billfold.'

'May I see it?'

I nodded, and reached for my coat pocket. I used one hand, moving slowly and deliberately so that I didn't startle him. I dug out the billfold and offered it to him. He handed the torch to Francis, who kept the beam trained on me. He held the billfold in the edge of the torch beam and flipped through it. He frowned. Then he looked at me again.

Now it was his turn to hesitate.

'What did you say your name is?'

'Stephenson,' I repeated.

'Right. So you did.' He said it kindly, calmly. But his free hand fell gently to the truncheon hanging at his waist. Right then I knew I was well and truly buggered.

His eyes didn't leave the billfold. 'Thing is, if that's the case, mind telling me who William Beauclerk is?'

'Shit,' I said.

Francis chuckled. 'Well. You've already seen to that, haven't you?'

Somewhere in the darkness, I heard the rattle of cuffs.

12 May 1940
Milkweed Headquarters, London, England

Blinding agony lanced through the stump of Will's severed finger. He'd never known such pain, never could have imagined such pain, as when Marsh had snapped shut the gardening shears. But the cauterization was worse because it never seemed to end. Pain like white-hot lava erupted from his mangled hand. It filled his veins, reduced his heart to charcoal, his brain to ash.

Will flinched, hard enough to yank his hand from the doctor's grasp. The doctor scowled.

'Sorry,' Will managed. It came out as a hoarse whisper. The ravages of Enochian, combined with mindless screaming through the wooden bit clenched in his teeth, had torn his throat raw. His teeth felt loose.

The doctor aimed a pointed look at Stephenson. Will didn't know the man's name. He was a naval medic, but probably attached to SIS rather than the Admiralty. That was a guess, but the doctor and Stephenson clearly knew each other. And the doc hadn't asked about the cause of Will's dismemberment, nor shown interest in anything other than treating the wound. Or so Will had gathered during the scant moments when pain wasn't threatening to drive him mad. He'd passed out just after the ceremony and felt like he might again any moment.

Stephenson grumbled, 'For God's sake, Beauclerk. You've nothing to prove. Take the bloody morphine. Or at the very least let brandy dull the worst of it.'

He tried to push a full tumbler into Will's free hand, but Will waved it away. The effort left his head spinning.

'No.' The pain threatened to make him sick up. But he'd endure anything to avoid the danger of becoming his grandfather. He'd never let himself follow in the footsteps of that wretched, twisted old drunk. Will had sworn off alcohol long ago. No amount of physical agony could make him relent. Not even this torture. He'd be a better man than grandfather, even if the effort destroyed him.

Will realized that sooner or later he'd have to explain the injury to Aubrey. Was it too severe for a plausible gardening mishap? That at least had a patina of truth to it. The shears had belonged to one of Bestwood's gardeners, long ago. Back in their grandfather's day.

Will almost passed out when he extended his arm to put his bad hand back within the doctor's reach. He managed to say, 'Please continue, doctor.'

The doctor sighed, looking wistfully at the morphine syrette lying unused on the desk. Stephenson leaned over Will's chair and used his weight to pin Will's forearm to the armrest. The one-armed man had a grip like bands of steel. The doctor hefted the iron again.

Will gritted his teeth. Yes, definitely loose.

A faint sizzle accompanied the wave of incandescent pain, hotter than the soul of the earth, that flooded Will's body. Delicate curlicues of blue-black smoke wafted around the stump, tracing greasy tendrils across the back of his hand. The stink of burnt flesh filled the old man's office.

Will cast about for a mental diversion lest the pain overwhelm him again. The few threads of his mind capable of conscious thought flailed for something upon which to focus. How did he get here?

The gypsy waif. Eidolons. Marsh.

What was she? What could she do? Why did she have wires implanted in her skull? What had von Westarp done to her? And how could the men and women on the Tarragona film perform such blatantly unnatural feats without appealing to the Eidolons? It was impossible. Yet the Eidolon's answer had been as unambiguous at its rage. The waif was not their handi-work.

What a straightforward answer. And all it had cost was a fingertip. This had been the height of foolishness, thinking he possessed skill enough to negotiate with the Eidolons. He had been fortunate. The blood price might have been far worse.

Stranger still . . . why would the Eidolons bestow a name upon somebody? What did it mean? And why had they chosen Marsh? It was as though they knew him. Acknowledged him. But the Eidolons didn't recognize individual humans. They perceived humanity as a stain upon the cosmos, an abomination, an infestation to be eradicated. Nothing more.

It was too disturbing to contemplate. Will forced his attention toward less chilling mysteries.

He had warned the others to expect strangeness. Though nothing could truly prepare a person for the way the world tended to warp and sag around the Eidolons like candles on the mantel of a burning house. Even seasoned warlocks had been known to go mad from time to time. Will remembered the servants' tales of his own father.

Tonight's negotiation hadn't been any different. Phantom scents, mysterious noises, alien sensations. Effects without causes. There had been a thump, as though something heavy had landed on the floorboards. And then Will's own voice, crying out in abject terror and mindless panic. More strident even than the scream that escaped him when Marsh severed his fingertip. The relentless pain made rational thought impossible. Was there another William Beauclerk somewhere, one who had experienced something worse than a severed finger? Witnessed something more dreadful than a Third Reich with superhuman soldiers?

Surely that was impossible.

12 May 1940
Walworth, London, England

Agnes's wrinkled red face traced drool on Marsh's shirt as he held her to his chest. He pressed his nose to her soft scalp and inhaled her scent, tickling himself with wisps of silken baby hair. She smelled so clean. So fresh, so wonderful. Like family.

'Our poor daughter will never know proper sleep,' Liv whispered, 'if you keep taking her from the bassinet.'

She came up behind him, slid an arm around his waist. A swollen breast brushed against his elbow. She winced.

'I'm making up for lost time,' he said. 'I'm so sorry I missed this.'

He'd been in France when Liv had gone into labor. Based on the time listed on Agnes's birth certificate, he'd been crossing the Channel with the Frankensteined gypsy girl when Agnes was born. He'd been doing his job. So why did serving the country feel like infidelity? The guilt clung to him tighter than a second skin.

Congratulations. It's a girl.

He'd rushed to the hospital as soon as he found Liv's note. But not before indulging in a fair bit of panic after finding the front door open, Liv gone, and the bedroom in disarray. The prisoner had found her way under his skin.

What was she? What were those hideous wires for? And how on God's earth did she know about Liv and the baby?

Liv said, 'Agnes might forgive you. Someday.'

'Someday?'

'Depends on how stubborn she is. Whether she takes after her father.'

'I'm not stubborn.'

Liv laughed into his shoulder. Long auburn hair draped across her face, tickling his arm. She hadn't put her hair up since returning from the hospital. 'Mulish, then.'

'That's better. And you? Am I forgiven?'

'There's nothing to forgive, love. You're here now.'

He said, 'I'll do everything I can not to leave again. I promise.'

'I know.'

Marsh brushed his lips across Agnes's scalp. He leaned over, gently cradling his daughter's head as he set her down. Her arm twitched, and her face scrunched into a new pattern of wrinkles while he covered her with the baby blanket. It was pink and embroidered with jolly elephants.

Liv laid her head against his shoulder. They stood together, quietly watching their daughter sleep.

'You should be resting,' he said. He took her hand, led her to the den.

'I'm not infirm, Raybould.' She clicked her tongue. 'You men. I had to tell Will the very same thing.'

Will's scream kept echoing in his ears. He couldn't forget the feel of the shears, the sensation of the handles in his fists as the blades crunched through flesh and bone.

But the Eidolon had been so much worse: the way it studied him like an insect under a magnifying glass, the intangible pressure of its presence, the titanic sense of malevolence, the skin-crawling dread. Marsh wondered if he'd ever sleep again. He drew a long, shuddery breath.

Christ. What a bloody wretched evening.

'Just because Will is Agnes's father,' said Liv, 'doesn't entitle you to be so jealous of him. You should be bigger than that.'

'Yes, you're right,' Marsh murmured. Then something she'd said snapped him back to the present. He frowned. 'Wait. What was that about Will?'

Liv tipped her head back and filled the room with melodious laughter. 'You went somewhere just now. I can always tell. It's in your eyes. But when you crack your knuckles . . . ' She touched the back of one slender hand to her face, pantomiming his habit. 'That's when I know you're entertaining particularly deep thoughts.'

She eased herself to the sofa. Marsh tried to help her, but she swatted his hands away. He sat beside her. Yawned. Rubbed his burning eyes.

Marsh said, 'Speaking of Will.' He pointed toward the entry-way. 'Did you know he left the door open when he took you to the hospital?'

'I do believe you've mentioned it. Once or twice.'

Congratulations. It's a girl.

'Liv, has anybody come around lately? While I was away?'

She shook her head. 'Just auntie. And Will.'

'Nobody at all?' Marsh thought about all the means the Jerries might be using to keep tabs on him and Liv. There were so many. How long had they been watched? It was the only explanation. He stood, paced around the room, double-checking the blackout curtains. 'What about ARP wardens?'

'No wardens.'

'You'd tell me if there had been, wouldn't you?'

A frown creased the space between her eyebrows. 'You know I would.'

'Has Will mentioned anything unusual? Strange visitors?'

'Raybould. Sit.' She patted the sofa cushion beside her. 'What is this about?'

He sighed. 'I worry about you and Agnes being alone while I'm at work all day.'

'And you're a dear for it. Now do stop before you smother us.'

He assumed a new tack. 'Perhaps the two of you could take a vacation in Williton. Go visit your aunt, rather than making her come to London.'

Liv said, 'We've already discussed this. I'm not leaving.' Her voice was tight with irritation. 'The first evacuation of mothers and toddlers was an utter waste of time. They all came back. It'll be the same again.'

'What if the Germans start bombing in earnest?'

'Stop it! You're frightening me.' She narrowed her eyes, looked him up and down. 'Did something happen while you were visiting the Yanks?'

Liv didn't know her husband was a spy for His Majesty's Government. As far as she knew, Marsh was a mid-level bureaucrat in the Office of the Foreign Secretary. Before Stephenson had sent him to the Continent to scrounge up information about von Westarp, they'd concocted an appropriate cover story. Marsh had told Liv that he was being sent to America, as part of a delegation hoping to procure aid from the Yanks. He'd worried that Will, who had no background in tradecraft and showed little facility for it, would inadvertently contradict that.

'Nothing. The entire outing was a loss, I'm afraid.'

That didn't allay her suspicions. 'Is something happening in France they haven't reported on the wireless?'

'I don't know any more than you,' he lied.

'They say the BEF is regrouping.'

Scrambling was more like it. Marsh had been just a few miles from the German advance. He'd seen firsthand the utter disarray of the British Expeditionary Forces as the Jerries sidestepped them on their lightning-fast incursions across the border. *The Germans have burned through Ardennes.* France would fall. Not immediately, but sooner than later. He knew it in his bones.

But he didn't want to alarm Liv more than he already had. So he said, 'They'll sort the Jerries out soon enough.'

'Then we have no reason to worry.'

'No. But I would feel better if you'd discuss the possibility of a visit with Margaret.' Liv answered silently with a scowl and a cocked eyebrow. The eyebrow meant she was sharpening the verbal barbs. Marsh quickly added, 'Tell you what. Things get bad here, we'll stay put, but send Agnes safely out of the city.'

Liv sighed. 'Well, that's a start.' She snuggled against him. 'It's settled, then. The Tommies agree to deal with Hitler. The Foreign Office agrees it won't send you away again. And Agnes agrees to go to Williton if she absolutely must.'

TWO

12–13 May 1940
Westminster, London, England

The coppers chivvied me into their car. It had been modified per the blackout regs. The slitted headlamps provided meager illumination for Francis, who drove.

I'd forgotten just how effective the blackout had been. It was one thing to stand in pastoral St. James' surrounded by a dark city, but the effect was altogether different when speeding through Trafalgar Square and realizing the night had swallowed Nelson's Column whole. London was a giant trying to hide in plain sight. It had seemed logical and effective the first time I lived through it. But the passage of time had changed my perspective; now I could see the ostrich for what it was. I knew, as nobody else could, that in the long run the blackout was ultimately pointless.

There was no hiding from the Eidolons. Even Gretel had managed to throw them off her trail just long enough to get what she wanted out of me.

But I hadn't spent a full hour back in 1940 before getting nabbed by the coppers. Did that mean I'd just tossed her entire scheme into a cocked hat?

Good. Fuck her.

All I cared about was saving my family. Agnes's death had been the thin end of the wedge that broke our marriage. But she wouldn't die this time around. I'd see to that if it was the only thing I did. None of this mattered a good goddamn if I couldn't save my girl. What point in saving the world if I couldn't save Agnes?

I'd lived with loneliness for so long that I didn't realize its extent until I returned to a world where my wife didn't despise me. All my failures of the past twenty-three years had been erased. The prospect of recovering my self-respect made me want to weep.

Things would change once I saved Agnes. But I'd have to keep a watchful eye. Make certain the Eidolons didn't steal John's soul again, leaving us with another hollow, howling monster. If there was a John this time around. Perhaps it wasn't fair, but I didn't know if I wanted a son after what had happened the last time.

One of the worst things I'd ever seen was my son's body put to use as a vessel for the Eidolons. His sightless eyes ... their legion voice ... Ill and exhausted as I was, I found myself dreading sleep because it would leave me defenseless against the memories seared into my mind.

I'd save Agnes. Everything would be right again. And Gretel could fend for herself.

That's what I told myself while the coppers motored carefully through the dark streets of Westminster. But I didn't share Will's capacity for self-delusion, meaning Nelson wasn't more than two or three streets behind us before the glaring flaw in my plan grew too large to ignore.

If I saved Agnes, but did nothing more, I'd be leaving her at the mercy of the Eidolons. Best case? She'd die as a young woman in her twenties. Gretel couldn't postpone the apocalypse beyond the early 1960s. When she'd laid it all out for me and Will, there at the end of the world, she'd told us that most of the time lines she'd studied had ended with the Eidolons much sooner. Meaning I could save Agnes from the Luftwaffe, but she'd still die as an infant.

I had to face the facts. Saving my family wasn't simply a matter of keeping Agnes out of Williton. *Truly* saving my family meant sealing off the Eidolons. And that meant eradicating the warlocks. But I wouldn't let Agnes grow up with Hitler's boot on her neck. Meaning I couldn't deal with the warlocks as long as Doctor von Westarp was merrily churning out *Übermenschen* for the SS.

The world was caught between Scylla and Charybdis: twin perils poised to devour those who veered too closely. Milkweed on one side, the *Reichsbehörde für die Erweiterung germanischen Potenzials* on the other. Or perhaps it was better to say they were the Symplegades, the deadly clashing rocks of antiquity.

I reckoned that made me the dove. I sure as hell wasn't Jason – he had a loyal crew behind him. Not me. I was all alone.

Unless . . . A new idea took root. I tucked it away for later.

Unconsciously, I made to crack my knuckles against my jaw. Most of the time I don't realize I'm doing it. Wouldn't have noticed it there in the coppers' car, either, but the cuffs made it cumbersome.

Point was, things weren't as straightforward as eliminating the warlocks. What really mattered was wiping out the *knowledge*. And not just the warlocks' knowledge of Enochian, the Eidolons' lingua franca, but the knowledge that such things were *possible*. Because once Whitehall got a taste of what the warlocks could do, they would forever be a part of our national defense strategy.

And the process of making new warlocks would be institution-alized, then sanitized behind layers of bureaucratic doublespeak. I knew because I'd seen it.

And it was much the same on the other side. As long as any-thing of von Westarp or the Götterelektrongruppe survived, people would seek to re-create that work. And Britain wasn't safe as long as that were the case.

I'd read the operational records; I knew how the doctor's pro-gram had begun. I knew about the orphanage and the mass graves. I'd come from a future where Whitehall had justified turning children into warlocks; in a way, it wasn't so different from what von Westarp had done to his early test subjects. So it didn't matter whether the research rested in German hands, or Soviet, or British. It all had to go. The farm, the batteries, the research, the Tarragona filmstrip . . . All of it. Which meant that on top of everything *else*, I had to find a way to wipe the doctor's 'children' from the face of the earth.

One of whom, it should be noted, could read the future.

But I couldn't hope to deal with either problem, Milkweed or the Reichsbehörde, from jail. They'd ship me off to an intern-ment camp on the Isle of Man. It's where they stuck the Germans and Italians who'd had the misfortune of living in the United Kingdom when the war started. British nationals of ques-tionable political leanings, too. By the time I got out of there, it would be far too late.

And just to top it all off, the nausea had returned.

I tapped my head against the window glass.

Shit. Shit. Shit.

How could I have been so careless? The cock-up that got me in bad with the coppers was one for the record books. Thank the Lord the old man – my mentor, John Stephenson – hadn't been there to see it. Just before he started the negotiation that sent me back to 1940, Will had tossed his billfold to me. He'd meant for me to take the cash, and I'd accepted, because there hadn't been any time to prepare. I returned to 1940 with nothing but the clothes on my back and the contents of my pockets when the Eidolons were moments away from erasing us. It was a good-faith gesture, a damn thoughtful thing to do in the face of such horrors. Thoughtful enough that it caused me a twinge of shame for how I'd treated Will. I had shunned him for decades, but in the end he was the noble one.

But it was also a futile gesture. And I would have seen that immediately if I hadn't been scared shitless and reeling from Gretel's revelations at the same time.

Cash? How many times had our currency changed between 1940 and 1963? We had a new *monarch*, for Christ's sake. I wondered if the coppers had noticed that yet. There probably wasn't a single piece of paper in Will's billfold that would stand up to scrutiny in 1940. Licenses wouldn't look like that for another ten or fifteen years.

Obvious now. But things had been so desperate.

It was hard for me to believe that there had been a time when tradecraft came naturally to me. I'd been rather good at it. You might say I'd been raised for that life. But I'd been out of the game for more than twenty years when Gretel and her brother emerged from behind the Iron Curtain. By that point I'd spent more years as a gardener than as a spy, and it showed.

When I had been a younger man, this kind of oversight would have been unthinkable to me. In fact, back then, I—

The idea I'd tucked away came surging back. I had the first inkling of a plan. But it was disturbing as hell. And I was nauseated enough.

The coppers took me to Cannon Row. I'd spent some time in various lockups during the years since my retirement from Milkweed, usually for drunkenness and a bit of brawling here and there. So I knew most of the stations by name.

They opted to toss me in the clink overnight rather than try to sort things out then and there. They held on to Will's billfold, and emptied my pockets. All they got for their trouble was my house key. I'd long ago made it a habit not to carry identification on me when engaged in work for SIS, and that had carried over to Milkweed.

But Leslie Pembroke's Milkweed, the Milkweed of the 1960s, was a slapdash affair. Somebody had made a bloody great oversight letting Will keep his billfold after his death had been so widely publicized. The fight with the Soviet agent had burned down half the crescent where Will's house had been. Milkweed had covered by spreading information about a ruptured gas main. They ought to have taken his ID when Will read his own obituaries in the papers.

Francis brought the key and billfold to the desk sergeant. 'Public indecency. And a possible burglary,' he said, nodding in my direction as his partner led me around the corner and into one of the two empty cells. It didn't differ significantly from others I'd known: cot, toilet, sink, and a single foot-square window set high in the bricks. This, like every other window in Britain, was covered with a blackout curtain.

The cell door clanged shut behind me, hard enough to rattle the springs on the cot. I listened for the lock; it snapped into place, a sharp metallic sound beneath the jangling of the copper's keys. I lay on the cot and began to shiver. The blanket smelled unpleasantly of sweat and cigarettes, which tweaked the nausea. So did the pillow stains, which gave off the odor of Brilliantine.

I wrapped the blanket around myself, but it did nothing to keep the trembling at bay.

They'd contact Will about his missing billfold. Meaning that soon enough they'd realize he was Lord William, which would only worsen things for me. How would Will react when the coppers told him they had his billfold? And how would the coppers react when he told them he was missing no such thing, and they took a closer look at its contents? Would Will recognize me? I shook my head, then winced when the coarse bristles of my beard snagged the blanket. The Will of this time knew a clean-shaven Marsh. But I had grown a beard to help hide the burns I'd received during an unsuccessful attempt to capture a Soviet wetwork specialist. The agent in question had been the product of Arzamas-16: the secret research city where the Soviets had reverse-engineered, reproduced, and improved upon Doctor von Westarp's achievements. Hence the fire that scorched me. Even if Will saw past the beard, the scars would prevent him from seeing Raybould Marsh's face.

The scars from that fight weren't only skin deep. Superheated air had blistered my throat, charred my vocal chords. I sounded nothing like my younger self.

Then it hit me. I knew, in a sudden flash of insight, exactly how Will would perceive me.

I looked and sounded like an old warlock.

This was a perfect opportunity. I knew exactly what to do. And for the first time since my arrival, I felt a twinge of hope. Perhaps undermining Milkweed wouldn't be as difficult as I'd feared. Even now Will was toying with the prospect of calling on the others to join Milkweed. I could intervene before that happened. Prevent Will from ever recruiting the warlocks in the first place.

I knew, based on conversations with Will in the original history, in the aftermath of our attempt to show Gretel to the Eidolons, that he suffered misgivings about his ability to handle further negotiations. So did we both after the mutilation those demons forced me to perpetrate against my friend. But Will knew we needed help. And he also knew there were other warlocks scattered throughout the country. Men like his grandfather. Men, I hoped, like me.

I'd tell Will the truth, of a sort: that I knew about Milkweed, and I knew what he was planning to do. I'd demand that I be the one to contact the other warlocks. After all, he was at best a novice, but I fit the role of an experienced elder. And after he'd pieced together the relevant information from his grandfather's journals (he'd done it once before, after all) he'd give me the whereabouts of the others. Speaking Enochian was out of the question, of course, but through my time in Milkweed I'd learned enough about the warlocks to pass as one of them. I'd have to hide my palms from Will, otherwise he might notice they weren't spiderwebbed with fine, white cuts like his own. But that was easy.

I would use Will as a means of tracking down Britain's warlocks. Just as the Soviets had done in the early '60s.

But I wouldn't kill them. Not right away. I'd keep them in reserve in case the war turned desperate again. I refused to throw Britain to the wolves.

And if it did become necessary to muster the warlocks, I'd retain one advantage. Will would be my eyes and ears inside the coven. I would turn him into a double agent.

It was stunning, the magnitude of my hypocrisy. I came from a future where Will was an unrepentant traitor to the country. Driven by grief and guilt over the things he'd done during the war, he had passed information about Milkweed's warlocks to the enemies of Britain. Enemies who systematically murdered the old men. I'd wanted to see Will's neck stretched for his collusion with the Soviets. But now here I was, deliberately planning to make him my own creature.

There was another option: I could tell him the truth. The whole truth. Tell him what the future held in store for us. Warn him about the blood prices, his morphine addiction. It was a seductive thought, having one true friend in 1940. A true ally. But I feared Will would make a hash of things. The man was incapable of discretion. And he'd be wary, given the strange things he'd witnessed on the Tarragona filmstrip. He'd go to Stephenson with this. And, worse yet, the younger version of me. And that pair would waste invaluable time chiseling into the bedrock of my story. Events could very well pass the tipping point by the time they reluctantly decided to take me at my word.

No. It was easier, and faster, to present myself to Will as something he was already prepared to accept.

I wasn't proud of how I intended to use Will. But it was a necessary evil for the sake of the greater good. Or so I told myself. It didn't lessen the disgust at what I saw myself becoming. Treating people like game pieces, evaluating them as means to an end? I was already thinking like Gretel.

The passage of time and my experiences in the future had given me an unforeseen advantage. I knew Will better than he knew himself. But there was one man whom I knew better than anybody. And if this was going to work, I'd have to turn him, too.

Everything relied on removing the threat posed by the Reichsbehörde. All the strategizing in the world would be pointless if I couldn't find a way to do that. The conclusion was despicable, but unavoidable.

I needed Gretel's help.

Acid clawed its way up my throat. I rolled off the cot, still tangled in the blanket, and kneeled on the slate floor while violent spasms ejected my stomach's contents into the toilet. When it was over, I lacked the strength to pull myself back on the cot. I stayed on the floor.

'You well?'

I looked up. Another copper had poked his head in. He stared at me, frowning.

I scraped the back of my hand across my mouth. 'Told you I was ill,' I croaked.

'You need a doctor?'

I shook my head. He withdrew, looking unconvinced.

Gretel. The mere thought of working alongside that raven-haired demon made me violently ill. How would I ever look Liv in the eyes – or *myself*, for Christ's sake – knowing full well that I'd willingly allied myself with the woman who'd killed our daughter? How would I ever look Agnes in the eyes? How could I work alongside Gretel without succumbing to the urge to murder her? Without despising myself?

It was vile. Another necessary evil.

As much as I was loath to admit it, I needed access to Gretel's power. I needed her knowledge of the future. Without it, this entire venture was doomed.

Gretel knew the score as well as I did. Better. She would co-operate as long as our interests were aligned. As to what would happen later . . .

A nimbus of gray light limned the bricks at the edges of the blackout curtain. A British sunrise, softened into a dull haze as the sun burned through a layer of rain clouds. I'd have known it anywhere.

The evidence of sunrise caught me by surprise. I hadn't expected to sleep. But I had, and now the night's jumble of fever dreams evaporated like storm clouds before the rising sun. I remembered little of it, except that John and his colorless eyes had figured heavily. Once again, my ears rang with the screams of a dying world.

Cold, dried sweat had stiffened my clothes and leeched the twin odors of tobacco and hair cream from the bedding into my hair. This roused the last traces of nausea still lingering dormant in my gut. My beard itched where the bristles edged the furrow of scar tissue along my jaw. I moved slowly, untangling myself from the blanket with careful deliberation. At least the throbbing behind my temples had retreated.

I don't know how long I lay there, lost in thoughts about the Reichsbehörde, before a copper came by. I didn't recognize him; I reckoned Francis and his partner had gone off shift. He slid a tray through a slot in the door. It held a plate of toast and a cup. I recognized the scent of weak tea steeped from the second or third use of the leaves. It was a common practice during the war.

'Thought I heard you moving about,' he said.

I took the tray. 'How much longer?'

'Depends on what Lord William says when he gets here.'

13 May 1940
Westminster, London, England

Cannon Row wasn't a five-minute walk from the Admiralty building, just a bit past Downing Street. Will strode through the Admiralty screen onto Whitehall, nodding to the marine sentries who manned the sandbag revetments. A handful of heavy raindrops pattered against his bowler. The leaden sky threatened to unleash another cold drizzle, as it had been doing on and off all day long.

He picked up his pace. He hadn't bothered with an umbrella; it was too much trouble with only one good hand. The Westminster Palace clock tower loomed over the Thames when Will turned the corner to Bridge Street. It showed a few minutes to three. He'd been absorbed in poring over his grandfather's lexicon, trying to make sense of the Eidolons' name for Marsh, when the strange message from the Metropolitan Police finally reached him.

Will checked his pocket again. No, he hadn't lost his billfold. What a queer mix-up.

The Cannon Row police station huddled beside New Scotland Yard, a nineteenth-century building that hulked over the Victoria Embankment. To Will's mind, it looked like nothing so much as a Victorian Gothic confection, a five-story layer cake of red brick and white limestone. Will inadvertently passed the station entrance, walking instead to where the Yard building itself fronted the embankment with two large iron gates. He had to get directions from a constable on duty at the gates. The clock tower was just chiming the hour when he finally managed the station proper.

He introduced himself to the desk sergeant, and explained that he'd been called down to claim some lost property. Except, he quickly pointed out, it wasn't lost at all, so wasn't it a bit silly to waste everybody's time over nothing? But the sergeant asked him to wait. He disappeared through a door.

By the time Big Ben chimed three in the afternoon, I was ready to climb the walls. But at long last I heard what sounded like a desk sergeant announcing there was a Lord William here, and had anybody called him?

Finally. Took your own bloody time, didn't you, Will?

Typical.

I ran a hand through my hair, trying to bring a semblance of order and dignity to the tousled haystack. I tried to imagine how an elder warlock like Hargreaves would receive Will. I'd barely dealt with the man – or any of the warlocks aside from Will, for that matter – and wasn't particularly saddened by it. Arrogant, standoffish, and nasty as the day was long. That's what I remembered. Sitting on the cot didn't seem quite right. Instead, I opted to stand in the center of the cell, hands clasped behind my back. One look at my face and Will would draw the obvious conclusion.

While I waited, I eavesdropped on the conversation that unfolded just around the corner from my cell.

The desk sergeant returned a moment later. He ushered Will through the same door, deeper into the station. Cannon Row was one of the stations responsible for policing the very heart of London, and as such, it was a busy place. The sergeant led Will through a warren of desks and filing cabinets, the room echoing with the clatter of typewriters, the ring of telephones, and a dozen conversations. They were met by a Constable Dennis something, and an Inspector Hill, at a desk along the rear wall close to a door with CELLS stenciled on its frosted glass pane.

'Lord William?'

'Hullo, hullo! I am tardy. Terribly sorry about that. Things have been just a bit manic. The war, you know.'

This was met with a general chorus of curses directed at the Jerries.

'Quite right! Now,' said Will. 'I must confess, I'm a bit perplexed as to why I'm here.'

One of the constables fetched a chair for him. Without thinking, Will used his injured hand to pull it closer.

'Ouch . . . double damn.'

The inspector asked, 'Why the bandages, sir? What happened
to your hand?'

'What, this? Ah.' Will paused to think up a plausible explanation, but then rushed ahead with the first thing to spring to mind
before his hesitation became awkward. 'Silly thing. Bashed it with
a spade. Victory garden, you see. Doing my bit for the war effort.'
He attempted a laugh, which came off halfhearted. 'Planting the
seeds of victory, you might say.'

He had always been a terrible liar. But this was the Will I remembered from the old days. Before Milkweed had changed him. It
felt good, hearing him be his old self again; I could picture him
waving his hands about as he spoke. But there was a lot riding on
this, and I couldn't help rolling my eyes with frustration. *Oh, for
Christ's sake, Will. Just get on with it.*

The constable asked, 'You keep your own garden?'

He couldn't hide the incredulity in his voice. It seemed he had
a hard time imagining Will, seated there in his Savile Row finery,
mucking about in the dirt.

'Yes,' said Will. 'For my brother's foundation. Leading by
example, you see. His Grace is dedicated to supporting the war
effort. As am I.'

'When did you hurt your hand?' asked the constable.

'Yesterday.' The constables shared a look.

'Just an accident, then?'

The skepticism came across clearly. Will couldn't understand why the police were so interested in his bandages. 'Indeed,' he said.

'Looks serious. You seen a doctor for that?'

'It's why I'm so very late, in fact.' At least that was true. 'But enough of my troubles,' said Will. 'What was this about a billfold?'

Constable Dennis relayed the story of an arrest he and his partner had made the previous evening. It was a strange tale. ('In the lake, you say? Good heavens.')

Inspector Hill took over after the constable finished his story. He said, 'You can see, sir, why we wanted to speak with you.'

'I appreciate your diligence. Truly excellent work,' Will said, 'but I suspect somebody is having fun with you.' He took care to reach into his pocket with his good hand. 'As you see, I haven't misplaced my billfold.'

The constable opened a desk drawer and produced a similar billfold. 'This doesn't belong to you, then?'

Will laughed. 'Gentlemen,' he said, 'I admit to a certain extravagance in my sartorial tastes. But that does not extend to owning multiple billfolds.'

Hill said, 'Is there any possibility you've misplaced some papers? Anything that might have found its way into this?'

'I doubt it. May I?'

'Please.'

Will thumbed through the contents of the mystery billfold. 'Sorry, gents. I don't recognize a scrap of this. I mean, look at this! Knightsbridge? That's no address I recognize. Certainly not mine. How I wish it were. Quite nice. Always struck me as a good place to settle down, Knightsbridge.'

'Do you recognize her?' The inspector pointed to a color

photograph (interesting, that) of a lady with striking blue eyes and a dusting of silver in honey blond hair. She looked a fair bit older than Will, but pretty just the same. Her expression was something between a smile and a scowl, equal parts irritation and fondness, as though the photographer were somebody dear to her and had surprised her in an unguarded moment. Will couldn't help but wonder who she might be, and who the photographer had been.

'Sir?'

Will realized he'd been lost in thought. 'Lovely lady,' he said. 'But I don't know her. Wish I did.'

The inspector unfolded another piece of paper. It appeared to be a driver's license. 'This is your full name? And your date of birth?'

'Yes.' Will looked at the date of issue, and frowned. 'But clearly this is a hoax. 1963? How silly.'

Dennis said, 'Yeah. We're a bit puzzled by that.'

'Any notion how your name might have ended up on these papers? Anything at all?'

'Not a crumb.'

The inspector referred to his notes. 'Do you know a John Stephenson?'

Will blinked. 'I beg your pardon?'

'That's the name this fellow gave. I see it's familiar to you?'

'I just spoke to John Stephenson not a quarter of an hour ago. Quite a riddle, isn't it? I'm as perplexed as you. Although . . .'

Will trailed off as another thought struck him. Marsh had been speculating about enemy surveillance. Was that it?

The inspector patiently prompted him. 'Yes?'

'Well, I'm not entirely free to discuss this, it's all very hush-hush, you understand, but I have been doing a bit of work for HMG.'

'What sort of work?'

'I'm sure you gentlemen will understand that the making of war occasionally raises issues of a sensitive nature. Suffice it to say that I've been asked to bring certain skills to bear on the problem.'

I wanted to punch the wall. Better yet, I wanted to punch Will. Anything to shut him up.

Jesus Christ, Will. Why don't you just come straight out and tell them about Milkweed and the Reichsbehörde while you're at it? I knew Will had read the Official Secrets Act. But I hadn't realized the basic idea hovered so far above his mental grasp. Stephenson would have been apoplectic had he known Will was practically traipsing over hill and dale, singing about his secret work for Whitehall to anybody who would listen to a few measures.

Right then I knew that I could never confide in Will if my mission was to succeed.

I couldn't believe what I was hearing. Nor, I suspected, could the coppers. What could this chinless toff possibly bring to the table?

'Skills?'

'I mustn't say any more,' said Will. 'But rest assured that we'll give Jerry what for, when the time comes. Yes, indeed.' He winked.

Dennis said, 'So you think your work for the Crown—'

'Not so loudly, if you please. The walls have ears, as they say.'

Inspector Hill sighed. Then said, 'Your *work* might be related to this?'

Will said, 'It's been brought to my attention that I might be followed. I could be under *surveillance*.' He paused before whispering, 'By the Jerries.'

*

God damn it. This was my own fault. I had warned him about the surveillance after I'd returned to Britain with Gretel as my prisoner. That had been long before I'd finally understood what she was. Enemy surveillance had seemed the only explanation for how she had known about me and Liv and our newborn daughter.

The constable said, 'Francis had figured the codger for a Jerry spy.'

'If he is, he's a poor specimen,' said Hill. 'The Jerries would at least make certain their agents in the country had real money on them. Not this rubbish.'

This provoked a general discussion among the policemen, who speculated about German agents at large in London. Which, I suddenly realized, was the root of the niggling itch at the back of my mind.

My legs buckled under the crushing weight of new remembrances. I kicked the wall and dropped to the cot; its frame groaned in protest.

'Oy, quiet down in there!' yelled a copper.

Will had lost his finger yesterday. But what I'd forgotten, until that moment, was that Klaus had come to pluck Gretel from the Admiralty building the very next evening. Which meant he was already in the country. Which meant the siblings would escape tonight. And I had to be there when that happened.

I knew, from reading the Schutzstaffel operational records long after the fact, that Klaus had arrived via U-boat, following instructions that Gretel had left in a letter prior to swanning off to become my prisoner. That sub was lurking off the coast right now, waiting to bring the siblings back to Germany and the farm.

Which meant free transportation to the Reichsbehörde. A golden opportunity. But the U-boat wouldn't wait forever.

I had to get my younger self on that sub.

And with that, another cog in Gretel's grand plan slipped into place for me. This was the one thing I'd never been able to square away: What purpose had it served for her to play at being my prisoner? Why did she let me take her to Britain, only to leave with her brother so soon afterwards? Long ago I'd given up on ever knowing the answer, resigned to the fact that Gretel and her machinations were inscrutable.

Now I knew my planning was on the right track, because Gretel's actions suddenly made perfect sense. She'd come to Britain to meet *me*.

But there was more I had to do. So much more.

Klaus's spectacular infiltration of the Admiralty building had forced us to acknowledge Milkweed's shortcomings. Which meant that unless I stopped him and changed the sequence of events, Will would leave tomorrow in search of the other warlocks. But that, at least, would take care of itself, as soon as the coppers escorted Will to my cell.

Or so I thought.

The policemen were deep in conversation, embroiled in speculation. Will hadn't solved the mystery surrounding the billfold's provenance for them, but he'd given them food for thought. They latched onto the surveillance issue, though with relief or dread, Will couldn't tell.

Either way, he'd done his part. They'd get it sorted. And Will wanted to get back to the lexicon while the Eidolon's declaration was still fresh in his mind. He cleared his throat.

'Well, then. If that's all?' He scooted his chair back. 'I'm sure you gents will put it right soon enough.'

Inspector Hill said, 'Very well. Though if we have further questions?'

'Of course. Do call on me as needed. Best of luck with your mystery man. Ta.'

Oh, no. Don't you dare, Will. Don't you dare walk out of here without first seeing me.

I cradled my face in my hands. Will was leaving without bothering to see who had been carrying his billfold. And the coppers let him.

You stupid, chinless toff! I wanted to scream. *Something strange has happened and you need to* follow it through! *You need to survey the situation. Gather information. For all you know your life could be at risk! And for Christ's sake, if you were under that level of surveillance, so were we all! It's your responsibility to find out what you can and report back to Stephenson. Report back to me.*

But it was too late. Will was gone.

Which left me back where I had started. I had less than twenty-four hours to get out of this cell, recruit my younger self and convince him to leave his wife and newborn daughter behind on an open-ended undercover mission, *and* to stop Will from recruiting the warlocks.

I had journeyed across twenty-three years to be here now. Yet still I faced the same problem as always: time.

THREE

Liv's fingertip traced the puckered knuckles of Marsh's hand where it rested on her stomach. She'd pulled his arm around her while spooning up against him after Agnes's 3 A.M. feeding. It had roused him from a horrible dream about gardening shears. He'd lain there half the night, listening to her breathe, watching the gentle rise and fall of her alabaster throat, inhaling her scent.

She'd been awake for a while before he'd realized it. It was a game she played, feigning the long slow breathing of a deep sleep and wondering if he'd notice. She was good at it. They'd lain awake together while the sun rose. They hadn't made love since they'd brought Agnes home. Not since long before France. But Liv hadn't been out of hospital long. He wouldn't press; he could wait until she was ready.

Her fingertip paused in its wanderings. She whispered, 'And what about this one?'

'Which one?'

She was counting his scars. He had a few.

'Ring finger. Just above the second knuckle.' She kissed the spot.

'Ah. That one.' He stroked the knuckle across her navel. Liv inhaled, flinching from the tickle. Her rump pressed against him. He kissed the nape of her neck.

'Well?' Liv feigned immunity to his attentions. But the flush rising on her skin put the lie to that. 'It must be quite a tale for you to remember it so vividly. How old were you?'

Marsh's fingers tapped her stomach as he counted off the years. 'Seventeen, maybe.'

'Aha!' she exclaimed in a stage whisper. 'Now I know I'm in for a truly fine story.' Liv delighted in the tales of his misspent youth – unlike so many women, who might have simply pretended their husbands didn't have a past. But he was glad she never asked how he'd managed a job with the Foreign Office given such a colorful record. So he'd never needed to account for how Stephenson had had his record wiped clean. Though of course his job had nothing to do with the Foreign Office.

'And where,' she asked, 'does the curtain rise?'

'Lympne.'

'What on earth were you doing there?'

'Seeing the sights. Rode down with some mates.'

'Right. Sightseeing. Of course you were.' She rolled over, hooked an ankle over his calf, and peered into his eyes. 'What was her name?'

'I'm wounded by the implication.'

'Mmm-hmmm.' She tapped his ring finger just above the pale crease of scar tissue. 'So. Sharp, are they? These famous sights in Lympne?'

'Not particularly. But window glass can be.'

'I've heard. How did you break a window?'

'Boosting a car.'

'Tell me you weren't.'

'I was in a bit of a hurry, Liv.'

'Were you, now?'

'Not by choice. The sights, after all. But there was this rather angry bloke.'

Now she feigned concern. 'Angry? With you? Whatever for?'

'It seems he'd come home to his flat to find somebody dangling from the bedroom windowsill.'

'Somebody.' Liv rested her forehead on his chest. Her warm naked body rubbed against him, shaking with suppressed laughter. It felt wonderful. He held her tighter. God, he loved this woman.

'Yes. But when he raced 'round back, and found me innocently collecting my shirt in the alleyway, he immediately leaped to conclusions. Unfounded conclusions.'

'The fiend.'

'Poor fellow. I would have boosted a different car if I'd known it was his.' He waited for her laughter to taper off. Then he added, 'His sister never forgave me.'

Liv dissolved into giggles. That was rare. The giggling became tickling. Then kissing.

Downstairs, the telephone rang.

'Bugger,' he said.

'Not just now. And the telephone will wake your daughter if you're not quick about it.' Her elbow nudged him gently in the stomach. 'Move, sailor.'

'Maybe they'll call again later.'

But Agnes began to wail on the third ring. Liv groaned. She yanked Marsh's pillow from under his head and hugged it over her ears. 'Go. And tell whomever it is to kindly sod off.'

Marsh levered himself into a sitting position. His foot tapped at the floorboards until he found his slippers. He staggered into the nursery, fumbling with the sash of his robe. He bounced Agnes in the crook of his arm as he descended the stairs.

The telephone rested on a table in the vestibule, next to the blanket and bowl of water Liv kept on hand for sealing the door in the event of a gas attack. Above the table hung the framed watercolor they had received as a wedding gift. The phone was still ringing when Marsh finally reached it. He croaked a serviceable hello into the handset.

'Why aren't you interrogating the prisoner right now?'

Marsh sighed. Rubbed his eyes. 'Good morning, sir.'

Stephenson said, 'We need to know why she's here.'

'Yes, sir.'

The stairs creaked under Liv's feet. She waved at the handset in Marsh's hand. *Hi, John*, she mouthed, while taking Agnes from him.

'Incidentally, sir, my wife wanted me to tell you she'd like you to so—'

She swatted at him. 'Don't you dare.'

'—to know she's cross with you for making me miss the birth of my daughter.' Liv knew he worked for Stephenson, and that they'd known each other for many years.

'Tell her to take it up with Hitler,' said the old man.

Marsh waited until Liv had passed into the kitchen, out of earshot. 'I've done my best with the girl,' he said. 'Perhaps somebody else should give it a go.'

'Perhaps you haven't noticed, but we're a bit short of hands.'

'There's Lorimer. Or Will.' The line fell silent for a long beat. Marsh conceded, 'Fair enough. Scratch that.'

Will's concept of discretion left something to be desired. He was still new to the world of tradecraft. Plus, in his weakened state, he was in no position to deal with her. The imperturbable gypsy girl would run circles about him. Only the Eidolon – Marsh shuddered – had evoked a genuine emotional reaction from her.

Fragmentary images from last night's dream, of shears and fingernails and butterflies with newsprint wings, fluttered across his mind's eye.

Stephenson said, 'Lorimer is busy.'

In the kitchen, Liv filled a kettle, simultaneously cooing to their daughter and dodging the fine spray of water that spat from the leaky faucet.

'Me, too,' said Marsh. He failed to keep a hint of pleading out of his voice.

'I'll pretend I didn't hear that.'

Liv lit the gas hob on the stove. *Click-click-whoosh.*

Marsh sighed again. 'May I eat breakfast first?'

'Only if you're quick about it. The PM wants answers.' Stephenson's voice faded and then came back, as if he'd paused in the act of hanging up to add: 'As do I.' *Click.*

Their refrigerator held no eggs, on account of the rationing, but their pantry was well-stocked with dried egg powder. Liv opted to try a recipe given in one of the Ministry of Food's War Cookery leaflets ('English Monkey,' from *Leaflet Number Eleven.*) Marsh would have preferred a different experiment, the so-called 'Spanish Omelet,' but it was too early in the season for herbs from the garden. And he'd been too busy capturing foreign operatives to get anything planted.

Marsh opened the cupboard while Liv crumbled the last of their stale bread into a bowl. The sleeves of his robe fell back as he reached up to fish out a pair of plates.

'Those are new,' she said, pointing at his forearm, the one she hadn't been studying in bed. Three thin scabs traced the contour of his arm, like a fragment of Morse code etched into his flesh. They were fingernail marks; the gypsy girl had clenched his arm in terror when Will's Eidolon arrived.

'That happened on the Tube yesterday,' he lied. 'Got a door slammed on my arm.'

'Poor thing. Those doors are evil, aren't they? I once had the hem of my skirt caught. On an express. I had to stand all the way to Paddington. Quite embarrassing.'

Marsh took the time to enjoy a proper breakfast with his family, and the old man be damned. Later, he would remember this morning, and weep with gratitude for the memory.

13 May 1940
Westminster, London, England

Precious moments slipped away while I rotted in that cell. I could feel every tick, every tock. Desperation had me on the brink of feigning illness serious enough for a doctor. I was assessing my chances of taking a hostage when something strange happened: the coppers let me go.

It was Francis's partner who came to give me the good news. Since Will hadn't pressed any charges, he said, there was nothing for them to do but set me free.

I asked, 'That's all, then?'

'That's all. Sorry for the misunderstanding, sir.' He smiled uneasily, and paused awkwardly as if debating whether to clap me on the back. 'But do stay out of St. James' from now on, won't you?'

Ha bloody ha.

'Straight home with you, sir. And don't leave the house without an ID next time. You'll be in a spot of trouble if you get nicked again.'

If anything, it seemed they were eager to see me go. Quite a change from the previous evening. And the mention of St. James' brought home another oddity. They'd dropped the public indecency charge. Not that I was keen to preserve that particular humiliation, but it was strange.

Stranger still: they returned Will's billfold complete with contents. And they glossed over my missing ID card. The coppers cut me loose knowing bloody well I still had no proper identification.

I emerged from the police station into a damp, gray afternoon. Looked like it had rained stair-rods while I was in the clink, though I hadn't heard a hint of it through the thick stone walls. Now the clouds had conjured a cold, thin drizzle that snaked beneath my collar. I missed my fedora.

I paused on the pavement, stretching and generally playing the part of a man sipping at freedom and relief in equal measure. It gave me my first real glimpse of the London I'd left behind long ago, in fact if not in spirit.

And dear God: I hadn't realized how much I'd missed this city. London had been such a proud city before Luftwaffe bombs erased centuries of our history and culture. The postwar rebuilding had been extensive, but soulless and perfunctory. London's postwar caretakers hadn't so much as nodded at the city's architectural heritage. But now I stood in the midst of London as it was meant to be.

I wiped my eyes while studying my surroundings. Little things had changed, as well. In 1940 it was still possible to find gas lamps. I stood beneath one.

After the look and feel of the city itself, I next noticed the cars on the street. I hadn't appreciated how much they'd changed over the years until the change had been erased. I supposed it had been a gradual evolution. And there were so few of them on the street; I'd forgotten about that, too. Part of that came out of the petrol rationing. But even accounting for the rationing, there were simply more cars on the street in 1963.

A placard pasted in the window of a chemist's shop exhorted me to LOOK OUT IN THE BLACKOUT. Other placards exhorted passersby to buy Victory Bonds and to spot enemy uniforms on sight. An ARP warden nodded to me from beneath the narrow brim of his metal helmet. I nodded back.

I took it all in. The sights. The sounds. The rainy smell of springtime in the city. This was where I belonged. Fighting a chiaroscuro war, black and white. I wasn't cut out to be a cold warrior. Events subsequent to my return to the service had borne that out.

The survey of my surroundings also enabled me to spot the black Vauxhall parked down the street from the station. Picked it out at once; SIS used modern descendants of that model into the '60s.

I realized what had happened. Will's departure incited a heated discussion between those who thought he was just another brainless toff, and those (probably the minority) who thought Will's claims merited closer attention. In the end, discretion won out. Next, a rapid series of telephone calls ricocheted from Cannon Row, to the Met, to the Home Office, to the Security Service, and back down the chain again. I reckoned the message from MI5 said something akin to: *Give us time to get down there. Cut him loose when we say. We'll send someone to pick up the file. After that, tell your men this never happened.*

At which point the coppers couldn't wait to see the last of me. Catching the occasional butcher who short-changed customers on their ration cards was one thing; cracking Jerry spy rings was a different kettle of fish.

This explained why they had set me free in spite of my dodgy credentials and lack of identification. Even the gentle advice to go straight home: so MI5 could track me. They'd returned Will's billfold complete with its original contents; I reckoned they might have added something, too. Something damning. The poisoned cheese of their rat trap.

I turned up my collar and started walking, careful to stay visible to the Vauxhall. After a few dozen yards I stopped behind a parked car, and stooped over to tie my shoes. I tried to use the car's chromed bumper as a mirror, but that had been painted over. Right . . . the blackout regs. I'd forgotten. So I watched the street behind me from the corner of my eye.

Sure enough. The Vauxhall eased into the sparse traffic the moment I disappeared from sight.

Splendid. I was officially under observation by the domestic intelligence services. They'd be running a standard box if they knew what they were about; I hadn't picked out all the watchers. Nor did I want to. Not yet. They'd get cross if they knew I'd picked them out so easily.

The residual ache in my knee twinged in warning as I hopped on the rear platform of a passing omnibus. These, at least, had resisted the passage of time, for which I was glad. Not for the comfortable familiarity, but because it meant I still knew a few tricks for dodging a fare.

The conductor frowned at me, clearly discomfited by my scars. 'That's dangerous,' he said. 'Wait 'til we've come to a proper stop, what?'

'Sorry, mate. Bit of a hurry,' I said. I took an empty seat behind a mother and daughter, and fished out Will's billfold. I plucked out a five-pound note and folded it into my hand while the clippie dealt with another fare. Then, while nobody was looking, I kicked the girl's seat. Her mother shot me a look that could have blistered paint, but frowned and turned away when she saw my wounded face. Didn't like doing it – I thought of Agnes – but it got the girl crying, loudly, which is what I needed.

When it came my turn to pay, I held the folded bill between my fingers so that the clippie could clearly see the '5'. I smiled apologetically, and rasped, 'Lost my pocket change at the pub. Help a fellow out, will you?'

He did. And he gave me change for the fiver: the crying kept him too distracted to give the bill a proper look. One of the oldest tricks around, yes, but that's because it works. You just have to know how to play it.

It wasn't much money, but it meant finally having some legal tender on my person, and enough to get me to Walworth.

A gas mask canister hung from the clippie's neck. It bumped against his chest when the bus lurched around a corner. Others – men, women, even the children – carried similar bundles. I didn't have a gas mask, but I wasn't worried; they'd been common in the first few months of the war, though by 1940 one could find folks who'd decided not to bother. More and more people opted to leave the masks at home as the war dragged on. They'd been right; Hitler never got around to lobbing mustard gas across the Channel.

I had to hope that piece of history wouldn't get rewritten. Only Gretel could tell me how things would change as my work unfolded. But I had to get to her before we could have that conversation.

I glimpsed a black Vauxhall trailing the omnibus when I transferred to another line. My eyes scanned the other traffic around us, what little there was of it, but I couldn't pick out the rest of the surveillance team. My fingers worried at the cold brass house key in my pocket. If I was going to break the box, I had to do it before I led them to Liv. And me. The other me.

The second bus wasn't as crowded as the first. Each time a lorry or fountain momentarily blocked the line of sight between the Vauxhall and my omnibus, I hopped a seat closer to the rear platform. The clippie looked bemused, or perhaps annoyed. But soon I was as close to the platform as one could be without physically standing on it. That was the best position for what I intended, but it would have tipped off my followers.

The dome of St. Paul's loomed out of the gray mist to my left as the bus trundled along Cheapside. I couldn't help but stare at the ghostly giant as though it were a long-lost friend; the Fire Watch had failed to save the cathedral from several direct hits in the autumn of 1940, after the systematic crippling of the RAF had given the Luftwaffe free rein of Britain's skies. After the war, the city had eventually filled the crater and turned the site into a municipal car park. But now Wren's masterpiece stood proudly over its neighbors, no less grand for the cloak of dampness. I hoped it fared better the second time around. I'd missed it more than I realized. I had my city back.

The omnibus slowed as we approached Newgate. I gritted my teeth, anticipating the flare of agony in my bad knee. The omni swerved onto St. Martin's Le Grand. I threw myself out of my seat and leapt from the platform.

My knee gave out when I hit the macadam. It sent me tumbling, but I managed to roll with the worst of it. Got soaked in the process. I dodged traffic, loping and limping to the entrance to St. Paul's station on the Underground while behind me the clippie cursed and tires screeched. I earned more curses with my elbows, squeezing past the throng on the escalator down to the ticket hall. I prayed a copper didn't see, and ask for my non-existent Identity Card. I'd have to do something about that damned ID problem.

The Tube was my best shot at breaking the box. I had lived in London most of my life. Although, in that regard, my extra twenty years spent riding the Tube might have been a liability. I vaguely remembered how this stop had been known as Post Office until it had undergone modernization, when the Underground had replaced the lifts with escalators and changed the name a few years prior to the war. But those alterations were recent to those around me.

I spent the next hour using every trick I knew for throwing off a tail: backtracking, choosing my direction at random, buying multiple tickets, entering cars and jumping out just before they pulled away from the platform ... My jump from the omnibus might have been enough to lose my followers, but I wanted to be damn certain.

It was late afternoon by the time I made it to Walworth. I knew exactly what I had to do; I'd had plenty of time to think in the cell. But it was one thing to formulate a plan, and quite another to put it in motion while standing on the doorstep of one's own home. Liv and I had bought the mock Tudor not long after our wedding in the old man's garden; we'd been lucky to find it.

I couldn't use the key in my pocket until I knew the house was empty. Accounting for my own whereabouts was easy: my doppelgänger was at the Admiralty. That I knew because I'd been at work most of the day when Klaus snuck in to free Gretel. But where was Liv?

I drew a steadying breath, then knocked. If Liv answered the door, I'd pretend to be lost and hope to hell she didn't recognize me.

No answer. I rapped more firmly the second time.

I fished the house key out of my pocket, just as I'd done countless times. The familiar divot in the brass cradled my thumb as I pushed the key into the lock.

The key and lock resisted each other. A frisson of panic wormed its way into my gut. What had I forgotten? I could have sworn we'd never changed the locks. But then the key jittered home, and I realized what had happened.

The house key I'd carried in my pocket from 1963 was the original mate to the lock on this door. But it was also twenty years older, meaning its teeth had worn slightly from decades of regular use whereas the tumblers inside the door were still sharp. So the key gave me a bit more resistance than I'd been accustomed to. It took a fair bit of jiggling before the bolt snapped open with a muffled clack. But it did, eventually, and then I was inside . . .

. . . and reeling from the onslaught of memories.

The first thing I noticed was the reek of fish stew simmering in the kitchen. The smell slammed into me with the force of an anchor chain snapping taut. If the other things I'd witnessed since my return to wartime had been a gradual sinking back into the seas of my past, this was a nighttime high-altitude drop without a parachute.

Austerity food. Hadn't experienced it for a long time, and I'd never missed it. But I'd know it anywhere.

Liv hated fish stew. We both did. But fish and offal were the only two meats not covered by the rationing system. By now they were already getting hard to find, forcing people to experiment with unfamiliar and unwelcome varieties; I shuddered at memories of nasty surprises from the fishmonger. We'd braved the whale steaks only once. The flavor of oily, fishy-tasting liver bubbled up from the recesses of my reinvigorated memory.

Simmering food meant Liv didn't expect to be gone for long. I had to hurry.

The house differed from the one I knew in myriad fine details. We hadn't kept a bowl of water near the front door since the war, and I hadn't laid eyes on that watercolor in years. Sunlight hadn't yet bleached the wallpaper in the vestibule; the banister glistened under a recent coat of varnish, still unblemished by the scuffs and scratches of coming years. But it was still the same house.

I thought I'd been ready for this. This was my own home, after all. I'd expected this visit to be easy and quick. But then I glanced into the den.

Where, alongside the wireless cabinet, sat Agnes's bassinet. Her baby blanket, the pink one with elephants, was draped over the bottom. The same blanket that had caught Liv's tears while I dug through the rubble of Williton with my bare hands.

Before I knew it, I was on my knees with that blanket pressed to my face. It smelled like my daughter.

Oh, God. It smelled like my living baby daughter.

It was real. This was all real. I was truly here, not in a dream. My daughter was here, and she was alive. She was with Liv right now.

In the early years after Agnes had died, we'd kept some little things around to remind us of her presence in our home and family. But as our marriage had withered, John's shrieking and yowling had transformed the constant reminders of Agnes from bittersweet mementos to instruments of torture. Liv packed away the blanket, and the rest soon followed. It had been so very long since I'd seen or smelled or touched any evidence of Agnes's existence aside from the single faded photograph—

—my head spun round to stare at the mantel, and there it was: the photo that would eventually go into my billfold.

I don't know how long I lingered in the den. My face was wet and the blanket damp when I finally stood. I wiped my eyes.

You're not getting her this time, Gretel.

First things first. I took the stairs two at a time, wincing at every throb from my bad knee. I went straight to our bedroom. Liv's wardrobe stood tidy in one corner. But she had more clothes than I did, so we shared the closet. I rummaged it, pushing aside shifts and shirts until I reached the very rear. And there it was, pressed against the wall, still hanging in its garment bag.

My naval uniform. *His* naval uniform.

I opened the bag and tipped it over the bed. The familiar blues of my uniform tumbled out, followed by the headgear. Then I hung the empty garment bag back in its spot in the closet and pushed the other clothes back into a semblance of their original clutter.

I dug out a slim briefcase before shutting the closet. It was almost new; I'd never been in the habit of carrying one. But it would be useful.

He would never miss the uniform. I probably hadn't laid eyes on it since the day I mustered out and started my real career with SIS. I'd made lieutenant-commander on my way out; a hair earlier than usual, and I was proud of that. Though it had never been the life for me, I'd served my country well. But the rank had counted in my favor when I joined the Firm. As the old man had known it would.

Next, it was back downstairs, through the miasma of austerity stew in the kitchen, and out the rear door. But rather than the garden, my destination was the Anderson shelter. Where Liv and I – and Agnes, in the early days – had huddled during countless bombing raids, listening to the wail of the sirens, the *chuffchuffchuff* of the ack-acks, the thunder of explosions as London disintegrated around us.

It had been our refuge. And though it was a tight fit, Liv had managed to stock a few supplies in case our house got bombed out. An oil lamp. Candles. A change of clothes. A few tins of food. And money.

We had stashed the glass jar in the corner, under the cot. I had sealed the lid with candle wax after we'd discovered how easily water seeped into the Anderson. It wasn't quite so musty in the shelter after I had cobbled together a sump pump out of an old bicycle tire pump. But that had been later in the summer, and so for now the shelter floor was damp.

I didn't have time to count it all, but it was enough to grease the wheels for a while. The paper money disappeared into my billfold. The coins, as well. It wasn't exactly stealing, I told myself. Not technically.

After that, I stripped out of the clothes I'd been wearing since 1963. The Anderson rang like a Chinese gong when I banged my head against one of the low curved steel sheets that formed the walls and ceiling. I folded the old clothes into the pile on a low shelf, then struggled into the uniform. It didn't fit as well as it might have; life as a hard-drinking fifty-year-old gardener hadn't left me as fit and trim as I had been as a thirty-year-old spy. But I managed to pull the trousers, shirt, and jacket on without popping a seam.

Liv had stowed a secondhand shaving kit in the shelter for me; a quick look in the mirror suggested I looked reasonably like a naval officer. The uniform was the man. Unless somebody knew what to look for, it would hide a multitude of sins. My shoes, for instance.

I didn't take the rest of the shelter supplies. Not yet. There was something else I needed, but it wasn't here. I knew that I – *he* – carried it with him. So I'd have to get it later. But I knew I'd be returning, depending on how things went at the Admiralty tonight. I was destined to spend the night bouncing back and forth between the Admiralty and my house like a badminton shuttlecock. A wearying thought. But time had grown very short, and it was crucial that my counterpart, the other Raybould Phillip Marsh, made that rendezvous with the U-boat.

Time to leave. And I started to, but had to duck back into the shelter when the kitchen door creaked open. Liv had come home.

She called, 'Love, are you about?' Just as she had always done. Back when she had still loved me. Back when her voice was still a dulcet soprano.

I opened my mouth to answer my wife – it was natural, the most natural thing in the world – but only caught myself as the first shivers of pain rattled through my ruined throat. She wouldn't recognize the rasp of my voice. Liv would never know me as her husband, by sight or sound.

Even the illusion was lost to me. I couldn't pretend – from a distance, for a few moments – to be her lover.

More than anything at that moment, I wanted to be Cyrano de Bergerac. To speak to my lady from hiding. To let her think that I was somebody else. But it was not to be. So I huddled in the shelter while she called again.

'Raybould? Are you home?' I wondered if she had heard me rifling through the shelter. Had she heard me rap my head? I leaned toward the finger-width gap in the Anderson door, straining to listen past the thudding of my heart and the faint tattoo of rain on the garden walk. 'Hmmmph,' she said, and closed the door. I recognized another creak a moment later; she had opened the window above the sink. I crept forward, still listening.

Liv said, 'Your father drives me mad some days. Sooner or later we'll get burgled because he can't see fit to close a door properly.' She paused for the sound of running water. Then she added, 'Or mend a leaky faucet.'

She was talking to Agnes. Oh God. Agnes.

I nudged the shelter door and peeked through the gap with one eye. Liv's auburn hair bobbed through the kitchen as she tended to the stew.

Agnes began to cry. I froze with my hand on the door. That sound. That wonderful sound. There was a hole in me where Agnes had been. But it shrank a little as my daughter wailed and her mother soothed her.

'Shhh, shhh, baby girl.' Liv sang a lullaby.

I closed my eyes, swaying to the sound of her voice.

Home. I was home again, my beloved wife and daughter just a few feet away. I could be with them in seconds. I could do it. I could approach Liv. I could tell her the truth, tell her her husband had finally returned from the longest journey. She'd know it for truth; I could convince her. I could whisper things only her husband knew, touch her in ways only her husband knew.

I could. I would. I would have my family back. I would take them back, and damn my doppelgänger. He didn't deserve them as I did.

I'm coming, love.

Still swaying to Liv's voice, I opened my eyes, reached for the door—

And glimpsed myself in the shaving mirror. Glimpsed my ugly beard, my ruined face, my sunken weary eyes. Saw myself as Liv would see me: a wretch, a horror, a burned madman in an ill-fitting husband costume.

And what of him? What of he, that other me, the other Raybould Marsh, the one Liv called husband and love? My homecoming would never be complete as long as he walked this world. Could I do that? When it was over, my mission completed, could I push him aside and take his place?

I wanted to believe I could. Wanted to believe it wasn't a fool's vanity.

I had turned back the years, but was the damage reparable? What bridge could span the vast gulf of years that separated me from the man I had been?

The gate didn't squeak because I tugged up on the hinge slats as I pushed it open. A trick I'd learned in the postwar years, coming home from the pub late at night.

But once safely outside, I paused on the pavement and wept along with my daughter.

FOUR

Marsh slammed the door to the storage room. He climbed the stairs and emerged from the Admiralty cellar just in time to find Will preparing to knock at his office. His coppery hair stood tousled like an ungainly haystack, except where the brim of his hat had rested. The raffish bowler was a peculiar affectation, one he'd adopted at Oxford, and which never looked more out of place than with Will's Savile Row finery. For now the hat hung from his uninjured hand.

'I'd think twice about that,' said Marsh, 'were I you.'

Will turned, surprised. Marsh pointed at the bandages on Will's upraised hand. Rusty bloodstains and splotches of sickly yellow had marred the pristine cotton gauze. The sight sickened Marsh with guilt.

Marsh said, 'I reckon that would hurt.'

'Ah. Yes.' Will lowered his hand, careful not to bump it. 'And indeed you would be correct.' He paused, awkwardly. 'A day later I find I'm still a bit careless.' Will smiled, though his face was peaked. Wan.

'Does it? Hurt?'

'When I'm not smashing it against locked doors, you mean? Hardly more than a toothache.' Again, his smile didn't touch his eyes. 'Such an ache wouldn't send me to the dentist.'

Marsh cracked his knuckles against his jaw. 'I feel like a right bastard, Will. If we—'

'Now, now. You mustn't blame yourself for this, Pip. It could have been worse. Much worse if you hadn't helped me.'

'Worse? I find that hard to believe.' Marsh shuddered. The demon's presence was worse than anything he might have imagined. And what it made him do to Will . . .

'Never doubt it where the Eidolons are concerned.' Will looked him over. 'I know that expression. Bad news for somebody.'

'Stephenson has me trying to question the girl.' Marsh shook his head, rubbed a hand across his face. 'Two sessions today.'

'Any luck?'

Marsh snorted. 'She's not right, Will. There's something very wrong about her. Lord knows I could use a pint after ten minutes in that cell with her.'

'Well, I'll pass on the pint, but I've heard tell of a place that serves only the finest horsemeat if you're in the mood for a chat. I did want to bend your ear.'

Will was a teetotaler. For the longest time, Marsh had only known that it was a personal choice. Something to do with Will's grandfather. But after learning a bit about warlocks and their practices, and witnessing a negotiation firsthand, he understood better what might have driven the old duke to his cups. Marsh had finally come to understand that Will's abstinence wasn't a moral statement, but an effort at self-preservation. He respected that. Not to mention the courage with which Will accepted the Eidolon's demand.

'Horsemeat?'

'I assume so. The chap said something about circus animals, you see, and I filled in the blanks. They use horses in the circus, don't they? Although I'm quite keen to try zebra if they have any,' said Will, warming to his subject. If not for the bandages fluttering about – Will talked with his hands – one might have believed nothing grim had happened yesterday.

The Ministry of Food had exempted restaurants from the rationing restrictions, a fact that brought little comfort to the many Britons who couldn't afford to dine out. But economic concerns were unknown to Will. Marsh tried not to take advantage of that unless Liv could share.

'We'll all be eating horsemeat, and worse, if the convoys don't start faring better. Bloody U-boats.'

'Perhaps the Yanks will help.'

Marsh snorted. 'Roosevelt faces reelection this year. He doesn't dare.'

'Pity, that,' said Will, looking somber again.

'Yes.' Marsh quietly berated himself. Will had been acting like his usual self again, and that was a fine thing to see. He pointed a thumb over his shoulder and changed the subject. 'I need fresh air. Let's walk.'

'Very good!' Will fell into step beside him. He tucked the bowler under his arm. They set off through the Admiralty corridors, paused briefly to allow a trio of matelots to pass.

'What did you want to bend my ear about?'

'Ah. Well.' Will's good hand gently touched the bandages. Marsh shook off a tremor of apprehension, tried not to let it show. 'You may have gathered that something a bit queer happened yesterday. And before you brush me off with another charming snort, I'm not referring to the finger business.'

'Name,' said Marsh. Memory bristled the hairs on his nape.
'You said the Eidolons had given me a name.'

'Yes they did, Pip. Yes they did.'

The low gray clouds and a tapering drizzle hastened the onset of
evening. I paid for a taxi from Walworth back to Westminster.
The return trip was fast and direct, but still twilight had swallowed the Admiralty by the time the cabbie pulled to a stop on
Whitehall.

A man in a lieutenant-commander's uniform like mine hurried across the street, trying to escape the rain, while I paid the
driver. A sentry saluted when he entered under the Admiralty
screen. I wasn't the only imposter here tonight. Klaus had arrived
to rescue Gretel.

What he did here in the next few minutes became a decisive
moment in the original history of Milkweed, prompting Will to
recruit the coven. Klaus and I eventually became allies later,
during the Cold War, after he'd finally broken with his sister. But
right now, he was the Klaus we'd come to fear: a wraith, an
Overman, a true believer in Doctor von Westarp and the REGP,
a man devoted to his sister the mad seer.

Tall sandbag revetments, and more sentries, flanked the
entrance to the Admiralty. I received and returned the same
salutes when I entered the building. Klaus was already searching
for a stairwell to the cellar. He'd get down there quickly enough.
I had to hurry.

I took my empty briefcase to the Milkweed vault. I'd last
opened this door in 1963, or less than two days ago by my own
reckoning. But the combination was different now; Leslie
Pembroke, the useless tosser, had managed a modicum of information security after taking over from Stephenson. He was a

piss-poor excuse for a section head, one of Gretel's most willing pawns, but at least he'd got that much right. So it took a bit of concentration to dredge up the old combination, but I managed.

The vault was mostly empty in these early days of the war. But its few contents were bloody dangerous – more than enough to kick-start the creation of Milkweed in the first place. They were arrayed on a low shelf near the door: a slim leather valise; a handful of pages from a memorandum, written in German; a photograph of a farmhouse. And, of course, the Tarragona film-strip. The original fragments, as well as the reconstructed version that Lorimer had cobbled together.

Some items, like the valise and photograph, ended in ragged scorch marks. Even now their blackened edges smelled faintly of smoke. Oddly, the fragments of burned film stock smelled of vinegar.

These were the meager fruits of my trip to Spain in the final days of the civil war. I'd gone to meet a man named Krasno-polsky, who had tried to warn the Secret Intelligence Service about the Reichsbehörde. But Reinhardt had killed him in rather spectacular fashion before he'd managed to come clean. Bastard nearly killed me as well. I'd snagged a berth on the last steamer out of Barcelona with nothing to show for the journey but a burnt valise, a name (Herr Doktor von Westarp), and an un-believable story.

Not very much. But enough from which determined investi-gators could piece together a story. We did.

Which is why I scooped it all into the briefcase. If my efforts in the past were going to work, I had to eliminate all traces of both Milkweed and the Reichsbehörde.

Speaking of the latter, the vault contained one additional item: the battery I had taken from Gretel when I captured her in

France. I tossed that into the briefcase, then snapped the locks shut.

Emptying the vault took seconds. In less than a minute I was back in the corridor with the vault secured firmly behind me. It would be several days before anybody noticed the theft. But I wasn't finished yet. Next, I headed for Stephenson's office. I had to get there before somebody recognized Klaus as an intruder; the hue and cry would only buy me a little time. So I did my best to hurry without drawing attention.

And found myself approaching two men heading from the direction of the Milkweed offices. Will Beauclerk I recognized at once. But his companion caused me to falter.

It was me. I was looking at a younger copy of myself.

Christ, was he young.

I resented his youth and strength. I envied his ignorance. I hated him for his loving wife and living daughter.

How long had it been since I'd seen that face in the mirror? Ever since my accident, mirrors had shown me nothing but a ruined man.

I wanted my face back. I wanted my life back.

I caught myself staring before he did. It took effort not to duck away. The closer they came, the more tempted I felt to scamper off and hide. But my destination was behind them, so I pressed on, hoping to hell they wouldn't recognize me. The beard and scars suddenly felt like a preposterous disguise. But it wasn't a disguise; it was my true face. I should have done more to hide myself from the one man who knew me better than anybody could.

Will and the other Raybould Marsh turned a corner just before we passed one another. They barely noticed me. They were deep in conversation. I caught only a fragment as they receded into a side corridor, but it was enough to set my head spinning with déjà vu.

'. . . fail to see the importance of this.'

'You don't get it, Pip. The Eidolons don't *do* that. It's quite unheard of.'

'They must have names for things, Will.'

Will was trying to explain how strange it was that the Eidolons had chosen to name me. He was right about that; how I wish I'd listened to him. Perhaps if I had . . . But of course I hadn't, and so we'd never unraveled that puzzle until it was far too late.

'Names for things, concepts, yes. But not for *people* . . .'

I glanced after them. And saw Klaus coming up the side corridor. In just a few more moments the other me would recognize him from the filmstrip in my briefcase. I picked up my pace.

The smell of Lucky Strike cigarettes ushered me to the old man's office. Swirls of blue-gray smoke eddied through his open door. I loitered in the hall where he couldn't see me, as though I were waiting politely to be summoned. A few startled shouts echoed to me from deeper in the Admiralty. The words were impossible to make out, but I knew what was happening. I waited.

'. . . don't care how valuable he is . . .'

Stephenson was on the telephone, haranguing some poor sod. The sound of his voice put a lump in my throat. Another thing long missed. But he didn't sound at all the way I remembered. From childhood on, my memory depicted John Stephenson's speaking voice as a deep, intimidating rumble. The voice of God. But now that I could listen to it again, his voice sounded delicate compared to my own rasp. Time was a cruel alchemist.

'Oy! Sir!'

As I'd expected, the old man's tirade was cut short. A fellow in civilian clothes came charging up the corridor and barged into Stephenson's office. His was another face I hadn't seen in a very long time: James Lorimer. One of Milkweed's first recruits. The man whom Stephenson had brought aboard to reconstruct the Tarragona filmstrip. And who suffered a grisly death on a cold December night.

Stephenson barked, 'What the hell is wrong with you? Can't you see—'

'It's one of those Jerry mingers from the film. He's in the building, probably came for the girl. Marsh is after him now.'

'Bugger me.' Stephenson smashed the phone into its cradle. Lorimer ran back out again with the old man on his heels. They went right past me. Stephenson passed so close that I felt the wind from the flapping of his empty sleeve.

I wanted so badly to reach out, to grab his good arm. *John, it's me*, I wanted to say. *I'm sorry I was too stubborn to visit when you fell ill. I'm sorry I didn't swallow my pride. I'm sorry we never put things right between us.* And I wanted to know, *Why didn't you see a bloody doctor?* He wasn't much older than I was now when the throat cancer took him.

But I held my tongue and my regrets. He was gone in seconds, and I slipped into his vacated office.

The old man always kept his desk locked. Given time, and the tools, I could have picked the locks easily enough. But when mounting blood prices had driven Will to the bottle, he'd discovered that a good jab with a letter opener did just as well. Time was short. I took Will's approach. But I wasn't after the old man's stash of brandy.

Instead, I rummaged the desk until I found a bundle of papers wrapped in a black ribbon. The pages were embossed with the full Royal Arms, effectively rendering each document a decree from His Majesty. I tugged out one of the blank transfer orders. With the new PM's backing, Stephenson had already been scouring the intelligence services for suitable recruits to wrangle into Milkweed when the debacle of Gretel's escape forced our hand. His plan to handpick a cadre of special operatives had been spiked by the wide-ranging chase through the Admiralty, which even now was leaving a trail of witnesses in its wake. Witnesses who would have no choice but to join Milkweed or face charges. A threat enforced by the Treachery Act, which Parliament would pass just ten days from now. I still remembered poor Lieutenant Cattermole, Milkweed's sacrificial lamb. Stephenson and I had chosen him from amongst the witnesses for execution under the new Act. He had been sentenced on false evidence of being a Nazi collaborator, but his true crime was talking. His death served Milkweed by convincing the others to keep quiet.

By now, the entire building had erupted into pandemonium. I could hear it through the closed door. Klaus had made it downstairs. He'd be pulling Gretel out onto Horse Guards Parade in a few more minutes.

Stephenson's typewriter sat on a credenza in the corner. The old man had had a secretary during his days as the head of T-section, but he hadn't taken Margie to the Admiralty with him when he created Milkweed. I ran the blank transfer order through his typewriter.

And promptly cocked it up. I'd never learned to type.

'Shit.'

I tore it out, crumpled the ruined page into my pocket, pulled another blank from the bundle, and tried again. This time my hunt-and-peck produced better results. Not superb, but good enough. I scribbled an illegible signature at the bottom of the form.

The forgery went into my briefcase, and the ribbon-wrapped bundle of papers went back into the desk. I closed it up again, made certain the desk lock clicked into place, and slipped out of the office. I was careful to leave the door wide ajar, as had Stephenson.

By now it was safe for me to run. It would look like I'd joined the chase to catch Klaus and Gretel. Which in fact I had. I went out through a side door, emerging into a moonlit blackout.

The rain had tapered off and been replaced with a misty fog. Nervous sweat dampened my too-tight uniform, and now that moisture turned chill in the night air. I huddled beside the Admiralty, waiting for my eyes to adjust to the darkness. It took a few moments before I could make out the mulberries in St. James', their rain-damp boughs limned in silver moonlight. I tried to remember exactly where Klaus and Gretel would emerge through the wall in the final moments of their escape. I counted down the row of windows in Milkweed's wing of the Admiralty building, then set off around the corner.

A sigh of relief escaped from my chest, so deep it verged on a sob. I was free and clear. A few seconds either way wouldn't matter at this point; I knew Gretel wouldn't leave without seeing me. Klaus had delivered a battery to her by now.

'Stop! You there, stop!'

I spun—

—saw somebody approaching—

—and blurted, 'Will?'

He stopped, taken aback. What the hell was he doing out here? Why wasn't he helping with the chase? A vague memory: Will had done something smart. He'd come out here hoping to intercept the escaping Jerry agents after they'd left the Admiralty. We'd compared notes later, during the postmortem of the

incident. But there had been something else, too. My sense of
relief became anxious dread, like a nagging itch that told me I
was overlooking something.

I hesitated. Should I try to talk to Will before meeting Gretel?
Could I convince him to see past the naval uniform, convince
him that I was a warlock? Talk him into delivering all information about the other warlocks to me? I probably could. But not
in thirty seconds. That was a longer conversation. And we would
have had it by now, too, if Will had had enough common sense
to peek into my cell when the coppers called him down.

But I would have to speak with Will at some point and gain his
trust. That meant I couldn't afford to let him see me with Gretel
and Klaus.

Will asked, 'Do I know you?'

I hated this, but it had to be done. I already owed Will a slew
of apologies. Still more regrets: the burden of my song. *I wish I
had listened to you. I'm sorry I turned my back when you needed help. I'm
sorry I didn't care when Milkweed destroyed you. I wish I had been a better
friend.*

Instead, I said, 'I wish I didn't have to do this,' and cracked
him with the briefcase. I tried not to break his jaw. His head
snapped around, he twisted at the waist, and then he collapsed
like a sack of grain.

I took a moment to unfold his crumpled arms and legs, hoping
he wouldn't be out long enough to catch his death from lying on
the damp parade ground. It was the least I could do, and I reckoned I owed him that much. I wondered what he would
remember when he came to his senses, what he would report to
the old man, what he would confide to his good friend Pip.

Itch, itch, at the back of my mind.

He would report he saw a strange man lurking outside the

Admiralty building. A bearded man. With terrible scars. Who addressed Will by name.

Itch, itch, itch.

Damnation. I knew exactly what Will would say. He'd told me this story twenty-three years ago. Told me of his encounter with a ghostly figure in St. James' Park. A ghostly figure who, I now realized, matched my description.

We had chalked it up as another side effect of the Eidolons. We'd seen stranger things in the Admiralty building over the course of that summer, while the warlocks negotiated night and day to keep the Channel impassable: spectral images, phantom odors, noises without any source. We'd thought the Ghost of St. James' had been one of those.

But we were wrong. *I* was the Ghost of St. James' Park.

My head reeled; pain flared in my knee. I had seen the ghost, too, albeit many months later. I thought back to that night, thought back to the figure I glimpsed in the shadows. Thought back to the ghostly figure who had pulled a gun and tried to shoot me in the knee.

What the hell had I been up to?

But I didn't have time to pursue that line of reasoning, because just then I glimpsed two figures in the park. A man and a woman. Inside the Admiralty right now, my younger counterpart was cursing.

Klaus had stopped, nervously surveying their surroundings. Probably heard Will calling to me.

Gretel watched my approach without a hint of apprehension. If anything, the bitch looked delighted. I had seen her smile before, but never like this.

'It's you,' she said. 'You came for me.'

'It's *you*,' I said.

We stared at each other. Sloe-eyed Gretel looked almost the same as the woman I'd last seen in '63. This younger version even wore her hair the same way, in two long raven-black braids. The only difference were the touches of gray missing from her hair and the crow's feet absent from the corners of her eyes. Her mannerisms, particularly the way she watched the world with an air of faintly condescending amusement, hadn't changed at all. Wires spiraled around her braids and terminated in the battery at her waist.

Klaus whispered, 'Gretel, do you know him? Who is he?'

She ignored him. Her eyes took in my beard, my scars. She had changed so little. But I . . .

The corner of her mouth quirked up. She said, 'The beard suits you. Very rugged.'

Very funny, you bitch. I'd heard that from her before.

'You know it all, don't you? The entire chain of events that sent me here.'

Gretel said, 'I remember all of it. Everything you did together. You and the other me.'

'*Together?* You—'

Klaus took her arm. In German, he said, 'We have to go.' He added, with a nervous glance in my direction, 'I assume this is why you came here. To meet him.'

She took my arm, hooked her elbow in mine. The fever heat of her body warmed my chilled skin, made it crawl. She grinned up at me. 'Shall we?'

Traveling by taxi, Tube, or bus was out of the question. There was no conceivable way the three of us would pass unnoticed. Even at night. Klaus's disguise did a decent job of hiding his wires from casual glances. But between my scars and her wires,

Gretel and I might have escaped from a circus. Their German accents didn't help. I could lose a tail and keep a reasonably low profile on my own. But the longer the three of us stayed in the open, the faster they'd find us. I didn't trust Gretel to warn me of impending trouble. Who knew what she intended now.

But, for the moment, she did appear to be working toward the same or similar ends as I. So I did, grudgingly, trust her to pick out a car. I boosted it. We got away clean.

I hated myself for working with her. For relying on her ability. For not avenging Agnes. Again and again, I reminded myself that it was a necessary evil for the greater good. I promised myself I'd find justice. But I tasted ashes in those words.

Klaus rode in the back. His sister sat beside me, in the passenger seat. I couldn't help remembering that the last time I drove with her; it had been through a London fallen under devastating attack. I kept one ear on the conversation flying back and forth between the siblings in a machine-gun patter of German.

Klaus asked, 'Where are we going?'

'To meet a man who can help us,' Gretel said.

'We don't need help. We can make the rendezvous on our own. But we'll miss it if we keep wasting time.'

If Liv's laughter was music, Gretel's was fingernails on slate. 'Dear, dear brother. You did read my letter, didn't you? They'll wait for us.'

'And who is he?' Klaus jerked his chin at me in the rear-vision mirror.

'A very dear friend.' Gretel patted my leg. I flinched so violently that we nearly went off the road. A lorry in the oncoming lane sounded off two short bursts of the horn. Gretel carried on, undaunted by my revulsion.

'He's fucking hideous,' said Klaus. 'He'll draw attention.'

I said, 'I'd like to point out, so there isn't any confusion, that I can understand everything you're saying. But if it makes things easier for you, I know about the U-boat. So please don't speak in circles on my account.'

Klaus scowled. This younger version of him was more intense than the one I'd come to know. Twenty years in the gulag had made him more thoughtful.

'Is he really a naval officer?'

'I was.' *Not in a long bloody time, mate.*

Klaus continued to address Gretel: 'What is he now? A double agent? Does he work for the Schutzstaffel?'

What a nauseating suggestion. The very idea made me ill again, though I knew better than to deny it outright. But Klaus had a point: by participating in their escape, I was guilty of treason against the Crown. Or perhaps treachery, depending on whether time travelers counted as British subjects under the law.

Necessary evils, I reminded myself ... I let the Queen of Evasions cover that question.

Gretel said, 'He's an ally. We can trust him.' She twisted in her seat to look at him. 'Trust me. Please. This is important.' The 'please' was a particularly nice touch. And it had the intended effect. Klaus piped down. He was, after all, still devoted to her in this stage of his life. Foolish bastard.

She settled back in her seat. I tensed as Gretel leaned closer, adopting a conspiratorial pose. 'He worries about me. But he means well.'

'He wants to see my country ground into dust beneath SS jackboots.'

'Well, yes. What do you expect? But he means well for *me*.'

'Very touching. I'll surely weep.'

'It is touching. Also frustrating.' She whispered, 'We'll have nearly the same argument again tomorrow morning.' She sighed, tossed a braid over her shoulder.

I drove our stolen car past the Walworth house. It was dark and shuttered, a hole in the night. Pangs of jealousy clawed at me, alternating with tremors of anger; I wondered where Liv had gone. Had she gone to one of her other lovers? The aftershave men?

Had she been doing this all along? Cuckolding me as far back as 1940?

But then I realized, with no small amount of shame, that the darkness arose from blackout curtains, not from vacancy. Liv's affairs hadn't begun until much later. After my anger and shame had pushed her away. After I failed to be there for her, after I became somebody other than the man she loved and needed. More than ever, I hated myself at that moment. Hated myself for being so unfair to Liv, then and now.

Of course Liv was home. Caring for their daughter while she waited patiently for her husband. As she'd always done. But her thrice-damned husband, the lucky sod, wouldn't be home for a while. The aftermath of Gretel's escape would see him and Stephenson scrambling to get a handhold on the situation. It wasn't a fond memory.

But it meant Liv was alone. Even now I struggled with the temptation to go to her. If only she knew I was home. If only she knew how badly I needed her warmth, her affection, her approval.

I took the car around the corner, parked on the pavement, killed the engine. The spot gave me a line on the garden gate, past the curve of the Anderson shelter to the kitchen door. I didn't need light to see these things. I knew the layout like I knew my own name.

'Why have we stopped?' said Klaus. Still to Gretel, still in German. Nobody answered his question.

We were in for a long wait. And I reckoned this was the only chance I'd have to try to suss out Gretel's angle in this new time line. I watched her. A distant expression had settled over her face, part rapture, part concentration. The moonlight was too faint for me to read the gauge on her battery.

I said, 'Do you—'

'Yes.' She didn't open her eyes.

'Don't do that.'

She said, 'I was trying to save you effort.'

'I want you to know that I'm not doing this for you. I couldn't care less if the Eidolons get you. Or me, for that matter.'

Exasperation in the backseat: 'What the hell is an Eidolon?'

I continued, 'You deserve to die screaming.'

'Hey!' The *click* of wires entering a battery. A ghostly fist emerged from my chest. Warning me. I froze. I didn't dare breathe.

'Klaus.' Gretel raised one hand, sharply. A pause. He withdrew. Another *click*.

She turned. Moonlight glinted on the whites of her eyes, and just for a moment I thought I could see something else lurking in those depths. But the shadows of her madness didn't unnerve me. Not I, who had been disassembled and reassembled by the Eidolons more than once. Who had spoken to the Eidolons directly when they took the guise of my son.

'You're still angry,' she said. 'You hate the thought of working with me.' She patted my leg again. 'Aren't we the strangest of bedfellows?'

Again I flinched away from her feverish touch. 'If this is to work, it has to happen in two parts, simultaneously. I can handle things here with the Eidolons and their . . . brokers.' Now it was my turn to speak in circles around Klaus. 'But I won't move against them unless it's safe to do so. I'd rather let the Eidolons take it all than condemn my daughter to growing up in the Thousand-Year Reich.'

I watched her eyes, those dark windows upon her malignant soul. She understood: I wouldn't sever humanity's link with the Eidolons if it meant leaving Britain defenseless against the REGP. Which brought me back to my question.

'Do you understand your part in this?'

That earned another sigh. 'Yes,' she said with exaggerated care. 'I'll help him.'

'I'm going to warn him about you.'

Gretel said, 'By all means. But don't spend too long at it. We do have a boat to catch.'

A car turned the corner. Glare from its slitted headlights briefly washed low against us. We hunkered down into the seats of our stolen car until it passed.

'Thing is, I can't help but wonder what happens later.' I nodded at her battery. 'After this is over. Assuming we're successful.' She smirked at that. 'What do *you* get out of this?'

'Oh, Raybould. You already know that. You were there. You saved me from the Eidolons.'

'No. That was the "other" you, wasn't it? To use your own words. But what did her sacrifice buy you?'

'Freedom. A new time line. The only time line that doesn't end with the Eidolons.'

She was careful in front of Klaus, but I filled in the rest: *The only time line where Gretel doesn't end with the Eidolons. And to hell with everybody else.*

'Oh, I've no doubt that's part of it. I know how badly they

terrify you.' I held up my arm, tugged down the sleeve of my uniform. The moon shone on a faint trio of crescent-shaped scars in my forearm. 'But that alone is too simple. It's never enough for you simply to break even. Your schemes always put you ahead. So I have to wonder. What do you want now?'

The corner of Gretel's mouth curled into the half smile that I had come to loathe. 'I have the same wants and needs as any woman. You don't believe that yet, but you will.'

She was right. I didn't.

I waited in the silent darkness for my doppelgänger to arrive.

FIVE

13–14 May 1940
Walworth, London, England

Marsh leaned against the front door, too tired to do anything but throw his weight against it. It flew open. He leapt to catch it before the slam woke Agnes. He bumped the telephone table, sloshing the contents of the water bowl across the floor.

'Damn it.'

He tossed his fedora on the banister finial, took the blanket beside the bowl, and tried to mop up the mess. The blanket wasn't very absorbent. It only succeeded in pushing the water about. But the thought of going into the kitchen for a proper towel left him feeling weary. The chase and its aftermath had taken all his reserves, mental and physical.

Liv shuffled in from the kitchen. She was in her dressing gown, the lavender one, and carrying a cup. She sipped at her tea, watching his ineffectual attempts to corral the water.

'You realize I placed that there knowing it would provide a bit of comedy,' she said. 'Gas attacks were just my excuse.'

He mumbled, 'Sorry, Liv. Didn't mean to wake you.'

'I wasn't sleeping, you mad fool. Here, leave that. It's just water.' She took his hand, pulled him up. 'You look knack-ered.'

'Long day,' said Marsh, shaking his head. He kept scouring his memories for everything the girl had ever said to him, trying to piece together those frantic minutes during the chase and her escape. He couldn't stop watching it in his head, the way the Jerry agent jumped through solid walls like they weren't there at all. Marsh could see they had weaknesses. The batteries, for one. And the ghost bloke couldn't breathe when he was in that state. But that seemed a thin thread upon which to hang the faintest hope.

Gretel – they knew her name now, for all the good that did – had known that bloke with the wraith ability was coming for her. The extraction had worked too cleanly for the operation to have been improvised. Von Westarp's people had planned this from the beginning. Why?

And worse, how did they know where she'd be? That was the question prickling Marsh's spine with needles of dread. The question that sapped his strength, for it was too heavy to budge. The Admiralty building was off the beaten path for SIS. The old man had chosen to put Milkweed HQ there for that reason. Gretel's rescuer hadn't made a lucky guess. He'd known.

And what was she? What could she do?

Whatever the answer, she and her rescuer were far away by now. Probably halfway to the coast at this hour. Together with Lorimer and Stephenson, Marsh had worked the phones, putting feelers out, quietly alerting every constabulary in southern England. But Marsh knew they wouldn't turn up anything.

"Long day," he says. Hmmm.' Liv studied his face. Her expression softened in the way that meant she was finished teas-ing him for a bit. A frown creased the bridge of her nose, rippled her freckles, tugged at her eyebrows. 'It's more than that.'

And she was right. As she often was. Because on top of the demoralizing and humiliating defeat they'd suffered at the hands of the Schutzstaffel tonight, there was also the issue of Will's encounter in the park. Marsh didn't quite know what to make of that. But the poor fellow did have a bruise where he said the stranger clocked him with a briefcase. Will was having a bad week.

As were they all. Because if the bloke who rolled him in the park was a naval officer ... The ease of Gretel's escape suggested a mole. Will's story, if true to the details, only corroborated that. Though it would take a rather bold kind of mole to show himself to Will like that. Very odd.

Ever since Marsh had returned from Spain, odd things had only meant trouble.

Liv was right. A long day, but so much more.

'Come,' she said. She pulled him inside, to where Agnes dozed in her bassinet. Marsh followed, half tripping while he kicked off his shoes. He collapsed into an armchair. Liv snuggled in beside him. She pulled his head to her shoulder. They swayed in time with her breathing. He listened to her heartbeat. She understood him so well. He could be vulnerable with her, and she knew when he needed it. And in spite of all the shit, she loved him. Sometimes Marsh felt as though Liv was his only human credential.

'Tell me,' she said.

Would that I could, Liv. Marsh cracked his knuckles. But what could he tell her? The truth, of sorts. *I failed you, Liv. I failed Agnes. I can't protect you.*

'Hitler kicked us in the bollocks today.'

'Don't let him do that too often,' said Liv. 'Agnes will need a little brother or sister soon.'

His daughter's face wasn't as red as it had been when he'd first met her. But still her eyes and lips were scrunched under little creases of baby fat, as though her dreams were matters of deep concentration.

'Have you thought more about sending her to your aunt?'

Liv's chest swelled with a long, steadying breath. 'Something terrible has happened. Something you can't say.'

'Yes.' What could he tell her? Again, he settled for simple truth. 'I'm afraid things may get worse, much worse, before they get better. We'd do well by Agnes to keep Williton in mind.'

Liv sighed. 'If we must.'

They held each other. Marsh closed his eyes. Drifted with the sound of Liv's heart, the smell of her skin. His stomach gurgled.

She asked, 'Have you eaten?'

'I . . . No. Not since breakfast.' He hadn't realized it until she asked. But now suddenly he was famished. And the house was full of the smell of Liv's cooking. How had he not noticed? That damn Gretel had him tied in knots.

'Well, there you have it. No wonder the Führer gave you such a drubbing today. You can't save Britain on an empty stomach.' She shifted out of his embrace, climbed to her feet. 'I'll get you a bowl.'

Marsh sniffed the air again. 'Fish stew?'

'Be thankful it isn't eel stew. It would have been, had I got to the fishmongers any later.'

Marsh ate while Agnes had her midnight feeding. He dozed off in the chair. Liv woke him some time later when she lifted the spoon and cold bowl from his slack fingers. It felt like only a few seconds had passed. 'You'll feel better if you sleep in a proper bed,' she whispered.

Climbing the stairs and undressing took just enough effort to jostle the gears of his mind back into motion. He fell into the sheets. And lay awake.

Had von Westarp or the Schutzstaffel placed somebody in SIS? Watching Milkweed? Was that how the gypsy girl had known about Liv's pregnancy? Marsh couldn't let it go. Like a dog with a soup bone, he gnawed on it from every angle. But it held no marrow. Only splinters.

He didn't know how long he had lain there before Liv's breathing eased into the long, slow breaths of peaceful slumber. She hadn't fallen asleep immediately; she was listening to him, too, wanting to know if he could rest. But he was too tired for sleep, his mind too agitated for true relaxation. He needed room to pace properly.

Marsh eased out of bed, taking care not to jostle the mattress. He dressed in the darkness and tiptoed from the bedroom. Agnes's face crinkled into a new pattern of wrinkles; her arms jerked in little spasms. Her blanket had slipped. He tucked it over her shoulders, caressed her chin with a fleecy elephant. She smelled of Liv's shampoo.

He crept down the stairs, stepping on the outer edges so the boards wouldn't creak, and into the kitchen.

'He's coming,' said Gretel.

I jerked back to wakefulness, my stomach full of butterflies. Soft snoring drifted to my ears from the rear seat. 'What?'

'Raybould is here. He's coming outside.' She paused; whether for theatrical effect or because she was reading potential time lines, I couldn't say. 'Try not to anger him. He's had an upsetting day. He won't receive you well.'

As though I needed the warning. Gretel knew everything he

might have done, but she still didn't know him as I did. I knew what he was thinking. What he was feeling.

I checked my pockets, double-checking the forged transfer order I'd created in Stephenson's office. My fingertips traced the embossed seal of the Royal Arms. It was my talisman, my only shield in the looming confrontation. And a bloody flimsy one at that.

Measured in terms of preparation, my mission tonight was a farce. And not a funny one. Beyond a considerable knowledge of the mark, my entire cover story rested on a single piece of paper. My plan made a mockery of proper intelligence procedures. A *real* SIS operation, even a halfway competent one, would have spent months creating an identity for me before I assumed it. Military service, school records, hospital records, birth certificate ... Anything an outsider might have used to corroborate my story we would have constructed and inserted into the historical record long before we put the ball in motion.

But I didn't have the luxury of time. Neither did my counterpart, and it was there I hung my hopes. He had one chance to infiltrate the farm. He couldn't do that and verify my credentials. So the lack of preparation wouldn't matter as long as he accepted my sales pitch.

I eased out of the car, but took care when closing the door lest the noise alert my doppelgänger. I leaned through the open driver's window and glared at Gretel. The moon had shifted, so now shadows cloaked her eyes.

I whispered through the wreckage of my throat, 'Don't go anywhere.' She stuck her tongue out at me. Klaus murmured in his sleep. Something about hay wagons.

The scraping of my shoes on wet pavement echoed impossibly loud in the night. I moved lightly, on the balls of my feet, trying to minimize the noise. Ours wasn't the only car parked on the street; another had appeared farther up the road while I dozed.

I'd just passed the hedge flanking the garden gate when the kitchen door creaked open. I spun, pressing myself to the hedge of barberries and holly so that he wouldn't glimpse my moonlit form lurking behind the gate.

The fluttering in my stomach made me stumble. I was hiding from a younger version of myself, waiting to have a conversation with him, in the garden, in the middle of the night. The entire situation was absurd. Since my arrival in the past, I'd been working to get to this moment. But I was nervous about meeting myself. Frightened, even. We had a temper.

I forced myself to work through the apprehension. I listened for my moment. Susurration: footsteps on dewy grass. *Pop-snap*: cracked knuckles. Then nothing. Knowing that small space so well, the way my garden shed crowded beside the Anderson shelter, I could tell exactly where my counterpart was standing. He had paused on his way between the house and my – his – garden shed.

What are you doing? Go inside.

But he didn't move. He merely stood there, like a statue in the darkness.

Marsh shuffled across the yard toward his garden shed. His best thinking happened there; he could pace and mutter to himself without waking Liv and the baby. He cracked his knuckles again.

A faint glimmer beyond the gate caught his eye. Moonlight on metal. He stopped. Squinted.

A car. Parked behind the house.

Marsh looked away, shunted the vehicle to his peripheral

vision. It traded acuity for sensitivity. He'd learned the trick at Fort Monckton before he joined the Firm.

Shapes coalesced from the darkness. Yes, there was a car. And it was occupied.

Somebody was watching the house.

Had they seen him yet? That depended on whether they'd heard the kitchen door. The moon was slightly behind the house, putting him in the deepest of the shadows.

He kept an extra revolver stashed in the shed. Liv didn't know about it; she hated guns. But he was glad he'd taken the precaution. Marsh sidestepped out of the car's line of sight, walking on the balls of his feet.

I knew he'd made us when he finally started moving again. Faster, more quietly. Were I in his shoes, I'd—

Bugger. He was going for the Enfield.

I tensed, listening. There was no shaft of light to tell me when he'd entered the shed. I had to go by the not-squeak of oiled hinges.

There. I tugged up on the slats again, as I'd done earlier in the evening, and stepped through the gate. I didn't let it clap shut behind me. No need to startle him. Forcing his hand would only make things worse.

My dark-adapted eyes easily picked out the shed's open door. He was already inside. I crossed the yard, knowing I'd be an easy shot for him when framed by moonlight in the doorway. I reached the entrance.

His voice came from somewhere in the darkness, past the familiar smells of mildew and potting loam. It brimmed with cold anger. 'There's a gun pointed at you,' he said. 'Try anything, anything at all, and I'll put a bullet in your gut.'

'No, you won't.' I stepped inside, feeling as though I'd already had this conversation long ago.

I knew damn well he was bluffing. He'd jump me instead. Nobody could answer questions while dying in agony from a gut shot.

'Try me,' he said. 'Who are you?'

'No,' I said. 'The real question is do you intend to have this conversation in the dark, or will you let me close the door so we can turn on the bloody light?' He didn't answer. 'I'm going to turn around and pull the door shut. I'll keep my back to you while you flip the light.'

'You don't move unless I say you do.'

Christ, what a belligerent sod. I wondered if everybody found me so abrasive. I took a steadying breath, turned around. Over my shoulder I said, 'If you do shoot me, try to aim for my head. I'd rather die cleanly.'

I closed the door, then raised my hands. There was a faint *click* and then weak, mustard-colored light filled the shed.

'Turn around,' he barked.

I did. We stared at each other for a long beat.

He said what I was thinking: 'Son of a bitch.'

The intruder was older than Marsh expected. Perhaps around Stephenson's age, or even a bit older, but it was hard to tell because one side of his face was a mass of scar tissue. The graying beard couldn't hide it. The scars might have been war wounds; he appeared old enough to have fought in the Great War. His throat had been damaged, too, judging by the sound of his voice. Mustard gas? Phosgene?

He wore a naval uniform. Lieutenant-commander.

'My God. I know you.' The codger's eyes widened to the size

of saucers. Marsh continued, 'You're the bastard who jumped Will in the park.'

The stranger let out a long, shaky breath. Marsh might have sworn it was a sigh of relief. The duffer asked, 'How is he?'

What?

'You nearly broke his jaw. I'm tempted to shoot you on his behalf.'

'Are you angry about his jaw, or feeling guilty about his finger?'

Only five people had been present for that. Marsh struggled to maintain an outward calm while his mind shuffled crisis scenarios. 'How do you know about that?'

The stranger gave Marsh a long, hard look. 'I know everything about you.' He nodded contemptuously at the revolver. 'And do stop with the threats. We both know Stephenson trained you better than that.'

'Who the bloody hell are you?'

'As of right now, I'm your immediate superior,' said the stranger.

He reached into a pocket. Marsh kept the Enfield trained on him. But instead of a weapon, the stranger produced a folded paper. He tossed it on the bench.

'Transfer orders,' he said. 'You work for me now.'

I recovered from the shock of thinking he'd truly recognized me by pushing to keep him off balance. Didn't push too hard, however. I stared into the barrel of his revolver, reminding myself that he had a bit of a temper.

The Enfield didn't waver an inch while my younger self unfolded the forged transfer orders with his free hand. His eyes scanned the page. I could see him mulling it over, trying to gauge the document's authenticity.

'Liddell-Stewart,' he muttered to himself. 'That's you, I presume.' He came to a decision a few seconds later. I crossed my arms and leaned against the workbench. But my relief became rage when he crumpled the paper and tossed it aside. I balled my fists, simmering.

Stubborn ass.

But I knew the man before me, and I knew the transfer had snagged his attention. But he refused to admit it. I wanted to strangle him. It would have felt good to try. But I reckoned he had the advantage of age. I clamped down on my anger. And nearly gave it all away: I raised a hand to crack my knuckles against my jaw, as I often did when agitated, but caught myself at the last second and scratched my beard instead.

I nodded toward the wadded paper. 'Perhaps you didn't notice the Royal Arms. You might not like them, but your orders stand. So do your goddamned job.'

'Work for *you*?' He shook his head. 'You helped them escape. That's why you silenced Will.'

'Beauclerk would have thrown everything into a cocked hat. Witless toff. I couldn't let him.'

My younger self sneered. 'I can see why you never made it past lieutenant-commander. You're an insult to that uniform.' He said, 'It'll be the gallows for you.'

Jesus. Was I always this self-righteous?

I thought about Stephenson, and tried to model my behavior on the old man. 'You don't understand a damn thing, lad.' He straightened, bristling at the condescension. But it was true. 'I'm not working for the Jerries. The girl is working with *us*.'

For the moment, anyway. But I didn't tell him that.

He hesitated. 'Preposterous. I—'

'She *let* you capture her. And don't pretend you haven't

suspected as much. By now you've already concluded it's the only sensible explanation. Or you should have.

'That's why I came to you. You're supposed to be the clever one.'

It was eerie, and maddening, the way this bloke seemed to anticipate everything. Something about him ... Had they interacted before? Marsh had a vague sense that they had, but surely he would have remembered that face.

Marsh said, 'Have we met?'

The plug-ugly codger sneered at that. 'You should get out of the intelligence trade if you can't remember a face like mine.'

You weren't born that way, thought Marsh. But he turned his thoughts back to Gretel.

'She couldn't have arranged her own capture,' he said. 'Nobody knew where I would be on that morning. Not even me. I made a decision in the field to take a quick foray toward the invasion front. What you're claiming is impossible.'

'Not for her,' said the stranger in his ruined voice. Amazing, how much emotion he could pack into that barren rasp. Sorrow, bitterness, anger. A man with heavy issues and heavier burdens.

Marsh asked, 'What is she? What can she do?'

'Gretel is clairvoyant,' he said. 'She knows the future.'

Of all the things Marsh expected to hear, this was not one of them. He reeled. The implications ... If it were true, that girl was the most powerful of von Westarp's creations. She would make the Third Reich unstoppable.

'That's—'

'Unthinkable? Incomprehensible? More ridiculous than a man who walks through walls?' The stranger also had an infuriating tendency to finish Marsh's sentences. Marsh balled his empty fists in frustration. 'By now you've already realized it fits all the facts.'

Damn him. He was right.

Marsh asked, 'Why would she help us?'

'It's one thing to see the future. Quite another to like what you see.'

That finally shut him down. My younger self stared at me through narrowed eyes. But I knew he wasn't seeing me. Liv and Will had always said they could tell when I was deep in thought. I finally understood what they meant.

He didn't set down the Enfield, but he did glance at the crumpled transfer order.

Warily, he said, 'Why have you come to me?'

Finally. I hadn't won him over yet, but at least now he was willing to listen. Took long enough. Never in my life had I met anybody so bloody obstinate. I wondered if people still saw me that way.

I'd given much thought to how I would answer this question. It had taken careful effort to make inroads with him. I wasn't about to piss it all away with a tale of the far future, cold wars, and time travel. He might just barely be able to accept that Gretel was an oracle. But only a madman would believe he was talking to an older copy of himself. He had seen a number of strange things over the past year or so, but when I was his age I still didn't fully understand what the Eidolons were and what they could do.

So instead I played on his fears. Which, of course, I knew intimately. 'Milkweed has been compromised. As amply demonstrated by tonight's farce at the Admiralty. We don't know how, but we do know the Schutzstaffel is well-informed about our efforts. They know we're watching von Westarp.' I skated past the thinnest ice quickly.

'Isn't this a bit baroque for an entrapment operation?'

'Playing prisoner was Gretel's idea. She has a particular way of doing things.' Lord knew that was the truth. Now to salt it with another falsehood: 'We knew that if Milkweed had been compromised, the SS would immediately send somebody to retrieve her. Which they did. His name is Klaus, by the way.'

'And you want me to root out the mole,' he said.

'No.' That caught him by surprise. 'Milkweed is a lost cause.'

Again, he bristled. I'd always known I had a short fuse, but I don't think I fully appreciated just how irritable I could be until I witnessed it firsthand. My younger self, I realized, was something of a thug. I hoped he could keep the anger in check, but knew he probably couldn't.

He asked, 'Did she tell you that?'

I ignored his objection and kept to my script. Kept spinning my lies. 'Milkweed does, however, have value. As long as the mole is in place and funneling information back to Germany, the SS will be focused on Milkweed's efforts to counter von Westarp's brood. Meanwhile, you and I are going to run a second operation. The real operation.'

'How do you know I'm not the mole?'

'You aren't.'

'You don't think it's Will, do you?'

'Beauclerk is a silly toff and an exasperating fool, but he's no traitor.' I hoped I managed to keep the note of irony from my voice.

'Does Stephenson know about this?'

We'd be in seven shades of shit if he breathed even a hint of this to anybody. 'Don't be daft.'

He rubbed a hand over his face. But I could see that he had bought my story. His mind turned to business. 'I'm only one man. What do you expect me to do?' But he answered his own question. He sighed. 'You're sending me to the Continent.'

'Yes.'

'I just returned! I've barely met my daughter!' He pounded the bench with his fist. Pieces of a half-built trellis tumbled to the floor.

'This is our only chance.'

'My wife will kill you for this.'

I said, 'She'll understand.'

'You don't know Liv.'

I thought, *Better than you do, mate.* But I said, 'If we don't do this, and von Westarp is allowed to refine his techniques, Britain will be overrun with people like Klaus and the rest of those monsters on the Tarragona filmstrip. Or worse.' I remembered how quickly and easily Soviet sleeper agents from Arzamas-16 had reduced swaths of London to smoking rubble. The rest of the city, the rest of Britain, would have followed if not for the Eidolons ... The ultimate case of a cure worse than the disease.

I laid out everything he had to do. It was a long list; he didn't look happy. And I shared everything I remembered about the REGP and the Götterelektrongruppe. How they were organized, how they were run. Told him what I knew of von Westarp and the others. Names, powers, loyalties, petty rivalries. And like a sponge, he soaked it all up. He had an intense focus to him. Strange to say, but my younger self reminded me of a coiled spring.

When I finished, he looked at me as though I'd asked him to flap his wings and fly to the moon. Perhaps that wasn't far off.

'This is impossible,' he said. 'It can't be done.'

'You'll have help.'

'Gretel.'

I nodded. 'Having access to her power will give you a tremendous advantage. Use it. As long as her interests align with yours, she will be an invaluable resource. But I want to make something very, very clear.' I moved closer. As close as I dared. 'Never trust Gretel. Never. She's the most powerful, and she's by far the most dangerous. They're all a little frightened of her, even if they don't admit it. And they should be. Even von Westarp doesn't understand what he created when he made her.'

'And yet you expect me to place my *life* in her safekeeping?'

'Gretel likes you.'

'How could you possibly know that?'

I told him the truth, of sorts: 'Gretel and I have a complicated relationship.'

'Oh, that's just bloody wonderful. Very reassuring.' He shook his head. 'How do I contact her once I arrive?'

'No need.' I nodded to indicate the street beyond the hedge. 'She's waiting in the car.'

A pause while he processed this. Then: 'You are fucking unbelievable, mate. Do you know that?'

'We need to move,' I said, glancing at my watch. 'Say your good-byes. And bring me your Identity Card.' He wouldn't need it in Germany. But, suitably altered, it might just save me from another night in the clink.

'Now?'

'There's a U-boat in the Channel, waiting to take you to Bremerhaven.'

He shook his head again. 'Fucking unbelievable.'

*

Marsh entered the kitchen on his way to break the bad news to Liv, his mind still wrestling with all the contradictions posed by the batty old duffer in the shed. There was something queer about him. But he seemed to know his business. He obviously knew Milkweed, and SIS. And he knew a damn sight more about von Westarp's outfit than anybody else on this side of the Channel.

But Commander Liddell-Stewart had appeared virtually out of nowhere. Marsh had never heard of him. Milkweed's autonomy meant Stephenson reported directly to the Prime Minister. Marsh would have sworn there was nobody in the chain between Stephenson and Churchill. Nor between Stephenson and Menzies, the head of MI6. Yet the stranger held such detailed knowledge . . . Who was he?

There weren't many possibilities. Perhaps he was political, somebody in the confidence of Churchill, or Menzies, or both. But that would be a superb position for a double agent. Was he the mole?

Marsh sure as hell didn't trust him. But he must have known that coming to Marsh in this fashion would earn suspicion. Hard to imagine a Jerry mole acting so brazenly. Meanwhile, everything the stranger said fit the facts. His claims about a mole meshed with the conclusions to which Marsh himself had been reluctantly drawn; his explanation of Gretel's prescience was unexpected, but again, it was consistent with everything Marsh had seen.

If the stranger were part of Jerry's infiltration of Milkweed, sending Marsh to Germany was a rather byzantine double cross. On the other hand, it would put him safely out of the way. What did the stranger have planned while Marsh was out of the picture?

Marsh let the stairs creak when he returned upstairs. He'd have to wake Liv, one way or another. Part of him loathed himself for doing this to her so soon after he'd returned. What kind of husband did this make him? What kind of father? A damn poor one.

He stopped at Agnes's crib again, and this time he took his sleeping daughter into his arms. Her yawn turned into a mewl. He rocked her against his shoulder, kissed the fine silken hair atop her head, inhaled her scent.

Would his baby girl grow up hearing stories about her absent father who hadn't been there for her birth and then abandoned her again a few days later? What if he never made it back? Would she grow up bitter and resentful? That thought frightened him more than infiltrating the REGP. It made him want to sick up.

'Papa loves you,' he whispered. 'He'll protect you.'

And that was the crux of it. More than anything else, he'd been swayed by the stranger's warning about what would happen if von Westarp's work continued unimpeded. The stranger had precisely reiterated Marsh's own deep-seated fears. The stranger might have been feeding him a line, but he also offered the chance to take down the REGP. And Marsh had to act on that. For Agnes's sake, and Liv's.

Just two of von Westarp's people had made a mockery of MI5, MI6, and the Admiralty. What could twenty accomplish? Two thousand? The commander offered perhaps the only chance to stop this.

Liv shuffled in behind him. She slipped an arm around his waist and rested her head against his free shoulder. 'Are you protecting her from sleep?'

Marsh kissed his daughter again, then laid her gently back in the crib. He pulled the pink elephant blanket over her. Marsh took Liv's hand, led her out of Agnes's room to where light from a bedside lamp spilled into the hall. He found it difficult to meet her eyes. She noticed.

Liv said, 'What is it?'

Marsh took her free hand. He squeezed both, staring at the floor and wishing he didn't have to do this. Wishing he didn't have to leave, wishing life didn't demand he wound her so deeply. She pulled away.

'Raybould, you're scaring me. What's wrong?'

'I have to go. They're sending me off again.'

Confusion flashed across her face, followed by disbelief. 'Now?'

'They've sent a car. It's waiting.'

'Tell them you can't go.' Her voice cracked. 'You've only just returned.'

He shook his head. 'I can't do that. They need me.'

'In the middle of the night?' Now Liv's voice dripped with disdain for the Foreign Office. 'Don't they know you have a baby at home? And a wife?'

'They do. But they don't care. They …' He faltered. There was nothing he could say to make this right. '… need me,' he repeated.

'Your family needs you, too.' She drew her robe tighter and glared at him. 'Is this how it will be? Agnes growing up without any idea of her father?'

That hurt. Liv's dart flew true and landed where he felt most sensitive, most guilty. She knew him so well. But he took what she hurled at him. He deserved it, and so much worse. He felt like shit.

'No. Of course not. But the war …'

'You said you wouldn't leave again!'

The outburst woke Agnes. She began to wail.

Marsh would have taken to his knees if he thought it would help. He hated the war, but he hated Liddell-Stewart far more at that moment. 'I meant every word, Liv. Every word. I can't read the bloody future. How was I to know . . . ' He trailed off, waving vaguely toward the street. He wished, for the hundredth time if not the first, that Stephenson had allowed him to share the truth with Liv when they'd first married. 'It's an extraordinary situation,' he said. 'I swear to you.'

That, at least, was true.

She frowned. This had cut deeply. He could see it in her stance, the sense of betrayal. Betrayal by her own government, which owed her time with her husband. But in the end, she was a British housewife in time of war. She had a duty, too.

Liv threw her arms around him and kissed him fiercely. Though he couldn't afford it, he waited while she took up Agnes. 'We'll make a cup of tea for you while you pack,' she said. 'Your kidnappers can wait a few more minutes.'

More awkwardness. Liv picked up on it at once. Marsh could feel the cracks zigzagging across the thin ice of his cover story. 'I'm not packing,' he said.

'No?' Up went the eyebrow. *Crack, crack.* 'Well, isn't the Foreign Office a truly fascinating place.'

Marsh started to object, but she waved it off. After that, he retrieved his Identity Card, and then it was time to leave. Liv, with Agnes on her shoulder, led him toward the front door. He shook his head. 'Garden.'

He kissed Agnes. 'Be good to your mother. Remember Papa loves you.'

Liv kissed him twice, on the lips and on the ear. 'Go. Go save the world,' she whispered.

*

It was a relief when my younger self went inside, and I found Gretel and her brother hadn't left us behind. I waited in the shadows outside the gate, where I could see both the garden and the car. The second car hadn't moved while I argued with myself in the shed. It was too dark to see the occupants, if it had any.

Again, I wrestled with the temptation to find out. Probably would have in my youth. But I'd learned a small bit of discretion over the years.

'You said you wouldn't leave again!' Liv's voice, equal parts anguish and anger, carried to me in the garden. I could hear Agnes crying, too.

Agnes's cries ripped my heart out. But, I'm ashamed to say, the sense of betrayal in Liv's voice filled me with guilty, greedy hope. The Jerries have a word for what I felt: schadenfreude. He didn't deserve her more than I did.

After that they fell silent again. He emerged from the house. Liv stood in the door to watch him go, and pity the poor ARP warden who might have tried to shut her back inside. I tried not to stare. But the kitchen light silhouetted her robed figure in the doorway, and I would have recognized that body even if it wore a ghillie suit. I'd never forgotten how beautiful she was.

Liv held our daughter. I recognized the blanket.

Like me, he knew how to open the garden gate silently. I suppose I shouldn't have been surprised, but I truly thought I'd picked that up later.

He held out his Identity Card. 'I'll need this when I return, you know.'

'It'll be waiting for you.' I reached for it, but he yanked it away. 'Why do you need this?'

I nodded toward the house. My house. 'It's for them,' I lied. 'If anything unfortunate should happen. They'll be looked after.'

But this wasn't his first time into the field. He knew better. 'That's not how—'

I grabbed his elbow and used my leverage to force his weight onto his weak knee. He stumbled into the hedge. A bit unfair of me, and unwise if he decided to tussle, but I had to distract him quickly before the doubts ate through the thin sheen of plausibility in the story I'd spun.

'This is deep cover,' I hissed. 'Not poncing about on a Spanish milk run.' He hadn't yet been on a deep cover mission. I had.

He shoved back. He was stronger. I retreated.

'This is a farce. You're sending me off without a cover identity and putting my life in the hands of that German bint. The one you warned me not to trust.'

'Your identity is Raybould Phillip Marsh,' I said. 'And the bint is your cover.'

I could see him weighing it over one last time. But I'd offered him a chance to infiltrate the greatest threat to his family and his country, plus an unbeatable advantage in doing so. He came round. Though it took a moment, the stubborn bastard.

He handed over the Card. He thought for a moment, then emptied his pockets. So I also took his billfold, spare change, and keys. Anything that could be used to identify him. Anything that would peg him as a Briton, should he get separated from Gretel's aegis.

We walked to the car together. Klaus had woken. Gretel watched our approach, though I could not see her eyes. She leaned forward in the open window.

'Hello, Raybould. I did say we'd meet again.'

'Fucking unbelievable,' he muttered.

'I know him,' said Klaus, still in German. 'He chased us tonight. What is this about, Gretel?'

'All in good time, brother.' She winked at me.

I asked my younger self, 'Remember the protocols?'

'Yes.'

I wanted confirmation when he arrived in Germany. Finding an unattended transmitter at the farm would be child's play with Gretel at his side. I knew, roughly, when to expect his arrival confirmation signal; I could arrange to be in a pub, near a wireless, for that.

I squinted at the other car, trying to make out its occupants. Something about this didn't feel right. To Gretel, I whispered, 'Our friends up the street haven't moved.'

'Of course not. They're here to watch over Olivia.'

'I had Stephenson put a team watching the house,' said the younger me, sotto voce. He gave Gretel a hard look. 'As a precaution against *them*.'

Oh, bloody wonderful. I'd forgotten all about that. The old man's watchers had already seen suspicious activity at the home of Raybould Marsh: a strange visit in the middle of the night followed by a sudden departure. This wasn't ideal, but it wasn't yet a catastrophe – the young agent Marsh's disappearance wouldn't be secret after he failed to appear at the Admiralty tomorrow morning. What worried me was the possibility the watchers might identify the visitors. If Stephenson learned his fair-haired boy had entertained two Jerry agents . . .

Our only saving grace was the blackout, which made it damn near impossible to count and identify the occupants of a car parked halfway up the street. I couldn't see the watchers, but they couldn't see our faces either. They'd only seen my silhouette coming and going, and I doubted they knew if there was anybody else in my car. So it seemed likely they hadn't yet made Gretel and Klaus.

My counterpart climbed in, taking the driver's seat that I had vacated earlier. 'Good luck.' I offered my hand through the open window. We shook. I had a strong grip.

'Don't worry,' Gretel said while he reached for the loose ignition wires. She handed me the briefcase. 'I'll look after him.'

'You might have a shadow,' I said, tilting my head toward the car up the street. 'Best if you lose them quickly.' He rolled his eyes. Then he started the stolen car, more skillfully than I had, and they were off. As they pulled away, I heard Gretel saying, 'Three streets, then turn right ...'

They disappeared into the night, that strange trio. I limped through a sleeping city and wondered what fate held in store for us.

Apparently Stephenson's watchers sensed something big afoot, because they pulled out before Marsh could get too far ahead. They ran without any lights at all, not even a slitted headlamp. That meant either careless drunks or trained professionals: driving in the blackout was bloody dangerous even with headlamps. The SIS men must have been confident in their decision: if they returned empty-handed after abandoning their post, they'd be chewed out good and proper. And probably spend the rest of the war scrubbing the loos at Fort Monckton.

Marsh reviewed his mental map of the neighborhood. Losing the tail at high speed wasn't wise; it was likely to attract more attention than it lost. At least one ARP warden was sure to witness the chase.

'Three streets,' said Gretel, 'then turn right.'

The commander said she could see the future. Was she doing that now?

Marsh cornered sharply after the third street, just slowly

enough not to screech the tires. The SIS car followed. It kept a discreet distance, hanging as far back as possible without running the risk of losing their quarry in the darkness.

'Now what?'

Gretel said nothing. He risked a momentary glance in her direction. Her moonlit silhouette sat with head tipped back as though dozing, or concentrating.

Marsh slalomed through another right, and a left, and a spin through a roundabout that tossed a cursing Klaus across the rear seat. But the SIS car kept a steady distance throughout. Marsh wondered if he knew the men in that car. He wondered how he came to be colluding with two enemy agents to elude his own colleagues. He wondered how he came to be abandoning his wife and newborn daughter. And for how long.

'At least tell me where we're headed,' he said.

Gretel said, 'Hush.' And pinched the bridge of her nose, either squinting or scowling. In the darkness they were one and the same.

Marsh addressed the vague form of Klaus in the rearview. 'If you want to make your rendezvous,' he said, downshifting, 'then give me a bloody destination.'

The engine noise of their stolen car hit a higher pitch. Their followers' motor followed suit a moment later, as though harmonizing. Marsh pressed on the gas.

Klaus was a sullen shadow. He rubbed his shoulder. Was he waiting for a yea or nay from Gretel? A strange pair, these Jerries. But Klaus reciprocated Marsh's utter unwillingness to trust them. That, at least, Marsh could understand.

He chanced another glimpse at the woman. Quietly, and without opening her eyes, Gretel said, 'Eyes on the road, Raybould.'

Marsh flicked his gaze back to the windscreen, just in time to suss out a shadow crossing the road between two unlit Belisha beacons. Marsh swore, wrenched the wheel. This time the tires did sing as the car skidded through the empty oncoming lane. He missed the warden by a whisker's breadth, close enough to hear the other man's fright and feel the crack of finger bones shattering against the side panels.

Behind them, a horn blared. Marsh struggled to right their fishtailing car without sideswiping a post pillar.

Sod this for a game of soldiers, thought Marsh.

'Klaus!' he said. 'Destination! Now.'

Klaus rubbed his scalp with the knuckle joint of a missing finger. In German, he said, 'We're supposed to meet the boat—'

Gretel's eyes snapped open. 'Stop!' she yelled.

Marsh punched the brakes. Their skid echoed up and down the lane.

'Back up,' she said. 'Second left.'

The transmission clanked. Marsh craned his neck, trying to see through the rear window. Klaus crouched.

'Perhaps you've noticed we're being followed,' said Marsh, squinting. 'By a black car running with no lights in the middle of a bloody—'

There. The MI-6 car loomed in the darkness, a blur limned by the faint glow of moonlight on matte paint. He cranked the wheel again, hoping to hell the other driver swerved accordingly, and braced for impact.

Metal screeched against metal. A flurry of sparks lit the night. Their side mirror shattered.

And then the SIS car was before them.

'—*blackout!*'

Marsh exhaled. He floored the accelerator, and threw the

car – still in reverse – around the next corner. Klaus tumbled across the rear seat again. 'Damn it!'

Gretel unplugged her battery. She clucked her tongue. 'I said *second* left.'

'How careless of me.'

The car creaked on its suspension when Marsh hit the brakes again. His foot slipped off the clutch. They lurched forward again amidst the grinding of gears and the faint stink of hot oil. They fishtailed around the corner. Gretel's wires swung wildly to tap against Marsh's arm.

The MI-6 car resumed the chase, this time in reverse while Marsh drove forward. Gretel's precious second left was a tight squeeze, barely wider than the car.

It was also a dead end.

Knows the future, does she? Ha.

'Oh, that's just bloody wonderful.' He caught a blur in the rearview as the SIS men rolled to a halt, blocking their only egress. 'Now that we've rogered the pooch so nicely, any further suggestions?'

'Yes,' said Gretel. She tossed her battery over the seat. It surprised Klaus but he caught it. She slid across the seat, rubbing her feverish body against Marsh. He suppressed a shudder. She arched her shoulders against the seat and pinned Marsh's foot beneath her outstretched heel.

'Drive faster,' she said.

The alley's end loomed in the dim glow of slitted headlamps. Marsh tried to knock her aside, but she was persistent.

'Look, you madwoman!'

But even the sharp jab of Marsh's elbow to her shoulder couldn't dent that damnable sangfroid. Gretel said, 'Brother. If you don't mind?'

Klaus righted himself in the rear seat. He peered through the windscreen at a rapidly approaching wall of masonry. He swore. '*Scheisse!*'

The faint click of his battery connector sounded like a gunshot. Marsh flinched again. He tried to object. 'No—'

But then he couldn't speak, for he was a ghostly man in a ghostly car, and the traces of ephemeral air in his lungs could push no sound. That didn't stop him from screaming. Brick and mortar ghosted through his pounding heart, along with lath and plaster and iron and glass. They breezed through obstructions like so much wind. It was far worse than when Klaus had run straight through him with ghostly Gretel in tow just a few hours earlier in the Admiralty.

Marsh's lungs ached. And still they drove. Through a parlor; through a den; through a foyer.

The ache in his chest became a tingle. A burn.

They emerged onto an unobstructed lane. Klaus did something – rather, stopped doing something – that felt like an inaudible *twang*, as though the car and everything in it were a violin string plucked in an impossible direction. The car rematerialized. Its occupants gasped for air in unison.

Marsh eased the car to a stop, still panting. 'Never,' he said, 'fucking do that again without advance warning.'

He writhed with the need to scratch an itch. But the phantom itch skittered along the inside of his bones, through the inner surfaces of his skull, where a house had been moments earlier. He slapped the steering wheel until his knuckles cracked and his palms stung. Just to feel something solid. To know his body was tangible again. When next he slept, Marsh knew he'd dream of being buried alive.

'They won't follow us now,' said Gretel.

SIX

14 May 1940
On the Sussex coast, England

They arrived at the coast just as the sky was fading from charcoal black to wet wool gray. Compared to the excitement of ditching the SIS shadow, the remainder of the night had been quiet except for the occasional navigational adjustment from Gretel. Marsh still rankled at playing chauffeur to a pair of Jerries. She'd directed them to an isolated stretch of shingle beach between Eastbourne and Hastings.

He set the parking brake and made to disengage the splice job that Liddell-Stewart had used to pinch the car. (A bit odd, that. Keeping an ultra-low profile was one thing, but no access to a motor pool? Stolen cars drew attention.) It wasn't a bad job, as such things went; Marsh appraised the work with a practiced eye. The commander knew his work.

Gretel laid a fingertip on Marsh's arm. He flinched away from her feverish touch.

'Wait,' she whispered. 'Flash the headlamps, twice.'

He did, wondering how far the light from the slitted lamps would carry. But moments later an answering flash came from

somewhere in the darkness of the Channel, a few hundred yards
past the tide line.

'I'll be damned,' he said to himself. It took a gutsy U-boat crew
to chance the Channel.

Gretel removed her shoes, then stepped out of the car. She
ambled among a handful of old fishing nets, green glass floats,
and other flotsam scattered along the beach. Pebbles tinkled like
chimes beneath her bare feet, creating an atonal counterpoint to
the hiss and thrum of breaking waves. A cool breeze carried the
tang of salt and foam from the sea and the faintest odor of fish
from the nets. The breeze ruffled Gretel's braids. It pressed the
hem of her skirt to her ankles.

Marsh emerged from the stolen car, making sure that Gretel
didn't disappear into the predawn shadows. He didn't trust her
any more than Klaus trusted him. Marsh stretched his legs,
cracked his knuckles. Good idea to stretch while he could; it
would be bloody cramped on the U-boat. Stretching helped keep
the collywobbles under control, too. He'd done more than his
share of reckless, dangerous things in his life. But this . . .

Klaus was the last out of the car. He draped the jacket of his
fake naval uniform over Gretel's shoulders. She turned and
smiled at Marsh. The whispering wind carried their conversation
to his ears, just audible above the static hiss of breaking surf.

Klaus asked, 'Who is he?'

'The future of the farm.'

He said, 'I don't trust him.'

She said, 'Do you trust me?'

He didn't answer. *That makes two of us*, thought Marsh.

He strained to hear the rest of their conversation, but either
they'd fallen silent or the surf grew louder. It wasn't long before
the first blushes of pink tinted the eastern sky when Marsh picked

out the faint creak of oarlocks. A rowboat coalesced from the shadows to ride one last wave and crunch against the shingle.

A Kriegsmarine petty officer vaulted over the prow. His boots splashed sea foam over Gretel's toes. She appeared not to notice. He carried an electric torch, its lamp entirely covered with heavy paper except for a narrow slit, much like the headlamps on the stolen car.

The submariner's eyes flinched away from Gretel's wires. Klaus's, too. 'You're late,' he said.

Gretel said, 'No, we aren't. Your orders were to wait until we arrived. We have now arrived.'

Marsh recognized a pissing contest when he saw one. Perhaps the Kriegsmarine sailors had heard rumors of the Götter-elektrongruppe. Certainly they had been ordered to defer to its members. But they had never seen Klaus or Gretel in action, which naturally left them wondering why these obvious examples of non-Teutonic stock were calling the shots. So there was friction, and Marsh was about to land in the middle of it.

The petty officer frowned. He pointed across the water, to where the shark fin silhouette of a conning tower was just visible against the brightening sky.

'A few more minutes and you'd have been stuck until nightfall. It's already too bright. Let's go.'

Marsh trudged down the pebbled beach to join the others at the waterline, each footstep crunching loudly on the shingle. He tried to swallow away the sour taste bubbling up from his stomach. *What am I doing here?*

'Who is that?'

Gretel twirled a finger through one braid, so that he and the other submariners couldn't help but see her wires.

'He's with us,' she said.

The sailors ferried their passengers into the Channel with swift German efficiency. Every stroke of the oars took Marsh farther from Britain, farther from Liv and Agnes. And with every stroke his heart beat more desperately, like a prisoner rattling his cage. He kept his wife and daughter at the forefront of his mind; it kept the panic at bay, knowing he did this for them.

Marsh followed Klaus and Gretel through the hatch into dark, cramped Unterseeboot-115 as the sun rose over the English Channel.

14 May 1940
Milkweed Headquarters, London, England

Stephenson had already worked himself into something just short of a foam-flecked tirade by the time Will arrived. Will glanced at Lorimer for a show of solidarity, knowing he was in for the brunt of it. Marsh hadn't yet arrived, but Stephenson let loose as soon as Will closed the office door behind him.

'How the *hell* did he know where to find her?'

Cigarette ash swirled around Stephenson as he paced. He used the cigarette like a baton, gesturing at his troops like a displeased commandant. Little white flakes settled on his suit and tie like dandruff.

He turned on Will. 'And *you*! What in God's name were you thinking? You insisted the prisoner wouldn't see anything she hadn't already seen. And then you bollixed everything up by *tipping our hand to the enemy*.'

Will stammered. It was hard to talk; his assailant in the park had given him a terrible bruise on his jaw. 'She – I mean, I – it was the only thing that made—'

But Stephenson had built up a full head of steam. His tirade continued, ricocheting from one source of irritation to another: 'And where the hell is Marsh?'

Lorimer and Will looked at each other, shrugged. 'Haven't seen him all day. Thought he'd be here already,' said the Scot. Will nodded.

But Stephenson turned his flinty gaze upon Will again. Will flinched. The accidental motion evoked another wave of agony from the bandaged stump where his finger had been. It felt like the lost finger itself was in pain; the doctor called it phantom limb syndrome.

If the old man's voice been any colder, it might have frosted the windows. 'Where is he, Beauclerk? You two have been thick as thieves since university.'

Will steeled himself to meet the old man's eyes. What he saw there put the lie to Stephenson's weary irritation. He was concerned. Concerned for Marsh, and concerned because they'd been infiltrated by an enemy agent.

'I truly don't know where Pip might be,' said Will. The swelling along his jaw rendered his pronunciation mushy. He had to concentrate to make himself understood. 'I expected to find him here. Though it pains me to contradict you, he doesn't, in fact, keep me apprised of his moment-by-moment activities.'

'The man does have a newborn at home,' said Lorimer. 'Probably running late.'

'Ah, well, that explains it, doesn't it?' said Stephenson. Tobacco breath puffed across Will's face as the old man continued, 'I'll just ask the Jerries that when next they intend to catch us with our knickers down, they kindly do it on a schedule more convenient to Commander Marsh, shall I? Better yet, I'll send cables to Hitler and Mussolini, explaining the situation. No doubt they'll conduct their war with more consideration for the commander's home life!'

'Knickers?' Lorimer's face twisted in indignation. 'How the hell were we supposed to catch that minger? Can't fight against something like that.'

Stephenson went very still, as though frozen in place with a veneer of ice. He approached Lorimer until the two men stood almost nose to nose. 'Allow me to remind you gentlemen that our mandate, as handed directly to me by the Prime Minister himself, is to do exactly that.'

Lorimer shouted, 'Did you promise him the moon while you were at it? There are only four of us! What does he expect us to do, pull a battalion from our arses?'

Yesterday's debacle had demonstrated just how badly Milkweed was outclassed by its adversaries, and now these men who were accustomed to being very good at what they did felt helpless. Tempers were running high.

Stephenson inched forward until the two men were almost thumping their chests together. 'Four? I count three men in this room, one of whom is soon to be—'

Will insinuated himself between Stephenson and Lorimer before their anger led to something truly daft. He used his hands to wedge the men apart. The Scot had a solid build; nudging him put enough pressure on Will's bandages to rip his breath away.

'Gentlemen,' he gasped. 'This is pointless. Let's save it for Jerry, what?' The pain made his voice thin and thready. He tried to get it under control as he turned to Stephenson. 'Pip will get here when he gets here. He knows this is important, and no doubt his tardiness will have an excellent explanation. In the meantime, let's make do without him, shall we?' To Lorimer, he said, 'I'm certain our esteemed paterfamilias is aware of the difficulties presented by our personnel shortages. So why don't we discuss the situation like civilized men, rather than a trio of raving savages?'

Will stood back, feeling faintly pleased with himself. Stephenson shot Lorimer another glare, but then stalked around his desk to take his seat, still simmering with anger. Lorimer did likewise, taking one of the chairs facing the old man's desk. Stephenson had moved his old office in the Broadway Buildings, including some of the furniture and most of the watercolors, into the Old Admiralty. The old man had parlayed all of his political capital into the oversight of an obscure four-man operation.

Four men, counting Marsh. But where was he?

'I blame you, Beauclerk, for this monumental cock-up.'

'What?'

'One minute you're telling us the Jerries must be using sorcery of their own, no question about it, and then after a brief interlude for some perfectly grisly self-mutilation – the reason for which I still can't begin to comprehend – you announce that no, in fact, the Jerries are doing nothing of the sort.' Stephenson took a long drag on his cigarette, snuffed it in a marble ashtray, lit another. 'You wasted months we couldn't afford chasing a will-o'-the-wisp.'

Stephenson said this last bit with such contempt that it struck the same chords in Will as did his grandfather's sadistic derision. It made him want to hide again. They might have been back in the glade at Bestwood.

The old man said, 'Now. How in the Lord's name did that Jerry bastard find her so easily?'

Realization struck Will like a jolt of electricity. The urge to hide became almost irresistible. Stronger even than the pain in his hand and jaw. He had a sickening feeling he knew exactly how that ghostly fellow had known Milkweed operated from the Old Admiralty building.

I truly am a witless toff.

'Not through the Eidolons,' Will mumbled. 'It was through human means.'

'Do you honestly think,' Stephenson said quietly, 'that bastard was human?'

Even Lorimer couldn't argue with that.

Will's mouth had gone dry. He coughed. 'I, ah ... What I mean to say is that there may be a rather straightforward explanation.'

Both men picked up on Will's hesitation. 'By all means, please enlighten us,' said Stephenson.

'It's something of a long story,' Will said. 'Perhaps I should wait until Pip arrives.'

Stephenson shook his head. 'Out with it, Beauclerk.'

They watched while Will fidgeted with the brim of his bowler hat. He took a steadying breath, then forged ahead before he could lose his nerve.

'I was contacted by the Met yesterday, you see.'

And so Will related the story of his visit to Cannon Row. Lorimer and Stephenson listened in silence, awestruck by the extent of Will's obliviousness, until he described the absurd copy of his own billfold.

Lorimer said, 'You bloody stupid tosser. You fucking idiotic toff.' He muttered obscenities and insults through the rest of Will's tale.

But Stephenson didn't say a word. Only the whitening of his knuckles as he gripped the ashtray betrayed any emotional reaction at all. Will expected him to hurl it across the room, or use it to bash in his skull once the rage overwhelmed him. It's what

Marsh would have done. Instead, the old man waited until Will's rambling and awkward confession wound down to its conclusion. When he spoke, it was as if he'd plunged so deep into rage that he'd come out the other side again, emerging into serene detachment.

He might have been commenting on the weather when he asked, 'And at no point did you consider having a look at this fellow they'd caught with your billfold?'

'It obviously wasn't my billfold and it obviously wasn't John Stephenson in their custody, so I thought the matter was settled.' Silence fell upon the office. Will rushed to fill it. 'I mean, surely the Jerries wouldn't be so careless. As forgeries go, the documents weren't even remotely credible. It had to be an elaborate hoax. A practical joke.'

But Stephenson was already dialing the telephone on his desk. It was particularly agonizing to listen along while, through a sequence of calls, the old man discovered that the fellow caught in St. James' Park had been cut loose. And that the police had done so on orders from 'higher up.' Will didn't understand the significance of that, but Lorimer and Stephenson did. The security service had put a tail on the mystery man. They were also watching Stephenson, whom the stranger had claimed to be.

MI5 didn't know about Milkweed. Nevertheless, the Security Service had stumbled upon evidence of German interference in Milkweed's affairs.

They'd been scooped. That was the pièce de résistance, the crowning jewel of Will's recent mistakes. So acute was the shame he wanted to bury himself. The fear of what he might have caused left his shirt damp under the arms.

Pip put his faith in me. How on earth can I possibly redeem myself? Will could think of one possibility. Two days ago, he'd have rejected it out of hand as being too extreme. Too fanciful. But now . . .

Stephenson said to Lorimer, 'We're left with no indication of who this mysterious prisoner might have been.'

'We know it wasn't the minger who sprang the lass.' Lorimer shook his head. 'At this rate, the four of us will be outnumbered by German agents by the end of the week. Bloody fuck.'

Four. That number again. But where was Marsh?

'Well, that's one place – the only place – where something good might come out of yesterday's debacle.' Stephenson opened a desk drawer. He produced a bundle of papers wrapped with a black ribbon. Each page was embossed with the full Royal Arms, making it equivalent to a decree from His Majesty. There had been dozens of witnesses to the chase, dozens of witnesses to a man who ran through walls as though they were a mirage. Those witnesses, Stephenson explained, were Milkweed's new recruits.

'Be ready to show the Tarragona film in a few days,' Stephenson told Lorimer.

'Aye.'

The talk of swelling Milkweed's ranks, of finally giving the organization the resources it needed for dealing effectively with von Westarp and his 'children,' convinced Will to voice his proposal.

He said, 'I fear that spies and soldiers won't ever be enough. No matter what von Westarp has accomplished, or how he accomplished it, the Eidolons are our best chance of countering it.' He held up his bandaged hand. 'And in that regard, my contribution has been less than exemplary thus far.' At that, Lorimer snorted. Will continued, 'We need true experts, not a dilettante like myself.'

What Milkweed needed more than anything else, Will

explained, was warlocks. Men descended from the bloodlines that had, for many centuries, secretly curated knowledge of Enochian. Will's grandfather, the twelfth Duke of Aelred, had been one of these men, as had Will's father. Aubrey, Will's brother, had been groomed for the peerage as was traditional for the older son. But Will had been raised in a different family tradition.

Though these men guarded their hard-won knowledge jealously, they were known on rare occasions to engage in trade with their colleagues. The old duke had done so. Which meant that his journals might hold records of other warlock lineages, or their whereabouts.

Stephenson listened with considerable interest while Will laid out his proposal. It didn't take long. Marsh still hadn't arrived by the time the meeting concluded. Will departed immediately on his new recruitment mission.

14 May 1940
Bermondsey, London, England

I dreamt of sea wrack and ravens, for how long I couldn't say, until the thrum of rain on a metal roof nudged me to consciousness. It was loud as an artillery barrage, or the Devil's own tattoo. Rainwater sluiced through a rust hole far overhead, drizzling me with cold water and ocher grit. I rolled over, groggily trying to escape the worst of it. But moving kicked up sawdust from the warehouse floor; the sneezing fit banished any hope of further sleep.

I yawned. Stretched. My joints ached. They popped and cracked from neck to ankles. Sleeping on the floor hadn't done my bad knee any favors. I blinked up at a row of windows streaked with sooty marks of the warehouse's past. A leaden gray morning loomed just beyond the glass and grime. It was raining stair-rods again.

I shivered in my underclothes. The rain had arrived from the sea, riding a line of squalls. Cool drafts swirled through the warehouse, mixing scents of the Thames and diesel fuel. The hoists and cranes above the warehouse jetty rattled their chains like Marley's ghost. I'd taken my younger counterpart's clothes from the Anderson; I went to the pile folded on a relatively clean spot of floor and dressed in civilian clothes. No uniform today.

I had slept like a dead thing. After sending my doppelgänger off with his Nazi escort, I'd headed for the river. It had been a long walk to Bermondsey on top of a very long and exhausting day. But I needed a place to work.

Back in '63, after the battle with the Soviet agent who'd given me my wounds, Milkweed had taken his body to a warehouse down on the docks. It was one of many properties secretly belonging to SIS throughout London and the UK. That particular warehouse had been damaged by bombing during the war. And, like so many pieces of London, it had never been fully rebuilt. Its derelict state had made it perfect for MI6. For now, the place was undamaged, but quiet, and slowly falling into disrepair. It wasn't yet an MI6 property, but attacks on shipping convoys had evidently reduced the flow of cargo to the point that the owners had been forced to consolidate. I'd have to move out before history repeated itself and it took a direct hit from a Luftwaffe bomb ... *if* history repeated itself. But for the moment, and as long as I was willing to share it with rats, bats, and pigeons, I had a space from which to run the second prong of my mission.

Which was the order of business for today. I'd taken my best shot at the REGP, but now it was out of my hands, and I wouldn't know for a long time whether my arrow had flown true. But Milkweed I could do something about.

Klaus's infiltration of the Admiralty had spurred a flurry of changes. I knew that in the original time line, today had been the day when Will took it upon himself to track down and recruit the warlocks. So today's job was simple: pay him a visit.

I wouldn't say that I felt relaxed – that was impossible, after a scant few hours of sleep on a wooden floor – but I did feel a temporary reprieve from the grinding weight on my shoulders. Dealing with Will was easy. It felt good to have a task well in hand.

My stomach rumbled, reminding me I hadn't eaten a thing since what the coppers had given me yesterday. And that I hadn't had a proper meal since 1963. There was still a fair amount of cash left out of what I'd nicked from the Anderson shelter. Enough for breakfast, if I could find it. But I didn't know the neighborhood, so it seemed more likely I'd be stuck with pub food, if I could find one open this early.

I glanced at my wristwatch. And cursed. Loudly.

It was mid-afternoon. I had slept most of the day.

Rain soaked past my bones and into my marrow while I pounded on the door of Will's Kensington flat.

No answer. But I kept at it because I didn't know what else to do.

Think. Think. Where was Will? With a bit of concentration, I could piece together his movements in the original time line.

I remembered how the old man had torn us new arseholes after the fiasco of Gretel's escape. Will had left straight from that meeting on his trek to find the warlocks. But he would have had to pack a bag before leaving. And then he'd needed his grand-father's papers. So he'd said good-bye to me at the Admiralty, made a quick stop here in Kensington, and then set off for his family estate at Bestwood, up in Nottinghamshire.

But events were unfolding differently now. I had changed things: Raybould Marsh wasn't at that meeting. How did Stephenson react to my absence? I reckoned it had made him even angrier. Further, that he took his anger out on poor Will and Lorimer. If anything, Will was probably more committed to finding the warlocks now than he had been in the original time line.

Was he still at the Admiralty? Had he already been to the flat? Or was he waiting on a train? I checked my watch again. My best chance for intercepting Will was at the train station. Assuming he was still in the city.

I dashed back through the downpour to the taxi. My clothes were uncomfortably tight. They belonged to a younger man, one who didn't carry the paunch of late middle age. Now they were sodden, and clung to my skin. But not so tightly as the renewed sense of failure.

The driver hadn't complained when I'd asked him to wait. My dithering was worth a princely sum. He folded up his newspaper and set it on the seat beside him.

'Your mate's not home, sir?'

'No.'

'Terrible day to be out and about, if you ask me. Where next?'

'St. Pancras station.' That's where Will would have caught a train to Nottinghamshire.

And so I wandered the platforms like a revenant spirit, haunt-ing each train bound for the Midlands until the last departure of the evening. But I was too late. There was no sign of Will.

'God damn it!'

My voice echoed through the mostly empty station. A solid kick sent a rubbish bin rolling off the platform, trailing newspapers and chip wrappers. I worked my way down the platform, booting every bin I could find.

'Son!' *Kick.* 'Of!' *Kick.* 'A!' *Kick.* 'Bitch!'

I remembered something the old man had said to me once, a very long time ago: *I'm quite impressed. When you cock something up, you do it good and proper.* How right he'd been.

I had missed my opportunity. Which left me powerless to do anything. Now there was nothing I could do about Milkweed until Will returned. I didn't dare set foot back in the Admiralty; by now everybody had heard of the stranger who had attacked Will in St. James' Park. Even now, Stephenson and Lorimer were busy rounding up all the witnesses to the escape. Slipping the King's shilling into their ale, so to speak. Very soon the old man would discover the vault had been cleaned out.

No, the Admiralty wasn't safe for me.

I limped out of the station before somebody could call the coppers to report the old codger who'd gone off his nut.

For dinner, I stopped in a pub and bought a piece of cod wrapped in newspaper. After a few bites, I waved down the barman and ordered a pint of bitters to wash away the taste of ink. In spite of this I finished the fish quickly, wolfing it down like the starving man I was. I ate as though with each bite I could snare Will, reel him back to London, delay his errand, keep my mission on track. The bitters went down equally fast.

This public house had a hearth on one wall, empty now but for a smattering of last winter's ashes. I'd met my wife in a pub not unlike this one. The clientele was a bit rougher here, but it reminded me of the Hart and Hearth. I had fond memories of that place. Will had introduced me to the Hart, and to Liv, on the same evening.

He'd blown it to pieces the following year. Part of the Eidolons' blood price in exchange for destroying an invasion fleet. Will had begun to drink before then, but I think that was the night that broke him. After that, the Eidolons' relentless demands for blood and slaughter hastened his decline. And relentless they were, for every drop spilled was another piece of the map, another Eidolonic fingerhold into our world. Thus Will and the others set fires, sank barges, even derailed a train. Atrocities committed against our own countrymen, all to fuel Milkweed's secret war against the Götterelektrongruppe.

I shook my head. Nothing I could do about it right now. I'd fix it when Will returned. What was one more item on the ever-growing list of things to put right this time round? Didn't seem to matter much at this point. The sodding list was already absurd.

My scars got looks, of course. By now I'd grown accustomed to the double takes, the stares, and the way people conspicuously looked at anything other than the ruined side of my face. But I discovered a bright side to looking like a wounded veteran.

The war dominated most conversations. And they took an optimistic tone, for the most part. The BEF was still putting up a fight on the Continent; most folks believed things would turn around once the French recovered from the Jerries' underhanded evasion of the Maginot Line. We had a new Prime Minister, one who clearly understood the Fascist threat. The possibility of complete and utter disaster hadn't yet penetrated the national psyche. Standing alone against our enemies hadn't yet become a grim possibility. We hadn't yet lost an army at Dunkirk.

And so it didn't take long before the conversation at the bar turned to the last time we beat the Boche. From there it was just a few pints before somebody approached the old duffer with the scars.

'You a vet, mister?'

'Yeah.'

'Great War?'

I started to shake my head, but caught myself. I was the right age for a veteran of the previous war. So instead, I nodded. 'Royal Flying Corps.'

'You were a pilot?' More men gathered round. The entire country hungered for good war stories. And there was nobody more flash than an ace.

'Yeah.'

One fellow said, proudly, 'My son is in the RAF. He'll give the Jerries what for.'

'God bless him,' I said, raising my glass. 'God bless all the fighting boys.' We drank to that.

'What'd you do, sir, if you don't mind saying?'

'Flew reconnaissance for three years. We stuck a camera under my Bristol' – I set down my pint, to better explain with my hands – 'then I flew over enemy territory. Snapped troop movements, artillery emplacements, and such.'

'Get shot at?'

'All the bloody time. Spent more time patching holes than I did in the cockpit.' That got a laugh. 'Once had a round come up through the seat and snap off my goggles.'

'It didn't.'

'Still have the pair to prove it,' I said.

'Do any dogfighting?'

I shrugged. 'Saw some combat.'

'How about von Richthofen? You ever fight him?'

'Red Baron? I'm still here, aren't I?'

That got another laugh from the group. Somebody slapped me on the back.

'Ever get shot down?'

The bloke who asked this got a couple of dark looks, but I pretended not to notice. 'Austrians got me. Shredded my plane out from under me, sent me spiraling down. God I loved that Bristol. I aimed for no-man's-land.' I swigged from my pint and set the empty glass on the bar. 'Woke up in a field hospital. That's how I got these,' I said, pointing to the burn scars on my face. That broke the ice, when they saw I wasn't shy about my experiences.

True story, almost every bit of it. Replace the burns with an amputated arm, and you had the story of my mentor, John Stephenson. He'd shown me the goggles.

I couldn't very well tell them the truth, could I?

Kept as close to the old man's exploits as I could. I could spin the story well and do justice to the old man's service. He didn't talk much about the old days, but I listened when he did. Usually over a brandy or three.

I wouldn't have done this if I weren't a vet. I might not have had any respect left for myself but I still respected the men in uniform. And I *was* a veteran. Of a secret war. And battles that hadn't happened yet, or perhaps would never happen in this new history.

And I'd been having a shit time of things for as long as I could remember. It was nice to be appreciated, just for a little while, and even if it weren't for the things I'd actually done for King and Country. It was good to have the gratitude of a few countrymen.

The details were irrelevant. I told Stephenson's story as a substitute for my own experiences, but it was my anguish that came out in the telling.

The fellow who'd first asked me about the war shook my hand. 'You done the country proud, sir. Thank you.'

And, God love them, the other fellows raised their pints to me. Nobody had ever thanked me for my service. Very few people knew the truth of what I had done and endured and suffered for the sake of Britain. But even they had never said a kind word about it. Not even the old man. I dug out a handkerchief and pretended to blow my nose so my new mates wouldn't see the water in my eyes.

But I couldn't help it. I was so goddamn lonely.

By the third pint I was feeling less constricted, less crushed by the weight of my responsibilities. Even played a few rounds of darts. My game was rubbish. But, God ... getting pissed with a few mates, ignoring my worries for a short while ... I couldn't say how long it had been since I'd done that. I'd started spending time in pubs after the trouble started with Liv and our son, John, but that had always been a furtive escape. Not genuine relaxation.

The barman clicked on the wireless a couple of minutes before six o'clock, giving the valves time to warm up before the BBC news. We suspended our dart game; conversations fell to whispers as the clock chimed.

'Here is the *Six O'clock News*, and this is Alvar Lidell reading it. German forces continued to cross the Meuse River today, pressing into France via bridgeheads established at Sedan and Dinant. After four o'clock today, the French Ninth and Second Armies were less than seventy-five miles apart. General Gamelin stated ...'

I finished my pint while the others listened. Didn't need to hear the broadcast. The Jerries would rout us, then slaughter the Tommies while they tried to evacuate. Hitler would make the French sign their surrender in the same railway carriage where the Kaiser's men had signed their surrender to end the First World War.

Nothing I could do about any of that. I'd traveled through time to stop the destruction of the world, but I couldn't work miracles. The world didn't spin according to my whims. I couldn't change the course of the war with a wink and a whisper. I wasn't Gretel.

Guess I'd lost track of my pints, because somebody asked, 'Who's Gretel, then?'

'The gypsy witch behind all of this,' I said, waving my arm and spilling foam on the bar. 'We're all just puppets to her. Fucking Punch and Judy. That's us.'

Maybe I had relaxed too much. No matter; they chalked it up to the old duffer being deep in his cups. Which I was, though that was beside the point. They still talked to me, still treated me like a human being. And for that I was grateful. I could have stayed all evening.

Though it was still raining, I opted to walk back to the warehouse rather than pay for a taxi. Tomorrow's errand would be expensive. I stripped out of my sodden clothes and immediately began to shiver in that drafty space. So I tipped the contents of my briefcase into an empty barrel, and set fire to the former contents of the Milkweed vault.

And nearly set myself ablaze. The fire was more energetic than I'd anticipated. The original fragments from Krasnopolsky merely melted, cracked, and gave off the smell of vinegar. Cellulose acetate. But Lorimer had apparently put the reconstructed Tarragona filmstrip onto cellulose nitrate film stock. The reel went up like a bloody Roman candle. Would've lost my eyebrows had I been a bit slower on my feet. I'd suffered enough burns for one lifetime.

A plume of blue-black smoke roiled from the barrel and wafted along the drafts swirling through the warehouse. It stung my eyes. But the flames provided warmth, so I endured the smoke while changing into dry clothes.

I couldn't burn Gretel's battery. Didn't want to bother taking it apart, either. Reckoned it was a regular witch's brew of corrosives and Lord only knew what else. Instead, I took the damn thing down to the jetty and hurled it into the Thames. It sailed into the night, then hit the dark water with a *splash* and *kerplunk*. And sank, I hoped forever, from the realm of human affairs.

The next morning, I gathered all the cash remaining from what I'd nicked out of the Anderson shelter and headed to Whitechapel. Fairclough Street was the place to go for illicit, contraband, or otherwise illegal purchases. Stephenson got his American tobacco from the black market here. This was also where Will had bought his morphine when alcohol could no longer numb the pain of fulfilling the Eidolons' demands for blood.

I brought my doppelgänger's ID card. The forgery cost me a substantial sum. It was a solid, though: the fence had a set of blank cards, the real thing, taken straight out of the National Registration Office. Didn't ask how that had been arranged. He even replicated the date stamps, and smudged them as in the original. I reproduced the original cardholder's signature easily enough, since it was my own. The cards didn't record the holders' date of birth. If they had, I'd have simply told the fence to push mine back twenty years to 1890.

An hour later, I held an exact replica of Raybould Marsh's ID card, identical in every detail except the serial number. The forgery was more than enough to keep the coppers happy if I got stopped again. They'd have to check with the NRO to catch the discrepant serial number, but that would only happen if I got hauled in again, or if the Security Service caught me, at which point the ID Card would be the least of my worries. Still, it was with no small sense of relief that I tucked the new card away.

The previous evening at the pub had given me a sense of comradeship, of being appreciated. But by morning the warm glow had faded and that thick familiar loneliness, cold like dead ashes, had taken its place. So I spent more cash on a decent shirt and tie.

And wore them both when I returned to Walworth for the third time in two days. I told myself it was simply to return my doppelgänger's ID card. A quick trip back. I'd wait for Liv to step out, slip inside, put the card back in its spot, slip out again. Not even five minutes. One less thing to worry about later, I told myself.

No. I didn't believe it, either. I'd done my best to save the world. Now I just wanted to feel like a human being again. To be in her space again. Just for a little while.

Didn't see anybody watching the house. But I was too lonely to care one way or the other.

I took a steadying breath. Hesitated. Gathered my courage. Knocked. Liv opened the door while I wrestled with whether to abandon this idiocy or to knock again.

Her eyes went directly to my scars, but just for an instant. She recovered well. 'May I help you?'

This was my first good look at her since I'd arrived. I'd become so accustomed to the faint wrinkles at the corners of her mouth, the age spots that had replaced her freckles. But now the passage of time had been reversed, and she stood before me as the woman I remembered. The woman I'd met at the Hart and Hearth. The woman who'd loved me. The mother of my children. My wife.

I didn't know if she could ever be mine again. But I would always be hers.

Speak, I commanded myself. *She won't recognize your voice.*

'Good afternoon. Mrs. Marsh?'

She raised an eyebrow. Liv's way of saying, *Yes, what?*

'My name is Liddell-Stewart. I work for the Foreign Secretary. I'd like to speak with you about your husband.'

Her eyes widened, her mouth fell open. It stabbed me like an icicle in the gut, the sight of her terror. I forged ahead before she drew the wrong conclusion. 'No need for alarm, Mrs. Marsh. He's perfectly well.' Or so I hoped. 'I'm not here in an official capacity. I understand you have a newborn at home. So I came to apologize.'

Liv looked me over. I saw the gleam in her eyes, and braced myself for a cynical retort. And it was forthcoming. 'Would this apology include groveling?'

Yes, this was my wife. But I made a show of being caught off my guard. 'I—' I stopped. Shook my head. 'I beg your pardon?'

'Sniveling would also be acceptable,' said Liv. 'Or cowering. I'm not particular. Though I do expect a magnificent apology.' Her gaze hardened. 'It's the least you can do.'

'Ah ... As you wish, ma'am.'

She chewed her lip, mulling things over. Then she stepped back, opened the door more widely. 'Come in.'

And I did.

INTERLUDE: GRETEL

She remembers the cipher future with the uncompromised clarity of a demigoddess. Sees every step the other-she takes to lure Raybould into the past. Remembers a quarter-century of prologue.

But now she stands at the headwaters of an entirely new time line. This universe is one day old. It is a hatchling, too weak and blind to fend for itself. Unshaped clay awaiting the sculptor's hands. Spider silk and golden thread awaiting the touch of a master weaver. Awaiting her.

Her Willenskräfte will be the loom that imposes form and structure upon this new time line. Like any youngling, this universe requires order. Purpose. She will impose it.

Brother comes for her. He delivers a battery.

The world fades behind a shimmering curtain of gossamer possibilities when she draws upon the Götterelektron. Her first true glimpse of the splinter time line. So beautiful. She wants to explore. Every thread, every tributary, every wispy one-in-a-million. What a delicious thrill to explore these vistas, to race off into the distant fringes of the not-quite-impossible. She can't resist. She skips ahead – a day, a week, a month, a year – following the luminous paths of potentiality for a peek at the world she and Raybould will create, the life they will have together . . .

Demigoddess as voyeur.

... And sees something entirely new: the futures lose their cohesion, melt into an indistinct blur. Her willpower outraces the birth cries of this hatchling time line! The ripples of creation have yet to perturb the inchoate primordial fog. It takes time to break the perfect symmetry of infinitely homogeneous, infinitely isotropic maybes.

She pulls back. There is much to do in coming days, many paths to explore in these first hours. In eleven minutes they will meet Raybould, her Raybould, in the park:

~~'You came for me,' she will say. 'I knew you would.'~~

~~And he will say, 'You fucking evil bitch. I didn't do it for you.'~~

No. Not nice.

'It's you,' she will say. 'You came for me.'

And he will say, 'It's you.'

That's better.

Raybould sheds little eddies of change with everything he does. Every blade of grass bent underfoot in St. James', every exhalation of sweet masculine breath while they wait in the car. Tiny perturbations at first, but they will grow.

Snowflakes will beget avalanches. A fallen tree will divert a stream, alter a tributary, reshape a river, etch a new topography into the vast, wide continent of time.

When she gazes upon Raybould through the shimmering tapestry of possible futures, he becomes a shadow, a silhouette limned with kaleidoscopic diffraction. The pattern is a framework, the garden trellis through which she will weave the vines of her Willenskräfte. Together they will grow a new axis mundi, a world tree strong enough to warp the universe to her liking. She and he are as Eve and Adam to this new time line. It is their offspring, the fruit of their labors. He, the man who traveled through time. And she, the woman whose vision transcends it.

She peeks again. But the leaden cloud bank of pre-creation still shrouds the far future.

No matter. She knows what she will see when the fog clears. The future no longer ends with the Eidolons. *She* no longer ends with the Eidolons. She and Raybould will be together. Given time, she can make him love her. There will be no Eidolons, no farm, no warlocks, no Götterelektrongruppe to pull them apart. No troublesome war to interfere with her desires.

Nothing to distract Raybould. No freckled whore. No mewling brat.

SEVEN

15 May 1940
53° 55' 41" North, 8° 14' 6" East

'It's impossible,' said Marsh.

He ducked through a hatchway as he followed Gretel through the cramped confines of the U-boat. She had changed out of her faded peasant dress when the watch officer announced they would arrive in port in a few hours' time, just a bit after midnight. Now she wore a crisp gray SS uniform clearly tailored for her petite frame. Three diamond pips on the left collar, one on her shoulders: SS-Obersturmführer, roughly equivalent to what the Royal Navy called a sub-lieutenant. So far, Liddell-Stewart's information was dead on target. But the tab on her right collar was something Marsh had never seen in any briefing: a skull cleaved by SS *siegrunen*. Marsh reckoned it symbolized the Götterelektrongruppe.

Kriegsmarine submariners made way for Gretel, though whether that was deference to her rank or revulsion at her wires, he couldn't tell. It seemed they didn't recognize the Götter-elektrongruppe insigne any more than Marsh did. The gypsy girl and her brother drew no end of wary glances from the crew. As did Marsh, though he earned those by virtue of being a hated Englishman.

It was frightening to walk among his enemies so openly. He carried the pretense of being a defector, but these sailors would be a fool to trust him for that. In theory, they didn't dare touch him, in case he truly was important to the Reich. But in practice his only beard was an inscrutable girl with 'mongrel blood.'

That was the most disconcerting thing of all. Liddell-Stewart had grown adamant when he spoke of Gretel. *She'll play innocent. She'll try to charm you. She'll even flirt with you. But never forget this: You are nothing more than a tool to her. Never trust her.* Yet somehow, for all that, he believed Gretel would protect Marsh.

Slipping an agent into the Reichsbehörde? Not even at their most wistful, their most brandy-sozzled, had Marsh and Stephenson dreamed of this. The commander had offered the one lure strong enough to drag Marsh away from his family.

And so his life was in Gretel's untrustworthy hands. Meaning his slim chance of survival hinged upon how well he understood the girl. So he kept tight on Gretel's heels as she sauntered through the cramped submarine.

It wasn't easy; the walkways were inches wide in places, and crates of provisions had been crammed into every available space. The boat reeked of diesel fumes, boiled cabbage, and other men's breath. The submariners slathered themselves in deodorant and cologne to mask the reek of body odor. The U-boat had been in port to take on Klaus not many days earlier, but that had been a rapid detour in the middle of a long patrol. Even the officers were unshaven.

Marsh laid a steadying hand on a cold steel reinforcement rib and shifted his weight as the decking tipped underfoot. The hull gave a long, low groan as the boat sliced up through the waters

of the North Sea on its final approach to Bremerhaven. He had
a good pair of sea legs, but he'd honed them on surface craft; it
wasn't the same on a submarine.

Gretel hopped into her fold-down cot. (And it was hers. She
was the only person on board, excepting the captain, who wasn't
subject to hot-bunking. A point of much grumbling among the
crew, especially the officer she had displaced. Worse still, the boat
hadn't fired any torpedoes on this run, meaning nobody could
bunk in the forward torpedo room.) She reclined on her side, one
hand resting on her thigh and the other propping up her head.
Such informality might have been considered inappropriate, were
a ranking officer to have seen this. Then again, so were the braids
that hung well past her shoulders. And her gender, for that matter.
But the Götterelektrongruppe received special dispensation, and
Gretel in particular. Which brought him back to the topic at hand.

'Impossible? Do tell, Raybould.'

Crossing his arms for warmth, Marsh leaned against the pressure hull. 'If you knew the future, everything slated to happen, it
would mean everything is predestined.'

'How do you know it isn't?'

'That would imply there's no such thing as free will.'

Gretel frowned as though he'd just said something obtuse. She
said, '*I* have free will.'

'Right. And so do I.'

A queer little half smile played on her lips as she regarded
him. 'Are you certain?'

'Of course I am.'

'I knew you'd say that.'

Klaus stumbled through the hatchway, forehead beaded with
sweat. He passed between Marsh and Gretel without saying a
word, then folded down the cot he shared on rotation with Marsh

and two seamen. His chest rose and fell with long, slow breaths. He'd been ill almost since the U-boat descended into the Channel.

The hull creaked. Klaus clenched his eyes shut.

Marsh asked, 'What's wrong with him?'

'Claustrophobia,' said Gretel. 'It's a side effect of the doctor's training methods.'

'I thought you lot do what you do with those things.' He pointed to the battery on her waist.

'The batteries are a tool toward a means. Not the means itself.' She fingered the tab pinned to her collar. 'We do what we do through acts of willpower, energized by what the doctor calls the Götterelektron.' That explained the insignia she and her brother wore. Divine lightning energizing the Willenskräfte. 'But first the willpower must be honed. In brother's case, it was through the supreme desire to escape his coffin.'

Marsh had yet to hear a single thing about Herr Doktor von Westarp that didn't suggest the man was a sadistic, first-class nutter. But he'd see for himself soon enough.

'In Reinhardt's case it was the cold.' Gretel shook her head. 'Junkman hates the winter so.'

'What about you? How'd he train you to see the future, if that's really what you do?'

Gretel leaned forward. 'I'm different from the others,' she whispered.

'How did you know about Liv? And our girls?'

Gretel's expression clouded over. She tried to cover – she did have one hell of a poker face – but she couldn't hide the way her eyes flicked down to her battery. He'd managed to instill the tiniest bit of doubt in her, but it was fleeting. She looked up, turned an icy gaze at him. Had she looked into the future to put the lie to his trick?

'Gotcha,' he said. 'That's twice now. Didn't think you'd fall for it the second time.'

If before her expression was icy, now it was arctic. Perhaps goading her hadn't been such a good idea.

'Would you like me to tell you about your son?' That caught Marsh off guard. And she saw it. 'Oh, yes. There are time lines where you and Olivia have a son. His name is John. He doesn't take after his father.' He recovered, but she pressed the point. 'Tell me, Raybould: What first drew you to Olivia? Was it the freckles? Or her voice?'

'You don't know anything about Liv.'

'On the contrary. I know quite a bit about your family. I know you were married in John Stephenson's garden. A small service. William was your best man. He—'

Marsh said, 'This is all guesswork.'

'Hardly. Olivia told me herself.'

'You've never met Liv.'

'But I have.' Gretel leaned forward again, met his eyes. He glimpsed something unsettling in those dark depths. 'Downstream,' she whispered.

Klaus hauled himself upright. 'Would you two shut up?'

'I'm sorry, brother. I'll be good.'

He stood, rounded on Marsh. Klaus shared the same olive complexion as his sister, but he hadn't inherited the eyes. Marsh didn't see insanity swimming there. Merely the cold-blooded fervor common to all true believers.

Klaus said, 'She says you're important for what's coming. Pray that doesn't change.' Marsh winced as sour breath wafted across his face. Klaus had been ill.

'Hand me to the RSHA, will you?'

'No, he won't,' Gretel interjected.

'When the doctor decides to dispense with you, he'll have you sent to the training field for practice exercises. Be thankful for that.' Klaus tapped a fingertip against Marsh's chest. 'I will make your death quick.'

Two voices vied for Marsh's attention. One was Liddell-Stewart's gravel-and-whiskey rasp rattling off the secrets of Klaus's psyche: *This is how to gain his trust, turn him to your cause* . . . The other was Marsh's own voice, and it countered with indignation: *Don't let this goose-stepping tosser think he can intimidate you.*

Stalemate.

Marsh cracked his knuckles against his jaw and drew himself to his full height. Klaus had a couple of inches on him. 'Who are you, Klaus? When you're not hiding behind your sister and that battery,' he said. And then, because he couldn't resist, 'Take it off someday, and then we'll see who gets the quick death.'

Gretel hopped down from her bunk. 'You've upset our guest, brother.' She patted Klaus on the cheek, then did the same to Marsh. 'It is flattering that you two would fight over me. But now is not the time.'

Unterseeboot-115 could accommodate over fifty crew members under normal conditions. Even then, there wasn't room in the cramped vessel for more than a fraction of the crew to eat or sleep at any given time. The presence of two SS officers plus an Englishman stressed the system. As did having a woman on board. The sailors might have made way for her, might have been unnerved by her, but that didn't prevent the resentful glances. But most of those were reserved for Marsh, and usually when he queued up to receive his share of 'rabbit,' which was what the crew called bread mottled with fuzzy white fungus.

Somebody sniffed loudly. 'I know that odor.' Something nudged Marsh in the small of the back. 'Ah, the pet Englishman.'

Another submariner said, 'Is it true that Churchill sent you away after you failed to service him?'

'I think he was sent away because of the smell.'

You're no bouquet of roses, Jerry.

The decking rattled underfoot as more sailors came to join the taunting.

'Perhaps he is a Jew,' said a third. The men taunting Marsh spoke variations on a Low German dialect. Frisian, from somewhere near the coast. It made sense they would join the Kriegsmarine if they'd grown up near the sea.

'Even a Jew isn't stupid enough to come here. They say he's a defector. I think he must be a spy.'

Marsh ransacked his store of evasions, searching for something that would deflate the brewing confrontation. Having a few words with Klaus was one thing, but getting jumped by a squad of Jerries wasn't an auspicious start to the mission. It could be his death if he lost his temper and slugged one of the Jerries; there was no guarantee an officer would break it up immediately. Small boat. How long could they turn a blind eye? A stomping might last a good while before somebody called an end to it. Marsh's fate rested on Gretel's word – implication, really – that he was crucial to the future of the Reich.

Marsh looked for a way to stop this. He came up short.

The first seaman, the one who had started the whole mess, squeezed in front of Marsh. Acne scars stippled his face. They boy looked to be about eighteen, twenty at the outside. Tufts of downy stubble covered his chin. Not particularly tall; the U-boat wasn't designed to accommodate height. His calloused hands had a few bruises, though whether from labor or brawling, Marsh couldn't tell.

'Which is it, Englishman? Are you a coward, or a spy?'

God damn you, Liddell-Stewart. Marsh grasped for the script he'd hastily prepared for himself on the drive to the coast. Mentally ran through all the ways he'd devised to express disdain for Britain and fawning admiration for the Third Reich. Then he tossed it all out.

'Is this German discipline? I'd expected more from the future masters of the world.'

'Do you hear that? Englishman thinks we're the masters of the world.'

'And you will welcome us when we come to your country?'

'Yes, I will.' He tried, but Marsh couldn't force the reluctance from his voice, the signs of a perfunctory performance. Could they hear it, too? 'Not only me. There are others like me. Others who wish for National Socialism to come to Britain.' Sadly true. *May they rot in hell for all eternity.*

One of the others said, 'Maybe you will introduce us to your friends.'

'And your women, too,' said another.

'*Ja*,' said the ringleader. The boy leered. 'Maybe you have a nice fräulein at home? Maybe you'll share her with us?' He shared a laugh with his mates.

A pair of hands gave Marsh a solid push to the shoulder blades. He stumbled into the ringleader. The boy shoved him back. Marsh concentrated on his hands, on keeping them from curling into fists while he bounced back and forth like a badminton shuttlecock.

Don't lose your temper. Don't lose your temper.

The ringleader said, 'I'll let the others watch when I take your fräulein. I hear the English whores are—'

Marsh's fist caught him square under the jaw, hard enough to slam his teeth together with an audible *click*. The boy squealed, doubled over, and spat out a piece of his tongue. Long streamers of blood and spittle dangled from his mouth. The blood kept flowing.

Shit.

A pair of submariners grabbed Marsh. He struggled, even managed to free one arm, but in the end it didn't matter. His resistance faltered with the realization that it was better to submit to the beating than to fight it; let the Jerries feel they'd come out on top. So they held him while the boy and a few others lined up for their chance to take a few swings at the Englishman. They had to work quickly: there was no privacy on a U-boat. They'd be severely punished for the breach of discipline.

A wide red streak trailed down the chin of the boy whom he'd hit. He looked slightly green behind the rage, as though sickened from a stomach full of his own blood. He brandished a pipe wrench.

Marsh struggled to free himself, tried to brace himself for the dreadful *crack* of shattered ribs. Wondered if it would puncture a lung. Closed his eyes. Tensed.

Somewhere, the *stomp-stomp-stomp* of a pair of boots rattled the decking.

The others backed away to give the boy more room to swing. As much as could be had on the crowded boat.

. . . *stompstompstompstomp.*

Clank.

Marsh flinched. Nothing happened. He opened his eyes.

The wrench lay on the floor. Marsh's attackers gaped at a section of hull. They backed off when Klaus emerged, ghosting from the cold dark space between the pressure hull and outer hull with the ringleader in tow. They rematerialized. Klaus released the boy. His victim dropped to the deck shivering and sopping wet.

It took a moment, struggling through the fog of pain, before Marsh realized what had happened. Klaus had dunked Marsh's assailant in the sea. Marsh saw that Klaus's forearms were wet, too.

'Dismissed,' said Klaus. The Kriegsmarine ratings fell over themselves to salute the SS-Obersturmführer and make themselves scarce.

Marsh turned to Klaus. 'Thank you,' he said.

'You'll wish I had let them finish you, if my sister changes her mind.' He strode away.

Marsh slumped against the cold hull. Beads of condensation, like the sweat of an iron leviathan, trickled down the plates to land in his hair and collar. He shivered. He sat there for a while, trying to get up the strength to find his cot, but his rubbery legs wouldn't hold him. *Close call.*

A new pair of boots sauntered across the deck. He didn't look up; he knew from the stride that they encased boney ankles.

'See?' said Gretel. 'You're safe with me.'

'You might have sent him sooner.'

'It wouldn't have had the same effect. The men fear you now, because they fear brother.'

16 May 1940
Bremerhaven, Germany

The mood on the boat was subdued during the approach and docking at Bremerhaven. Nobody gave Marsh any further trouble. Thus validating Gretel's cruel calculus.

Exiting the U-boat meant climbing a ladder up to the hatch, then descending on a series of rungs welded to the outer hull. The beating made this difficult. Marsh found himself standing on a jetty within the U-boat pen, an immense shelter of reinforced concrete.

If France fell, French ports would give Kriegsmarine U-boats direct access to the Atlantic. But for now, Bremerhaven was Germany's main base for U-boat operations in the North Sea and North Atlantic. As such, it had been designed to withstand direct hits from English bombers.

Marsh blinked, shielded his eyes. The klieg lights felt mercilessly bright after the shadows of U-115. The proximity of open ocean helped to flush the lingering odor of diesel from his nose. The ferroconcrete cavern shook with the rumble of idling engines and the clatter of heavy equipment. It echoed with the bark of orders and the harbor master's announcements over the PA system.

He followed the siblings through the bustle. The Reichsbehörde had sent a car to retrieve Gretel and Klaus. The driver balked when he saw Marsh, but the scene unfolded much as it had at the beach. Gretel got her way.

The captain of their submarine called after them as Gretel climbed into the Mercedes. 'Your cargo is taking up valuable space!'

Cargo? Something didn't add up. The easy rendezvous, for starters.

She called back, 'It stays where it is. I'll retrieve it when I need it.'

Once they were settled in the car, Marsh asked, 'What did he mean by *your* cargo?'

'Spare batteries,' she said. 'My instructions were quite specific.'

Instructions? A mole hadn't arranged Gretel's escape from the Admiralty. She'd arranged it herself.

'That miserable bastard lied to me.'

'Yes. But you're here now. It's all that matters.'

Liddell-Stewart was going to have a bad day when Marsh returned to England.

Traffic around the port was light during the first few hours of the new day. Soon they were on the open road, headed toward Weimar. Klaus snored through most of the drive. Marsh tried to sleep. But he couldn't put his mind at rest, nor could he ignore the butterflies in his stomach. Each mile took him closer to the REGP. And then what?

Getting to von Westarp's farm was the easiest part of this mission. Marsh could imagine – if he indulged in Will's brand of naïve, wide-eyed optimism – that he'd find a way to destroy the farm. Gretel might help with that.

But destroying the farm wouldn't be worth a tinker's cuss if the paperwork didn't disappear, too. It seemed to Marsh that Liddell-Stewart wanted the Reichsbehörde not just destroyed but *erased*. And the commander was quite certain the Schutzstaffel had a separate store of operational records pertaining to the REGP, and that those records were stored in the cellar of 9 Prinz-Albrecht-Strasse.

SS HQ. In Berlin.

But even if the SS accepted Marsh's cover story as a British defector, it would keep a very close eye on him. It seemed rather unlikely he'd have the latitude to pop over to Berlin for a long weekend. Even less so that he'd be able to swan in to SS Haus and pinch their goodies.

Indeed. If he ever found himself on Prinz-Albrecht-Strasse, inside the deepest heart of the Third Reich, it almost certainly meant something had gone very, very wrong.

Gretel caught him staring at her. 'Try to sleep. You have quite a day ahead of you.'

The sky faded from black to gray to blue as they neared Weimar. According to Stephenson's dossier on von Westarp, the family farm stood roughly a dozen kilometers southwest of the town. Sunrise found them in a forest. The first light of day pierced dark stands of oak and ash, winter-naked boughs covered in a delicate fringe of greenery.

The road itself was tarmacadam. An odd thing for what must have been an old farm track. Somebody had replaced the original roadway with something more suitable for important visitors. Perhaps Himmler didn't fancy bouncing along through ruts and mud.

When they emerged from the forest, the ring of tires on tarmac became the clatter of crushed gravel. The roadway of chalk white pebbles blazed in the sunrise like a silver ribbon. It crossed a wide clearing dotted with clumps of spring wildflowers. A wooden sign arced over the lane. It confirmed these were the grounds of the Reichsbehörde für die Erweiterung germanischen Potenzials: the Reich's Authority for the Advancement of German Potential.

One could tell quite a bit about the narcissistic mastermind behind the REGP just from observing the layout. There, in the center, stood the farmhouse itself. Marsh recognized it from the half-burnt photograph he'd salvaged from Krasnopolsky's valise in Tarragona. But it was larger than shown in the photo; it had grown along with the doctor's stature within the Reich. The three-story farmhouse was the tallest building in a complex that comprised dozens of other structures. Wide windows adorned the farmhouse's top floor. They enabled von Westarp to lord over his domain, figuratively if not literally.

The arrangement of the other buildings put Marsh in mind of ducklings huddled near their mother. Buildings that housed the REGP's most important functions were situated closest to the farmhouse and, by extension, the doctor's shadow. These included laboratories and a warehouse (battery storage or manufacture, Marsh surmised). The next set, a bit farther from von Westarp's house, included an armory and barracks. The buildings that von Westarp deemed inconsequential – such as the pump house, icehouse, mess hall, and the infirmary for mundane soldiers – were relegated to the fringes of the compound.

The ground shook. Thunder boomed across the clearing. Small artillery.

As the Mercedes slowed along the final curve on the approach to the farmhouse, Marsh glimpsed an extensive training field through the gaps between the buildings. The overall layout was that of a large U. The farmhouse formed the base, the other buildings formed the arms, and the field filled the center. The top of the U abutted the forest.

Once again, Commander Liddell-Stewart's intelligence proved spot on. Just who *was* that plug-ugly codger?

Marsh counted dozens of support staff members and mundane soldiers. If the commander's intel held, he'd find the soldiers had been assigned to the REGP from the LSSAH, the elite SS unit spawned from Hitler's personal guard.

They pulled up alongside the farmhouse. Klaus stretched and yawned; the artillery had awoken him. Their driver pulled the parking brake, then waited for the trio of passengers to emerge from the idling car.

Marsh gritted his teeth before following Gretel out of the car. His bruises were tender, and the long cramped ride and mounting anxiety had caused his knee to stiffen. He'd been too long without sleep. That, along with dehydration, had put a persistent dull throb behind his left temple. His eyes felt as though they'd been lubricated with a slurry of axle grease and sand. No amount of swallowing could wash away the bitter taste in his mouth. He knew that taste. It was fear.

The car clunked into gear and pulled away as soon as they were clear. In moments it passed again beneath the arch and continued into the surrounding forest.

Gretel took Marsh's arm. She knew damn well that he didn't dare shove her aside. Not here in her home territory. 'So many introductions,' she said, looking up.

Three men – two in uniforms, the other in a dressing gown – peered down at them from a third-floor window. The man in the dressing gown was considerably older than he'd been in the single photograph Milkweed had been able to scrounge up. One of the uniformed men looked distinctly unhappy. A shimmer enveloped Klaus for the briefest of moments. Marsh thought he felt a flush of heat, but it dissipated too quickly to be certain.

Klaus muttered, 'Swine fucker.' He entered the house.

Marsh followed, Gretel's arm still linked in his. The soles of their boots clicked against pink marble. Sunlight glinted from the gilded balustrades of a wide staircase. The stairs adjoined a wraparound balcony. A rosette stained-glass window illuminated the landing at the top of the first flight. The window depicted a man in a white lab coat catching a lightning bolt. The swastikas didn't match the style; later additions, obviously. Marsh suspected the original farmhouse had been more humble than this.

He followed the siblings past the grandiose stairwell. They passed a kitchen where a half-dozen women dressed a pair of game hens, sliced tomatoes, slathered marmalade on toast. Marsh caught a whiff of bitter coffee and eggs frying in bacon

grease. His stomach did a somersault. He hadn't known a breakfast like that since before the rationing. It didn't surprise him that
the doctor ate well. He wondered if the hens were for lunch or
dinner.

He salivated at the prospect of eating meat more than once
per week. But then he thought of Liv, and felt selfish.

The corridor beyond the kitchen was dusty, with a faint odor
of formaldehyde. A window in one wall looked into what
appeared to be a surgical ward. Shackles and straps dangled from
the operating table, alongside a rack bristling with saws, drills,
retractors, scalpels, and forceps. A neck brace and round clamp
dotted with set screws topped one end of the table. Nearby stood
an electrical console the size of a large armoire. A looped bundle
of wires similar to those affixed to Klaus and Gretel hung from
a hook on the console. It was tipped with a sharp wire probe.

Marsh had inspected Gretel's wires after dosing her with ether
on the passage from France to England. Her scalp, he remembered, was riddled with surgical scars.

She said, 'This is the doctor's personal laboratory. The original.'

A series of doors lined the corridor across from the laboratory.
Marsh tried one, but it was locked.

'What's in here?'

'Incubators,' said Klaus.

The servants' stair was narrow and dark. No marble, no
stained glass, no gilded balusters. They had to wait at the bottom
while a woman descended. Her porcelain-pale skin made her
look like a phantom compared to Klaus and Gretel's darker com-
plexions. The newcomer mouthed something to Klaus as she
jogged down the final few stairs.

She glanced at Marsh. He did a double take, tried to get a

better look at her eyes, but she was already past them on her way outside.

Mismatched eyes. One blue, one brown. A Twin.

The commander had mentioned the Twins in his summary of the farm and its inhabitants. Twin psychics forever linked, forever seeing through each other's eyes. Ideal for secure communications.

Klaus went up first. Gretel followed, then Marsh. He caught her arm and spoke into her ear as softly as he could, so that Klaus wouldn't hear over the creaking of the stairs.

'What is she doing here?' he breathed. 'I thought they were both deployed.'

Gretel patted his hand. 'They were. But I suggested she be temporarily moved from the OKW back here.'

Well. That addressed one of the commander's concerns.

Klaus waited for them on the landing. Gretel trotted up the stairs. Marsh hurried after her. She said, 'These are our quarters. The doctor likes to keep his children close at hand.' She pointed back and forth across the corridor to each in a series of doors, rattling off names as she did so. 'Heike. Rudolf. Brother. Me. Reinhardt. Kammler. Oskar.' The last room at the end of the corridor had housed both Twins, before they were deployed. 'They'll give you Rudolf's room. He doesn't need it any longer.' She squeezed his arm. 'I'll be right next door.'

Liddell-Stewart hadn't mentioned a Rudolf or Oskar. Marsh wondered what had happened to them.

Klaus made to climb the narrow stairs to the top floor, but scowled and reluctantly stepped aside as somebody stomped down from above. They were joined by one of the uniformed men that Marsh had seen in the window. The unhappy one. He wore the same rank of SS-Obersturmführer as Klaus and Gretel, and a similar battery harness. Marsh recognized his face from the Tarragona filmstrip. This man had melted an anvil with his bare hands.

If looks could murder (and couldn't they, here of all places?) the newcomer's contempt would have made a corpse of Klaus. He sighed theatrically when he saw Gretel.

'Hello, Reinhardt,' she said. 'Did you miss us?'

'I'd hoped I'd endured the last of your company. I should have known better.' Reinhardt turned to Klaus. 'And where the hell have you been the past few days?'

Klaus smiled. 'Serving the Reich,' he said. 'Carrying out my orders.' Klaus said it with obvious relish. Prior to that moment, Marsh had doubted Klaus was capable of smiling at all.

Reinhardt stared. 'I don't believe you,' he said.

'It's true.' Gretel toyed with a braid. 'The doctor will be *most* pleased with my brother.'

Little tendrils of smoke curled up from the wooden boards beneath Reinhardt's boots. Marsh stepped back. A floorboard creaked. It caught Reinhardt's attention. He finally noticed Marsh, tossing contempt in his direction as he looked him up and down.

Reinhardt's eyes were the palest blue that Marsh had ever seen. This was the man who had murdered Krasnopolsky. Did that mean he'd seen Marsh in the Alexandria's bar? A bead of sweat trickled down Marsh's brow.

'Who is this?'

Gretel said, 'This is Raybould Marsh. He's come from England to join us.'

Reinhardt asked, in perfect English, 'You're British?'

Marsh responded in accentless German. 'Yes. I grew up in London. St. Pancras, mostly.'

'How fortunate for you to be here now. It won't be long before we unleash our Willenskräfte upon Britain. And when we do, there will be nothing left of your home but smoking rubble. How does that make you feel, Englishman?'

'Our Raybould is the future of the farm,' said Gretel. 'We mustn't keep the doctor waiting.'

Reinhardt's bored expression suggested he either disregarded or distrusted almost everything she said. He pushed past Marsh to descend the stairs. 'If you should see Heike,' he said over his shoulder, 'tell her I wish to speak with her. Privately.'

'Pig,' said Klaus.

Marsh muttered, 'Thanks for the support.'

'Reinhardt's attitude is your problem. Not mine.'

Klaus followed Marsh and Gretel up the second flight of stairs. It ended at a narrow landing and a closed door with a peephole. A pair of Wellington boots stood on the landing beside the door. They had been covered with mud, but it had since dried and cracked away. The landing was covered with clods of dirt.

'Those,' said Gretel, 'are the doctor's galoshes. And this is the doctor's study.' She knocked.

Somebody said, 'Enter!'

The Reichsbehörde's inner sanctum was part antiquarian bookshop, part sunroom, and one hundred percent Mad Hatter. Sunlight flooded through the east-facing windows to illuminate bookshelves packed to bulging. They occupied much of the wall space not devoted to windows, except for a pair of closed doors and where a gramophone rested on a sideboard. Loose papers, covered in handwritten notes, peeked from between the pages of many books, or even from the spaces between the books on the shelves. It looked like a cyclone had ripped through a book bindery.

Here and there, a gap had been pried between the books; the

doctor used those spaces to store what appeared to be specimen jars. Pale tissues floated in murky solutions. Marsh couldn't begin to identify them. Part of him desperately didn't want to.

The doctor's desk was situated before one of the wide windows that overlooked the training field. The books and loose papers were more orderly here. There was also a battery similar to the ones Klaus and Gretel wore, but bulkier, as if an older model. For a paperweight, the doctor used a human skull; several long wires had been riveted to the cranium.

A small skull. Not an adult's.

The wires made for a convenient placeholder. They had been draped across the open pages of a leather-bound journal. The doctor's notes covered one page. Marsh spied a stack of similar volumes under the skull.

Dust eddies glittered like powdered silver in the sunlight. It wasn't hard to find the source of the dust: the doctor's chalkboard looked as though it hadn't been properly washed down since Marsh had been a schoolboy. Which, given the long history of the doctor's orphanage, might not have been far from the truth. It was difficult to gauge the original color of the board because attempts at erasure had merely smeared the chalk rather than removed it. Chalk dust lay so thick in the tray that the felt eraser lay half buried in it. The doctor's peculiar crabbed handwriting scrawled over earlier passages and across old sketches. It wasn't a chalkboard so much as a palimpsest documenting multiple phases of the doctor's investigations. But one corner of the board had been kept clean and legible; the diagram within appeared to be half human anatomy, half circuit diagram.

A dining-room table stood alone in an island of order. The table could have accommodated six. It was bare except for a single place setting.

Another muffled explosion rattled the china.

Doctor Karl Heinrich von Westarp stood alongside his desk, gazing across the training field. The doctor wore a gown over the uniform and twin oak leaves of an Oberführer. The senior colonel wore slippers in lieu of boots.

The third man Marsh had glimpsed wore the uniform of an SS-Standartenführer. Only a single oak leave adorned his collar tabs. His name was Pabst, according to Liddell-Stewart, and he was in charge of training and discipline at the REGP. Pabst was the equivalent of a colonel. Quite a high rank for such lowly responsibility. Odd.

Klaus saluted. 'Herr Doktor! Standartenführer!'

Gretel followed suit more casually.

Von Westarp turned to face the new arrivals. He was bald but for a graying tonsure. The lenses of his eyeglasses were round as marbles. The waist sash of his gown hung to the floor. A tattered fringe traced curlicues in the chalk dust on the floor.

The doctor looked at Klaus, then to Gretel, then back to Klaus. He didn't appear to notice Marsh standing between them. He might have been gazing into a microscope, studying a specimen, for all the emotion he showed.

He said, 'You were successful.'

Klaus said, 'Yes, Herr Doktor.'

'That pleases me. You will breakfast with me on Sunday.'

Klaus stood even straighter. 'It will be an honor.'

Von Westarp acknowledged this with a dismissive wave. He turned his attention back to the window.

Pabst cleared his throat. He spoke slowly, gently, in measured tones. 'Pardon me, Herr Oberführer, but there is still the matter of Gretel's desertion. And it appears she has brought somebody to meet you.'

Ah. So that's *why Pabst is here.*

The Schutzstaffel wasn't stupid. Even Himmler probably recognized that he had a first-class nutter running the asylum here. An indispensible nutter, perhaps even a mad genius, but mad just the same. Pabst's real assignment was to keep an eye on him.

Any hint of gentleness evaporated from his voice when he addressed Gretel. 'You are guilty of dereliction of duty. You disregarded your orders, abandoned your station, and willfully surrendered to the enemy.' He crossed the study, came closer. 'A mundane soldier would be executed for that.'

Gretel said, 'The invasion was destined for success. My guidance was immaterial. France will fall. I had more important issues to attend to.'

'More important than doing as you are told?' Pabst spun her around with a vicious backhand. The breeze ruffled Marsh's hair. She'd have a terrible bruise tomorrow. Marsh started to intercede, but caught himself before he moved to her defense. When Gretel straightened, she was smiling.

'Please meet Lieutenant-Commander Raybould Marsh. Raybould was a key member of the British intelligence unit monitoring the Reichsbehörde until he decided to join us.'

Pabst glared at Marsh. 'Is that what he told you? Absurd. He's a spy.'

'It was my understanding,' Marsh said, 'that it's impossible to deceive Gretel.'

Pabst couldn't argue that point without calling the doctor's success into question. 'Why are you here?'

The question had come from Pabst. But Marsh addressed his answer to von Westarp. 'Once I came to terms with the true nature of the work carried out here, I knew, beyond any doubt, that this was the future.'

Pabst looked extremely skeptical. He started to counter, but the doctor interjected. 'How did you learn of my work?'

'We were contacted last February by a man named Krasnopolsky. MI6 sent me to Spain to collect him and the information he carried.'

Von Westarp said, 'The turncoat was silenced. He gave you nothing.' He turned his back to Marsh, once again putting his attention on the training field. 'My children saw to that.'

Krasnopolsky had refused to hand over anything until he was safely off the Continent. Reinhardt had torched him a few minutes later. Marsh had been lucky to escape the conflagration with a few charred fragments. But this was an opportunity to bolster Klaus's position against Reinhardt. It was clear the two had a powerful rivalry. Keeping Klaus on top of the pile was in Marsh's best interests.

Marsh answered, 'Krasnopolsky burned to death. But not before he passed everything to me.' He had to raise his voice to be heard above the chatter of a machine gun. 'The filmstrip, in particular, has been invaluable.'

Silence fell over von Westarp. Then he began to tremble. Quietly, almost to himself, he said, 'Reinhardt deceived me. He claimed to have carried out his orders successfully. But that was not the truth.' A bit more loudly, he added, 'My own son has lied to me.' His anger hit a crescendo: 'Humiliated me!'

'Have Reinhardt punished,' he snapped to Pabst. 'Make it known my disappointment is profound.'

'And the newcomer? I strongly suggest he be removed. He's seen more than he should.'

The colonel was absolutely correct. But von Westarp outranked him, and Gretel knew how to play the doctor's ego.

She said, 'The British are in a panic over this farm. You'll want to hear what Raybould has to say. They're embracing desperate measures.'

The doctor considered this. He muttered to himself. Then he said, 'Board him downstairs. Find him work.'

Pabst's eyes hardened, but he saluted. He paused beside Marsh on the way out. 'I will know the truth of you,' he said quietly. 'She won't protect you forever.'

Gretel took Marsh's arm again. Her jaw had already begun to swell. 'Hungry?'

23 May 1940
Reichsbehörde für die Erweiterung germanischen Potenzials

Again and again during Marsh's first week at the Reichsbehörde, Commander Liddell-Stewart's analysis proved correct. Gretel was an invaluable ally.

The information Marsh carried about British intelligence efforts was deemed too important to lose to a momentary lapse of discipline like that on U-115. So, rather than bunking him in the barracks occupied by the mundane soldiers, he was assigned to Rudolf's room in the farmhouse. As Gretel had foreseen.

And, two nights after their arrival, she helped him sneak in and out of Pabst's quarters. He used the colonel's transmitter to send a terse volley of dots and dashes into the ether: 'Sailing monarch.'

The first word flagged the message for Liddell-Stewart. The second verified the association with Milkweed. If the commander was listening, he'd know Marsh had arrived.

Of course, nobody trusted Marsh. His credentials consisted of Gretel's say-so, but it quickly became clear that Pabst and von

Westarp had problems of their own with her. And the mundane soldiers went out of their way to avoid her. Even the other members of the Götterelektrongruppe regarded her with emotions ranging from outright hostility (Reinhardt) to fear (Heike).

Marsh didn't have many opportunities to observe training sessions. Pabst and von Westarp kept his interactions with the others to a minimum. The exception was Kammler, who was profoundly mentally deficient. They didn't want him interacting with the technicians, either. Nor did they want him handling sensitive equipment, such as the batteries. So, when they weren't debriefing Marsh, they assigned him the most demeaning tasks they could find short of cleaning latrines.

Minding Kammler occasionally involved latrine duty.

Hauptsturmführer Buhler, Kammler's handler, was the only person at the REGP who welcomed Marsh's arrival. Not Marsh himself – Buhler didn't trust him more than anybody else did. But he welcomed an extra pair of hands. It freed him from the tedium of dressing, feeding, and cleaning the muscle-bound imbecile. Were he a regular citizen of the Reich, an unfortunate fellow like Kammler would have been a candidate for sterilization or euthanasia. But he was also the farm's resident telekinetic, capable of crushing a tank as though the steel were beeswax, or hurling an antiaircraft gun as easily as a snowball.

He couldn't speak. He couldn't feed himself. But an army of Kammlers could crush anything that stood in Hitler's way. Britain included.

Buhler kept him on a leash. When Kammler wasn't wearing the leash and his battery harness he was harmless, and Marsh's responsibility. Buhler was happy to eat without his meal getting cold while he struggled to get a spoon into Kammler's mouth.

'G-g-guh—' said Kammler. He rocked back and forth, wafting

the faint smell of sour milk across the table. It was time to bathe him again.

Marsh held a spoonful of applesauce to Kammler's mouth. 'Have a little more. Can you do that for me?'

'Careful, Englishman. Sometimes he bites.' Buhler laughed to himself, ran one thick hand through the stubble along his scalp. A semicircular scar creased the skin along one side of his hand.

Kammler's head lolled sideways, as though the bulging cords of muscle in his neck had gone slack. He rubbed his head affectionately on Buhler's shoulder. 'Buh-buh-b-b-b—'

'Not me, you idiot.' Buhler knocked his head away with a sharp shrug.

Marsh lifted the bowl, held it where Kammler could see and smell the applesauce. They made it with cinnamon here. Marsh hadn't even smelled cinnamon since before the war. Even the Third Reich's most pitiable soldiers ate better than he and Liv. He struggled to keep a lid on the indignation, lest it became rage.

Instead, he concentrated on humility. Concentrated on his task. Concentrated on staying alive.

Feed Kammler. Destroy the farm. Destroy the records. Go home.

He tried again with the spoon. 'Here, son.'

Chronologically speaking, he probably wasn't a great deal older than Kammler. But it was difficult not to think of Kammler as a child. When it became difficult to maintain his patience, Marsh thought of Liv, and tried to channel her kindness. He thought about Agnes, and tried to imagine that instead of a perfect little girl he and Liv had had a troubled boy instead. They'd talked about having another child. What if it came out like Kammler? They'd still love him, wouldn't they? Marsh wanted to believe he'd learn to love his damaged son. Wouldn't every parent?

Perhaps not. It wasn't hard to imagine how Kammler had arrived at von Westarp's foundling home. Had he been abandoned? On the other hand, it seemed unlikely the doctor would have taken in a damaged child. Had Kammler been broken by the same process that made him so powerful?

Kammler chomped down on the spoon. His teeth clicked. Marsh's mind had wandered; it caught him unprepared. The large man rocked backwards, easily yanking the spoon from Marsh's outstretched fingers. Kammler giggled to himself. Clapped. Rocked back and forth.

'Sp—! Sp-pu-p-p—'

The spoon clattered across the table. He spat applesauce over himself and the people sitting beside him.

Buhler flicked a speck of food from beneath his eye. He tossed his own silverware down on his tray. He stood.

'Fucking idiot.'

It wasn't clear if he meant Kammler or Marsh. He departed without elaborating.

Marsh had managed, with no small amount of effort, to clean the food out of his hair and to get most of the rest of it into Kammler's mouth when a soldier entered the mess hall. Marsh chewed cold corned beef, watching him approach.

'You're wanted in the farmhouse.' The messenger didn't bother to look at Marsh. He watched Kammler, who was now licking sauce from the table. His lip curled in distaste.

'By whom?'

'You're wanted. Now.' Marsh was an enigma to everybody here, free only because fear of Gretel exceeded distrust of him. But he didn't rate courtesy.

More interminable debriefing. It had to be.

Marsh stood. He touched Kammler's shoulder. 'See you later.'

To the soldier he said, 'Kammler must be cleaned prior to his training session this afternoon.'

'That's not my—'

'I have been summoned by the doctor. Kammler hasn't. He can't be left alone.'

The soldier shook his head. 'I'm not—'

'Really? I'll tell the doctor,' said Marsh.

He left the messenger and the telekinetic to sort themselves out.

The trees had been almost bare on the day of Marsh's arrival. But spring had brought green life to the forest in a very short time. Fresh leaves rustled in the breeze, a delicate susurration beneath the clatter of heavy artillery and muffled explosions. The nearby fields were a patchwork quilt of wildflowers. They perfumed the breeze with lavender. Gretel spent much of her time there. Blood-red corn poppies grew closer to the farmhouse. They made Marsh think of Stephenson.

Marsh's path from the mess to the farmhouse took him along the edge of the training field. He slowed his pace as much as he dared. He'd had precious few chances to watch the other members of the Götterelektrongruppe at work.

Reinhardt stood in the center of a plot edged with sandbags and trenches. Marsh spied mundane troops crouching behind the revetments. Three technicians in laboratory coats watched from behind a blast shield. One called through a bullhorn: 'Begin!'

Whoosh. A corona of blue fire engulfed Reinhardt. A soldier popped up, tossed something at him, and immediately dived for cover. Reinhardt gestured at the incoming projectile with a contemptuous flick of his wrist. The dummy grenade flared into harmless vapor. It continued like that – soldiers popping up to toss things at him, Reinhardt vaporizing the projectiles in midair – until one quick soldier managed to land a throw at the salamander's feet. Reinhardt incinerated the grenade, then reduced a row of sandbags into glassy slag as a warning.

Jesus, God. Despair was ever close at hand when Marsh considered his mission. *How in the hell . . .*

Closer to the farmhouse, Marsh passed a solid block of brick and steel. It was forty feet long, fifteen deep, and ten high, chalked with an elaborate pattern of circles, squares, crosshatches, and Xs around the perimeter. In other places, it was adorned with switches or levers. No doors. No windows. Its purpose escaped him.

Until a ghostly hand emerged from the steel, just inside one of the chalked circles. It withdrew just as quickly. A finger's width of mortar crumbled from between a line of bricks, roughly following a zigzag pattern traced in blue chalk. Klaus withdrew again into the immense slab, then his arm popped out further down. He emerged just far enough to engage a switch, then withdrew again. All this happened under the observation of two technicians. One held a stopwatch, the other a clipboard.

Marsh had heard Klaus refer to an obstacle course. He'd wondered what that meant to a ghost. The training display wasn't as impressive as Reinhardt's, until Marsh realized that Klaus couldn't see while inside. He must have been moving entirely by memory. Marsh also knew, by virtue of having chased Klaus through the Admiralty, that Klaus couldn't breathe when he was insubstantial. Marsh wondered if there were other tricks, other obstacles, where only Klaus could encounter them.

An empty uniform stood downrange of a machine rifle. (The gun looked to be an MG 34. Marsh made a mental note.) It looked like the uniform had been arranged on a tailor's dummy. The boots, the trousers, the shirt and jacket were filled out, yet the collar opened to thin air, as did the cuffs. The elbows bent, bringing empty cuffs to hover over the jacket buttons. The invisible woman disrobed.

Now there appeared to be nothing except a pile of discarded clothing between the machine rifle and another obstacle course. A dozen numbered pennants hung from chains accessible only by traversing narrow pipes, or dangled atop rope ladders, or peeked from the ground past coils of barbed wire, or nestled in equally inaccessible locations.

A technician clicked a stopwatch. 'Begin!'

Somewhere, bare feet slapped across the ground. Pennant number six flipped into the air and fluttered to the ground. Marsh inferred the purpose of this test: Heike had to pull all the flags without giving herself away. The gunners sent a burst toward where the downed pennant had hung. But they were too slow; now pennant number two was whisked from the ground by invisible hands.

And then a chain jangled, nudged by something invisible. The gunners immediately swung the barrel of their rifle toward the disturbance and raked that section of the course. The rounds traced a line along the wall, the last few stopping in midair.

The woman shrieked. 'Ahh!'

She reappeared, naked, already falling from the rail. She thudded to the ground. Marsh could hear the wind rushing from her lungs, even above the ticking of the MG's barrel. 'Hoomph.'

She'd taken a direct hit. She should have been perforated. But her wounds were lime green. The splotches covered her thigh, belly, breast.

Wax bullets. The color chosen to make the impacts distinct from bleeding wounds.

He averted his eyes, realizing that he'd already seen Heike

naked on the Tarragona filmstrip. He felt terribly embarrassed for her. But he reminded himself that she was an enemy soldier, and dangerous as hell. What if the SS released her into the field? Into Britain? How could Milkweed deal with an invisible assassin stalking the PM?

'Gorgeous, isn't she?'

Marsh turned. Reinhardt stood behind him, still wearing his battery harness. He stared across the training field to where a medic kneeled beside Heike. And the look on Reinhardt's face . . . it was raw. If Marsh caught a bloke staring at his wife like that, he'd knock the bastard's teeth out the back of his head.

Couldn't do that with this one. The man could kill with a thought.

Reinhardt said, 'You want to look. And she wants you to. She does this to tease me.'

Marsh stared at him, trying to figure if this was what passed for humor at the REGP. It wasn't.

'I'll have her. Gretel has predicted it.'

'Thought you didn't put much stock in what she had to say,' said Marsh.

Reinhardt said, 'She is a gypsy charlatan. But you are the liar.' He poked Marsh's chest with a hot fingertip. 'You spread lies about me to the doctor. Told him I failed my mission. Now Klaus dines with him while I endure the incubator.' Air shimmered around Reinhardt. Marsh stepped back. 'Can you understand the humiliation that causes? I am the best! But the doctor thinks me a failure.'

He composed himself, tamping down the anger with visible effort. The shimmering aura diminished, then vanished. He stalked away.

'I won't forget this, Englishman.'

Marsh smelled smoke. He looked down. Reinhardt's fingertip had charred a shirt button. Marsh patted his shirt. The button crumbled to ash.

Marsh entered the farmhouse through the old servant's entrance. Only special visitors, high SS, and members of the Führer's staff used the main stairs. Salamanders, invisible women, telekinetics, psychics, wraiths, oracles, and suspected spies used the rear.

A sentry, another mundane soldier, stood outside the closed debriefing room.

'I've been summoned,' said Marsh.

'Wait.'

There was nowhere to sit. He leaned against the wall opposite the door. Gretel's throaty voice was just audible from inside the debriefing room.

'... timing is critical. Everything depends on this. Kleist's panzer group must halt its advance to the coast. It must do so tomorrow ... Yes, both of them. Guderian's corps as well.'

Marsh couldn't make out the other voices as easily. He strained to listen; he hadn't had any news of the war since coming to the farm, and it was driving him barmy. It didn't help, knowing that the German High Command and the Führer's staff regularly received strategic advice from a clairvoyant. He caught a reference to the British Expeditionary Forces and a town on the coast: Dunkirk.

To another muffled reply, Gretel said, 'Irrelevant. This is a task for Herr Göring and his Luftwaffe. You will want to keep the heavy armor in reserve for Case Red.'

That must have been the code name for an upcoming offensive. Now her questioners sounded more animated. But she was unaffected, or unimpressed, with their objections.

'Herr General von Runstedt.' Gretel spoke with exaggerated patience. 'If the Wehrmacht and Luftwaffe do as I advise, there will be no British soldiers left fighting in Europe within two weeks.'

Her questioners sounded mollified by this.

She said, 'Remember. Explain to the Führer that the panzer divisions must stop on May 24. And they must not resume before May 26.' She paused. 'I've seen the futures where they don't. I've studied them quite closely, Herr General. There is no Thousand-Year Reich in those futures. There is *nothing* in those futures.'

Gretel's pronouncement raised the hairs on Marsh's arms. It reminded Marsh of something Commander Liddell-Stewart had said. *It's one thing to see the future. Quite another to like what you see.*

Most of the time, Gretel sounded like she didn't take anything seriously. Like she didn't give a good God damn about anything. So it was chilling when she did become somber. What could possibly frighten her? Only the Eidolons, as far as he could tell.

Gretel's meeting ended soon after that. Two men of extremely high rank filed out, followed by Pabst.

Gretel sauntered out behind the men. She had ditched her uniform soon after their arrival at the farm. Now she was back in her peasant dress, and barefoot again. She had tucked a corn-flower into each raven-black braid. Her wires spiraled around the braids and connected to the battery at her waist. She touched Marsh's arm.

She did that often. Put her feverish touch upon him.

'Hello, Raybould. How is Kammler?'

He didn't flinch away this time. Instead he tipped his head closer to her. Should any of the officers look this way, it would look like they were flirting.

Marsh nodded almost imperceptibly toward the men conferring with Pabst farther down the corridor. Quietly, he said, 'Friends of yours?'

'Admirers. It's very flattering.'

He whispered, 'What the hell were you telling them?'

'You look troubled.'

'Troubled?' Marsh stopped himself. When he was sure he could continue at a whisper, he said, 'I've had a good look at this place. The commander expects me to pull off a bloody miracle.'

She squeezed his arm. 'You'll think of something.'

'And then there's the little matter of Berlin.' Marsh hadn't yet formed a plan for dealing with the farm. The thought of dealing with the REGP files in Berlin was an overwhelming complication.

'Trust me,' said Gretel. Something dark moved behind her eyes, like a shadow upon her soul. 'I know what to do.'

Marsh started to ask, but the visitors had left. Pabst called to her.

'Get away from him.'

'Jawohl, Herr Standartenführer.'

Gretel released Marsh's arm and traipsed down the corridor, trailing flower petals in her wake.

Marsh followed Pabst into the briefing room. Pabst ordered him to sit. Pabst took a seat across the table and started a wire recorder.

'Tell me about the demons,' he said.

Marsh's mission, and his survival, relied upon his ability to convince his hosts of his sincere desire to join their cause. But he hadn't had the time to prepare a cover for his knowledge of Will's family and those creatures called Eidolons. The only way to guarantee consistency across multiple questionings was to tell the truth. And he hated himself for it.

It was a gamble. And a damn dangerous one at that. Marsh could envision scenarios where the knowledge Will carried could become the crucial hinge upon which Britain's fate turned. What if he gave the Jerries the insight they needed to overcome Britain's supernatural defense?

Would Gretel tell him if he had? The commander had been vehement about not trusting her.

The only saving grace, to Marsh's mind, was the fact that he knew damn little about any of it. Just bits and pieces Will had dropped about his grandfather from time to time, and what Will had told them on the strange afternoon they attempted to show Gretel to an Eidolon.

'Tell me everything you know about these warlocks,' said Pabst.

And so Marsh did. Again.

EIGHT

30 May 1940
Walworth, London, England

I don't know how he did it, but two weeks after my doppelgänger
arrived in Germany, history changed.

Clever, clever bastard.

Well, I liked to think he had something to do with it. But I
couldn't deny Gretel's hand lay heavy over the events described
daily on the wireless and in the papers.

The defense of France was failing. The Wehrmacht had outmaneuvered the British Expeditionary Forces and their French
allies. They'd been routed. Completely. Utterly.

Same as last time.

Now the allied soldiers were holed up along the coast. Hundreds of thousands of men on the beaches of northern France,
all waiting for rescue. Waiting for evacuation. Waiting to see if
friendly ships would come to take them across the Channel
before the Jerries finished them off.

Same as last time. But.

This time, they were holding out. This time, the ships were

coming in. Tommies were coming home by the thousands. By the tens of thousands.

Last time, they'd died on those beaches. Jerry had slaughtered them to the last man. Hundreds of thousands of soldiers. Britain had lost an army.

But now, several days after the Dunkirk evacuation had been expanded to include civilian boats, the flow of rescued soldiers showed no sign of abatement. The Miracle, some folks had begun to call it.

I'd never been a student of the details of history. Living through the war, fighting in it, had been more than enough. Never felt much need to reexamine it. So I couldn't begin to guess which troop movements and armored column maneuvers were holdovers from the original history and which were fresh alterations, carefully chosen by Gretel for this new time line. Detailed information of that nature was too sparse anyway, and would be for years. But I could see the general shape of how she was doing it.

The Germans relied heavily on the Luftwaffe to pound the encircled refugees and prevent ships from approaching the beach. I'm sure it seemed like hell on earth to the men trapped there, but it was a damn sight better than it could have been. Last time around, they'd forgone the aircraft and moved in with heavy armor. At least one entire panzer division had arrived at Dunkirk before the first rescue ship could begin hauling waterlogged Tommies aboard.

Last time around, Göring hadn't been in charge of the Luftwaffe. Gretel had had him removed early in the war. I wondered how she would sell the evacuation to her superiors. They couldn't be pleased by it.

Liv set our tea service on the low table in front of the sofa. The service was new, but it had been a chipped and battered thing when last I saw it.

'Thank you.' It was weak, brewed from twice- or thrice-used leaves. But the company made up for it.

She sat across from me, within reach of the wireless. Close enough to touch.

'Do you take your tea with sugar, Commander?'

A formality, of course, and I declined. My first experience with rationing had forced me into the habit of taking my tea without sugar. A habit I'd never broken; it served me well now that I was stuck with rationing again.

'Raybould hates his tea without sugar. I think the rationing might drive him mad.' She unfolded a cloth serviette to reveal a treasure: a whole sugar cube, glittering in the afternoon sun.

I coughed. Sat upright, narrowly avoided spilling tea all over myself.

'Where on earth did you get that?'

Liv had a particular smile. It could make you feel like you and she had just shared something deeply private, deeply important. Something funny, dire, sexy, frivolous, and momentous all at the same time.

She flashed that smile at me now as she gently scraped her tea-spoon along one edge of the cube, dusting her tea with sugar. 'Raybould thinks he knows all my hiding spots.'

I did. I could have sworn I did.

'I think perhaps he has underestimated you.'

'Oh, he's clever in his own way.' She sipped. Fixed me with a sly look. 'I suppose that's why you chose him.'

During the course of my afternoon visits I'd managed to give Liv the impression that I was responsible for having Raybould Marsh tapped for another protracted Foreign Office errand. She

couldn't come out and say how much she resented it, of course –
that would have been unpatriotic – but she had been a bit frigid
at first. She supported King and Country and husband but that
didn't prevent her from being brusque, all sharp edges and cutting wit at first. But it didn't last. I knew the woman. Knew her
so well.

That was the hardest part. Pretending I didn't know how to
woo her. Pretending I didn't want to. Pretending part of me
didn't fixate on how I could steal her away so easily once she
stopped seeing my scars. When I'd first won her heart, I hadn't
known her half as well as I did now. What if her husband never
came home?

No. She wasn't my wife, I reminded myself. My wife had died
at the end of the world. I had to take what I could, and I did. I
was grateful for every moment of her company. Because if, luck
willing, we won this war and Liv's true husband returned, would
I have any choice but to fade into the shadows like a lonely ghost?
I couldn't bear the thought of it. I had to find a way to stay close
to Liv and Agnes.

Liv clicked on the wireless. Her hands shook when she took
her teacup again. She covered her nervousness well. But I knew
the questions tugging at her mind. How long could Britain's luck
last? Would this be the day it broke?

Every Briton followed the news from Dunkirk. And although
every day brought more soldiers home, the nation was caught
between optimism and terror. France was going to fall. The
evacuation was fragile; it could collapse at any moment. How
many Tommies were fated to die on the beaches?

All of them, the first time around.

I remembered that day. That terrible day. She'd dropped a
dish when the first news came. Liv and I sat in the den, practically

glued to the wireless, listening as the details unfolded. Much like we were doing now, and had done for the past several days.

Funny thing. Go back in time twenty years and the huge events change while the little things repeat themselves.

Sometimes Liv twirled a finger through an auburn lock while she listened to the dispatches. Sometimes she pursed her mouth, hard enough to whiten peach-pink lips. Sometimes she frowned. She put on a brave face, but I knew she was concerned. Frightened.

It was so goddamn hard not to stare at her.

I had to play along, feign the same apprehension. Had to play the part of the grizzled naval commander, projecting fragile confidence as events teetered on a knife edge. Had to be a regular Englishman, worried that our army was soon to die on the beaches.

Even though that wasn't going to happen. I knew this because I knew Gretel. Knew her well enough to understand what she was doing.

Every soldier rescued from the French coast was one more soldier put to the defense of Britain if Hitler tried to invade. Each and every evacuated soldier lessened Milkweed's incentive to trust our national defense to the warlocks. Lessened our dependence upon the Eidolons.

Gretel had worked a miracle. Not her first, and unfortunately not her last, probably, but the first I could appreciate. This was concrete proof that my mad mission wasn't impossible. Proof that things could change.

It opened up so many possibilities I couldn't begin to catalog them all. For the first time, I had a glimpse of the world through Gretel's eyes. History was a mutable thing. It could change, like a river carving a new course, changing the fates of armies and nations. And so, too, could the course of individual lives change.

Agnes's life could change. She could *have* a life.

I was grateful for the gift. Even if it did come from the Devil herself.

The radio warbled with static. We sipped our weak tea in cordial silence while Agnes napped in her bassinet. Every day, every hour with Liv was less awkward than the one before. She was slowly warming to the commander. She'd warmed to Raybould Marsh very quickly, and he to her. I had to keep reminding myself that I was here as a different man. That other me would throw all of this away without even realizing it. Stupid, stubborn ass.

The six o'clock news confirmed my suspicions about Gretel's strategy. What little German armor was present to dog the allied soldiers had been withdrawn. In its place, the Luftwaffe unleashed another day of heavy attacks on Dunkirk itself.

Interesting that Gretel had left Göring in charge this time around. What mistake would he make? What would he overlook? What would he underestimate?

Well, the RAF, for one. It was engaging the Luftwaffe, providing cover for the retreating troops. That hadn't happened last time. It hadn't been possible.

Official estimates said upwards of fifty thousand men would be rescued by the end of the day, British and French together. Almost twice the total number of men who had escaped Dunkirk during the first two days. The evacuation was accelerating.

Liv finished her tea. She turned off the wireless with a shaking hand. Released a long, pent-up sigh. Her eyes met mine briefly. I knew that look. I suddenly realized why the news from France had her wound so tightly. She didn't believe her husband had gone to America. She suspected otherwise.

But just then Agnes awoke and distracted both of us.

Agnes mewled. One little arm poked from beneath her

elephant blanket. It shook with the jerkiness of baby muscles. I concentrated on my tea. Tried to ignore the icicle piercing my heart.

Liv lifted our daughter. Their daughter. 'Shhh, shhh, baby girl.' She held Agnes close, rocked her. 'Are you hungry?' She rocked and hummed while Agnes mewled. 'No, not hungry. Do you need a change?' More humming, and a sniff. 'No, not that. You miss your father, don't you?' Agnes settled, calmed by her mother's voice.

'Me, too, baby girl,' Liv whispered. 'Me, too.'

It was agony, seeing this family but not being a part of it. The wanting burned hotter than the fire that had taken my face.

I couldn't stand it. I gathered my courage. 'Mmm . . . May I?'

Liv's eyebrows went up. She hadn't pegged the commander as one for children. And she didn't know me well. Or, that is to say, she didn't realize she knew me very well indeed. But she looked at my face, and whatever she saw there, it changed her mind.

'You'd be doing me a kindness. I must put supper on, or I'll be eating at midnight.'

She started to show me how to hold a baby, but I knew what to do. It came back so quickly. Liv laid Agnes in my arms. My baby was lighter than a snowflake and smelled just as clean. Cleaner.

I'd forgotten the little creases of baby fat under her eyes. Forgotten her tiny fingernails. Forgotten the way she scrunched her face in her sleep.

Oh, God. My baby daughter.

I didn't kiss her. God knew I wanted to. But it would've been the end of Liv's courtesy if she caught me at it. And I think my beard would have been too tough, too scratchy, for Agnes's newborn-soft skin.

It couldn't have been more than a few seconds before Liv returned. She surprised me. I didn't look up. Didn't want her to see the wetness on my cheeks.

'You're very good with her. Do you have children, Commander?'

'No,' I said too quickly, shaking my head. But something broke inside my already ruined voice. Liv heard it. 'Not anymore,' I confessed.

'I'm so sorry,' she said.

I knew it was dangerous, spending time with Liv and Agnes. But I told myself it was the best thing I could do.

There was nothing I could do about the Reichsbehörde at the moment. I'd trusted that to more capable hands. As for the warlocks . . . well, Milkweed didn't have a cadre of warlocks yet, and it wouldn't until Will returned. After his travels about the country, tracking down every last warlock in Britain, he'd instantly know me for an imposter. Though I'd missed the opportunity to make him think I was one of them, I still felt confident I could make Will my personal double agent within the Milkweed coven.

But the issue of Gretel remained. She'd killed Agnes the first time around, but what now? What were her intentions toward my daughter? My wife? Something cold scudded behind Gretel's eyes when she spoke of Liv.

I was glad Gretel had changed the course of events at Dunkirk. But that didn't make me inclined to trust the bitch. We had too much history for that.

And so I told myself I was being smart. Whatever her intentions toward Liv and Agnes, I knew Gretel wouldn't let anything happen to me. After all, I was her savior.

That meant Liv and Agnes were safe as long as they were with me. I'd make certain they wouldn't leave London if the bombs came. They'd be under my umbrella. As long as we were in the same city, I could protect them from Gretel.

Just until her husband returns, I constantly reminded myself. *This is an illusion, this oasis of domesticity.* It couldn't last. He'd come back, and then she'd be his forever and ever. But if he didn't return ... No. I refused to acknowledge the evil thoughts that smoldered like banked coals in the fire pit of my soul.

What had Gretel done to me?

Things would be well again. If I could stave off the growing compulsion to confess everything to Liv. If I could suppress the urge to reveal myself. If I could overcome the jealousy I felt toward her husband.

I handed Agnes back to Liv, whose face had grown long with pity and compassion.

She hesitated. Asked, 'Won't you stay for supper?'

If I could resist the temptation to come home.

6 June 1940
Reichsbehörde für die Erweiterung germanischen Potenzials

Along with the major objectives of Marsh's mission – destroy the farm, destroy the records – Liddell-Stewart had included one particularly strange requirement. Marsh didn't know why the commander wanted a blood sample from one of the Twins, but the abrasive codger had been insistent.

Marsh knew the request must have had something to do with the Eidolons. He remembered how Will had shed his own blood to draw their attention, and how he'd used a sample of Gretel's blood to show her to them. But at the time, Marsh had been more concerned by the mechanics of the order than by the twisted logic behind it. The problem, as explained by the commander, was that the Twins had been deployed in the field. And he didn't know where.

Marsh had been prepared to write it off. Bad enough he still hadn't a clue how to scuttle the Reichsbehörde records stored in Berlin. He couldn't orchestrate that, and the destruction of the farm, *and* accommodate the commander's eccentric addendum. Not when the targets could have been anywhere in the world.

But Gretel had taken care of that. And so the strangest of Liddell-Stewart's demands also became the easiest to fulfill. Not simple, but straightforward.

He watched the Twin as much as he could manage. He tried to note the frequency of her visits to the loo, though it was difficult to watch her that closely. But it didn't take much attention to he see how much time Pabst spent alone with her. Ostensibly the debriefing sessions were used to retrieve information from her sister. But more than once Marsh heard the faint, rhythmic squeaking of wooden table legs across a tile floor, or the jangle of a belt buckle. Followed afterwards, of course, by the smell of sex, and the glimmer of tears in mismatched eyes.

Marsh had been at the farm three weeks. Today his menial task was to keep Kammler occupied while a trio of technicians readied the morning's test. Buhler lounged in the shade behind the icehouse, waiting for the test to begin. He spent no more time with Kammler than he had to.

Clouds drifted across a patchwork sky. Hot sunlight accompanied a breeze cool enough to make the shadows uncomfortable. It rustled oak leaves in the forest and fluttered swastika banners atop the farmhouse. Marsh didn't mind the chill; the wind washed away the sour-milk scent of Kammler. Off to the west, a line of lower, darker clouds made a strategic advance upon the farm. Rain by lunchtime.

Mundane soldiers dumped fine golden sand from a supply truck into a pit in a distant corner of the training field. Reinhardt oversaw their work. Wind tore the falling sand into sheets and ribbons. It carried across the field to Marsh and stung his eyes with grit. Kammler seemed not to notice. But Marsh tugged at the larger man's arm, turned his face out of the wind.

'Here. This should be better for you,' he said.

'Mmmmmm. Muh,' said Kammler.

That was new. He usually said, 'Buh.' Which was as close as he could come to pronouncing 'Buhler.'

Marsh felt grateful that he didn't have to use the leash. But they only fastened the collar on Kammler when he had a battery, and they didn't let Marsh near the telekinetic when that was the case. Buhler, for his part, relied heavily upon the choke collar.

Marsh kept up a steady string of encouragements and kindnesses. No reason to expect Kammler understood any of it. But it made the imbecile familiar with Marsh's voice and manner. It achieved, superficially at least, a sense of comfort and familiarity. And it kept the large fellow calm.

From his vantage alongside Kammler, Marsh watched Pabst escort the Twin from the mess hall into the farmhouse, and, undoubtedly, the debriefing room. He wondered where her sister had been deployed, and whether it was strategically important enough to justify the standartenführer's constant need to question the girl.

You fucking pig, he thought. *I won't have any qualms about plugging you when the time comes. Your victim, though . . .* He didn't like thinking about what he'd have to do to Kammler, either, when the time came.

As always, von Westarp oversaw everything from his study while the technicians arranged cameras and equipment for Kammler's test. They struggled with dollies and jacks to spread a half-dozen rusty metal-bound crates across the field. Heavy things, too, judging from the way the ground shook each time they rolled a box from the dolly. Looked like they were planning to stretch Kammler's limits by making him focus on multiple objects.

Good luck, thought Marsh. Meanwhile, Kammler picked his nose and rubbed a hand across his shaven scalp.

The technicians made final adjustments to the cameras. Pabst emerged from the farmhouse. He slammed the door hard enough that the *bang* made Kammler jump. The colonel stalked across the field toward Reinhardt's sandbox.

Marsh thought, *Oh, ho. Got tired of you, did she?*

But he saw no scratches on the colonel's face, nothing to suggest she'd resisted him. She didn't dare. Pabst had changed his mind. And didn't look happy about it. But he'd been as eager as ever to have it off with her not ten minutes ago.

What could snuff a man's ardor like that? There were times, a few particular days out of each month, when he and Liv didn't . . . Pangs of regret, fear, and loneliness speared him in the chest and stole his breath. *Oh, Liv.*

He shoved aside the gnawing ache in his mind and heart. Concentrated. This was his opportunity to fulfill one of Liddell-Stewart's goals.

Marsh watched the techs from the corner of an eye made rough with grit and wind. One of the men made final checks to the camera arrangement. He nodded to the others, then called to Buhler. The hauptsturmführer levered himself to his feet and slung Kammler's leash over one shoulder. His footsteps left trails in the dewy grass as he approached.

Marsh made a show of inspecting Kammler. 'God damn it,' he said, loud enough for Buhler to hear before he came too close.

Buhler said, 'What?'

'He pissed himself again.' Marsh reached up to Kammler's neck and fished the long wires out from under his shirt. He shook the bare copper connectors, as though flicking away beads of moisture. Then, for good measure, he frowned in disgust and wiped his hands on Kammler's shirt. 'It's everywhere.'

'That's why,' said Buhler, 'you're supposed to take him to the bathroom before we start a test. Now we have to wait.' He shook his head. 'You're worse than Kammler. At least he has an excuse.' He sauntered back to the shade.

Marsh tugged at Kammler's wrist. 'Sorry about that,' he whispered. 'Let's go inside for a minute.'

The farmhouse had two lavatories. Von Westarp's study had its own en suite accommodation. His children shared a single facility on the ground floor. Support staff used the outlying buildings. Past renovations to the farmhouse had included an upgrade to the plumbing, but only halfway. There were several sinks but still only one toilet – and that in sore need of cleaning (no doubt they'd hand that task to Marsh as soon as somebody thought of it). It allowed several people to shave or brush their teeth simultaneously, but gave no privacy to anybody who otherwise needed to use the facility. But they'd been raised without such expectations, and thus understood nothing else.

To his credit, Kammler knew what the bathroom meant. He pushed his pants down and shuffled toward the toilet with his trousers around his ankles.

Marsh knelt on the hard tiles beside the rubbish bin. He took care when reaching into the bin, not knowing what he might find. The nub of a pencil. An empty tube of dentifrice. The cold, wet trail where somebody had blown their nose on a serviette. Something hard; a chip from the handle of a cheap straight razor.

And, shoved near the bottom, a wad of bloody linen. Marsh fished it out. The material was still tacky with clotted blood. He gave it a sniff. Menstrual.

It might have been Gretel's, or Heike's, but given what he'd seen of the sudden change in Pabst's behavior—

The door opened. Reinhardt barged in. He froze, taking in the scene: Kammler standing over the toilet with his pants down, mumbling to himself; Marsh hunched over the rubbish bin, studying a bloody rag.

Marsh froze, too. *He can't possibly understand what I'm doing*, he thought. *Whatever he makes of this, it won't be the truth.*

He fished around for a quick and plausible explanation, but Reinhardt obviated it with barking laughter. 'I knew it! You fucking pervert.' He pointed at Marsh. 'I knew there was something wrong about you the moment Gretel brought you home. Anybody who'd willingly make himself her pet had to be bent.'

Reinhardt went to the toilet and pushed Kammler aside. Unbuckling his belt, he said, 'Is that Gretel's discharge? No, no, don't tell me. I don't want to know.' He voided his bladder. Over the loud ring of water on porcelain, he added, 'You two are even more disgusting than I'd imagined.'

Marsh shoved the moist linen into his pocket while Reinhardt had his back turned. Reinhardt shook, rebuckled, pulled the chain to empty the bowl. Marsh re-dressed Kammler while Reinhardt washed his hands.

'Englishman, you've made my morning,' said the salamander. He departed, still chuckling to himself. Marsh led Kammler back outside, a sample of the Twin's blood tucked firmly in his pocket.

8 June 1940
Milkweed Headquarters, London, England

Will shrugged with relief when the Admiralty came into view through the windscreen. He rode in the first of a line of three cars that had been sent by Stephenson. And, just as soon as Will made the appropriate introductions and explanations, the men in these cars would be the old man's responsibility. Not soon enough. Will felt ridiculous playing mother duck to the men he'd recruited. He could endure a bit of silliness for the war effort. But it wasn't concern for his dignity that gnawed at Will. It wasn't the desire to be a proper host and ambassador to his charges that caused chilly tendrils of doubt to cling to him like winter fog.

He'd had grandiose dreams of raising an army. Of returning to London triumphant with Britain's saviors at his heels. He'd imagined the warlocks as genteel but eccentric old men, united by a common goal.

How wrong he'd been in every detail. Will hadn't raised an army. He'd found less than a dozen men. Of those, several were too far gone to be of use. Too mad, too ruined, or both. Nor were the remaining men the gentle protectors he'd envisioned. He'd gone in search of patriots, men like the father he barely remembered. Instead, he found men like his grandfather. Not evil, necessarily, but amoral. Cold. The questions they asked ... the things they sought ... The sooner he handed them over to Stephenson, the better.

Stephenson would sort them out. These men were dangerous.

Some of the warlocks, like Pendennis, were old enough to be Will's grandfather. (And thank the Lord that drunken devil had passed away long ago. Bad enough dealing with this lot without tossing familial abuse into the mix.) Others, not much older than

Will. But even the least of them wielded more power than the King. These men communed with forces beyond the fantasies of any monarch, potentate, or despot.

One by one, the warlocks had made their way to London. They'd needed accommodations in the city, so Will had reserved a block of rooms at the Savoy and charged it to his brother. Will had made the reservation open-ended, because he hadn't known how long it would be before he'd finished tracking down the warlocks. The manager had been happy to meet Will's unusual request; the war had been terrible for business. Will's earliest recruits, like Shapley, had been at the Savoy for several weeks. White, the last recruit, had only been there for two nights. Will suspected the final bill was quite impressive.

He'd returned to his Kensington flat just long enough to bathe, shave, and change into a suit that hadn't been on the road for weeks. The telephone rang twice in that short amount of time. Aubrey had not been happy.

Will emerged from the foremost car. The warlocks followed his lead. Two more emerged from the rear seat of his car, another pair from the following car, and another pair from the car behind that.

The most experienced warlocks, like Hargreaves, spoke in voices like shattered granite cloaked in shadows and cobwebs. The painful, inhuman sounds of Enochian had permanently etched the soft tissues of their throats. And they all had visible disfigurements. Every warlock, even Will, had a spiderweb of fine white scars on the palm of one hand. But as blood prices went, those marks were a trifle, a token fee. The scarring grew worse in accordance with the time and effort spent studying the Eidolons. Shapley's knowledge of Enochian was just a bit advanced beyond Will's; the mass of scar tissue on his hand caused his fingers to curl like claws. Most of White's nose was missing; he wore a prosthesis in public. One of Webber's eyes was a sunken, milky orb. Pendennis kept his dead arm concealed in a glove that extended to his elbow. Something had pockmarked every inch of Grafton's skin. Hargreaves had burned.

Nobody looked twice at Will's severed fingertip.

These men lived in a world divorced from the petty concerns of war and tyranny, King and Country. They were hermits and misanthropes. They maintained minimal interactions with the greater world, existing almost entirely separate from it. And they would have been impossible to find without his grandfather's notes as guidance.

He'd learned quickly that appealing to their sense of patriotism was a dead end. What brought these men to London, what piqued their interest enough to meet Stephenson, was the chance to practice their craft with a freedom that hadn't been known in centuries. The chance to perform real negotiations, the chance to bend and break the laws of nature. The opportunity to bargain with the Eidolons as hadn't been done in generations. The occasion to fuel those negotiations with blood prices of a scope unattainable to solitary, secretive men.

The warlocks wanted to try things of which they'd only dreamed. They wanted government sanction. Hargreaves had looked positively bloodthirsty when the possibility had dawned upon him. Hence the gnawing doubt that had become Will's constant companion in recent days. How wise was it for Milkweed to throw its lot together with such powerful men when their concerns and motivations barely overlapped?

Was this a mistake?

Will would have to speak with Stephenson privately, to warn him. But he already had a strategy in mind for dealing with the blood prices. Will knew he'd rest more easily after he and the old man worked out the details and established some guidelines for the other warlocks.

Will thanked the driver, then ushered the warlocks past the marine sentries posted beside the sandbag revetments at the Admiralty entrance. The marines stared, but didn't intervene. Stephenson had sent word down to expect guests.

Milkweed's portion of the Admiralty had changed while Will had been away. The offices were no longer empty, and the corridors showed actual signs of life. Lorimer and Stephenson had done their own recruiting, too.

Rather than crowd into Stephenson's office, the old man brought them to a conference room. A well-appointed space with leather and brass, it smelled of wood polish and cigarette tobacco. High-backed chairs flanked the windows and the empty hearth. Marsh wasn't present, but Lorimer was. Will nodded at him.

It was a bit surprising Marsh wasn't there. Disappointing, too, if Will allowed himself a moment of selfishness. He'd finally made a useful contribution.

Stephenson took the head of a long inlaid table; Will sat at the other end, and the warlocks joined them. Lorimer took a seat beside Will. A closed folder lay on the table before Stephenson.

One by one, Will indicated the men sitting along either side of the table. 'Mr. Hargreaves, Mr. White, Mr. Webber, Mr. Pendennis, Mr. Shapley, Mr. Grafton: please meet Captain John Stephenson. The captain—'

Stephenson cut in. 'I represent the Crown.' He looked Will in the eyes, as if in warning. 'And before another word is spoken, I need each and every one of you to understand that the Crown puts the highest premium on secrecy. From now until the end of time, as far as the world outside this room is concerned, the conversation we are about to have never, ever happened.' He opened the folder and distributed copies of the Official Secrets Act. The empty sleeve pinned to his shoulder fluttered like a flag. 'You'll see there's nothing for you to sign. This is a formality. A courtesy, if you will. This Act is law within the United Kingdom, and you're bound by it, whether you're aware of this or not. Take a good look, especially at the bit about penalties and prosecution, and think seriously about whether you want to stay in this room. Take the time you need until you're satisfied.'

It was essentially the same speech Stephenson had given Will the previous summer. Less profanity this time.

Paper rustled while the warlocks studied the documents Stephenson had distributed. They read with more attention to detail than Will had done. But, after all, these were men who lived and suffered and died by nuances of wording.

Nobody backed out. These men were not easily swayed or impressed by human threats.

'Excellent,' said Stephenson. 'Now. Lord William tells me that you gentlemen have certain skills that might be of use to His Majesty's Government.'

Hargreaves rasped, 'Politics do not concern us.'

'Perhaps you've heard that we're at war.'

'We are not soldiers to be called up at your leisure,' said Pendennis. 'You know nothing of us. You should know nothing of us.' He glared at Will. 'You don't understand what we do. No outsider could.'

'I've seen what Lord William can do in a negotiation.' The warlocks looked torn between dismissing Will's competence (he couldn't blame them for that) and looking dismayed that Stephenson appeared to know the terminology. Stephenson continued, 'He tells me your command of Enochian is far greater.' This earned more dismay, more angry glances at Will.

White said, 'He does not speak for us.'

Perhaps I'm not one of you, thought Will. *That didn't stop you from taking me up when I offered a room at the Savoy, did it?*

'And yet here you are,' said Stephenson. If he was unsettled by the disfigurements arrayed around the table, he showed no sign. Then again, a one-armed veteran of the Great War was no stranger to grievous injury. 'Something lured you out of hiding.'

'An arrangement,' said Hargreaves. 'Our assistance in exchange for the latitude to practice our craft. That is what we were told.'

Stephenson said, 'You're the most secretive men in the country. If not for Lord William, we'd have had no idea you existed outside of fairy tales. Nobody knows you exist. You already have latitude to do as you wish.'

'Beyond a certain point, the practice of our craft faces limitations. We lack resources.'

They were dancing around the issue, the warlocks and Stephenson both. Nobody wanted to come out and state the issue. Will wasn't about to let them sweep the ugliness under the rug. This arrangement could turn very dark if handled poorly. He'd see it wasn't.

He jumped in. 'They're referring to blood prices. Human blood secures the Eidolons' cooperation.'

Will hated the way Stephenson very much did *not* look dismayed by this. *Well, I suppose one doesn't become King of the Spies without knowing how to affect a certain level of aplomb.*

'I've seen a blood price in action,' said Stephenson, nodding to Will's injured hand. It didn't throb as much as it had in the days immediately after the injury. The seepage had stopped; Will had removed the bandages midway through his cross-country sojourn. 'And forgive me for saying it, but it seems to me you gentlemen have expended no shortage of blood and pain in pursuit of your craft.'

'Nevertheless,' said Hargreaves, 'there are some actions our blood will not purchase. But if you have experienced the Eidolons, then you know in your bones and your heart they exist outside physical laws. Nothing is beyond them.'

'You're saying that given the proper resources' – Stephenson put a slight emphasis on that word, slipping comfortably into euphemism – 'you gentlemen could bend the laws of nature?'

'I am saying that with the proper resources, the laws of nature become irrelevant.'

Stephenson fell silent while this sank in for a beat or two. A clock ticked on the mantel. He cleared his throat.

'Why do they need blood to fuel those acts?'

'They don't. They use the blood to study us. The acts are inconsequential to the Eidolons. An afterthought. A means of acquiring blood, and thus a means of learning more about the human stain.'

If Stephenson wondered what Pendennis meant by that, he didn't inquire. He pulled the conversation back to his original point. 'No doubt the metaphysics are quite fascinating. How much blood?'

'It depends upon the—'

Stephenson knocked on the table with his knuckles. 'I'm sorry. You seem to have confused me with somebody content to deal with generalities. So let me put this another way. You lot are negotiators. But how good are you? Must people die?'

At last, the opening Will had hoped for. He threw himself into the conversation. 'Certainly not,' he said. 'In fact, I've devised—'

But Pendennis spoke over him. 'Not necessarily.'

Not *necessarily*? Was he mad? The only acceptable answer was an emphatic, 'No.'

But then something disturbing happened: Stephenson didn't balk. Will shivered. What was that saying about when somebody walked over your grave?

Stephenson said, 'In that case, I would like to retain your services. Welcome to Milkweed, gentlemen.

'Now let me explain some background. The story begins early last year, when one of our agents retrieved a remarkable film in Spain. His contact was a man who claimed to have worked in a deep cover Schutzstaffel unit testing exotic technologies. The film was damaged in transit. I brought on Lorimer here, who reconstructed it.' Lorimer nodded at the newcomers. 'What we saw left no doubt the Jerries had achieved something extraordinary. Unnatural.'

Will said, almost to himself, 'This will make sense once you've seen the film.'

Stephenson shot him a look that could have etched glass. But he ignored Will, continuing, 'I'll get to the details in a moment, but we believe the breakthrough is the work of a man named Karl Heinrich von Westarp. A medical doctor . . .'

Lorimer tapped Will on the arm. Will leaned over. The Scot whispered, 'It's missing.'

Will spun to face him. 'What?'

'Aye. The film vanished. Along with everything else in the vault. Probably happened when the lass escaped.'

'Good Lord.'

Will excused himself while Stephenson continued the précis on Milkweed's backstory. Somebody had pilfered the vault. The Germans had outmaneuvered them yet again. He had to clear his head.

Will took a seat on a bench near the stairwell. Several of the offices had opened their windows, attempting to dispel some of the early summer stuffiness. He could smell the lake in St. James' Park.

It had seemed like such a good idea, such a noble cause, finding and recruiting Britain's warlocks for Milkweed's secret war effort. And it seemed Milkweed needed help more than ever. But the warlocks had turned out to be bloody-minded wretches, while Stephenson proved perfectly blasé about the blood prices. But perhaps that was the spymaster's natural cunning at work. Perhaps he was being careful, getting a feel for the warlocks before he made the crucial decisions. *Yes*, Will thought. *That had to be it.*

Doubtless the old man would put the warlocks to work. And sooner than later. That meant Milkweed needed access to human blood. Done wrong, that could lead to atrocity. But done right it would weigh on nobody's soul. Will had given this thought during interminable hours spent in automobiles and trains. He closed his eyes, tipped his head against the wall, reviewed his ideas.

Some time later, Stephenson emerged from the conference room. Pendennis and Hargreaves were arguing; it sounded like a pair of granite boulders in full rut.

The old man fished a pack of cigarettes out of his pocket, shook one out. 'Good work, Beauclerk.'

Well, now. That was nice to hear. 'Thank you.'

'We need those men.'

'In that case, we'll need blood. I'll make arrangements with the blood banks. It can be done through my brother's foundation, with a fair amount of legerdemain.'

Stephenson shook his head. 'If this goes forward, we are not leaving a paper trail.' Almost as an afterthought, he added,

'The hospitals are going to need their stores of blood. The Jerries will have France locked up soon enough. It won't be long before they've stationed fighters and bombers. Then they'll start coming over the Channel.' He scraped a safety match along the wainscoting. Around the cigarette dangling from his mouth, he said, 'Let me worry about the blood. I have another job for you.'

Will pointed. 'If we're not careful those men will push as hard as they can to get the sanction they crave.'

'I told you I'd handle it,' said Stephenson.

It wasn't the least bit reassuring. A bit of history came back to Will, whence he didn't know, but enough to make him realize he was wrong. He *had* returned with an army at his back. And they had just crossed the Rubicon.

Stephenson touched the flame to his cigarette, blew out the match, tossed it aside. The cigarette glowed marigold orange when the old man puffed on it. Tobacco smoke stung Will's eyes. It tasted like a bad decision.

'Marsh is missing.'

This brought Will up short. His teeth clicked together. 'I beg your pardon?'

'Nobody has seen him since the night of the prisoner's escape.'

The bottom fell out of Will's stomach. *Good heavens*. And that was probably when the vault got cleaned out. 'You don't suspect Pip was complicit in that?'

'I don't suspect anything yet because I don't have solid information. Pay a visit to Olivia.'

'Wait one moment. Marsh has been missing for weeks but you've waited until now to investigate?'

Pearly smoke jetted from Stephenson's nose. 'Don't be obtuse. SIS has men watching their house.' Will frowned, but

Stephenson quickly added, 'At Marsh's own request. Perhaps you've forgotten that the prisoner knew a great deal about Marsh and his family.' Ah. That. He hadn't forgotten. Stephenson continued, 'We need to know what Olivia knows. You're the man for that job.'

That was probably true. Stephenson was something of a father figure to Marsh, which made him an in-law to Olivia. She seemed fond of Stephenson, maybe even found his gruffness endearing. (Will suspected that was possible only because she had never dealt with the man in a work environment.) But Will was a close friend.

Or he had been ... Perhaps that changed when Marsh returned from France with that cipher of a Jerry girl in tow. His reaction to the way she spouted impossible knowledge of his family was to isolate Liv and Agnes from anything that might connect them back to Milkweed. Thus Marsh had forbidden him from visiting. Will still hadn't met their daughter.

'I'll do what I can,' said Will.

'Good. Find Marsh.'

9 June 1940
Kensington, London, England

The woodpecker in Will's dream spoke fluent Hungarian, wore jodhpurs and a forage cap, and was very, very persistent. *Tap tap tap*. It was trying to get into Will's cupboard. The locked one, where he kept his beetles. *Tap tap tap*. Splinters flew. Soon the diamond beak would reduce all the carpentry to flinders. The bird had a rationing book tucked under one wing. It paused in its relentless tapping, peered at Will with a pale rheumy eye, as if to commiserate. 'Getting so that an honest bird can't find decent blood for love or money these days. Curse the Jerries.' *Tap tap tap*.

Something jostled Will. It dragged him into wakefulness, where the last echoes of a sonorous rumble still lingered in his ears.

Awareness slowly percolated through his cottony mind. His mouth was open. He'd been snoring. Hard enough to rouse himself. That only happened when he was knackered beyond words. Which he had been, after weeks of traveling back and forth across the United Kingdom.

He cracked one eye. Pale light limned the bedroom shades. Morning, then. But early. And he hadn't slept in a decent bed since leaving London. He closed his eye, rolled over, sank back into warm silk sheets.

Knock knock knock.

Damned woodpecker. Will pulled a pillow over his head.

Woodpecker?

He pushed the pillow aside. Listened. It came again, a few moments later. Tapping. Or knocking. But it was too early for visitors.

Knock knock knock. Too early for polite visitors.

He'd already given the issue too much thought. His mind was waking up, even if his body wasn't. Nothing to do for it but answer the door. He slid out of bed, grabbed his robe from the back of the chair over which he'd thrown it all those weeks ago, and shuffled for the stairs.

Knock. 'Just one moment, please,' Will called.

He hoped, halfheartedly, that it might be Marsh at the door. Perhaps the whole thing had been a misunderstanding.

Will had gone immediately to Marsh's house after the

conversation with Stephenson. Nobody answered the door. He'd lingered in Walworth, endured a perfectly mediocre supper at a pub not far away, then returned. But neither Marsh nor Liv, nor Agnes for that matter, were present. He'd begun to worry in earnest. Until that point he'd been able to convince himself that Stephenson had been somehow mistaken. The street hosted a handful of parked cars; Will had wondered if one of those belonged to the SIS surveillance team, and if so, whether it would be worth trying to speak with somebody. In the end he'd decided against it and resolved to return in the morning.

No, it wouldn't be Marsh. Stephenson, perhaps. He was ex-military, wasn't he? Early risers, those types. Someone from the Admiralty? One of the warlocks? Aubrey? A very persistent and very upset Aubrey? Will sighed.

He pulled the robe around himself and drew a deep breath, expecting to find Stephenson, a warlock, or a grim-faced Duke of Aelred.

What he didn't expect to find was the man who had attacked him in St. James' Park.

My God. He looked so young.

By '63 – when Gretel came back, when everything went to hell – I hadn't seen Will in the flesh for nigh on twenty years or so. We'd both aged by then. He a little better than me. Money can do that for you. But still there'd been creases beneath his eyes, and a weariness within them. Milkweed had made its indelible mark upon him, stamped his clay and tossed him into the kiln. Years of hard living after the war etched that mark more deeply. And though he'd made up for it later with a decade or more of the pampered life he'd been born to, the look in Will's eyes had never fully recovered.

But the Will Beauclerk standing before me now was nothing but fresh clay. Clean, unblemished, naïve clay. I'd expected this to be easier than meeting myself, easier than meeting young Liv again. It wasn't.

This was the original Will. The real Will. The cheerful Will. My long-forgotten friend. It was difficult not to break into a smile. The pleasure at seeing him again hit hard. I realized just how badly I'd missed him, realized again just how acute my loneliness had become. And I accepted, truly accepted for the first time, what a right bastard I'd been to this man. Including when I'd walloped him in the park a few weeks ago.

He remembered. A flicker of recognition played across his face. His gaze alternated between my scars and my uniform. Was I a warlock or a sailor?

Will rubbed his jaw. He straightened, wrapped himself in indignation. 'I don't know who you are, sir, but I have half a mind to—'

'My name is Lieutenant-Commander Liddell-Stewart. I'm here to talk with you about Milkweed.'

Will blinked. Crumbs of sleep had dusted the corners of his eyes. A second too late, he protested, 'I don't—'

I bulled past him. Last time I'd been here, this flat had been the home of an alcoholic and a morphine addict. Not this time. This was the unremarkable home of an incorrigible bachelor and sometime rake. No clothes on the floor, no piles of old papers, no dishes and cutlery piled on the settee. No noisome squalor. Just Will, spluttering.

'I'm quite impressed,' I said, parroting something said to me long, long ago. 'When you cock something up, you do it good and proper.'

Will managed, 'What?' It came out sounding strangled.

'Milkweed, son. It's barely set sail, hardly past the jetty, and already you've found a way to sink it.'

'I'm sure I don't know what you mean.' Well, he was trying. I had to give him credit.

'Oh, come off it. I know Milkweed better than you. I know you work for John Stephenson. I know you were recruited by an agent named Raybould Marsh. I know the Admiralty was recently compromised by one of von Westarp's progeny. And, more to the point, I know you've just returned after several weeks spent tracking down every warlock you could find. The end result being that you've let a half-dozen complete strangers in on Britain's most important secret.'

'Why don't we back up a bit, shall we? Because you've conveniently omitted the part where you assaulted me. In fact, I think I'm going to call the police.' He reached for the telephone on the end table in the entryway.

'I wasn't assaulting you. I was saving your life.'

Not true, but at least it stopped him. His hand hovered over the receiver. 'You nearly broke my jaw.'

I said, 'If you had accosted the Jerries when they came through the park, it would have been a fatal mistake. There was more to that evening than you realize.' Profoundly true, that bit. 'Think about how easily they orchestrated that rescue. They must have had help from inside the Admiralty. And if you'd given chase, it's highly likely the traitor would have killed you.'

'This is absurd,' said Will. 'There were only four of us at the time. Do you truly expect me to believe that Stephenson is a traitor? Or Lorimer? Or Marsh? You don't know that man at all, if that's what you believe.'

Well. That was touching. Christ, it was good to see him.

'It could have been anybody in the Admiralty building. Or in

SIS. But the point remains. Milkweed's operations have been compromised. And you've managed to make the problem worse.'

'I'd have to say the most suspicious character in our little drama thus far is you. A complete stranger, to use your phrase.' He lifted the telephone receiver.

I sighed. 'Don't be such a fool. A mole has to be inconspicuous. Do I look like a fellow who passes unnoticed everywhere he goes?'

Will frowned. 'Are you . . . ' He glanced at my hands.

'No. I'm not one of your warlocks.' That's what I would have claimed a month ago. And I could have pulled it off, as long as I sidestepped the Enochian. But now, after his recent adventures, Will was probably the foremost expert on the history of warlocks in the UK. 'But that's the point. How much do you truly know about those men?'

There was something familiar about the wretched fellow. He reminded Will of John Stephenson, if the old man's personality had been dragged by its ankles through a slurry of broken glass and vinegar. Same with his voice.

Will shook his head, trying to cast off the last cobwebs of sleep. He desperately wanted tea.

'Look,' he said. 'If you're so knowledgeable, you must understand how badly we need their help. Without the Eidolons, we haven't a prayer of holding back von Westarp's brood. I mean, my God, man. Have you seen that film?'

The commander rasped, 'Yes. Yes I have.'

A warning klaxon went off inside Will's mind while a chill raised goose pimples on his arms. Prior to the escape, only five people had seen the film: Marsh, Will, Lorimer, Stephenson, and the PM. And then the reel had disappeared. So when did this fellow see it?

Will decided not to point out the discrepancy. Not yet. Not while this stranger was inside Will's home, close enough to shoot or stab or even strangle Will. He'd already demonstrated his willingness to use violence. Will tried to hide his anxiety, gauging his chances of making it out the door while the commander continued.

'I repeat. Milkweed has been compromised. The ease of the prisoner's escape should tell you just how badly.' He paused. 'And I assume you know about the vault?'

Now how in the world could he know about that? Well, he'd know if he'd been the one doing the pilfering . . .

'How do I know you're not behind that?'

But the commander ignored him. 'The Reichsbehörde has been playing us since the beginning. Since Marsh returned from Spain with that damnable film.'

He spoke with the fervor of a fanatic. His claims were slightly absurd. And he knew a staggering amount.

I was getting through. I could see it. He didn't trust me – nor should he – but I had his attention.

Will asked, 'Do you mean to say that the creation of Milkweed is all part of Hitler's master plan?'

'Not Hitler's, but a plan, yes. A very thorough, very dangerous plan.' Gretel's plan. But I skirted that issue. Didn't want to get lost in a long digression about the Nazi oracle. 'And that's why you're going to be my eyes and ears within the warlocks.'

'Aha. I see. For what, exactly, shall I be watching?'

'Anything unusual. Anything out of the ordinary.'

Will laughed. I knew the man, knew it wasn't intended

unkindly. But people of his station had a way about them, a way of turning the tiniest gesture into a class statement. And so it was with him now. Gentle condescension.

'I'd say that sums up everything the warlocks do. It's their raison d'être.'

'Tell me something, Wi—' I caught myself. '—Lord William. If Hargreaves and the rest launched into negotiations on behalf of Milkweed today, how confident are you they couldn't slip something past you? Some peculiarity of Enochian grammar, or a snippet of vocabulary not in your grandfather's lexicon?'

I'd surprised him again. But he conceded the point.

He said, 'You think there may be traitors among them.'

'We must be aware of the possibility.'

Will asked, 'How do you know I'm not the traitor?'

My doppelgänger had asked the same question. I gave the same answer. 'You aren't.'

This Will, the Will of 1940, was poised to endure terrible things for King and Country. And he had. Only much later had he sold us out to the Soviets.

He said, 'I would be a traitor if I did as you say. You speak of turncoats and spies, yet you'd have me be one of them!'

It was easy to underestimate Will. Easy to forget there was more to him than just another chinless toff. He was Milkweed's guilty conscience. He would betray the project, if he believed it was the right thing to do. And I knew how to push him there. I knew the shape of the dark worries that scurried through the back of his mind even now.

'Tell me something else. Have you spoken with Stephenson about the blood prices yet?'

He blinked, fell silent. Quietly, warily, he said, 'What could you possibly know about that?'

That's when I knew I'd set the hook. Yes, Will was concerned. He'd seen the shape of things to come. And even if he hadn't yet admitted it to himself, he desperately wanted an ally in the ethical firestorm to come.

'You've spent so much time recruiting those men. Surely you have a plan in mind for what to do when the negotiations begin. Something humane, something sensible.'

Will said nothing. But he looked at me as though I'd just read his mind.

I said, 'Mark my words, Lord William. Stephenson won't go for your hospital idea. It will be worse. Much worse.'

'I don't believe you,' he whispered. Did he look pale, or was that my overeager imagination?

'You might change your tune after they've trained you in planting explosives.' Will looked appalled. But I kept the pressure on. 'Let me guess. You suggested blood banks, but Stephenson waved it aside. He cited concerns about leaving a paper trail.'

He chewed on this for a long moment. Then he looked at me again, squinting. 'Who are you?'

I said, 'Just think about what I've told you. And don't let the warlocks engage in any activities without first reporting their plans to me.' I stood. 'I'll check in regularly.'

And together, with you as my cat's-paw, we'll keep them from doing anything whatsoever.

Will said, 'Excuse me, but don't you think you're being just a bit overconfident? You're making some rather stunning assumptions about me.'

God bless him, the man was trying so hard.

'You'll come around.'

'I am not remotely comfortable with this conversation.'

'Unnecessary.' I stood. 'Just keep your mouth shut and your eyes open.'

Will followed the commander to the door. The rising sun was a smear of light in a thin, gray sky.

The commander paused on the landing. 'Your bell is broken, by the way. You ought to mend that.' He donned his hat. 'Good morning.'

He was doing this intentionally. Leaving before Will could get his thoughts in order. Before he could start asking questions. The older man trotted down the stairs. But there was one thing Will had to know immediately.

'Marsh,' said Will. The commander missed a step, nearly tumbled to the pavement. But he caught his balance. Turned, slowly. A strange expression had crossed his face.

Will asked, 'Where is he?'

Liddell-Stewart hesitated. He seemed unsure for a moment, almost relieved, as though he'd been expecting Will to ask a different question.

'I couldn't begin to guess,' said the commander.

9 June 1940
Reichsbehörde für die Erweiterung germanischen Potenzials

The betrayal happened while Marsh was eating breakfast.

Buhler had just led Kammler away on his leash, leaving Marsh a few free minutes to tuck into his eggs. They were still warm; he was getting better with Kammler.

'Yes. That's him.'

Gretel's voice. Marsh looked up. She stood in the entryway of the mess hall, pointing at him. Pabst stood behind her. They were accompanied by an SS-hauptsturmführer whom Marsh didn't recognize.

Elsewhere, the sound of a table sliding back. Marsh took a quick glance over his shoulder. Two mundane soldiers had circled behind him.

He looked again at the captain with Gretel. The patch on the bottom of his left sleeve differed from what Marsh had become accustomed to seeing at the farm. Two letters inside a black diamond: SD.

The officer was from the Sicherheitsdienst RFSS: the SS security service. Party intelligence.

Gretel looked straight at Marsh and said, 'He's a spy.'

The SD officer barked an order. 'Bring him.'

The soldiers grabbed Marsh's arms before he had time to realize what was happening. A little crowd gathered outside to watch while the SD man had him bound and dragged to a black Mercedes idling alongside the farmhouse.

Reinhardt paused in the middle of another training session. He watched with arms crossed. His mouth twisted into a smirk.

Buhler and a trio of technicians abandoned their conversation. Kammler saw Marsh. Clapped. Tried to say his name. 'Mmm – muh – mmm.'

Von Westarp watched it all from the window of his study atop the farmhouse. The last thing Marsh saw, before the bag went over his head, was Gretel. Winking at him.

It was a long, dark ride to Berlin.

NINE

'Haven't you been a perfect stranger!' Liv threw her arms around Will and gave him a hug. Agonizingly brief. Yet long enough to convey the tickle of her hair, the milkiness her skin. He tried to overcome the twinges of envy toward Marsh. Tried, for the thousandth time, not to imagine the body beneath her dress.

He returned the hug as chastely as he could manage. 'I've been out of town.' His voice cracked. 'Traveling quite a bit, in fact.' He dared to look at her, truly look at her. 'You are lovely as always, my dear.'

Liv blushed and looked away. 'You'd say that if I were draped in sackcloth and ashes.'

'And it would be equally true.'

Liv gasped at the sight of his injured hand. She hadn't seen him since before he'd lost the fingertip. 'William, what have you done to yourself this time?'

The question didn't register because Liv was touching his hand, and the waves of heat pulsing from the gentle contact softened his knees like candle wax. Her brows tugged together in a frown that creased her freckled skin, a rough and devastating thing that ripped the breath from his chest.

Will remembered himself before she caught him staring. He pulled his hand away, though he hated to do it.

'What, this old war wound? I think I've already told you, haven't I? Bashed myself with a spade.'

Liv bit her lip, as though unsure of whether to laugh or frown. 'Will, that was a month ago. This injury's fresh.'

'Yes, well, we *are* at war. And Hitler still plans to do us in with gardening mishaps.'

She laughed because he wanted her to, and because they both knew it, and because hers was a kind heart. It was a selfish thing to do. But that laugh ... He'd feel guilty later. Guiltier.

'You haven't met our daughter yet.'

'She hadn't arrived, last I saw you.' When last they'd seen each other, a month earlier, Liv had been in labor. Will had escorted her to the hospital because her husband the spy was in France at the time, though she believed he had gone to America. Will had hastily packed a bag for her.

'I've never thanked you properly for that,' said Liv. 'You were my champion, Will.'

He followed her to the den, where a baby-shaped bundle of blankets rested in a bassinet. Liv bent over the bassinet; Will's gaze lingered on her backside for a moment before he tore his attention away. Long enough to revive the memory of packing for her. Long enough to cause shameful speculation about the undergarments currently beneath her dress.

Will cleared his throat. 'It was my pleasure.'

Liv cradled her daughter. The baby yawned, shifted. Quietly, Liv said, 'This is Agnes. Say hello to your Uncle William, baby girl.'

Agnes was tiny, and fragile, and utterly foreign. Will couldn't fancy himself a father. Couldn't fancy himself a husband, for that matter. He supposed that nobody who knew him could imagine such a thing. And so he'd never had a Liv. Probably never would.

Will and Liv chatted, over watery tea, of matters small and large, profound and inconsequential. Less than a week after its conclusion, the Miracle at Dunkirk was still fresh on everybody's minds and lips. Almost 340,000 British and French soldiers had made it off the beach. They had left most of their equipment behind, but that could be replaced. People couldn't.

When the opportunity presented itself, Will asked, with as much nonchalance as he could muster, 'And speaking of not seeing people in ages, where is your dashing husband? He's been rather scarce these past few weeks.'

Liv fussed with Agnes while her lower lip trembled with the struggle to contain something. She took a shaky breath before answering him. And when her hazel eyes shimmered like puddles during a rainstorm, Will knew her smile was fragile as spun sugar. One tear would dissolve it.

It skewered him, this momentary glimpse at her sorrow.

'Off again to America. I tell you, I don't know what the Foreign Office would do without him.'

Will inquired further, as gently and casually as he could manage. She confirmed her husband had departed late on the thirteenth. The night of the prisoner's spectacular rescue from the Admiralty cellar. Coincidence or cause and effect? Either way, it was disconcerting.

He wished he could read Liv more effectively. Had Marsh lied to her, or was she lying for him?

'Well,' said Will, 'at least he's safely across the Atlantic. Seems as if the States are the only part of the world not stuck in this war.' Europe, Africa, Asia, Australia, and South America all were touched by the conflict, which promised to surpass the Great War in scope and suffering. 'Aside from the Antarctic, I suppose.'

He had to make her smile again. 'Now that I'm in London again it would be my pleasure to visit more regularly. I imagine it must be lonely without Pip making noise in the garden.'

The hesitation was so slight that Will thought he might have imagined it. 'That would be brilliant. Cheers, Will.'

The garden gate had come unlatched, so when Will took his leave of Liv, she asked him to go out through the back and close the gate on his way. He was happy to oblige. It gave him a chance to duck into Marsh's garden shed in the hopes of finding some clue as to where, and why, he had disappeared. But if some clue had indeed been hidden in the arrangement of tools and sacks of potting soil, it was lost on him. Certainly there was nothing so straightforward as a note. The gate gave off a tooth-shaking squeal when he pulled it closed, loud enough to scare off the Jerries.

Back at the Admiralty, Will reported to Stephenson.

'As you feared, Marsh departed late on the thirteenth, or very early the fourteenth. The night of the escape. According to Liv he'd been sent back to the States.'

'By whom?'

Will shrugged. 'Foreign Office. The same cover he used when you sent him to France, yes?'

'He could be anywhere.'

'Yes.'

Stephenson said, 'The observation team reported a visitor to his house late that night and some activity. I'd convinced myself he'd been snatched by the Jerries, Gretel and her rescuer.' He crushed a cigarette in the marble ashtray on his desk. Ashes drifted across the blotter. 'But if he had time to tell his wife he was off again . . . '

'Yes.' Will shook his head. 'I refuse to believe he's turned on us.'

'I don't know what to think.'

An alarming confession from the old man. He and Marsh were quite close. Will stood to leave, not wanting to intrude on Stephenson's anxiety.

'Good work, Beauclerk. Go mind your ducklings.'

Will hesitated, debating whether he ought to tell Stephenson about the visit from Lieutenant-Commander Liddell-Stewart.

'Something else?'

Will remembered Stephenson's words from the previous day: *Let me worry about the blood.* And the commander's words from earlier that morning: *It will be worse.*

The commander might have been winding him up. And what reason was there to trust him? None. And yet the things that man knew . . . What if he were right about the blood prices? What if the doubt that chewed at Will every quiet night as he crisscrossed the country had been gnawing on the truth? Will decided to wait. Just for now.

To cover for his hesitation, Will said, 'Any problems with the new recruits?'

'The day is young,' said Stephenson. 'How long until they're ready to contribute?'

'We must collate our individual lexicons and journals, to bring them into agreement. It could be rather perilous otherwise. Inconsistencies would play merry hob with the negotiations. Merry and deadly, I would wager.'

'How long?'

'Difficult work. A few weeks? Perhaps a month.'

'Damn,' said Stephenson. He bowed his head, rubbed his forehead. 'Not as soon as I'd like.'

But in fact . . .

'Do you remember the day Pip returned from France?' Will asked. 'I'd been on my way to find you.'

Stephenson looked up, his eyes bright for the first time since Will had returned to the city. 'Yes! You said you'd been cooking up a way to find Marsh.'

Will had been worried Marsh might have been caught up in the invasion of France. He wanted to know if his friend had found himself on the wrong side of the front.

Will nodded. 'Yes. It might not have worked, had we tried it then. But it should be straightforward now. The Eidolons have seen his blood.'

Not only that, but when they did see Marsh, the Eidolons gave him a name. Maybe Pendennis or Hargreaves or one of the others could make sense of that.

'Excellent. Make it happen as soon as you can. Come straight to me with any problems. I'll ensure you get what you need.'

Will took his leave of the old man. What would it cost, this effort to find his missing friend? He'd see the price paid, if it meant an end to Liv's misery. But would it be the beginning of the descent? Is this what the commander warned him about? *It will be worse . . .*

17 June 1940
Westminster, London, England

I've killed for my country. Oh, yes.

I once strangled a man with a garrote and my bare hands. Shot another in the temple the same afternoon. But it was war, and they were the enemy. A thin comfort when caught without a coat in a cold autumn rainstorm, or all the times I woke in the middle of the night to find Liv's side of the bed cold and empty. But there it was. And I've never killed a countryman, though I suppose Cattermole's shade might disagree. I've been many things, but never a murderer. But now, watching the people coming and going from the Savoy, I wondered if that was soon to change.

Age and ruin lay heavy over the man I'd been following. He walked with a peculiar shuffling gait, as though one leg bone had fused to his hip. His arm swung listlessly; I'd watched him long enough to suspect it was dead, or lame. I'd contrived to get a solid look at him earlier in the afternoon when he took his leisure in the Savoy's tearoom. His good hand, the one that wasn't shriveled inside a leather glove, was ribbed with fine white scars.

A doorman tipped his hat, opened a door for the warlock. I checked my watch, memorized the time, and tossed another handful of crumbs to the pigeons at my feet.

I wondered how he'd rated a room at the Savoy. He appeared to be one of the oldest warlocks. Perhaps they did things by seniority. That was consistent with what I remembered of Will's interactions with them, and my own. Either way, for a reclusive misanthrope – and weren't they all, these sorcerers? – he certainly seemed to be enjoying the accommodations. Probably had the others staying in hovels over in Limehouse, bloody hypocrite.

His name started with a P. He'd died of a heart attack in August of 1940. Killed by the strain of keeping the Jerries' invasion fleet out of the English Channel. Will's warlocks had been running round-the-clock negotiations that summer.

He was, in short, a bloody dangerous bastard. He knew

Enochian; he could talk to the Eidolons. He carried knowledge that would one day destroy the world if it became the tool of Whitehall.

I didn't *want* to kill my countrymen. Even twisted old codgers like these. But I wouldn't have to kill them immediately, if Will fed me the information I needed to sabotage the negotiations. Stephenson would give up on the warlocks right quick if they failed to deliver results. They'd still be around in case of emergency.

Once my counterpart carried out his mission at von Westarp's farm, the warlocks would become superfluous. The key was to ensure that Whitehall never embraced 'Enochian realpolitik.' For now, I'd start by discrediting the warlocks. Later, after they had been cast out and were no longer worthy of Whitehall's attention, I'd kill them.

Which is why I'd been tailing this warlock for the past four days. Like the warlock before him, and the warlocks I'd study after him. Learning his routine, seeing how he made his way to the Admiralty and back, picking out his protection. (Blue fedora, gray trousers, shoulder rig. Flat cap, coveralls, pistol tucked behind the breast panel.)

Stephenson had put two SIS minders on every warlock. Just like last time.

Every warlock except Will, that was. He had refused. Said it wouldn't do for the Duke's brother to be seen about town with two bodyguards everywhere he went. That would raise eyebrows and invite questions. He was right.

I tried not to think about Will. What would you do if you knew, beyond any possibility of doubt, that your best friend carried knowledge that would one day destroy the world? And what if you knew that determined persons could rip it from him?

Because if it wanted to, Whitehall could force Will to reveal the process for creating more warlocks.

Destroying their credibility was essential, if I didn't want to murder my friend.

22 July 1940
Kensington, London, England

Took me over a month to learn all I could about the warlocks from the outside. During that time, the Luftwaffe started regular attacks on shipping. By the time I neared the end of my surveillance campaign, the Jerries had begun air operations against ports along the Channel, too. But their strategy was haphazard, almost spasmodic. It lacked the cold precision with which they'd dismantled our air defenses the last time around. I wondered how Gretel was framing her advice. Somehow, she had the OKW believing this was the best possible scenario. Then again, she and I were the only people on earth who knew firsthand of scenarios that played out much better for the Luftwaffe.

Though things were better than they'd been the first time around, they weren't good. France had folded in late June, and now the beleaguered Royal Navy was tasked with blockading the Continent. Meanwhile, the Ministry of Aircraft Production took up a collection. 'Saucepans into Spitfires,' they called it. We were weak. Weak enough that the British Empire could offer no resistance when Japan demanded closure of the Burma Road. Hitler made a final 'peace offering' to Britain a few days ago, with predictable results. Even America rebuffed the overture: Roosevelt signed an act that would greatly expand the Americans' naval presence in both the Atlantic and Pacific. (I didn't remember that from the first time around, but it was becoming difficult to remember such details. It was a challenge to keep straight both versions of this accursed war.) The most chilling reminder of the original history came when the Soviet Union annexed Lithuania, Latvia, and Estonia. I watched, and wondered if Stalin would take the rest of Europe as he'd done last time.

Will and his colleagues had also been quite busy during those same weeks, as he reluctantly explained to me when I returned to his Kensington flat.

'We've done nothing that would be of interest to you,' he said. 'Merely paperwork.'

He didn't want to tell me anything. Couldn't help but respect him for that. But I had to know what was happening inside Milkweed. I said, 'Tell me.'

Will sighed, running a hand over his face. 'Before we can collaborate on negotiations, we have to ensure that we share a common frame of reference. A canonical text, if you will.' He delivered this explanation in a bored monotone, as if by rote. I reckoned he'd gone over this more than once. I saw shades of my mentor's impatience in that. 'Every warlock has his own journal. And his own lexicon. A personal, idiosyncratic record of Enochian. These documents are old and, sometimes, unreliable. They've been passed down for generations. Centuries in many cases.'

'You're combining them. Writing a master lexicon.'

'Master lexicon.' Will scratched his chin. 'Yes. I suppose you could call it that.'

'Quill pens and parchments. I take it Milkweed hasn't found a use for you.'

I tried not to let my eagerness show. But with the war evolving so differently this time, the circumstances that had forced us to rely upon the warlocks to blockade the Channel hadn't crystallized. With France under heel, the Jerries had of course looked across at Britain and begun to salivate. But this time we had an army with which to repel the invasion force. And, so far at least, we still had the RAF.

Invasion was still a threat. But if the world was lucky, we'd find a way to counter it without magic. *Perhaps*, I thought, allowing myself a glimmer of optimism, *we'll manage to fight this entire war without magic*.

But it's never that easy.

'I'm happy to say,' Will said, 'that we're poised to do something rather valuable.'

I concentrated on a neutral tone: 'Oh?'

'A Milkweed agent went missing two months ago. I mentioned him to you. Marsh. Quite a good friend of mine, in fact. We're going to have the Eidolons locate him.'

Shit. This was a disaster. The problem immediately sprang to mind: If the warlocks delivered on this promise and managed to discern that my doppelgänger was in Germany, Stephenson would have to draw one of two conclusions – either Raybould Marsh had defected, or he had been trussed up and shipped to the Continent against his will. But both paths of reasoning led to the same place. Whether willingly or under torture, it ended with Raybould Marsh giving up everything he knew about Milkweed.

Stephenson would have no choice but to order the warlocks to find a way to silence my younger self. They wouldn't kill him outright. That was their one ironbound rule, and God knows I'd learned to respect it. But there were other ways. Subtle ways.

I asked, 'Can you do that?'

'It's complicated, but yes. The key is that they've already seen his blood. The Eidolons, I mean. They know him,' said Will. 'In fact, they seem to be rather fascinated by him.'

Will was still trying to decipher the name the Eidolons had given me. Poor sod. It took us twenty years to get the answer to that particular riddle.

Your map is a circle. A broken spiral. That's what the Eidolons had told me through the empty husk of my son.

'Whose idea was this?'

Will said, 'Mine.'

Damn it, Will. Why do you have to be so fucking helpful at the worst possible time?

So I aimed for his weak spot. 'And the blood prices? How will those be paid?'

'It's just information we seek.' He flexed his hand, glanced down at his wound. 'The price should be minor.'

He didn't add, 'This time.' But I could see from the look on his face that it was on his mind and on his tongue. So I gave the hook a little twist.

'Are you certain?'

His only answer was to go a little pale. I didn't enjoy it, but I had to undermine his faith in Milkweed. Meanwhile, if the warlocks located Raybould Marsh, it would ruin everything. I had to stop them.

26 July 1940
Berlin, Germany

Nobody knows I'm here.

It was a deadly, dangerous thought. A loose pebble, bouncing down the towering scree of piled-up fears. The first rumble of an avalanche that would bury hope.

Marsh had fended off despair as long as he could manage.

Kept his body active with stretches and exercises. Kept his mind occupied with plans, strategies, tactics. He'd even devised a plan for destroying the Reichsbehörde, if he ever returned there. But after nearly seven weeks in a lightless prison, sleeping on a cold hard floor, steeped in the smell of his own bodily functions, unable to block out the screams of prisoners in adjoining cells, his resolve had weakened.

He spat out another torn piece of fingernail. Reviewed what he knew.

They'd kept the bag over his head for the entire journey from the farm. But Gretel had sent him here for a reason. That implied he was deep underneath SS Haus, the Schutzstaffel headquarters that Himmler had placed inside the former Prince Albert luxury hotel.

There couldn't be many cells down here. They would be reserved for the prisoners of highest interest to the SS.

He'd inferred that based on the screams.

He'd spent every day waiting for his own turn with the interrogators. But they hadn't come. Not yet. They were patient. Wearing down his resolve before they laid a single finger upon him. They let the cold and wet and hunger soften him. He knew that, in the part of his mind still capable of evaluating the situation objectively. But that part of him had atrophied while the rest of him rotted away.

Nobody knows I'm here.

But if she had sent him here for the Reichsbehörde files, how long did she expect him to wait for his opportunity? Nothing short of a miracle would enable him to deal with the files and get out of Berlin.

Nobody in Britain knows I'm here.

Yes. That was true. Manifestly true. Commander Liddell-

Stewart didn't know. John Stephenson didn't know. Will didn't know; Lorimer didn't know.

Liv didn't know.

An icy fist gripped his heart. He couldn't breathe. Panic heavier than a mountain settled over him, forced the air from his lungs. Guilt seared like acid in his veins. Liv would spend the rest of her days wondering what had happened to her lost husband. Agnes would grow up without ever knowing her father.

Iron bands of despair constricted around his chest like straps of wet canvas drying and shrinking in the sun. He cast about for something strong, something bright.

He remembered the last morning he'd had with his wife and daughter. Liv and he had made breakfast together: a recipe with dried egg powder. They'd had no toast. But they'd laughed at the absurdity of the wretched austerity food, fed each other, reveled in togetherness. A single shining memory, etched in diamond and set in gold.

Tears burned trails down his face. He resolved to keep that breakfast firmly in mind when they finally came for him. He'd make it his dying thought.

26 July 1940
Milkweed Headquarters, London, England

'Our task,' said Will, 'is to find Raybould Marsh.'

The warlocks sat with the world spread at their feet. Will's blood had stained the floorboards here, though now the rusty blotch lay hidden beneath a sprawl of overlapping maps. Several depicted the Continent in great detail; Ireland and the UK had similar coverage. Slightly less detailed were the maps of Mediterranean

Africa and the western Soviet Union. Lorimer had brought a map of North America, which had been added to the mix on the off chance that Marsh had been telling the truth when he told Liv he was off to America. They'd also taken the Mercator world map from the wall in Stephenson's office.

Each warlock held a copy of the master lexicon. Stephenson had insisted on attending. He leaned against the closed door, looking grim. Lorimer was busy in his workshop.

Will stood beside a low table, upon which rested a maritime binnacle compass. The gimbaled compass was well over a century old and, back in the days of Nelson, had adorned the deck of a 104-gun ship of the line. In more recent decades, it had adorned a pedestal outside the office of the First Lord of the Admiralty. Until Stephenson liberated it for, as he'd said, 'Purposes related to security of the Crown.' The binnacle itself was a tall dome of polished brass, smooth and round except where a slanted pane of glass provided a view of the compass rose.

Another table, across the room, held a miscellaneous assortment of objects: a doorknob, a frying pan from Lorimer's kitchen, a box of tenpenny nails. It was the best they could do on short notice; pure iron had become hard to find these days, as more and more of it went into foundries to make weapons and equipment for the war effort. Even the ornamental railings in city parks had disappeared.

In Nelson's day, the compass would have been flanked by a pair of iron correcting spheres. The spheres compensated for compass deflections caused by the iron in the nails used to build the ship. Today, the odds and ends would be used to realign the compass after the Eidolon arrived.

The warlocks had been over the essentials and had come to

an agreement on how they'd phrase their request. Will briefly reviewed the situation regarding Marsh. Then he rubbed his hands together. 'Shall we begin?'

I returned to the Admiralty in civilian clothes. One side benefit of the weeks I'd spent shadowing the warlocks was that I easily knew enough to pass as one of them. I already looked and sounded like the old bastards. Today I carried a carpetbag.

Easy enough, as long as Will didn't see me. Stephenson and Lorimer, too, for that matter, since they'd have recognized me based on Will's description from our encounter in the park.

But, if I knew John Stephenson, he'd be with Will and the others. He'd want to be there when the Eidolons located my doppelgänger. Lorimer, on the other hand, wouldn't come within a quarter mile of the negotiations if he could help it. Lucky bloke.

I went to the room where I'd landed during my arrival. The warlocks were next door. I closed the door and set the carpetbag on a filing cabinet. I pulled a drinking glass from the bag, held it to the wall, and listened.

The inhuman syllables of Enochian pierced Will's throat like caltrops. The shriek of dying stars. The hiss and crackle of a cooling planet. The thunder of creation. The perfect silence of a lightless, lifeless universe. Ur-language ricocheted through the room, a chanting interplay of seven distinct voices.

Will chanced a quick look at Stephenson. He'd gone rigid, eyes and fists clenched as he withstood the assault.

The warlocks converged on a single line, a single rhythm. The maelstrom of language scraped reality down to an onionskin veneer.

'Now,' said Pendennis.

As one, the warlocks unfolded their pocket knives and slashed their palms. Blood flowed freely.

The wall flexed, the floor canted. I stumbled. The glass shattered at my feet. And reassembled itself.

Their Eidolon had arrived.

An awareness seeped into the room, flowed through cracks in time and space like a vast ocean forcing itself through hairline fractures in a dike. It filled the world with the crushing pressure of an ageless, boundless intellect. The heartbeat of the universe pulsed with malignance.

The clock stopped. Ticked forward, back, sideways. Tocked in directions unknowable to human minds. The compass slewed, the floor shifted underfoot. The air tasted of diamonds and daffodils, gangrene and starlight. Somewhere, a thousand eons ago, a glass shattered.

Eidolons were intelligent manifestations of the malevolent universe. Milkweed's warlocks had successfully caught the attention of one.

Pendennis pointed at Will. The others fell silent while Will took up the line of Enochian laboriously transcribed during a long, contentious afternoon. Will had been present when the Eidolons first noticed Marsh, and so he was the one to express the desire to know his whereabouts.

He stammered twice, each misstep more jagged than a mouthful of broken glass. Something warm and wet ripped inside his throat. The final syllables of his declaration tasted of hot salted iron.

The Eidolon responded, a century or millisecond later, declaring a blood price for the humans' request. Pendennis,

Hargreaves, Webber, Shapley, White, and Grafton engaged the Eidolon with a round-robin chant, the call and response of supernatural negotiation. Refusal, counteroffer, refusal, counter-counteroffer, refusal.

Will saw, in the part of his mind that could still think rationally, how the experts struggled to reduce the blood price for such a simple act. Left on his own, this negotiation would have cost far more than a fingertip. What would happen when they asked for more than simple information? When they started fighting a war?

Agreement: A single blood map, but new and unknown.

Will beckoned to Stephenson. He coughed. 'It must see new blood.' To his credit, Stephenson extended his arm without hesitation or question. Will hefted his pocketknife. He said, 'It's going to look at you. Brace yourself. This won't be pleasant.'

He pricked the pad of Stephenson's thumb. A scarlet bead welled up. Will blotted it with a handkerchief, and then offered John Stephenson's blood to the Eidolon.

I couldn't understand the back-and-forth in Enochian while they negotiated a blood price. But I knew they'd come to an agreement when I felt a shift in the demon's attention.

I'd been through this enough times to know what it meant. The Eidolon had focused its attention somewhere. On someone. It was reading his blood like a map, studying the entire course of his life from birth to death. Taking him apart, scrutinizing him from deep within every atom of his being. I wondered who got stuck playing Milkweed's tethered goat, the poor bastard.

The wall flexed again. The Eidolons had acquired another

blood map. And incrementally widened their beachhead within the human scale of reality.

I banished thoughts of my son, John, and pulled the pocket-knife from my carpetbag.

'Good job, sir.' Will touched the old man's shoulder. A pale-faced Stephenson returned unsteadily to his corner.

The price had been paid. Now the Eidolon would extend its volition toward the task at hand.

Will cleared his throat, swallowed the taste of blood, and repeated his query. A pause, and then the universe within that tiny room rumbled again with the language of creation. Pendennis and Hargreaves glanced at each other in surprise.

I'd heard that sequence of alien noises frequently enough to recognize it. My name. My Enochian label.

The Eidolon sought Raybould Marsh.

The compass spun. Will readied a handful of nails, but the damnable thing wouldn't stop.

The Eidolon spoke too quickly for him to catch it all. Something about broken, something about reflection, locality, presence. Two halves.

Marsh jerked violently awake. He panicked, thinking they'd taken him for interrogation while he slept. His pulse hammered in his throat.

But he was alone. No, not alone. Something else was here. Something *other*. Something that studied him from the inside out.

He'd felt this once before. These were the first tendrils of an Eidolon's attention.

Milkweed had come to the rescue.

Marsh staggered to his feet. *God bless you, Will.*

'Here I am.'

I cut myself and extended my bleeding hand toward the Eidolon's sphere of influence.

The compass rose shattered.

It is here, said the Eidolon. *It is far away.*

The Eidolon withdrew. Marsh's prison cell snapped back to the illusion of reality. It left him reeling. Confused.

Very well. It had seen him. What now?

The Eidolon saw me.

The floor underfoot canted as though the earth had popped off its foundation. I could smell starlight and taste the cooling sizzle of a primordial universe not our own.

It repeated my name. Oh, yes. I had its complete and utter attention. I stood at the center of my own personal bubble of unreality.

I tightened the bandage on my hand, gathered the carpetbag, and walked into the corridor. I hurried past the room where Will and the others had convened. But after that, I took the long route through the busiest, most populated parts of the Admiralty.

The Eidolon's attention followed me. And, like earthly tides obeying the pull of moon and sun, the warp in reality flowed around me.

Hargreaves, Pendennis, and two of the others jumped from their seats. 'Oh, no,' said Will.

Stephenson shouted above the chaos, 'What happened?'

The Eidolon didn't retreat to the crawl spaces of the universe. It merely ... turned its attention elsewhere.

'It isn't leaving!' Will cried.

I stumbled through wood-paneled corridors, wearing the Eidolon's fascination like an albatross. Panic followed in my wake. The world rippled around my footsteps.

The Eidolon maintained its extension into the human scale of space and time, but it was no longer interested in the warlocks. The room snapped back to reality, ephemeral and quiet as a candle flame.

Until Will heard the screaming.

It followed me outside. The sentries huddled behind their sandbags, eyes clenched and knees hugged to their chests. Nobody would remember seeing me. They'd remember the fleeting touch of something *other*.

And to Stephenson's point of view, it would look like the warlocks had lost control of an Eidolon and sent it roaming about London. Their credibility had just taken a torpedo below the waterline.

I was halfway to Westminster Underground station when the Eidolon withdrew.

Marsh waited, counting heartbeats in the darkness. Nothing happened. He sank to his knees. *Come back*, he wept. *Please.*

But the Eidolon didn't return. It abandoned him, just as Gretel had, in the dungeons of the SS.

TEN

7 Sept 1940
Walworth, London, England

History continued to change throughout the summer.

My sabotage of the warlocks' first negotiation threw their abilities into doubt, but not without consequences. I knew, from Will's reports, that news of the 'disturbance' in the Admiralty building had reached the PM. The bulldog had turned round to take a bite out of Stephenson. Stephenson had taken it out on the warlocks. Furthermore, there was a general befuddlement among the warlocks themselves about how the negotiation had gone so severely wrong. I gathered they were a bit gun-shy now. All to the good.

The bad news was that Milkweed still intended to use the warlocks, and planned to isolate them lest another Eidolon got loose. Several Admiralty staffers had been driven mad by the roaming demon; one marine sentry had shot himself. So construction had begun on a new structure that bordered the Old Admiralty, Horse Guards Parade, and St. James' Park. Right where I'd clocked Will, in fact. The public believed the Admiralty Citadel to be a bunker for government functionaries, particularly in the event of invasion. Doubtless it would be used for that. Primarily, however, it would house the warlocks during negotiations. An unwelcome complication, from my point of view.

No amount of reinforced concrete could bar the Eidolons, should they choose to go roaming again. But Churchill had demanded changes, and so changes were made.

All through the summer, the Royal Air Force gave the Jerries hell while barrage balloons sprouted like toadstools. In mid-August, the Luftwaffe started attacking RAF airfields. There were places in the south where picnickers could watch the aerial ballet of Hurricanes and Junkers, Spitfires and Messerschmitts; a hot hail of spent casings rained upon flower shows and tennis courts. Late August and early September saw attacks on Fighter Command air bases. Both sides lost planes and pilots every day, but so far, at least, and by a slim margin, the numbers held in our favor. The Luftwaffe strategy to achieve air dominance over Britain sorely lacked precision. It lacked Gretel. And any fool could see that control of the skies was a necessary precursor to invasion. Thus far there was no need for supernatural defensive measures.

Or so I'd thought, until Whitehall issued a precautionary invasion warning on the morning of September 7. And so I was sitting in the kitchen, listening to the peal of church bells, wondering what I had missed, when the banshee wail of air-raid sirens shattered my concentration. The cacophony launched me from my seat and sent my thudding heart into my throat.

This had to be a mistake. It was the middle of the day. Liv's house was miles from the nearest RAF base. But even before my thoughts settled, I felt in my gut the *crump* of explosions to the east of us. A milk-bottle flower vase rattled on the windowsill above the sink.

Liv had stepped out to change Agnes. Now she ran into the kitchen, baby clutched to her chest. Our crying daughter's nappy dangled half unpinned. She wailed, too.

'Agnes's bag,' I said, 'is it still in the shelter?'

Liv nodded. I laid my hand on her shoulder and chivvied her out the back door, through the garden, to the Anderson shelter. Little puffs of gray smoke pimpled the eastern sky. More smoke blossomed while I watched. It looked like every ack-ack battery between London and the Thames estuary was filling the sky with flak. I couldn't see the bombers, but there was no doubting their presence. Only as we descended into the shelter did I realize my mistake. I hoped that in the confusion Liv hadn't noticed my poor choice of wording.

Heat pulsed through my palm in time with my heartbeat, the skin moist where it had touched hers. But Liv didn't flinch away from my touch. I yanked my hand away from her shoulder. Hard enough to rap my knuckles on the Anderson's steel arch. Hoped she didn't notice that as well.

She's not your wife, I reminded myself. *She belongs to somebody else.*

I slammed the door behind us. The summer heat hadn't yet broken; the stifling Anderson reeked of mildew. Liv stood in the darkness, consoling our child, while I scooped up the oil lamp from the nail by the door. In moments I had a bit of light going. Liv had taken to growing courgettes in the layer of earth atop the Anderson, so now the soil and plants overhead muffled the sirens, but the rumble of distant explosions drew steadily closer.

Somebody else who may never return.

Liv laid Agnes on the cot and fixed her nappy. Then she sat, facing me, humming and dandling the baby on her lap. The cot hung low over the damp earthen floor. The hem of her dress rode up, revealing smooth calves, lustrous in the dim lamplight.

The heat in my hand washed through the rest of my body. Breath hitched in my chest like cockleburs in a wool sweater. I turned away to coax more light from the lamp. In spite of the mildew and faint odor of the lamp oil, all I could smell was Liv. I couldn't get away from it. Her scent surrounded me. Infused me. The smell of her hair, her glowing skin.

I checked the door. Made certain it was solid, that it wouldn't blow in under the blast from a nearby hit. Next I counted the candles. Checked the charcoal filters in the gas masks. Anything to take my mind from the forced proximity to Liv.

She watched me fidget, one eyebrow cocked. Faint amusement tugged at her lips. She waited until I'd run out of halfway plausible things to keep me occupied. She caught my eye. Her hand slid down to pat the empty patch of canvas on the cot beside her.

'Do sit, Commander. We could be here a good while if Hitler's got his dander up today. It wouldn't do for you to stand at attention throughout.' Had she noticed the tightness in my trousers? I prayed to God, if there was one, that she hadn't.

'I'm not sure there's room,' I managed.

'It's perfectly safe,' she said. 'I promise you'll not get drummed out for being PWP.'

PWP. Pregnant Without Permission. Liv had been in the WAAF. Up with a lark and to bed with a Wren, as the saying went ...

I wondered if she'd always teased other men like this when I had been her young husband. But I wanted her to do more than tease me. Oh, yes.

I sat, gently. My clothes stuck to my skin in the close air of the shelter. The heat left me delirious. Sitting on the low cot roused the ache in my bad knee.

Liv sang quietly to our baby. Agnes's eyes slid closed when she drowsed off, but opened again when the thunder of the bombing raid shook the ground beneath our feet. A reverberating crash left the Anderson ringing.

We sat in the half light, sweat trickling down our skin, while Jerry rained bombs on London. The explosions drew closer, sweeping across the East End until they were all around us.

When Liv inhaled, her weight shifted just enough to brush my knee with hers. The slight pressure pushed all thought from my head and filled the void with a crushing awareness of her. I silently wished her to hold each breath, just to prolong the contact for a few seconds. Just once. Just for me.

She's not yours, I told myself.

We might have been killed at any moment. But the bombing raid was the furthest thing from my mind. The effort to ignore Liv left me trembling.

'Are you frightened, Commander?'

I swallowed. 'Yes.' But not of the Germans, not of the Luftwaffe. Not at that moment. No, I was afraid of myself. Afraid of what I wanted.

I wanted my younger self never to return. I wanted him to leave Liv a widow.

Wanted to scoop her up. Wanted to lay her down.

Would Gretel grant me that boon? Would she destroy him, that I could live? I could take up his life so easily.

Airily, Liv said, 'You have something on my husband, then.' I flinched. Liv must have noticed, but she made no point of it. 'Raybould would never admit to being frightened by a few Jerry airplanes.'

'He's a fool.' Maybe I'd have a reprieve if I got under her skin. Drew out that sharp tongue. But Liv was having none of it. Instead she fell silent for a moment. I could feel her eyes on me, studying the wreckage of my face.

'It was queer, what you said earlier.'

'Hmmm.'

'"Is it still in the shelter," you said.'

Damn. 'Nothing strange about that. It seemed reasonable you'd have a bag prepared in the shelter.'

'I suppose,' she said. 'Odd way of phrasing it.'

Inwardly, I sighed. That was Liv. Once she got something into her teeth she wouldn't let it go. My discomfort drew her as blooded water drew a shark. Dishonesty riled her, but condescension infuriated her, and now she sensed I was guilty of one or both.

Once she decided I was hiding something she'd pick and pick again until I relented. It drove me mad. Because it didn't matter one jot whether I was being truthful; once she got it into her head that I wasn't, nothing could convince her otherwise. More than a few fights had started this way.

'Don't you agree?' she prodded. She shifted Agnes in her arms. Now Liv's knee rested against mine. Physical contact stoked the fire inside me; searing desire torched a hole through my ability to think clearly. The tightness in my trousers became a pinch.

'Why—' I caught myself. Dared to look at her.

Auburn hair shining with lamplight. *Not yours.* Sweet breath. *She's not yours.* Freckles on milk-pale skin. *You're not her husband.* Breasts . . .

I wasn't strong or brave or honorable enough to stand and distance myself from her. Instead I leaned, just enough to break the contact. A fraction of an inch, but room enough to think. My inclination was to rise to Liv's bait. Defend myself. Become defensive. But I didn't dare act naturally. What would Raybould Marsh never do?

'You're right, Olivia. I apologize. I waited here in the Anderson before speaking to your husband.'

She narrowed her eyes. 'I knew it.'

'I truly am sorry.'

The cacophony of battle swallowed Liv's response. The drone of bombers, the *chuff-chuff-chuff* of antiaircraft guns, the ceaseless crash and rumble of detonations. Agnes began to cry. Another nearby hit shook the earth and nearly tossed Liv to the floor. I caught her.

We held each other while the Luftwaffe did its best to destroy London.

7 September 1940
Berlin, Germany

Marsh's captors finally came for him a month and a half after the Eidolonic visitation. He'd tried to convince himself that it had been a nightmare. Why would Milkweed locate him, then leave him to rot? It didn't make sense. If they didn't intend to set him free, Stephenson's only alternative would have been to silence him. But that hadn't happened either, though Marsh had prayed for it.

At first he thought the scrape and rattle of a key in the lock was also an echo from some deep corner of his imagination. But then light flooded into his cell, painful as railroad spikes to the eyes. Strong arms hauled him to his feet, but Marsh could stand on his own. They'd fed him regularly. Marsh reckoned that was Gretel's doing.

A hard shove sent him stumbling into the corridor. The light here was even worse, painful even through his eyelids. He lowered his head. Long, greasy strands of hair fell over his eyes, helped to shield them from the glare.

'Shit, he reeks,' somebody said. 'How long has he been down here?'

'A few months.'

Marsh couldn't smell anything. He'd become inured to the smell of the privy bucket.

'We can't put him in front of the Reichsführer like this. He won't tolerate it.'

'He won't care. He's seen worse.'

'He hasn't smelled worse. Not in his own office.'

Marsh swallowed. They were taking him to Himmler. This had to be why Gretel sent him here. She wanted Marsh to be in Himmler's presence on this day. Why? What was he supposed to do? Why didn't she tell him? And what would happen if he got it wrong?

'Well, let's hose him down. Quickly.'

They pushed him along the corridor into a room that echoed, as though it were a large empty space with walls of brick or concrete. Stripped him. Sprayed him with frigid water, hard enough to leave welts. It pounded at every aching part of his body, all the bruises caused by sleeping and exercising on bare concrete. The chill penetrated to the marrow in his bones. His breath came in gasps.

Marsh had rolled into a ball on the floor before they finished. He clutched his knees, teeth chattering.

By the time the guards had wrestled him into clothes that

weren't crusted with grime, his eyes had remembered how to filter out the worst of the light. He could crack them open without overwhelming pain. His first glimpse of SS Haus showed nothing but a slotted drain in the center of a slick gray concrete floor. Water trickled through the stubble of his beard, dripped to his feet. The too-small shoes pressed painfully against his overgrown toenails.

They pulled his arms behind him and cuffed them at the wrists. From the shower they led him through a series of doors in what appeared to have been a laundry at one time but which was now filled with filing cabinets. Marsh also spied a cavernous room carved into the bedrock beneath the hotel. It had the look of a wine cellar, though this, too, was filled with row upon row of shelves and files. Somewhere nearby resided the Schutzstaffel operational records of the REGP. Marsh staved off dispiriting thoughts of needles and haystacks by concentrating on his mission. Gretel had put him in place to do this, and now it was up to him to seize the opportunity when it arose. If Himmler didn't have him executed.

The Reichsführer's office resided on the top floor, three stories above Prinz-Albrecht-Strasse. It was, in every way, the diametrical opposite of von Westarp's nest at the farm. Where the doctor's inner sanctum embodied chaotic disorder, the Reichsführer-SS kept his office clean, precise, orderly. The stacks of paper on his desk were clearly kept to a minimum, and their arrangement reminded Marsh of soldiers at parade inspection: not a single corner out of true, all aligned with the straight edges of the desk. On the walls hung photographs of Himmler with the Führer; Himmler inspecting Waffen-SS troops; Himmler at a rally, a little girl in blond braids on his lap. The girl must have been his daughter, Gudrun.

Sunlight glinted from the wings of a glazed porcelain eagle on Himmler's desk. Several more pieces of Allach porcelain adorned the shelves. Each was pure white, like the eagle, and decorated with a different arrangement of swords, swastikas, eagles, and wreaths. Some were stamped JULFEST 1937, JULFEST 1938, JULFEST 1939. The most colorful object in the room was a gilt and painted porcelain figurine depicting Frederick the Great on horseback.

Himmler himself sat with hands rested flat on the desk, framing a pair of folders laid before him. The trimmed and manicured nails on his soft, pink hands came off distinctly feminine. He had a round, puffy face which, coupled with one of the weakest chins Marsh had ever seen, gave him a neotenic appearance. Like von Westarp, he wore wire-rimmed spectacles with round frames, though the lenses in Himmler's pince-nez were thinner than the doctor's. Himmler's blue-gray eyes reminded Marsh of Reinhardt, but while the salamander's gaze shone with fanaticism, the Reichsführer's unemotional stare might have been at home on the face of a banker or actuary.

Himmler dismissed the guards. They left Marsh standing in the center of the office, hands still cuffed behind him. The leader of the Schutzstaffel hardly moved while Marsh was brought before him. Only when the two men were alone did he show any sign of being something other than a wax figure.

He opened the folders side by side. Marsh glimpsed the word REICHSBEHÖRDE on one; AHNENERBE, WILIGUT, and IRMINEN-SCHAFT on the other.

'Tell me about the warlocks,' said Himmler. 'Tell me about their magic.'

Marsh kept his eyes downcast. It gave him the posture of an obedient prisoner. It also enabled him to read the filing numbers stamped on the folders.

12 October 1940
Walworth, London, England

A month of bombing rendered Marsh's neighborhood unrecognizable. The Germans had attacked London every night for a month straight with no sign of stopping; they'd sent bombers during daylight, too, for most of September. That had begun with a particularly heavy pounding of the East End. It was as though a band of fairy-tale goblins stole into the city each night, but rather than pinching children from their beds and replacing them with changelings, they swapped entire buildings for heaping piles of shattered brick, broken timber, shards of glass and heirloom china.

Will made it a point to check on Liv regularly. She refused to leave the city. She wouldn't put words to it, but he knew she was waiting for her missing husband to return. Foolish girl. He'd have nothing to return to if the Anderson shelter in the garden took a direct hit.

In fact—

The taxi slid to a halt. Ice congealed at the bottom of Will's stomach when he looked through the windscreen. A new rubble pile, still smoking in places, had slumped into the roadway. Just a few streets from Liv's house. One of Jerry's bombs had cratered a terraced house, obliterating the center and leaving the homes on either side open to the elements. Will glimpsed a Wren uniform still hanging in a wardrobe. It fluttered in the breeze. Wreckage of the pulverized unit had run into the street like a landslide, tearing down everything along the way except for a bright red postbox sticking up straight and proud from the debris. The top of the rubble was heaped higher than the top of Will's taxi. A quartet of rescue men clambered over the pile, carrying a stretcher. Will looked away.

His visits to Walworth had become a study in anxiety. Liv's luck wouldn't last forever. Nobody's would, if the bombing didn't let up soon. He didn't much care if the Kensington flat took a hit. But if something were to happen to Liv or Agnes while Marsh was away …

Traffic inched past the obstruction under the direction of a man in denim overalls far too large for him and a forage cap far too small for him. His armlet was printed with the letters L.D.V. though the Local Defense Volunteers had months ago become the Home Guard, on Churchill's suggestion.

Will could smell gas. Not uncommon these days. But the rescue men were about in force, and the Home Guard were letting traffic through, so the leak must've been plugged.

The driver cleared the obstruction and accelerated again. Will's mouth went dry, as it always did when they rounded the corner. But the house came into view looking apparently none the worse for the previous night's bombing. He released a pent-up breath.

His voice cracked when he said, 'Hi, hi, driver, you can let me here, thanks.'

Will tossed the man a five-pound note. The taxi driver blinked twice. He opened his mouth to object, but Will was already on the pavement.

'Wait here a bit, won't you? There's a good fellow.'

The driver shrugged. He maneuvered the car aside so that it didn't block the road, then killed the engine. He pulled the brim of his flatcap across his eyes, crossed his arms, and dropped his head until the second of his chins brushed his chest.

Will walked the rest of the way, struggling to conquer the cold hollow in his gut. It seemed concern for Liv's well-being had taken months off his life. He'd found a gray hair in the mirror yesterday.

He rehearsed his arguments, vowing to convince her to put her stubbornness aside and get out of the city while she could. She could be mulish as her husband at times. Will supposed that made them a good match, although he'd always thought Liv to be more sensible than that.

Things didn't look as if Marsh were likely to return any time soon. Not that he'd mention that.

It is here. It is far away.

Almost three months on, and the warlocks still hadn't deciphered what the Eidolon had said about Marsh before it decided to go on a stroll and terrorize half of Westminster.

Nobody understood how *that* had happened, either.

Musical laughter came from inside the house. Liv had company. Will was glad for that. Things had been difficult for Liv since her husband had up and disappeared someplace even the Eidolons couldn't articulate.

He knocked. She opened the door, still talking over her shoulder to somebody in the den. Her eyes widened, along with her grin, when she saw him. 'Will! Hello!'

He doffed his bowler. 'And hello to you, my dear. Thought I'd drop in, be certain that you and the little one are none the worse for last night's festivities.'

Liv's expression clouded over. 'Dreadful thing. Let's not dwell on it.' She ushered him inside, closed the door, and brightened. 'But I'm glad you're here, Will. I'd like to introduce you to a friend.'

Will followed her into the den, where he stopped in his tracks, and found himself speechless. For sitting in the den, rocking Agnes's bassinet, was none other than Lieutenant-Commander Liddell-Stewart. Will couldn't have been more shocked had she been playing hostess to Mussolini and Hitler.

An awkward silence pervaded the room, pregnant as a doe rabbit in June. They blinked at each other. Liv jumped in, smoothing over the unease she interpreted as Will's reaction to the commander's scars.

'I'd hoped for a chance to introduce you. I think you'll get on famously,' she said. 'Commander, this is my dear friend Lord William Beauclerk. Will, this is Commander Jonathan Liddell-Stewart.'

Liddell-Stewart stood. 'Lieutenant-commander,' he mumbled in his broken voice.

Will tried to recover as best he could. He crossed the room, stuck out his hand. 'A pleasure,' he said.

'Likewise,' said the commander. A stiff and cordial handshake. 'Olivia speaks highly of you. Lord William.'

'Just Will, if you prefer.'

'I wouldn't presume to be so familiar.'

The commander was rigid. Uncomfortable. As well he ought. Just what the devil was he doing here?

'I hope I wasn't interrupting anything important.'

Liv said, 'Heavens, no. The commander had kindly offered to mend the kitchen sink, but when you knocked I was just explaining that I'm saving that for Raybould. It's one of the first things I'll have him do when he returns. Even if I have to chain him in the kitchen until it's done. He'll spend hours in that garden of his, but ask him to mend a leaky faucet and you'd think I asked him to wrestle down the moon. But you don't care to hear about that.' She motioned Will to sit, pointed at the tea service. 'Cup?'

Will declined. 'I won't be long.'

The commander said, 'Indeed? Then what brings you by, Lord William?'

'Oh, I like to check on our Olivia and little Agnes from time to time. Especially now that the Luftwaffe has taken to visiting so regularly,' said Will. He again turned to Liv. 'I had a bit of a scare in the taxi just now. Did you know there was a hit just a few streets over?'

Liv nodded, sadly. 'We felt it in the shelter.'

We? Now *that* was interesting. At least the commander had the grace to look embarrassed.

'Perhaps,' Will said, 'you should consider what I said about visiting your aunt.'

The commander sat ramrod straight, fast enough to slop tea over the lip of his cup. 'No!'

Will and Liv both turned to stare at him. He wiped his hand on his trousers, rasping, 'I think that's a bad idea.'

Liv explained, gently, 'The commander thinks we're better off in London.'

Ah. So that's it. That's why Liv hasn't seen fit to leave the city for a while. Liv's obstinacy isn't the issue. It's the commander. But why?

'Does he, now?' Will pointed to the window. 'Excuse me, but have you seen it out there?'

But the commander's attention had fallen on sleeping Agnes. He laid his hand on the bassinet again, slowly rocking it forward and back. 'Williton isn't safe,' he said.

'Really? Is there a second bombing campaign we've not heard about? Because unless that's the case, I think you're talking nonsense.'

The commander said, 'Olivia and Agnes mustn't leave London.'

'Her husband would want her to leave,' said Will.

'Since when does she do everything her husband wants?'

'I happen to know,' Will said, 'from several conversations with him, that he's always felt she should leave the city if and when the Jerries started bombing. Which, if you haven't been paying attention, they have.'

'She isn't—'

'*She* would like to say something!' Liv looked back and forth between Will and the commander. 'It's my decision. I'll evacuate if absolutely necessary. But I'm not having Raybould come home to an empty house if I can avoid it.' She looked down, and just for a moment her resolve faltered. Liv bit away the trembling of her lower lip, though not before Will and the commander both saw it. 'He's been gone long enough. I want to know the moment he's back.'

She collected the tea service, the commander's cup, and herself. 'I can see I was wrong about the both of you. You're getting on like a pair of caged badgers. I hope you get it worked through by the time I return or I'm putting you both out on the street. Especially if you upset Agnes.'

She went to the kitchen. Will rounded on the commander. His whisper came out like a hiss.

'What on earth have you done? You've poisoned her against all reason.'

The commander started to rise from his chair. But, with visible effort, he stopped himself. He looked to Agnes. His own whisper was like the grinding of rocks. 'I'm trying to help her. Help them both.'

'Then for God's sake, man, tell her to leave!'

'Why must you be so pigheaded?'

'Are you completely mad?' Will said. 'They're safer outside London.'

'You don't know that!' said the commander. His attempted whisper had become a low rumble; Will had got under his skin.

'You're guessing! You don't know what may come.' He paused, shaking his head. 'Nobody does.'

His gaze went inward. Very far away. 'You don't understand,' he said.

Will started to respond, but just then the commander did something quite unexpected.

He cracked his knuckles against his jaw.

I caught my mistake a half second too late. I pulled my hand away from my face, but Will had already seen it. My tick, the thing I did unconsciously when I was agitated, or deep in thought. As at that moment, when I was both.

Will had known me for years. He'd seen me do this – seen his friend Pip do this – a hundred times.

His eyes went so wide it seemed there was nothing left to keep them in. I saw the wheels turning. Yes. He knew.

Our eyes met.

His mouth fell open, but no sound came out. I must have looked much the same. Liv returned before I could corral my scattered thoughts.

She said, 'Well. You're not biting each other, so I gather it's safe to return.'

I stood. Shakily. 'Indeed. It's been a pleasure, but I must be off.'

Will leapt to his feet. It knocked his bowler to the floor. It rolled along the brim, came to a rest behind the bassinet. 'I'll share a taxi with you.'

'I wouldn't dream of it.'

Liv asked, 'Commander, will I see you tomorrow?'

From the corner of my eye, I saw Will watching me with Liv. Now his eyes narrowed.

'I . . . can't say. I don't know. Thank you for the tea. Good day.'

I was out the door before Will had gathered his hat. Behind me, I heard Liv say, 'Are you certain you must go? You've only just arrived.'

'I'm afraid I must,' he said. I didn't hear the rest because I was already on the pavement, heading for a taxi parked up the street. Behind me, Will bid Liv good afternoon. I picked up my pace. Practically hurled myself into the taxi. It woke the driver, who had been snoring.

'Bermondsey,' I said.

The driver craned around to look at me. 'Can't, mate. Already waiting on a fare.'

'He changed his mind.'

'No, there he is. See? Just coming along now.'

Will's shoes crunched along the pavement, louder with each step. I fished in my pocket, tossed a few coins to the driver. Don't know how much. 'Just drive, man!'

He collected the cash. Added it together. 'The other bloke paid me a flimsy just to wait.'

My fingers felt around for more coins, but by then it was too late. Will opened the suicide door and settled in beside me, just as calmly as though we hadn't been on the hairy edge of a footrace moments earlier.

'Ah, there's a good chap,' he said to the driver. 'Thank you for waiting. Take us to Kensington, if you please.' He recited his address.

I considered jumping out. But I knew it would have been a pointless and foolish gesture.

The taxi pulled onto the street. Will relaxed into his seat. He looked at me. I mean, really looked at me. But I didn't look at him. I couldn't bear it.

'It seems an odd thing to say,' he said, with a quick glance out the rear window to Liv's house, receding in the distance, 'but I suspect you're quite a long way from home.' His attention snapped back to me, and it had an intensity I hadn't often seen in Will. Not in the early days.

'Aren't you, Pip?'

INTERLUDE: GRETEL

The fog does not dissipate. How curious.

It exists in every future, like a pearlescent shroud; every sequence of choices leads to the impenetrable primordial chaos. The birth cries of the new time line and its universe have yet to wreak a coalescence of discrete future possibilities. This is not the enraged oblivion of the Eidolons. Of that she is certain. It is the dull homogeneity of a trillion indistinct maybes.

Sometimes, late at night, if she strains her Willenskräfte in a way not done since those first feverish glimpses of the future, she perceives movement in the fog. She lies awake at night, watching it swirl, watching it engulf the distant threads of gossamer possibility. She drains whole batteries this way.

It is *not* moving closer. She is *not* worried.

She wants to see the entire web again. Wants to watch it glisten and sparkle, infinite in all directions. But the fog is opaque. She wants to watch the glorious coruscations as the future reconfigures itself. Wants to make it dance to the music of her whimsy. It does, but only as far as the fog. The fog does not succumb to her Willenskräfte.

She examines it merely to sate her own curiosity. She is *not* revisiting Raybould's return from Berlin. She is *not* wondering what has taken so long. She is not wondering when they will be together again. He will be back soon. Of course he will. Because she planned it so.

The warlocks try to find him. She recognizes their work because the Eidolons' attention makes the lines of future possibility thrum like electrified violin strings. They vibrate and bifurcate and tangle and thrum with the terrible music of uncreation until the entire tapestry threatens to shred into disparate pockets of unreality and she is cast into the void screaming screaming screaming into the between place outside the time lines where dark things lurk and they see her ohGodtheyseeher—

She must prepare for Raybould's return to the farm.

He will return in ~~six days four months~~ two weeks. She will bring him ~~lunch in the flower field breakfast at~~ dinner in the forest. He will be ~~furious violently enraged~~ angry at her for sending him to Berlin. He will call her ~~a bloody miserable bitch a bloody miserable bitch~~ a bloody miserable bitch. He will be ravenous and she will take care of him. They will ~~picnic among the butterflies~~ huddle in the dark. She will bring him a coat because he is cold. He will ~~be grateful and lay her down among the wildflowers~~ shiver in the snow and ask about Olivia.

Olivia, freckled tart.

Olivia, who laughs like an overpriced courtesan.

Olivia is the most upsetting problem of all. But dealing with her is straightforward. That particular course is well charted.

Olivia will not be a problem forever.

ELEVEN

12 October 1940
Kensington, London, England

Though he didn't partake of it himself, Will had often found it worthwhile to keep a bottle on hand at the Kensington flat. The sherry proved useful when visitors dropped in. Such as his brother, or a time traveler.

Marsh had drained a glass and had started on another, sinking deeper into the green baize armchair with each sip. Will let him take his time. His own thoughts were twisted about like myriad strands in a ball of twine and he couldn't untangle them. He'd always been rubbish with knots.

This aged man sitting before him. This scarred, battered, and aged man sitting before him. It was Marsh. And yet, it wasn't. Clearly it wasn't.

Finally, Marsh spoke, mostly to himself: 'Damn.'

'I don't even know where to begin with my questions.'

'Let me start, then. Yes. I am Raybould Phillip Marsh. Whom you call Pip.'

'But ... you're clearly not the Marsh that *I* know. You're not the fellow I met at Oxford.'

'Oh, I am. But that was much longer ago for me.'

Will's speculations had been inching in this direction. But to hear it confirmed so straightforwardly ... It was too abrupt. He had to come at it sideways, from the edges, lest it send him reeling. Well, it did that anyway.

The tension lay so heavy it threatened to suffocate them both. Something had to be done about that; this promised to be a long conversation.

'I see,' said Will. He made a show of looking Marsh over. 'Did you come back a hundred years?'

Marsh scowled. But Will allowed himself a little laugh, just to test the ice, and the scowl faltered. Became laughter of a sort. Sharp, gulping laughter, just this side of weeping. Will let him have his space. Marsh regained himself, and when he did, his grimace touched the corners of haunted weary eyes. And thus the ice was broken.

Marsh said, 'Feels like it some days.' He shook his head. 'Twenty-three. I departed from the summer of nineteen sixty-three.'

'You used the Eidolons, I presume.'

'Yes.'

'Who sent you back?'

'You did.'

Will started. To think he'd still be speaking Enochian decades from now. Would he be conducting negotiations for many years to come? *What a horrifying thought.* 'That's a surprise. Am I ... well? In the future?'

Marsh gave a little nod. (Tinged with sadness, or was that Will's imagination?) 'Happily married.'

'Pull the other one.'

'Things were good for you in sixty-three,' said Marsh. It looked like he was about to add something, but stopped.

'Quite an extreme measure, sending you back.' Will paused, afraid to say it. 'We lost the war.'

'No. We won. In large part owing to you and the other warlocks. But it was bloody expensive, and the victory changed everything. Changed the way Britain fought wars, changed the way it defended itself.'

'Why, then? I can't imagine what forced you to this.'

'Your one unbreakable rule. We broke it ... I broke it. I've seen what happens when the Eidolons extract their own blood prices. You're right to say you can't imagine it. The end of the world,' said Marsh.

He drained his glass. His hand shook. He turned inward again, gazing at some atrocity that only he could see. Will turned away, to give Marsh a bit of privacy while he contemplated private horrors.

He said, 'You know, I'm tempted to join you in that. Normally I wouldn't, of course. But perhaps an allowance can be made, just this once.' He rose to fetch a glass for himself.

'Don't!'

Will paused, halfway to the sideboard. The tone of Marsh's voice prickled his scalp. Beneath the ruined croak, there was a hint of desperation. Warning.

'You shouldn't,' he said. 'You have ... I mean, he had ...' Marsh sighed. Collected his thoughts. Nodded toward the bottle. 'The Will I knew had problems.'

'Oh dear.' Will sat. 'Well, then. Perhaps you should start at the beginning.'

Commander Liddell-Stewart melted away while Marsh told his tale. With the help of a generous amount of sherry, the stiff, abrasive mannerisms became the maudlin storytelling of an old university chum. The burden of being somebody else had been lifted from Marsh's shoulders. With no small amount of relief, evidently. By the time he concluded his long, incredible exegesis of future history, he'd become Marsh again. Older, sadder, and lonelier, but still the same man.

'For what it's worth,' Marsh said, 'you were right, and I should have listened. I'm sorry I didn't. And I'm sorry I hit you in the park.'

No. Perhaps not quite the same man after all.

Will sensed that Marsh had skipped or simplified great swaths of his story. In places, his storytelling became vague, and they stood out because he told the rest of his story with such passion. But mostly Will suspected he was omitting details because his own name barely entered the story until the end. What was Marsh not telling him? He'd have to get the full story someday.

'Why the charade, Pip? You know you could have come to me in confidence.'

Marsh laughed. A looser, more relaxed laughter than earlier. The alcohol had done its job. 'I mean no offense by this, honestly, but telling you a secret is a bit like printing it in *The Times*.'

'I'm not that bad.'

'I was there at the police station. I heard you hinting around about Milkweed.'

Will wished he could deny it. But this was the truth. 'I suppose that's fair. But if not me, why not tell your younger self?'

Marsh leveled a flat gaze at him. 'You know me. You know him. How would we handle something like that?'

Will thought aloud. 'I suppose you'd suspect it for a Jerry trick.' He chuckled. 'Yes, I can see it now. First you'd fly into a rage. Then you'd attack yourself. And then, after you'd beaten each other silly, you'd have yourself arrested.' He paused to wipe his eyes. 'I'd like to see which one of you would win that fight.'

'Let's hope it doesn't come to that.' Marsh frowned. 'I didn't expect it to take this long. Not with Gretel helping him.'

'We tried to find him, using the Eidolons. But—' Will's eyes grew wide. 'That was you, wasn't it?'

'Ah. Look. About that—'

'I knew it!'

'Listen. If Stephenson had learned that my younger self was in Germany, he'd have no choice but to blame it either on abduction or defection. He'd see both as a grave threat to Milkweed. I know him. He'd have ordered the warlocks to find a way to silence my counterpart.'

'I can't believe he'd do that to you.'

'He's a hard man, Will. But this is beside the point. Didn't matter what you fellows were doing. I had to sabotage that negotiation to undermine Whitehall's faith in the warlocks. They must never become an instrument of foreign policy.'

'It's hard to argue with your point about the warlocks,' said Will, 'given what you've told me about the future.' He stood, stretched his legs, and crossed to the sideboard. His shirt stuck to his back; the tale of Marsh's plight had him sweating. Pouring himself a tonic water, he continued, 'But I can't help but notice that I'm still drawing breath. As are the others, or so they were until quite recently. And that seems out of character for you.' He swished the water in his mouth, swallowed. 'If the warlocks are such a threat, there's a very simple way to counter it. So I can't help but wonder why we haven't expired yet.'

A truck rumbled down the street with a detachment of Home

Guard volunteers. It backfired, loud enough to rattle the china in Will's kitchen. Marsh waited until it had receded into the distance.

He said, 'Unless and until the younger me has completed his task on the Continent, I don't dare do anything permanent to the warlocks.'

'You're trying to have it both ways. Saving the world, but only on your terms.' Will took another swallow. 'It's good to know you're the same old Pip. Stubborn as always.'

'What would you do in my situation?'

'I'm not saying I disapprove.'

'Good. Because I need your help.'

Will set the empty glass down, then held up his hands. 'We still have quite a lot to talk about. But I, for one, am famished. When is the last time you had a real meal?'

Marsh shrugged. 'I'm not sure.' He looked away. 'Not so long. Sometimes Liv invites me . . .'

It was hard to tell if the man could still blush, under the beard and scars.

'I thought so,' said Will. 'At some point we'll have to talk about Liv, as well. But later. Because right now I'm buying you dinner. I happen to know a fine little place that serves—'

'Circus animals. I remember the joke, Will.'

'Your younger counterpart found it amusing.'

'I know. I was there.' Marsh tossed back the last traces of his sherry, then set the empty glass on a side table. He gritted his teeth and winced as he rose to his feet, but waved off the hand Will offered.

'Just my knee. My advice? Don't get old.'

'It must beat the alternative.'

*

13 November 1940
Berlin, Germany

Himmler questioned Marsh three more times in the months after his first encounter with the Reichsführer-SS. The head of the Schutzstaffel liked things neat and orderly, and he did not care for offensive odors, so Marsh was cleaned and groomed before each session. Marsh kept his eyes downcast while being questioned, as expected of any obedient prisoner. He memorized a dozen filing numbers.

Himmler had read the report from Gretel's debriefing after her escape from Milkweed custody, and so, to a certain extent, Marsh had to play it straight. Himmler's eyes shone at the thought of eldritch powers and dark summonings. He wanted to see an Eidolon, yearned to witness its power. But Marsh didn't know how the warlocks had come by their lexicons, nor could he speak a single word of Enochian. There was little to say about the warlocks that Himmler didn't already know or suspect based on Gretel's report.

The internal mechanics of Milkweed were another matter. Marsh lied to the best of his ability when Milkweed became the topic of interest.

Back in his lightless cell, when he wasn't mentally reciting the filing numbers and wondering if he'd ever have a chance to make use of them, he spent his days exercising, dreaming about his wife and daughter, and waiting for torture that never came. Even after Himmler had grown impatient, then angry, then enraged with Marsh's inability to lay out the secret to summoning an Eidolon.

Still, the physical coercion never materialized. They even gave Marsh a cot. Gretel's handiwork, no doubt.

Marsh started his third round of sit-ups of what he guessed

was evening. The cold stone floor ground against his spine, almost hard enough to knap chips from his vertebrae. His shirt was cold and slick against his back, dampened by sweat and caked with grime from between the floor stones. The cot's taut canvas cut into his toes where he'd wedged them for stability. His stomach muscles burned. Sweat salt stung his eyes.

Thirty-one. Left elbow to right knee. Thirty-two. Right elbow to left knee. He'd long ago stopped noticing the odors of his cell, but now his sweat smelled impossibly of hyacinths and mashed garden slugs.

The floor shifted on rep thirty-three. Marsh stopped, panting. It shifted again.

Somewhere in the darkness, somewhen, a vast presence oozed through fissures in reality. Marsh sensed the walls of his cell flexing, genuflecting before the Eidolon.

The demon enveloped him.

'He may be in Berlin,' said Will through clenched teeth. 'Someplace small. A cell, I think.'

'Damn.'

I had to think fast, before Will lost the Eidolon. It had taken him almost a month of surreptitious preparation before we could make this attempt.

I paced through the shards of a broken compass. A syringe of blood lay atop the map of Europe spread on the floor of my warehouse. When Pendennis's minders went to rouse him in the morning, they'd find the old codger had died in his sleep. I just hoped they didn't find the puncture mark. I'd chosen Pendennis because I knew he was likely to kick as soon as things got heavy. He'd died of a heart attack in the original history.

The Eidolon's malice swirled around me like a cold draft from the Thames. Somewhere in Germany my younger counterpart was feeling something similar, because to the Eidolons we were two aspects of the same blood map.

'Two things,' I said. 'Tell it to let him out. Then it must stay with him. Surround him.'

'One or the other,' Will managed. 'Our secret negotiation bought us a single action. No more.'

Damn. If the Eidolon let him out of his cell, but then disappeared, my doppelgänger had no chance of leaving Berlin without the distracting shroud of the Eidolon's presence. But if it stayed with him in the cell, would it warp things enough for him to escape? It depended on so many things we didn't know, not least of which his physical state.

How bad was he? Could he move? Was he shackled? Broken? 'Pip—'

'All right! Tell it to focus on him. Stay with him for' – I thought about my experience swanning through the Admiralty building with an Eidolon in tow, and did some quick arithmetic – 'seven thousand heartbeats.' I reckoned that was more than an hour of elevated heart rate.

Will didn't seem to like it, but he couldn't spare the extra effort to argue. The only other time he'd dealt with an Eidolon by himself had cost a fingertip. From his open mouth came an impossible basso profundo rumble. The Eidolon responded with the static hiss of a moribund cosmos.

The unrelenting scrutiny of something immense and unknowable threatened to drive Marsh mad. He'd been through this once before, and so far that experience inured him to the worst of it, but back then he'd only held the Eidolon's attention for a few moments. The small part of his mind that could still function cowered from the overpowering maleficence. The Eidolon's presence became a chisel on the mortar of space and time. Reality twisted outside-in. The Eidolon swirled about him as though it were a cyclone and he the eye.

It didn't speak. It didn't act. It waited. For what?

Marsh managed to stand, though the floor continued to sway underfoot. Somewhere, rusty chains rattled in a chill wind that smelled of river water. He approached the door. The bubble of unreality moved with him.

A prison cell cordoned off a volume of space for long periods of time. In human terms, it created a pocket of here-and-now inaccessible to the rest of the universe. But that distinction was meaningless to an Eidolon.

He laid his hands upon the cold steel of the door. When seen through the prism of an Eidolon, the darkness in Marsh's cell became a blinding glow compared to the perfect dark of a lightless universe. Marsh peered through streamers of melted here-and-now, past the pigeons cooing on the Champs-Elysées, past the molten seas of a primordial planet, to the shattered spacetime where the lock mechanism had been.

Please, he thought. *Please work*.

He pushed. The door opened.

Will said, 'He's moving.'

'Thank God.'

Marsh emerged from his cell into a long corridor. He concentrated on two things: filing numbers, and not going mad. His dark-adapted eyes felt no flare of pain from the corridor lights, because when passing through his Eidolonic shroud the shining bulbs became distant starlight. The smell of chlorine burned his sinuses. A phantom chorus called to him in a dozen dead languages.

A guard shouted. Marsh looked to where an SS-Schütze, a private, stood drawing his pistol. Narrow corridor. Easy shot. Marsh didn't know what would happen to a bullet as it passed through the region of warped reality, but there was no guarantee it would protect him. He charged the guard, veering drunkenly across the swaying, uneven floor.

The private didn't shout a second warning. His arms snapped up, putting his Walther at the tip of a triangle, just as he'd been trained. Too close. No way he'd miss. The guard frowned. Marsh gritted his teeth and dived for the floor. The Eidolon's malign presence swept over the guard. His eyes went wide. Marsh bowled him down.

The soldier curled up in a ball, screaming. He clapped his hands over his ears, one still holding the pistol. Just for an instant, his flesh hissed and shifted like loose sand, then became solid again. He didn't struggle when Marsh wrenched the gun away. Marsh smashed it against his temple before the screaming summoned an entire battalion into the cellar.

He listened, but it was difficult to know what was happening outside the Eidolon's sphere of influence. Nobody came to investigate. The men down here were accustomed to screaming prisoners.

Marsh tried to lift the unconscious guard. He couldn't. The boy wasn't very large, but Marsh had lost more strength than he'd realized during the long months of his incarceration. He settled for dragging the unconscious soldier back to his cell. Once there, he stripped the guard of his uniform and piled the clothing on the cot, away from possible blood spatter, before shooting him.

He pulled the trigger. Warm, wet droplets dusted his face. Marsh's fingers came away from his upper lip glistening red.

The Eidolon unleashed an onslaught of Enochian. It redoubled its scrutiny of Marsh, turned him inside-out. He collapsed. The cell reverberated with inhuman howls, shrieks, and rumbles. All the fury in the universe was focused on the specks of a stranger's blood on Marsh's face and hand. The rest of the world disintegrated.

Marsh remembered the way Will had cut himself before summoning the Eidolon that studied Gretel, and the way he'd shown a drop of her blood to the Eidolon. He remembered how her fingernails had drawn his blood, too, and the way the Eidolon had reacted to it.

Time lost all meaning inside the Eidolon's bubble. Marsh was incapacitated while it scanned him and the blood of the man he'd killed, but when he returned to himself the sheath of unreality hadn't dissipated. He staggered to his feet under another volley of Enochian.

Blood. It wanted more blood.

The dead guard's uniform didn't fit. The boy was too small. Marsh couldn't even pull the trousers on. His hands hardly fit through the wrists of the jacket. The pockets contained a knife, a few coins, three cigarettes, and a packet of safety matches. He kept the knife, the Walther, and the matches, but abandoned everything else.

Back in the cellar, he headed toward the archives, retracing the route he'd memorized on his first summoning to Himmler's office. The Eidolon's attention kept pace with him. Ripples of impossibility followed in his wake.

He couldn't tell how long it took to reach the filing cabinets in the former laundry. A millisecond, perhaps, or a millennium.

Marsh had to dodge the ghosts of former washerwomen in order to read the labels on the cabinets. He followed the sequence of filing numbers as though it were a trail of bread crumbs. It led him to the wine cellar.

Barrel vaults had long ago been carved into the bedrock. But filing cabinets and freestanding metal shelves now occupied the spaces where wooden racks had once held countless dusty bottles of wine and port. Bare brass fixtures revealed the spots where gas lamps had lighted the hotel's early days. But the Schutzstaffel had affixed electrical cables to the ceiling, providing power for the bare light bulbs that now cast shadows through the archives.

When Will had shown Gretel to the Eidolon, the entire ordeal hadn't taken very long. But now the Eidolon's prolonged presence distorted reality in ways Marsh had never imagined. Inanimate objects hissed at him, the Eidolon's loathing made incarnate. Shadows writhed like angry tentacles in Marsh's wake.

One of the slithering shadows whipped a tendril at his ankle bone. A stab of pain shot through his bare foot. The tendril left a ring-shaped burn and the odor of burnt flesh. The shadow bulged and undulated like the silhouette of a python swallowing a rat. Marsh kept to the light.

He found an unoccupied desk. The archivist wasn't on duty. He didn't know if that meant it was later at night than he'd realized, or because the man had heard the commotion and gone to investigate. Judging from the dates on the topmost paperwork, it was mid-November. He'd lost track of the days. Felt like a century since he'd seen Liv.

She probably thinks I'm dead. Might have even come to terms with it by now. Has she moved on? She has Agnes to care for; she needs a husband.

If he let them, he knew, the fear and sorrow would cripple

him. This was his only chance to see Agnes and Liv again; he had to move quickly. There would be time for mourning later.

He forced the tears aside and concentrated on rifling through the desk. He found more cigarettes, more matches, more money, and a flask. When he unscrewed the cap, the fumes numbed his nose and made his eyes water. It smelled like the loneliness of a medieval scholar. But there was something else, too, beneath the Eidolonic distortion.

Homebrewed schnapps. Apricot? He prayed to God, if there was one, that the schnapps was genuine.

Marsh dumped out the rubbish bin. He placed all of his matches and the flask inside it, then set off again in search of the files. Another century passed while Marsh found the operational records of the REGP, and the IMV before that, and the privately funded orphanage before that. An entire niche of the former wine cellar had been dedicated to von Westarp's work. There were other records back at the farm, records of that madman's research, but the Schutzstaffel kept the only operational records close at hand.

The shelving kept the paper files packed too tightly for adequate airflow. He couldn't simply touch a match to the lot. Carelessly dumping the files on the floor wouldn't help. He had no choice but to be patient and feed the fire slowly until it built up enough heat to generate a suitable draft. He had to do it right. This was his only opportunity. How long would the Eidolon stay with him?

Marsh splashed a bit of schnapps into the rubbish bin. The fumes burned with a pale blue flame. Precious centuries ticked away while he fed the first of thousands of pages of documentation into the bin. The flames turned from blue to orange to yellow, growing above the lip of the bin as he fed the fire with doses of paper and schnapps. Soon, the niche smelled of ash and apricots.

He couldn't watch the fire. It hurt his mind. The Eidolon's proximity transformed the flames into serrated saw teeth that grated past one another while crystalline spindles whirled through the troughs.

The fire grew brighter and hotter, casting more shadows into the archives. Marsh had to keep circling the fire, practically dancing about it like a pagan loon on Midsummer's morning, lest his bare feet get melted off by acidic tendrils. Sidestepping the angriest shadows and nursing the fire kept him occupied.

He didn't hear the shot.

A thumb-tip-sized portion of the limestone arch exploded into chips that nicked Marsh's face, hands, and feet. He hit the floor. Shadows burned his feet and hands. The Eidolon repeated the mad-making gibberish that Will had once claimed was a name.

I clamped my hands over my ears. There it went with my wretched name again. *Your map is a circle. A broken spiral.*

'Why is it doing this?'

'I think he's bleeding,' said Will.

Marsh pulled the Walther, but shelves obstructed his view in every direction. He couldn't peer past the rippling interplay of light and shadow. But the angle of the shot constrained the shooter's location.

There: movement at the end of an aisle. Marsh rolled behind the rubbish bin to line up a shot. But the ruby-tipped flames had retreated to a lowly sizzle. He couldn't let the fire die. He reached up to slide an armload of files from the nearest shelf. A bullet whistled past his hand, *pinged* from a nearby strut, and lodged into a stack of reports from late 1938 detailing Kammler's efficacy against Spanish Republican mortar emplacements.

Marsh yanked back his hand, and dove. *Bloody fuck.*

No chance of charging his attacker this time. Attackers? He'd been lucky in the corridor, but that had been a straight run. Too many obstacles here. He had to be patient, work his way closer one aisle at a time, until either he had a clear shot or the Eidolon drove the Jerries mad. Assuming it lingered that long.

There had to be more than one of the bastards down here by now. If the shooting hadn't attracted them, the smoke had, and if the smoke hadn't, the constant disintegration of reality must have raised a few eyebrows. Marsh splashed more schnapps on the fire. Emerald flames leapt from the rubbish bin. He fired off a covering shot and heaved another armload of papers into the bin. Fire licked at the edges of the new pile. That would buy him a few minutes.

He crept in the direction of the last shot. Another volley of screeches and chthonic rumbles echoed through the cellar. The Eidolon had made these noises after Marsh shot the first guard. Demands for more blood.

'If you want it so badly,' said Marsh, under his breath, 'kill the bastards yourself. Or feed the fire. Anything. Just help me.' But the Eidolons weren't listening, even if they had given him a name.

More movement, in front of him, a few aisles down. And to the right ... The goose-steppers were circling around behind him. Cutting him off from the fire.

Silently cursing Liddell-Stewart, Marsh retreated.

There was no way to know how many men were in the archives now, loitering outside the range of his gun and the

Eidolon's cyclone of unreality. Probably half the bloody Reich. But they only had three avenues into the Reichsbehörde niche. The arrangement of shelves constrained his attackers as much as they constrained him. More so – they had to take care not to shoot their own men. And they feared to rush him because of the Eidolon. Did they know what was happening? *Here's your chance, Himmler.*

Marsh chose an aisle. He fired two shots into the shadows, then pressed himself behind the limestone arch. Over the whisper of star-driven winds and the chiming of a ghostly trolley, he could just make out yells in German. Return fire carved more chips from the wall. He leapt out, rolled behind the bin, then shot into a different aisle.

While jackboots shuffled in the distance, he unsheathed his stolen knife and climbed the shelves. It enabled him to reach the cable bolted to the ceiling. The bare bulbs that provided light for the archives hung at regular intervals from cables like this one. A few moments of frantic sawing were repaid by a jolt hard enough to knock him to the floor and the overwhelming taste of copper.

Now the only light in and around his section of the archive came from the fire. The very unnatural fire.

And if the Jerries were playing it safe, their scout would be approaching down the central aisle. Marsh's gunfire had, he hoped, ensured the other avenues were covered, and there wasn't room between the stacks of files to fire around a scout.

Marsh watched through a gap in the shelves as a pair of SS guards came creeping forward. Their boots clicked on the stone floor. Both held their sidearms in shaking hands. They'd entered the Eidolon's sphere of influence, where the air burned like frostbite, the shadows writhed like serpents, and the archives echoed with the death cries of ancient stars. The play of ghostly firelight made a grotesquerie of their faces.

Marsh pressed his back to the shelves and heaved. Nothing happened. He'd lost too much strength during his incarceration. He strained. A grunt escaped him. The shelves tilted.

One scout turned. 'What—'

Slowly, more slowly than the turning of the seasons, the shelving unit toppled, showering the men with crates of files. It didn't hurt them badly. But it knocked them down.

Into the writhing, snapping shadows. Tendrils slithered over the men. One soldier dropped his gun, slapped at his bare hands and face. But he couldn't fend them off. Dark tendrils sizzled against his upper lip. Greasy smoke wafted from the wound. Within moments the shadows enveloped his companion, too.

The men beat themselves bloody, trying to stave off the assault from an altered reality.

And the Eidolon pounced.

I clamped my hands over my ears for the second time that night. 'For God's sake,' I yelled, 'what is it now?'

'Something about blood maps.' Will had gone pale from the exertion. His hoarse voice called to me over the din of Enochian: 'I think it's sampling blood. New blood.'

A chill sweat percolated through my skin. I knew what that meant. My doppelgänger was in a fight. And every man he wounded or killed meant another blood map that widened the Eidolons' beachhead into our world. I'd seen firsthand what could happen if they perceived enough of it.

Marsh killed the scouts. Their screams had driven the other Jerries to retreat a safe distance outside the Eidolon's sphere of influence. It gave him time to strip the men of their weapons and, in the case of the smaller fellow, clothes.

The fire had grown. Marsh tossed another armload of files on the fire, then doused the pile with the last of the schnapps. He changed into an SS-Schütze uniform by the light of burning medical records. But the fire cast no warmth, offered no relief to his cold, emaciated flesh. The crystalline flames and their impossible shapes sucked heat from the room. Serpentine darkness snapped at the gooseflesh stippling his legs and arms.

More than half of the Reichsbehörde files had been reduced to ashes. Many of the files comprised films and photographs, too, which the fire had reduced to blackened slag. Marsh fed the fire as quickly as he dared while the Eidolon's non-wind sculpted the ashes into impossible shapes that hurt to behold. If he worked too quickly, he risked smothering the fire. But he had to finish the task before the Jerries regrouped. They wouldn't play it safe on the next assault. They'd come in force.

And so they did. Marsh threw himself behind the arch at the first sign of new movement in the shadows. A barrage of gunfire winged through the flames and chiseled new gouges in the limestone. They'd brought machine pistols.

Marsh leaned out, squeezed off two shots, ducked back. He didn't hit anything. But the maneuver did enable him to confirm his suspicions. Guards advanced on the fire along all three aisles. Each carried an MP 34 submachine gun. Together, they probably had close to ninety rounds available, just in the current magazines.

The pistol in Marsh's hand held one remaining cartridge. The other Walther held a magazine of eight.

He had to protect the fire. If he could hold on just a few more minutes, he'd have accomplished half of his mission in Germany.

Except ... it was a meaningless gesture. Burning the files was pointless without also destroying von Westarp's farm. The farm produced new records every day.

Marsh risked another shot. Deafening return fire kept him pinned behind the limestone arch. When the echoes died down, he heard urgent murmuring and the scuffle of boots. The Jerries weren't bothering to hide their intentions from him. They knew he was alone and outgunned. He dropped the empty pistol and drew the second.

Marsh's thoughts turned, as they always did, to his wife and daughter. *I'm sorry, Liv. I should have told you the truth. I hope you find a man who makes you happy. A man who'll be a good father to Agnes. I love you both.*

Please tell her good things about me.

The guards charged. The Eidolon engulfed him again. Marsh closed his eyes, firing blindly past the fire. His body peeled apart in myriad directions—

The Eidolon's howls blew out the windows. Glass tinkled to the warehouse floor. I shoved Will under my makeshift desk before the worst of the shards rained upon us. Glass crunched all around, like hailstones.

'What the hell is happening?'

'I don't know!'

—and then back again.

Marsh opened his eyes. His gaze fell upon a trio of dead SS troops arranged around the dwindling sapphire flames. Each man had taken a single bullet in the back of the head. Like the other guards Marsh had killed. But he sure as hell had never shot like that, not even under controlled conditions.

He couldn't stop shaking. His lungs burned. The Eidolon had neglected to put air in his chest when it reassembled him. Marsh's inhalation sounded like a long, shuddery gasp.

The Eidolon had protected him. It must have deduced, perhaps by virtue of the blood it had already absorbed, that bullets brought life histories to an end. Apparently it found that perfectly acceptable as long as Marsh's history wasn't the one brought up short. Marsh suspected it had come to see him as a vehicle for receiving still more blood to sample.

He pulled down another armload of Reichsbehörde files. Three matches remained. But he lost two of those to the uncontrollable shaking of his hands. He gritted his teeth and clenched the muscles in his atrophied arms, forcing himself rigid while he lit the final match. Flames licked at the corner of a report written by Standartenführer Pabst regarding the death of a test subject named Oskar. The crystalline flames resumed their impossible dance.

He took a gun and a spare magazine from the dead guards. Jerry would be hard-pressed to bring heavier armaments down here; anything much larger than a submachine gun threatened to destroy the archives they were fighting to protect. They probably had potato mashers upstairs, but explosives were right out. Likewise phosphorus smoke grenades, which had the potential to make a mockery of Marsh's feeble fire by turning the entire archive into an inferno. They might have resorted to poison gas to flush him out, but not without first evacuating SS Haus.

No. He reckoned they were waiting for him up top. There was only one way out of the archives, after all.

On another guard, he found cigarettes and enough matches to finish the job. He made short work of the remaining files. After that, Marsh straightened his uniform, checked the MP 34, and headed for the lift.

Tactically, in a world where the laws of nature hadn't been shredded, stairs would have been preferable. But he didn't know where they were, and couldn't spare the time to look. Normally, the lift would have been a quick route to the firing squad. But it didn't matter as long as the Eidolon escorted him. And if it abandoned him, he didn't stand a chance regardless of how he tried to escape.

The no-man's-land of unreality moved with him. He addressed it, under his breath. 'Stay with me. Just a bit longer. Please.'

Ice crusted the walls. Black vines sprouted from the ice, topped with wet, pulsating blossoms.

The lift still featured rosewood paneling, a vestige of the building's previous life as a luxury hotel. The doors closed; the floor pressed against the soles of Marsh's stolen boots. He leaned against the brass railing, trying but failing to control his breathing. He'd begun to tremble again. The walls of the lift pulled apart like soft caramel, a thousand leagues wide.

Ding.

The doors opened. Marsh had never seen the lobby of the former hotel because he'd had a bag over his head the previous time. But he doubted the line of gunmen was part of the usual arrangement.

He emerged from the lift. The gunmen unleashed a hail of gunfire into his Eidolonic cocoon. The bullets ceased to exist before they touched him. The Eidolon howled, shaking the heavens with its demand for blood, but Marsh didn't need to return fire. The Eidolon's presence swept across the lobby like a tidal wave of crushing malice. The Schutzstaffel men collapsed to the bare marble floor. Some clutched their heads, others curled into fetal balls.

Some screamed, some sobbed. The Eidolon swirled through a frieze of bas-relief plaster eagles, turning them into blazing phoenices. The world smelled of warm raspberry tarts, a wet dog, and poorly tanned leather. Marsh tasted bile not his own.

The Eidolon withdrew.

Reality snapped into place around him. Gone were the phantom smells, the impossible visions, the carnivorous shadows, the waves of incapacitating hatred.

'Shit.'

Marsh sprinted across the lobby. The most stalwart troops wobbled to their feet as he burst through the doors onto Prinz-Albrecht-Strasse.

Marsh used his uniform and gun to requisition the first passing vehicle. Once alone, he wept all the way to Weimar.

TWELVE

Liv took a blue pullover from the pile of clothes on the sofa, folded it, and placed it in the suitcase on the floor. She frowned. Then replaced it with a red one.

Will said, 'I thought you'd intended to stay.'

'I did, Will. I really did.' The skin beneath her eyes had become dark and papery. As was the case, lately, with every Londoner. 'But they say the Jerries might resume the bombing any day. I can't take another night alone in the shelter with Agnes. I thought I could do it, but I can't, Will. I simply can't.'

The Luftwaffe had taken to tossing bombs like confetti. They'd come for fifty-seven nights in a row. Stephenson said the raids had averaged over 150 bombers per night. The last several days had seen a reprieve, but nobody with a shred of sense expected it to last.

Liv continued, 'The commander's company made it bearable. But he hasn't come to visit in days.' She shook her head. 'I imagine he's quite busy.'

Just what do the two of you think you're doing? Will wanted to say. Marsh's duplicitous re-courtship of his own wife – for that's what it was, regardless of his refusal to admit it – curled Will's toes. When confronted about it, he pleaded honorable intentions and having missed his dead daughter for so long. He knew it was impossible for him and Liv to be together, and yet . . .

Marsh refused to stop seeing Liv. He claimed it was to protect her from Gretel, but that was only part of it. He'd fallen in love with his wife all over again. He couldn't fool Will on that front, who had already seen them fall in love once before. His friend had become an old man not because he was burdened by the passage of time, but because he carried an unrelenting weight of sorrow and loneliness. One only had to look into the man's eyes to see that.

'I'm certain he'd be here if he could,' said Will. 'He'll be back soon, no doubt.'

And Will supposed it might very well be true that Marsh's proximity was keeping his wife and daughter safe. Marsh, the older Marsh, knew far more about Gretel than anybody else. And if just a fraction of what he'd said about her were true . . .

Agnes gurgled in her bassinet. Will wrinkled his nose. She had wet herself.

Liv took a blouse from the pile on the armrest. The blouse brushed a newspaper that lay folded open on the end table; it fluttered to the floor. Liv had circled a piece about the presidential election in America, where Roosevelt had won reelection over his opponent, Willkie.

'I was saving that for the commander,' she said. 'He follows news from the States. But I suppose I can toss that paper in the bin. It was on the wireless.'

Will suppressed a shiver. Sweat trickled from his armpits. He had to stop her from leaving.

He said, 'The commander was dead set against Williton, as I recall. He probably had good reason.'

'I haven't broken my promise, if that's what you're wondering. I'm not taking Agnes to Williton.'

'Where, then?'

'Coventry. Auntie knows people there. She made introductions for us.'

Will had to bite his tongue. The most sensible thing would have been to invite Liv to Bestwood. But Marsh had forbidden it. They had to assume Gretel knew about the family estate. They also had to assume, based on Marsh's final conversation with her in the original time line, that she no longer had a need to keep Will or any other Beauclerk alive. The estate was a viable target.

'Unless I'm mistaken, the Führer has been known to send his hounds to Coventry, too.'

'Not since summer. And never so terribly as here. Any place is better than London,' said Liv, her voice cracking.

'Well. Don't worry on your husband's account. I shall take it upon myself to keep him informed as to your whereabouts, the very moment he returns.'

Liv fidgeted with the buckle on the suitcase. 'Oh, Will . . .' Her shoulders slumped. 'He's never coming back.'

And then she was shaking, struggling to gulp down air and force the words past the sobs at the same time. 'He's gone . . . forever . . . and our daughter . . . won't . . .'

Will crossed the den to stand beside her. Liv pressed her head against his shirt. Awkwardly, uncomfortably, he put an arm around her. He'd wished for a chance to hold her for such a long time, but he'd never wished for this. But she needed a friend. And he could be that.

'Shhh, shhh, Olivia. Don't give up on our Pip just yet. He's still out there. And we'll see him again before long. I have a nose for these things.'

He hoped that were true. The younger Marsh had certainly been alive when Will had bade the Eidolon to hover near him. And he'd been on the move. And, apparently, engaged in some rather vicious fighting. But as to the state of affairs when the Eidolon departed on heartbeat seven thousand and one, Will couldn't say.

14 November 1940
Weimar, Germany

Marsh arrived in Weimar before dawn. He ditched the truck in a cobbled alleyway not far from the local Schutzstaffel garrison. Autumn had put a chill in the air, glazing the cobbles with frost. Marsh's chest ached from the effort to suppress his shivering. The lure of warmth and a chance to bathe, perhaps even a chance to pinch an overcoat, made it tempting to enter the garrison.

But that would have been suicide. By now the word of his escape had been flashed to every corner of the Reich. So instead, he took a mildewed tarpaulin from the truck bed, folded it under his arm, and set off through the side streets and alleyways of Weimar. He needed to put at least a couple of miles between himself and the truck before he secured transportation for the next leg of his journey. He left a trail of sparkling breath in the still autumn air and hurried past the darkest shadows. He stuck to pavement where he could, lest he twist an ankle on the uneven, frost-slick cobbles.

Minding each footstep took too much mental effort. His brain had been stuffed with cotton, doused with schnapps, ignited, snuffed, and buried as a pile of cold ashes. The Eidolon's cries of rage had become physically painful toward the end, and now Marsh's ears were clogged with coagulated blood that muffled the sounds of the real world.

Real?

As much as he feared recapture by the SS, he feared even more what he'd see inscribed on his eyelids when he tried to rest. The Eidolon had departed hours ago. Yet the world still lacked the plausibility of a Christmas pantomime. When Marsh had driven through the city center, he'd flinched with disgust because a pair of men inside a bakery had appeared to be grotesque parodies of paper dolls – until Marsh had realized they weren't dolls animated into a semblance of life, but flesh and blood human beings.

The rising sun tinted orange the clouds of the eastern sky. He had to hurry. The SS uniform was good for deflecting people who weren't inclined to look further, but no more than that. Anybody who saw him boosting a car would stop to watch, and from there it was a short hop to noticing the stubble, long hair, dirty fingernails, and bloody ears.

On the next street, Marsh found an Audi, an Opel, and a Mercedes. He approached the driver's door of the Opel, grabbed the handle, and waited for the shifting currents of reality to loosen the lock enough for him to work it free. His breath fogged the glass. The ache in his chest spread into his back, neck, and shoulders. Still he waited. Nothing happened.

And then he remembered how the world was supposed to

work when the Eidolons weren't paying attention to the affairs of men. The world where solid objects remained solid. Where cold fire didn't twist itself into impossible shapes. Where shadows didn't burn unprotected flesh.

'Are you well, sir?'

Marsh spun. A lady stood on the stoop of a block of flats. She wore a brown wool overcoat two sizes too large for her. For an instant, Marsh saw her lying on the pavement, her coat gone, sapphire flames illuminating the bullet hole in her temple while a demon howled for a taste of her blood. He flinched.

'Sir?' She frowned. Stepped closer.

Marsh forced himself to focus. 'Good morning. Yes, I'm well. Thank you for your concern.' He smiled, but not too widely, for fear of how she might respond to his teeth. They had to be yellow.

'You looked confused,' she said.

'Merely tired. I've been on patrol all night.'

'They work you boys so hard,' she said, shaking her head. She descended the stairs to the pavement. Her attention shifted to her footing. 'Even when the war is so many miles away.'

False memories called to him: *Spill her blood. Take her coat.*

Marsh said, 'It's my duty.'

'That's what my nephew says, too. We're proud of him.' She set off in the direction of the city center. Probably headed for the bakery he'd passed.

'I hope so,' he said, to her retreating back.

As soon as she'd turned the corner, he wrapped the tarp around his elbow and jammed it against the window. But the glass held. A flare of pain shot through his forearm and numbed his hand from wrist to fingertips. He'd overestimated his strength again.

He discovered, on the third try, that the car was unlocked.

The drive from Weimar took Marsh past the turn for a place called Buchenwald. From there it was a short drive to the forest on the outskirts of von Westarp's farm. Autumn had stripped the trees, coating the forest floor with a mulch of desiccated oak and ash leaves. He pulled off the farm track and parked the car behind an overgrown embankment. A nearby thicket of wild blackberry bushes provided a passable blind. The thorns tore his hands open. Marsh braced himself at the sight of the blood welling from his cuts, but this time there was no Eidolon to shake the cosmos with its dissatisfaction.

Back in the car, wrapped in the tarp, he fell asleep.

14 November 1940
Kensington, London, England

I paused in the act of filling a glass at Will's sideboard. 'What in the hell do you mean she's gone?'

Will said, 'I'm sorry, Pip. I gave it my very best, I assure you. But Olivia was quite determined.'

A nauseating dread hit me so hard I thought I might sick up then and there in Will's parlor. They had slipped away, out of my reach, to where I couldn't protect them. It was exactly the kind of momentary lapse that Gretel could exploit. It was exactly the waking nightmare I'd struggled to avoid. And this time I was going to lose them both.

'Obviously, you didn't try hard enough,' I said. 'And don't call me "Pip". Save that for *him*.' We'd never found a convenient shorthand for discussing my younger self. But Will knew my meaning. 'Otherwise you're likely to make a hash of things.'

I slammed the glass down hard enough to crack it. 'I have to get to Williton. Now.'

Will perched on the edge of a chaise longue upholstered in long stripes of royal blue and sunflower yellow. He raised his hands in a gesture of supplication. 'I think you can relax just a bit. They're safe.'

'They're *not* safe. They're safe when they're close to me. Gretel won't kill me. Everyone else is expendable.'

'But they're not in Williton. She did take your warnings to heart.'

A frisson of panic ricocheted through me. If Liv had gone to her aunt's house, I'd know where to find them. But if she wasn't there ... 'Did she tell you where she was planning to take Agnes?'

'Coventry,' said Will. He fished around in his billfold. 'I gather auntie made introductions for her and the little one.'

'Coventry is full of factories, you fool!'

Will handed me a slip of paper. I recognized the stationery from the pad Liv kept on the hallway table beside the telephone. She'd left an address. No telephone number.

'When did they leave?'

'Yesterday.'

In moments, I was out the door and hailing a cab. I gave the driver an address in St. Pancras. The taxi itself might have served my purposes, but I didn't have time to worry about petrol. But I knew a place where I could find a reliable car along with a spare petrol canister.

Funny how the big things change, while the little things stay the same.

*

14 November 1940
Reichsbehörde für die Erweiterung germanischen Potenzials

Marsh woke with the sun low in the western sky. His breath had frosted the inside of the windscreen, spreading the sunset into a soft, pink glow. The stink of mildew from the tarp was permanently frozen into his nostrils.

Though the temperature had already dropped with the sun, and the coming night promised to be unseasonably cold, Marsh left the tarpaulin in the car. It was too stiff, too prone to getting caught on underbrush, too loud. A quarter of an hour passed while he picked his way under half-fallen trees, around brambles, and over the occasional hillock. Tiny mounds dotted the forest floor around the farm. Weather and the slow encroachment of the forest had softened their contours to the point they were almost invisible to the eye, but they became apparent as Marsh trudged over them. They were too uniform in size and distribution to be natural formations. Dozens of tiny graves, they were.

Marsh huddled in the underbrush a dozen yards from the tree-line. It gave him a decent view of the farm. It was just as busy as it had been on the day he'd been taken by the SS. Things had begun to wind down with the onset of evening, but Marsh could see Heike limping to the mess hall from what appeared to be a new version of the obstacle course. Behind her, LSSAH men collected the flags she had successfully dislodged.

Light from the farmhouse windows shone on the gravel drive and the black Mercedes parked there. Probably a staff car from Berlin, ferrying members of the OKW for consultations with Gretel.

The underbrush rattled in time with Marsh's trembling. He

clenched his muscles to suppress the shivering, which drew out the ache in his chest and shoulders. The cold ground evoked agonizing throbs from his bad knee. He tasted salt; his nose had run, trickling wetness across his upper lip. His face was too numb to feel it.

The farmhouse door opened. Marsh ducked. Jaundice-yellow lamplight stretched halfway to the tree line. Two men emerged from the house, followed by the silhouettes of von Westarp, Pabst, and Gretel. Marsh couldn't make out the visitors against the glare from the house, but neither had a size and gait to match what he remembered from his brief glance at von Runstedt.

Bits and pieces of the parting conversation drifted to Marsh's muffled ears. He caught something about the Luftwaffe, and London. Marsh strained to listen as Pabst bid good-bye to the visitors: Generalfeldmarschall Keitel and Reichsmarschall Göring.

Gretel stood in the doorway, staring into the forest.

Marsh retreated into the brush as the car rounded the gravel drive. He huddled behind the gnarled, mossy roots of an oak while the car's headlamps raked the trees. Soon the Mercedes entered the forest and was gone.

Twilight slid into full darkness. The farm fell silent, but for the occasional murmur of conversation as mundane troops departed from the mess hall in pairs and trios. His stomach gurgled. How long since he'd eaten? The incarceration had weakened him. Now the cold, hunger, and lingering disorientation from the Eidolon conspired against him. He awoke to the sound of footsteps crunching through the underbrush. He fumbled for his pistol.

A voice in the shadows: 'Hello, darling. Have you missed me?'

'Missed you?' Marsh had to force the words past the gauntlet of his chattering teeth. 'I nearly rotted in that cell, you bloody miserable bitch.'

Gretel clucked her tongue. 'I thought you wanted my help getting to Berlin.'

'If I'd wanted to get arrested, I could have managed that on my own.'

'Yes, that's true.' She plopped down beside him, sitting cross-legged in the brush. She wore a leather coat over a dark blouse and gray trousers. She held a thick bundle in her lap. 'Although the torture would have left you incapable of completing your mission. Oh, well. I'll know better next time.' She handed the bundle to him. 'I brought this for you.'

It was a wool overcoat. Marsh recognized the scent of aftershave on the collar. 'This is Pabst's coat.'

'He won't be needing it after tonight.'

Marsh flung the coat over his shoulders. Savoring the warmth as he fished around for the sleeves, he said, 'I see you're still in Berlin's good graces. What have you been telling them while I was away?'

'Very little,' she said. 'They want advice on where to concentrate the bombing campaign.'

That explained Göring's presence. He commanded the Luftwaffe, or did earlier in the year, before Marsh had been hauled off to rot in an SS prison cell.

At least Britain was still in the fight. Seemed like a lifetime ago since he'd been taken to Berlin. What was the state of the world? The war? His family?

Bombing campaign. The chill in Marsh's body seeped through to the pit of his stomach. 'How long has this campaign been on?'

'They shifted to civilian targets in September.'

My God. Liv. Agnes.

'I'm sure it's been a grand success thanks to you.'

'Oh, Raybould.' She laid her hand on his forearm. He flinched away. 'The war could evolve so much differently. You've no idea.'

Moonlight shone briefly on her teeth as she smiled at him. She leaned closer, affecting a conspiratorial whisper. 'I tell them what they want to hear. Tonight, for instance. Coventry was already on their list.'

'What's going to happen to Coventry?'

Gretel stood. 'You must be quite hungry. You'll be safe if you wait here.'

She headed toward the farm, in the direction of the mess hall. A few crunching footsteps put her out of earshot of the loudest whisper he could muster. Marsh hugged his knees to his chest, folded the hem of Pabst's coat around his legs, and pulled his hands inside the cuffs. The shivering hadn't subsided, but the pain in his muscles was tolerable now.

More tolerable, anyway, than the aching despair in his mind and heart.

His home had been subject to months of bombing. His wife, if she still lived, surely thought him dead. And what of Agnes? He'd missed so much of her first year. She wouldn't be his new-born baby any longer ... if he ever saw her again. Where were his wife and daughter at this moment? Were they warm and safe? Did they have a home? Had Liv already grieved for him and moved on? Agnes needed a father.

The Eidolons' perfect, lightless, lifeless universe had nothing on the chasm separating Marsh from everything he cared about. The things he saw in the presence of an Eidolon were alternate unrealities, distortions, might-have-beens. Mere phantoms. But the gulf between a cold patch of ground in a Thuringian forest and a cozy mock Tudor in Walworth was undeniably real, and crushing in its immensity.

Isolation. Alienation. Loneliness. A bramble of thorns lodged in his chest. He couldn't breathe.

Marsh wiped his eyes when Gretel returned carrying a covered tray. Wisps of steam escaped through a hole in the lid. Marsh's stomach gurgled.

Gretel knelt beside him. From a coat pocket, she produced a fork, knife, and spoon. Marsh took them. She pulled a cloth serviette from her other pocket and tried to tuck it into his collar. He knocked her hands away. She stuck her tongue at him; it glistened in the moonlight.

One plate contained stewed cabbage, carrots, and onions, all swimming in butter and black flakes he took to be pepper. Another held a steaming slab of corned beef. She'd taken a thick slice of brown bread, too, and laid it atop a bowl of stew.

'Thanks,' he said.

'I wanted to bring milk, but it didn't fit on the tray,' she said.

He tucked in. Gretel tied yellow ribbons into her braids while he ate. After a few moments, she said, 'You'll make yourself ill if you don't slow down.'

An uncomfortable churning in his gut proved her right. He forced himself to chew more slowly. But once the food had blunted the razor edges of his hunger, he questioned Gretel while devouring the rest of his dinner.

'What's happening at the farm?' If Gretel's colleagues had been deployed into the field, tonight's efforts would be for naught. 'Is everybody here tonight?'

'No,' said Gretel.

Shit. 'Give me a rundown.'

'I warned the doctor and Pabst that the farm would fall under attack. They recalled Kammler and Buhler from the North Atlantic to help with the defense. And they postponed further deployments of Reinhardt and my brother until the crisis has passed.'

That was a good start. But: 'What about the others?'

'Heike has made great strides with her training. Pabst was preparing to send her to England. You have good timing, Raybould. Oh, and one of the Twins is at OKW headquarters in Berlin.'

'And her sister?'

Gretel shrugged. Did that mean she didn't care, or didn't know? 'She isn't here.'

Nothing they could do about the Twins tonight. Marsh would just have to hope that fulfilling the commander's odd requirement would lead to closure on that front.

Marsh tore the bread in two. The melted butter had congealed again in the cold night air, but it suffused the bread with a creamy slickness. Delicious.

He chewed, slowly. 'And how is Liv?'

'Keep eating. You need your strength.'

'How is she?'

Gretel sighed. 'She's alive. I don't know details.'

'I think you're lying.'

'I see the future. I'm not omniscient.'

Marsh scraped the bread around the bottom of the bowl. The last flecks of stew had gone cold, but he didn't let a drop go to waste. Gretel hummed to herself. Her eyes were dark as his cell in Berlin. Darker.

He said, 'You know why I've returned, and what I plan to do. Why are you so pleased?'

The corner of her mouth quirked up. 'I've finally solved a long-standing problem.'

14 November 1940
On the road to Coventry, England

I raced the fall of night in a stolen car, haunted by the ghosts of never-were and might-still-be.

A memory of Liv occupied the passenger seat. She'd come with me the last time I stole the old man's car. And she was there now in my mind's eye, clutching a pink blanket covered with elephants and baby stains. *What if she's cold*, Liv had worried.

The sweet-sharp tobacco scent of Stephenson's Lucky Strikes leached from the upholstery into my clothes and hair. But in that other time line, the car had smelled of Agnes. Only Agnes.

That history had never happened. And it wouldn't repeat itself. No. It would be worse this time. Tonight, Gretel would attempt to kill Agnes *and* Liv.

A curve in the road forced me to downshift. I stomped the clutch. The engine screamed in protest. So did I, inwardly, begrudging every bit of lost speed, every wasted moment. Stephenson liked his Rolls Royce Mulliner because of its smooth ride. Now, though, that suspension made the car sway like a sloop in a gale as the tires screeched across macadam.

The headlamps slewed across marshland and hedgerows. I had ripped the grilles from the headlamps, so I was driving in violation of the blackout regs. But I'd never find my way to Coventry otherwise. Didn't know if I could find the place in bright daylight, much less now. I'd never been to Coventry before. I'd committed Liv's forwarding address to memory, but I had no map of the town.

One thing at a time, I reminded myself. *First thing is to get there.*

The wild sway of the headlamps settled on another dark, tree-lined tunnel. The clutch *clanked* under my foot. I slammed the car back into gear and gunned the engine. A heavy thud shook the car; the canister in the boot had just tipped over. Nothing to do about it but hope the lid held.

I sniffed the air for the scent of spilled petrol, but still all I could smell was Agnes. That memory had never faded. Not during all those lonely, accursed years. But it was stronger now, after weeks and months of stolen time with my wife and daughter. My main memory of Williton – the Williton of the other time line, the Williton that Gretel had subjected to nine hours of bombing – was the mingled smells of baby powder and high explosive. That mélange had insinuated itself into countless nightmares over the years.

A dip in the road evoked another groan from the suspension. The engine whined again as the drive wheels lost their grip on the macadam. Last time, I'd more or less destroyed the old man's car. I'd gutted the undercarriage first by navigating a road of pulverized macadam, then by forcing the Rolls over heaps of rubble during our futile race to find and save our daughter.

To his credit, he'd taken it well. The old man wasn't without empathy. Empathy for his surrogate son, Raybould Marsh. But a stranger had stolen his car tonight.

I blew through a crossroads. The headlamps flashed on a bare signpost. Most signs had been taken down or painted over in preparation for the invasion. If the Jerries came, they'd have to find their own bloody way around England.

The memory of Liv cried beside me. *What if she's hungry? We didn't bring her food.*

Phantom splinters tore into my calloused fingers. Broken

timbers, shards of glass, and pulverized masonry had torn my hands while I searched the rubble for our daughter. I hadn't realized what I'd done to my hands until much later. The scars were still there, beneath the calluses.

It wouldn't be like that this time, I tried to reassure myself. Last time, we'd hit the road after the BBC had reported the bombing. But the skies over Coventry had been clear when I left Will's flat. Maybe they'd stay clear. Maybe I was overreacting.

But with Liv and Agnes out of London, they had passed beyond my sphere of protection. And Gretel was nothing if not patient. I knew as surely as I knew the sun would rise in the east, if Gretel still had designs on my family, she'd send the bombers to Coventry.

14 November 1940
Reichsbehörde für die Erweiterung germanischen Potenzials

Marsh said, 'How long are we going to wait here?'

'Until it's time,' said Gretel. Her hand went to the battery at her waist. A faint click told him she'd unplugged her wires again. But her gaze didn't waver from the farmhouse. She'd been watching it over an hour.

Sod it all for a game of soldiers, thought Marsh.

He stood. 'Look. I'll die of exposure if I sit out here much longer. I'm in a bloody uniform. Nobody will question me. And if they do, they won't recognize me in the darkness. Once we're in the farmhouse, you'll warn me if things are looking to go pear-shaped.' He strode away.

Gretel whispered, 'Raybould, wait.' He sighed. Turned. She said, 'We have to get a battery first.'

'What?'

She pointed toward the battery storage shed. 'We need a battery for Kammler.'

'We don't have time for that. We'll use yours.' Marsh reached for her battery harness, but Gretel flinched away, eyes wide and dark.

'No!' Her shout pierced the darkness.

They both froze. Marsh tensed, waiting for blinding kliegs to shred the darkness, waiting for the farm to explode with shouts of alarm. He started to tremble again. But no searchlights raked the forest; no guards boiled forth from the barracks. Marsh exhaled.

Gretel recovered her composure. She added, 'This isn't fresh. He'll need a fully charged battery. And a spare.'

'Oh, this is just bloody wonderful,' said Marsh. 'You might have taken care of this ahead of time, if you knew I'd be back tonight.'

An expression flitted across her face, too quickly to read in the dim light. Marsh cursed the inconstant moonlight. Her gaze settled on him, and it was harder than granite. Which matched her tone of voice.

'Of course I knew.'

He'd seen a protracted version of that expression once before. When she stood, frightened, before the Eidolon.

Von Westarp's farm was infested with monsters, but all of the human variety. And Gretel was the queen bee. What did she fear now? What had changed since he'd been away?

'You lead,' he said.

She hiked through the underbrush. He followed a few steps behind, trying and failing to minimize the crunching and scraping of his footsteps. Soon they hopped over the fringe of tall grasses that lined the clearing. From there it was a straight shot to the battery storage shed. Gretel led him there without pausing and without veering.

The shed's single entrance faced the center of the Reichsbehörde campus, like most of the facilities that bordered the training field. They had arrived in the rear. Marsh pressed himself against the cold bricks and inched toward the corner. But Gretel waved him back.

'Wait here,' she whispered. Then she disappeared around the corner into the semicircle of light cast by the lamp above the shed door.

A breeze caught Marsh's breath, pulling it into long silvery streamers that drifted past the edge of the shed and into the moonlight. He backed away, one carefully measured footstep at a time, lest his breath give him away. The breeze snaked tendrils through the buttonholes of Pabst's coat. He tried not to shiver. And wondered how long Gretel would make him wait this time.

Around the corner, footsteps approached from the direction of the farmhouse. Marsh tensed, and listened.

'Good evening. How was your dinner?'

'I got your note,' said Klaus. 'It's cold outside. So why am I here?'

'I need you to do something for me,' she said.

Klaus might have sighed – Marsh couldn't hear him well enough to know – but the man didn't miss a beat. 'Why am I stealing a battery for you? You're already wearing one.'

'Not one battery. Two. And it's a surprise.'

'I don't like the sound of that.'

'Do you remember what I told you in England?'

'You said I need to trust you. That what you're doing is vital.'

'Yes.'

'And this is part of that.'

'Yes.'

Nothing happened for several moments. The silence was Klaus's way of mulling things over. Did he really believe he'd stand up to her? Klaus wasn't capable of resisting his sister. As aggrieved as he felt at times, he was, in the end, devoted to Gretel. He always would be.

'If I do this, will you tell me what it's for?'

'No. But you'll find out soon enough.'

'Will I get in trouble?'

'No more than I will.'

A few footsteps, then Klaus fell silent again. This silence lasted a bit longer than the previous one. Gretel broke it a minute or so later.

'Thank you, Klaus.'

'I'm going to bed.' His footsteps receded into the night.

Gretel rejoined Marsh behind the shed. She carried a battery in each hand. Patchy clouds scudded across the dark sky, blocking the moon. Marsh couldn't read the gauges.

They waited before setting off again, this time toward the farmhouse. The door to the servants' entrance creaked, then thudded, when Klaus entered. Gretel led Marsh to the main entrance.

Shifting moonlight coaxed a pale glow from the stained glass window on the landing. The swastika banners inside the window cast soft ruby light upon the gilded balustrades. It waxed in brightness as another cloud bank cleared the moon. Marsh looked away, to better preserve his night vision. They headed for the kitchen. He turned to tell her to look for sweets, but she went straight to the walk-in larder without his prompting.

Marsh searched the rest of the kitchen while Gretel rummaged in the larder. The faint aroma of baked trout wafted from the ovens. A sliced lemon lay atop a saucer on one of the butcher-block tables in the center of the kitchen. It reminded him of Will.

I've been away so long. Is he still alive? Has he visited Liv? What must they think of me? What of Milkweed? What does the old man think? Can I ever make this right with any of them? Will Agnes know me, if I ever see her again?

He packed the worry and wistfulness aside before they crippled him. He checked the cabinets and the iceboxes, but didn't find anything that was likely to garner Kammler's cooperation. Not unless the poor fellow enjoyed calf liver, which appeared to be on the menu for the doctor's dinner tomorrow.

But he did find a nearly empty sack of flour. Marsh dumped the flour into the rubbish bin, rolled up the cloth sack, and tucked it into his belt.

Gretel emerged from the larder with a paper bag in one hand. She held something lustrous and white in her lips. She plucked the stick from her mouth, offered it to him.

'Peppermint?' she whispered. He declined.

Back to the entryway. Marsh took care to step at the edges of the stairs, where they were less likely to creak. Although it felt like six days had passed since he'd returned to the farm, and even though each tick of the clock meant another opportunity for things to turn sour, he suppressed his impatience and the temptation to take them two at a time. That would have put more stress on the boards and, thus, might have been louder. He crouched in the shadows beneath the rosette window.

Gretel followed. Straight up the middle. Sounded like a bloody rhino.

Marsh turned for the flight that led to the top floor, which housed von Westarp's sanctuary. But Gretel entered the corridor that led to her quarters, and those of the doctor's other 'children.'

'Not yet,' he whispered. 'I'm paying a visit to the doctor first.'

Gretel shook her head. 'We need Kammler.'

'I can't bloody well pinch the doctor's journals with Kammler in tow. Your stepbrother isn't particularly quiet, in case you haven't noticed.'

Her eyes were darker than the surrounding shadows. 'You weren't ordered to take his journals.'

'I'm not leaving here without them.'

Silence fell. A faint *click* echoed across the landing, louder than a gunshot in the quiet farmhouse. Gretel closed her eyes.

Something about this wasn't sitting well. Even by her standards, Gretel was acting oddly. But he couldn't quite put his finger on it. When he tried, it slipped away, like the name of an old acquaintance who bumps into you at a Tube stop. And since when did she entertain suggestions?

She opened her eyes. 'Kammler first. And hurry.'

I killed the headlamps once I blew into the outskirts of Coventry. Last thing I wanted was to make it easier for the Luftwaffe to find the damn place. I didn't slow down until I nearly embedded a postbox into the grille of Stephenson's car. And so I prowled through sprawling Coventry by the light of a full moon.

I'd never been here before, and hadn't realized the extent of my task. Liv had left an address in Stoke Aldermoor, which I reckoned to be part of the residential ring around the city. But I knew little more than that. And Coventry was a damn sight larger than Williton.

I had no hope of finding her address on my own. Had to find somebody who knew the city. Probably a succession of somebodies. That meant either stopping at a pub or flagging down an ARP warden. But, just like a copper, neither was there when I needed it.

Moonlight shone on the corrugated metal roof of a long, tall building that loomed over the street. Factory or warehouse, I reckoned. No sounds of industrial machinery greeted me when I lowered the window. But the fence, the sandbag revetments, and the army sentries suggested either an aircraft factory or a munitions plant. It wasn't the only shadow factory I passed.

Coventry's industrial base would provide Gretel a convenient excuse.

Factories meant men thirsty for a drink. There had to be a pub in the area. But damned if I could find it. I chose another street at random, wending toward the city's medieval heart.

Sod it all, I decided. *Let the wardens come to me.*

I leaned on the horn.

Kammler recoiled from Gretel when she woke him. But he let out a cry – half squeal, half grunt – when he finally recognized Marsh.

'Shhh!' Marsh snatched the peppermint stick from Gretel's mouth and waved it under Kammler's nose. The large man took it in his fist, shoved it in his mouth. He rubbed his head on Marsh's arm, chewing and drooling. The candy didn't silence him, but it did reduce the volume of his utterances to a low murmur.

A sour milk odor wafted from Kammler. The room smelled of peppermint and shit. Kammler had soiled his sheets.

Kammler slept in his underclothes. There wasn't time to dress him fully, much less to clean him. Gretel fetched his empty battery harness from its hook behind the door. Kammler again recoiled from her. She shot a look at Marsh.

Marsh whispered in his ear. 'Easy, son. I'm glad you remember me. I was gone for a time, but I thought about you quite a lot while I was away.' He did his best to keep up the soothing patter while Gretel buckled the harness around Kammler's waist. Marsh eased a battery into place. He endured a rib-bruising embrace from Kammler when he fished around for the man's wires. They'd worked their way down the back of his nightshirt. Poor fellow had been sleeping on them. The bare copper connectors were damp, though whether with sweat or urine, Marsh couldn't tell. He ran a fold of the cloth flour sack over the connectors to give them a cursory drying, then plugged them into the battery at Kammler's waist.

The large man shuddered. 'T-t-t! G-g-g-guh ... '

'For Christ's sake,' Marsh whispered. 'You insisted on getting him first, so you keep him quiet.'

She waved another sweet before Kammler's face. And nearly lost a finger when he chomped at it. But she didn't flinch.

'Stay here,' said Marsh. 'I have to do something.'

He crept into the corridor and shut Kammler's door. In moments he was back inside the room they'd assigned him, the one Gretel had said once belonged to a man named Rudolf. Silver moonlight streamed through the window. Marsh pulled the cot away from the wall that separated this room from Gretel's. He felt along the floor for the loose segment of trim, pulled it aside, reached into the hollow.

The rag was still there. Still stiff with what he hoped was a Twin's menstrual blood.

With Kammler in tow, Marsh and Gretel crept past the other occupied rooms – Heike snored – to the servants' stair. The width of the stair forced them to go single file. Marsh went first. Behind Gretel, Kammler emitted a low whimper that grew in pitch and volume as Marsh ascended. The only way to mollify him was to send Gretel up first, followed by Marsh, then Kammler. In that order, they climbed to von Westarp's study. Gretel opened the door. Marsh gave Kammler another peppermint stick, then handed him back to Gretel.

Shadows and moonlight bleached all but the slightest suggestion of color from the doctor's inner sanctum. Marsh crept through a chiaroscuro warren. Past the bookshelves, past the gramophone, through eddies of chalk dust swirled up by his footsteps. He approached the doctor's desk. Toward the empty-eyed leer of a child's skull. Toward the glimmer of polished steel rivets.

A wet *click* rattled on the floorboards behind him. 'K-k-k-buh-bbbb!' Kammler squealed and clapped.

Marsh wheeled, crouched, froze. His thudding heart smashed against his breastbone, chiseling for escape. Long seconds passed while he watched the door to the doctor's bedroom. Gretel snatched something from the floor and pushed it back into Kammler's mouth. If she saw the dirty look he shot her, she showed no sign.

His breath came out in a long, ragged exhalation. His hands shook. He leaned against the desk until his jackhammer heart didn't threaten to pulverize his ribs to so much gravel.

He traced the wires from the skull-cum-paperweight. The doctor used them as a bookmark, Marsh recalled. His fingers traced cool copper to the soft leather of a blotter, past the sharp facets of a glass inkwell, across the slick oiliness of polished wood. He brushed a fountain pen, sent it rolling across the desk to clatter on the floor. He searched the entire desktop by touch, feeling for the roughness of paper, the contours of embossed leather, the filigreed brass of corner clips. But the wires ended on a bare desk. No journal.

Tipping the skull back with one hand, he slid his fingers under the dead child's teeth. When he'd been here before, the skull had rested on a pile of journals. But not tonight.

Drawers rasped open when he rifled the desk. With dark-adapted eyes he glimpsed stationery; rubber stamps; paper clips; calipers; a magnifying glass; multiple file folders; an empty salt-cellar; a cracked sugar bowl inscribed with gradations and imperial volume measurements; a medal inlaid with opals and diamonds. No journals.

God, where were they? Marsh reconsidered the jumble on the bookshelves. The true hopelessness of his self-appointed task washed over him. He didn't have time to search the entire room. The moon was already lower in the west than he liked. They had to finish this.

The journals would have been such a boon ... But it would take an hour to search the shelves in the dark.

Click. The ceiling fixture erupted with electric light, banishing the shadows. Marsh winced from the flare of pain in his eyes.

Marsh hissed, 'Kill that bloody light!'

Behind him, von Westarp said, 'I'll do no such thing.'

I flashed the headlamps a few times, too, for good measure. It worked. ARP wardens swarmed to me like picnic ants to an open jam pot.

The first was a pudgy fellow who came trotting up the street, huffing and wheezing, a hand holding the forage cap to his head. He looked to be in his late sixties. 'Oy!' he managed, before doubling over to catch his breath. 'You can't ... do ... that ... '

He trailed off, still a dozen yards from where I leaned against the Mulliner. Brilliant. Poor bastard was likely to kick before I could get directions out of him.

I reached inside, flicked the lights a couple more times. Gave the horn another blast, too.

The second warden came running around the corner at a good clip. 'You! Kill those bloody lights now!'

Much better. Young fellow, this one. It surprised me to see somebody so young and healthy working for the local Air Raid Precautions. Ought to have joined up. But as he approached, swaggering with righteous indignation, moonlight shone on the gray hair at his temples, and I realized he had to be in his mid-forties. Not so young. But younger than me. Young enough to remind me what it had been like to sprint without my knee giving out, to raise my voice without the inevitable agony from the wreckage of my throat.

Came right up to me, this one. 'What the hell is wrong with you? Might was well be signaling the Luftwaffe, what?'

'Stoke Aldermoor,' I said. 'How do I get there?'

That brought him up short. 'What?'

Behind us, the pudgy warden had caught enough breath to stagger over. 'What?'

I grabbed the younger warden by the collar of his oversized coat. The wool scratched at my knuckles like tiny ineffectual hands scrabbling for release. 'Stoke Aldermoor! I need directions!'

Guess the moonlight gave him a glimpse of my face, because he blanched. But he shoved me back, hard enough to knock me against the old man's car. Strong chap. 'You broke the blackout regs for this? Are you barmy?'

I pulled Liv's address from my pocket, waved it in his face. 'Can you tell me or not? It's life and death, man!'

'I don't care if the Prime Minister sent you, mate. You're breaking the regs. That could mean life or death for everybody in the city.'

He tried to snatch the paper from my hand. I ducked under his arm, sidestepped, pulled his arm through the rest of the arc to overbalance him. He toppled facedown in the street. I knelt on him, locked his other arm behind his back, clamped my free hand on the back of his head.

'Stoke Aldermoor,' I growled. 'Now.'

Something scuffled off to my left. I turned just in time to turn the kick into a glancing blow. Fat coward. Rage boiled up from deep within me. Unfocused anger had been my companion for so long that it had long ago become part of the background noise of my daily life.

I remembered the first man to speak to me after Liv and I arrived at the ruins of Williton. He spoke with compassion and reason, told me there was nothing I could do. He dared to suggest I stop digging in the rubble with my bare, bloody hands. Dared to suggest I abandon the search for my infant daughter. So I shattered his jaw with a brick. There were times during the long, dark years after the war when I wondered what became of him. Usually late at night, when I lay in bed alone, Liv having taken a lover just to avoid sleeping under the same roof as our son. Most natural thing in the world, questioning the path of your life at times like that. But there had been just as many times, in earlier days, when I remembered how good it felt, how right, to give the grief a violent outlet.

I released the armlock on the younger warden and leapt on his colleague. Fat man went down fast. It felt a bit like kicking a puppy, but I didn't care. All I needed was one miserable question answered, but these tossers wouldn't help me. I needed to find Liv, but their obstinacy was killing her. I couldn't lose Agnes again. I wouldn't.

The younger warden tried to pull me off him. He got an arm under my shoulder, jammed his thumb and forefinger against my windpipe. His other hand clamped down on the back of my neck, as I'd done to him.

'What's so bloody important about Stoke Aldermoor?'

I broke free. 'I'm trying to save my family!'

'From what, for chrisssakes? There isn't—'

But the rest of his protest was lost in the banshee wail of air-raid sirens. Doors opened all around us as people ran for shelter in their nightclothes. I pointed at the sky. Over the earthshaking chatter of ack-acks, I screamed, 'From *that*!'

Von Westarp stood in the doorway that opened on the main stair-case. He wore a tattered silk dressing gown. Its colors had faded long ago; when he moved, the wispy sleeves and hem waved like cobwebs. He might have been a sepulchral visitation, a revenant spirit. No shortage of those at the farm. In one hand, the doctor held a white porcelain plate stacked high with pieces of black-ened toast; his other held one of the missing journals. He'd been reading it.

Bloody fucking hell.

He must have gone down to the kitchen for a midnight snack while they were dealing with Kammler. He'd come up the front stairs while Gretel and Kammler held the servants' stair. Speaking of whom—

Gretel and Kammler were not in evidence. Had she foreseen the doctor's interruption and slipped out to give Marsh surprise reinforcements? Or had she sold him out again? She was overdue for a short, intense conversation.

Von Westarp said, 'I knew you were a problem the moment my daughter brought you home.'

'You're not the first man to say so.'

Keep him talking. Keep him busy. Take him before he raises the alarm.

Marsh gauged the distance separating them. He sidled around the desk.

Von Westarp dropped the plate of toast and pulled a short-barreled pistol from the sagging pocket of his gown. He had it trained on Marsh before the toast and porcelain fragments came to rest underfoot. When he strode forward, his hairless legs poked through the opening of his gown. His sash was coming undone. He was pale and skinny.

'Stop,' said the doctor.

The Luger in his hand predated the Great War. Marsh wondered if the half-naked madman knew how to use it. Probably. What sort of lunatic carried a gun in his dressing gown?

Marsh said, 'I doubt you fully understand what's—'

The doctor cut him off. 'This isn't a conversation. I'm no fool.' And he raised the Luger at Marsh's face.

He was too close to miss. The barrel looked a foot wide. Marsh tensed, rose to the balls of his feet, prepared to dive as the doctor's finger tightened on the trigger. Tendons stood out in bas-relief beneath the doctor's papery skin.

A door scraped open. Von Westarp's gaze flicked from Marsh's face to something behind him.

Marsh clenched the bundle of wires on the desk. He swung the skull at von Westarp's outstretched hand. It connected with a solid *crack* at the same moment von Westarp fired.

A dead child's teeth clattered to the floor like hailstones. Somebody gasped.

Marsh leapt on the doctor. He wrenched the Luger from his grip and broke a couple of his fingers in the process. A punch snapped the doctor's head back hard enough to daze and subdue him, but not before von Westarp screamed to raise the dead: 'Help! Children, help me!'

Well, we're in the shit now, thought Marsh.

He said, 'Gretel! Get Kammler ready! We're going to have company in about ten seconds.'

Then he shot von Westarp. The bullet split the doctor's glasses at the bridge of his nose. A jet of blood and brain matter geysered from the neat round hole between his eyebrows. Warm blood spatter stippled Marsh's face for the second time in as many days, but this time no Eidolon swirled about him to demand greater carnage.

'Somebody should have done that long ago, you twisted bastard.'

That made two gunshots in the doctor's study. Shouts echoed up the rear stairwell. The rest of Von Westarp's children were awake and agitated.

Bloody fuck.

He kicked the dead man for good measure, for frustration's sake, for time spent rotting in Berlin, for time lost watching Agnes grow . . .

. . . and glimpsed the rest of von Westarp's journals crammed on a shelf between a pair of specimen jars.

He yanked the flour sack from behind his belt. Unfurling it, he said over his shoulder, 'Don't kill Reinhardt until the house is burning. Let him do our work for us.'

Marsh shoved the doctor's snack-time reading into the bag. Then he ran to the shelf, swept the other volumes into the sack, and spun it closed.

Two doors. Two exits. Two entrances.

He slammed the door that opened on the front stairwell. Marsh hooked a mahogany armchair with his foot, wedged it under the knob. It wouldn't keep everybody out, not in this nightmare factory, but it would keep the mundane soldiers out for a minute or two. Long enough. If he and Gretel were still barricaded in the doctor's study when the soldiers broke in, it would mean their bid to destroy the Reichsbehörde had failed.

Next, he turned for the rear stairwell, where Gretel's perfectly timed entrance had distracted the doctor. Von Westarp's desk looked to be half an acre of solid oak. Pain rippled through Marsh's knees and shoulders as he strained to force it across the room to barricade the door.

Couldn't get it there in one go. He wedged himself under the edge of the desk, strained, forced the damn thing past where Gretel knelt on the floor, slammed it against the servants' door.

Right. Now we can make a good run at this.

'Doctor!' The servants' stair reverberated with footsteps and panic, the scuffling sounds of a brainwashed family scrambling to be the first to leap to the aid of its insane paterfamilias.

Marsh said, 'Gretel, get ready.'

Then he looked down.

Kammler lay slumped against the wall. All color had drained from his face. He stared up at Marsh, wide-eyed and afraid. He was crying. Gretel's braids hung in disarray. She had tied her ribbons around Kammler's left thigh. Her hands were the color of stewed beets, as was the long smear of blood from Kammler's gunshot wound.

'God damn it!'

'Temper,' said Gretel. Her face was unreadable.

'Can he work?'

Kammler was the key to everything. What was Gretel's escape plan?

The door to the servants' stair rattled. The edges turned black. Marsh scooted away from the heat. Tongues of flame licked into the study while Reinhardt assaulted the door with fists and Willenskräfte.

Reinhardt called, 'Doctor! Let me in!'

Klaus yelled, 'You idiot, you'll kill him! Give me that battery!'

Marsh knelt over Kammler. Gretel's tourniquet hadn't staunched the bleeding. She was too small, and the ribbons too slippery, to pull tight enough. Marsh's belt, or even a stick to twist into the knot, might have done the trick. But they hadn't time. Heat poured off the door in waves thick enough to crisp Marsh's hair.

The chair barring the other door screeched backwards half an inch, tracing bright gouges in the dark varnish of the floorboards. Another good shove would snap it apart.

Marsh took Kammler's face in his hands. 'Look at me, son. Remember me?'

The fear and confusion on Kammler's face softened under Marsh's attention. He shrunk away from Gretel's touch. He smelled like sour milk and peppermint, shit and warm iron.

'M-m-m—'

Marsh gave a little smile of encouragement.

'That's right. I need your help.' He pulled one of Kammler's arms over his shoulder. Gretel did the same. Marsh lifted the telekinetic to his feet. Christ, but he was heavy. Klaus passed through the barricade like a ghost wreathed in smoke and anger. He disregarded the growing flames. Marsh fired at him with the Luger, but the shot passed harmlessly through him to crack the chalkboard. But then Marsh started to lose his grip on Kammler, and he had to keep the large man on his feet.

Klaus rematerialized. Stumbled over the doctor's body. Howled. Spun. His gaze paused on Marsh for an instant, just long enough to recognize him, but Gretel and Kammler were the targets of his rage.

'You sick bitch! And you, you fucking retard. *What have you done?*'

He rushed them.

Marsh pointed. To Kammler, he said, 'Crush.'

Gretel's bombers had arrived at Coventry. Stealth was out of the question now. I left the headlamps on and drove like a demon while the Luftwaffe unleashed hell behind me.

The bombers came in waves, the heavy thrum of their engines creating a basso profundo counterpoint to the hysterical soprano shriek of the sirens and kettledrum percussion of ack-acks. This wasn't a routine bombing run. They'd come to pulverize the city, burn it to ash, salt the earth. They'd come to redraw the map.

Gretel wasn't taking chances. She was thorough. And who was I but a scarred and sweaty madman railing against the woman who twirled history around her fingers like so much yarn?

Explosions like flashbulbs strobed the night and shook the earth. Thunder rolled over me. The steering wheel danced in my hands, tried to shake free of my grip.

On I drove.

The farmhouse disintegrated.

Klaus disappeared into a cyclone of debris. So did the floor, wall, and ceiling behind him. The agitated yelling became screams of panic, shrieks of the injured.

The blow from Kammler's Willenskräfte tore through wood and glass and stone with equal ease, squeezed the shattered pieces together, then flung them apart like confetti.

It didn't disturb one hair on Marsh's head.

Cold night air swirled around him. Overhead, beyond the missing ceiling, a faint cloudy halo wreathed the moon. Firelight shone on the training field. Kammler shivered. The floor shifted underfoot. One of the doctor's bookcases toppled into the jagged hole where the floor had been, followed by the chair Marsh had used to barricade one door.

A handful of mundane soldiers – those who hadn't been standing where Kammler had smashed part of the balcony to flinders – burst into the room.

'Crush,' said Marsh. And Kammler did. An invisible, impenetrable wall punched down from the sky like the fist of God. It slammed down on the men and most of the farmhouse behind them, crushing three stories of farmhouse into a volume not two feet tall. Kammler swung his open mouth toward Marsh, wanting another peppermint stick.

Gretel yelled, 'Raybould!'

Searing heat rolled over them. Kammler mewled. Marsh glimpsed Reinhardt blazing with fire and fury. But then the devastated farmhouse shifted again, and the floor lost its fight against gravity. It tossed the trio into the hole. Marsh lost sight of Reinhardt.

He landed on what was left of the floor of Heike's room. Kammler slammed atop him, hard enough to bruise bone and empty lungs. Gretel landed on the mattress and bounced daintily to her feet.

Kammler wailed. He rocked back and forth, crying.

Marsh couldn't breathe. He couldn't get his lungs to work, not with Kammler rolling on top of him. He'd been pierced by debris in a dozen places, and something in his chest was fractured. He looked to Gretel. Her face shrank at the end of a dark tunnel. Above him, the ragged remains of the doctor's study burned like a torch. The fire had no shortage of debris on which to feed, and an open sky from which to breathe. It inched downwards.

Gretel took Kammler by the hands. The large man rolled away from her, which made the pain still worse, but it freed Marsh. Air trickled into his lungs. The spasms in his chest stopped, and he sucked down a lungful of breath in one explosive inhalation. Razor-sharp pain in his ribs threatened to flay Marsh wide open.

Night became day. All around them, klieg lights bathed the Reichsbehörde in stark white brilliance. The light streamed through the void where Heike's outer wall had been. So, too, did shouts, screams, orders. LSSAH troops scurried back and forth. Pabst was there, shivering in the cold without his topcoat. Under his orders, the soldiers took positions in a loose line surrounding the farmhouse.

The colonel called for Buhler. The captain and the colonel's brief discussion ended with Buhler running toward the farmhouse. They recognized the pattern of destruction. Perhaps they lacked a complete picture of the situation, but they certainly knew Kammler's work when they saw it.

Marsh stood, then took Kammler's arm over his shoulder again. The mentally deficient man left a thick red smear on everything he touched. Gretel's ribbons had come undone in the fall.

'Hold him up,' said Marsh. He slipped off his belt, flipped it around Kammler's leg, and pulled until the large man cried. It wouldn't hold forever, but it was better than the ribbons. Tears and snot traced wet trails down Kammler's face. His skin had gone gray.

'Get us outside.'

They couldn't demolish the rest of the house from inside. Any one of them, or all three of them, could have been impaled on debris in the fall. Another blow from Kammler was likely to bring the rest of the burning structure down on their heads.

'G-g-g—' Kammler mumbled to himself. 'T-t-t-t.'

Gretel led. Kammler – shivering, weeping, and limping – was a heavy burden. Marsh pushed as hard as he dared, but he couldn't move very quickly while supporting the confused tele-kinetic. It would have been impossible to descend the servants' stair side by side, but Kammler's assault had torn away several load-bearing members, so the stairs now sloped away from the remains of one interior wall. It made the stairwell precarious but passable.

The damaged house fell apart around them. Overstressed timbers creaked and snapped; warped windowpanes spat shards of glass. They passed the doctor's laboratory, the incubator rooms, the kitchen. Their footsteps crunched on fragments of the stained-glass window. Marsh swept the floor with the soles of his boots; Kammler was barefoot.

Kammler's confused mumbling trailed off. He grew heavier, partially owing to Marsh's exhaustion, but mostly because the man was weak with blood loss. He shivered with cold and the onset of shock. Marsh doffed Pabst's coat and put it on Kammler.

Stay alive. Just a few more minutes. Please.

Buhler's voice called from deeper in the ruins. 'Kammler! Where are you?'

'B-buh-buh!' Kammler perked up. He squealed and clapped, weakly.

Marsh pulled von Westarp's Luger from his belt. Gretel reached up and covered Kammler's eyes with the palms of her hands. Buhler crept around the corner, flinching at every groan from the slumping farmhouse. Marsh put two bullets in his chest.

Gretel pulled Kammler away before he glimpsed his dead handler.

They paused to check the gauge on Kammler's battery. A bit more than half its original charge remained.

Marsh glanced out the window. Another line of soldiers had formed up along the gravel drive, rifles at the ready, facing the main entrance. Marsh started to point through the window, but Gretel stopped him.

'He needs an unobstructed line of sight. He'll think you want him to break the window.'

'They'll fire the second I kick open that door.'

'No, they won't.'

Gretel opened the door. As one, the soldiers aimed. Hands up, she stepped into the glare of the kliegs. 'He's taken Kammler!' she said. 'He's going to destroy the farm.'

The soldiers hesitated. Which bought Marsh just enough time to pull Kammler into the doorway. Gretel dove aside as Marsh pointed. 'Crush.'

Kammler pounded the soldiers into the ground like tent pegs. Another blow extinguished the spotlights and snapped the masts like matchsticks.

They pulled shivering Kammler outside. Marsh took him by the hand, coaxed him deeper into the darkness toward the forest. The sack of von Westarp's journals slapped against Marsh's leg, threatening to trip him. But they needed distance. The more Kammler could see of the farm at once, the better.

'Smash,' said Marsh. 'Crush!'

A final blow flattened the burning farmhouse into a raging bonfire. A funeral pyre. Next, Marsh directed Kammler's willpower against the chemical hut where batteries were manufactured: two blows to destroy it, a third to grind it into powder.

The debris cloud roiled with black smoke that carried the eye-watering sting of ammonia.

Spotlights swept the grounds, accompanied by the chatter of a machine gun. Soldiers had turned the heavy armaments from the training field toward defense. They didn't rush Marsh's position; instead, they hung back, keeping to the shadows behind the lights. Nobody wanted to be caught in the open where Kammler could see them.

A light raked across them, swept back, pinned the trio in its glare like butterflies beneath a stickpin. The defenders unleashed a fusillade from rifles and pistols. Marsh tackled Kammler aside as bullets sizzled through the night. The light followed them. Kammler sobbed in pain.

He pointed and yelled, but Kammler just gaped at him. Gretel snapped a peppermint stick and waved it under Kammler's bloody nose. He stuck out his tongue. She placed a fragment of candy on it.

The next blow took out the spotlights and the gun emplacement.

Barracks: destroyed.

Surgical ward: pulverized.

Each flattened building revealed the portions of the farm behind it, bringing more structures into Kammler's field of view. Some structures, like the icehouse and pump shed, weren't worth the expenditure of battery life.

Marsh pointed to the battery storage shed. 'Crush!'

Kammler scowled at the low brick building. It shuddered, then nothing. Spittle trickled from one corner of his mouth, faint pink in the moonlight.

'Crush!' Again, nothing. The defenders got another spotlight up.

Marsh checked the gauge on Kammler's battery. Just about empty.

The light slewed across the grounds, carving zigzag patterns in the darkness in its search for the assailants before another blast of Willenskräfte destroyed the light.

The light hit Marsh just as he undid the latch on Kammler's harness. 'There they are!'

Marsh dropped the dead battery into his sack, then tackled Kammler again. Gretel tossed him the spare. He fumbled it. The soldiers unleashed another fusillade.

Somebody, perhaps Pabst, called an order to kill the spotlight. They'd reacquired Marsh and company, but didn't want to provide Kammler with another target. The light died, yet still the darkness retreated, as though the night had suddenly come to fear the farm.

Marsh inched forward on his stomach, toward the battery he'd dropped. Night became day. He looked up, dreading what he'd see.

A figure stood in the center of the training field, sheathed in a swirling corona of violet flame.

Reinhardt blazed like a vengeful sunrise.

My world was chaos. Peals of man-made thunder deafened me, suffocated me, slapped me. My eyes burned from constant readjustment to darkness and light. As the bombers overflew me, so, too, did their payloads catch up, then surround me. Every explosion strobed the night and etched a still life of the dying city into my eyelids.

Miles behind me, a massive detonation turned night into day. I knew, before the shockwave hit, that the Jerries had punched through the roof of a munitions factory. The swirling fireball rose over the city, large enough for me to see in the mirrors. Its light outraced the thunder, but the concussion reached me a few seconds later. The earth shook with such violence that the Mulliner's wheels left the road. I lost control.

Drive wheels pushed to starboard, I steered to port as I skidded into a roundabout. Stephenson's car slid right across it and slammed to a halt against the empty fountain at the center. My door dented inward, head-butted by a cherub with pursed lips. Shattered window glass winged through the cabin like grapeshot. A jagged crack appeared in the fountain's empty basin. My arm felt as though I'd just been kicked by a pony.

The dent had me worried I'd permanently beached the car on the fountain. Not so, though freeing myself did mean shearing off most of the paint on that side of the car. So much for the old man's beloved vehicle.

I rejoined the race to find Liv and Agnes before the Luftwaffe got them. A spur off the roundabout took me speeding into Stoke Aldermoor. Residential. Everything looked the same to me. The headlamps didn't do a damn bit of good. I needed a bloody street sign. But of course they'd all been taken down as a precaution in case of invasion.

The Rolls Royce made short work of the first postbox I came across. Letters and envelopes went fluttering into the deadly night. I chased them. Another ton of ordnance rained on Coventry while I sifted through the addresses for a clue to my location, and Liv's. I read by the glow behind me as Coventry burned and dwindling searchlights crisscrossed the sky.

It took five more postboxes, but I found Liv's street. Question was, where was Liv? I'd passed a few municipal shelters on the way through. Had she scampered to one of the brick bunkers dotting the neighborhood? Or did this place have an Anderson?

I'd expected a terraced house. But this was nicer than our

place in London, I was sorry to see. Nicer than anything I'd ever been able to give her. Set back from the road a bit, lined with a little privacy hedge, brick pathway curving through the gate. Cedar shingles, new paint. The kind of place we'd always assumed, wrongly, we'd make our own one day. That we wouldn't be stuck in Walworth forever. Wrong, wrong, wrong.

I left the car running and didn't bother to knock. Anybody still inside – assuming they'd be that daft – wouldn't hear it over the whistling and concussion of Hitler's bombs drawing closer with every second. A gas main went up a few streets over. The explosion slammed me against the door. I tasted blood. Compared to the resulting fireball, the headlamps from Stephenson's car were a candle flame held against the sun.

'Liv!' I shouted. No response.

The foyer took me to a den. There Agnes's bassinet lay tumbled sideways on the floor, draped with a swath of pink elephants. I snatched her baby blanket on my way through. The fibers were damp. My daughter had sicked up. Liv hadn't had a chance to wash out the stain.

'Liv!' Empty house.

Please, God, let there be a garden.

Through the den, through the dining room, through the kitchen. A plate of reconstituted egg had gone cold on the table. Midnight snack? A door beyond the kitchen hung open, spilling light from the house into the rear garden. A breeze pushed on the door and pulled a creak from the hinges. Somebody had come through here in a hurry, reckless with haste.

Then I was outside and sprinting toward the familiar silhouette of an Anderson. The shelter rang like a gong from the pounding of my fists. I must have startled somebody, because my Agnes started to cry. I would know that sound anywhere.

'Liv! Olivia! Open up, damn it!' My ruined throat turned it into the bellowing of a madman.

'Oh, crumbs,' said the voice of an old biddy. Most definitely not my wife.

The door opened. A man squinted up at me. He looked roughly my age, though he wore the years a hell of a lot better. Also unlike me, he wore a clerical collar. I couldn't see into the dim lamp-lit shelter. He took in my scars, and what could have only been a wild-eyed expression on my face, with an impressive grace.

'Sir,' he said, taking my arm, 'you're safe now. Join us, please.'

Had I been a bereaved congregant, the tone of his voice would have been exactly what I needed. With a gentle tug, he tried to coax me inside. Brave fellow: all this while the whistle of free-falling explosives grew louder and the concussion of bomb blasts surrounded us.

The next hit to the neighborhood knocked us on our arses. Debris like a rain of knives pelted my head and shoulders. It sounded like hailstones on the Anderson.

The vicar jumped to his feet and tried to physically drag me into the shelter. I called for Liv again.

Movement in the shadows. An older lady moved aside, and then there she was, my Olivia, standing with a baby on her shoulder like a disheveled Madonna. She gaped at me.

'Commander?'

Reinhardt's brilliance cast knife-edged shadows in all directions. Every brick in the rubble, every strand of autumn-dry grass stood at the focus of its own spotlight. Heat shimmer rose from his body in waves, distorting everything around him like a desert mirage.

'Raybould. Hurry.' There was an edge to Gretel's voice. That was new. Marsh didn't like it.

The zone of heat shimmer expanded around Reinhardt as though he were inflating a balloon. Wider. Wider. Trampled grass flared to ash where his Willenskräfte scoured the earth. The crushed gravel drive became a scar of bubbling slag in its wake. Stray pockets of moonlit snow flashed into superheated steam.

Marsh scrambled for the fresh battery, snatched it, rolled. Glimpsed a twinkling moon. Reinhardt's wall swept toward them, too wide to dodge.

Gretel held Kammler's connectors at the ready. Marsh slammed the battery into his harness, hard enough to tear the buckle. She drove the wires home. *Click.*

Marsh pointed toward the tidal wave of invisible death speeding toward them. 'Wall!'

Kammler scowled. Frowned. 'W-w-w.'

There was nothing to see. He didn't understand.

'*Wall!*' screamed Marsh. His breath no longer steamed in the autumn night.

Nothing. Kammler moaned.

Marsh slapped him. '*WALL!*' Kammler's face twisted in confused anger. The night turned warm, too warm, like when he sat too close to the hearth at Will's favorite pub. Marsh hit Kammler again. 'Wall, damn it, wall!'

Kammler flailed at Marsh, confused, hurt, and angry. Marsh gasped at the pain in his ribs when the muscular imbecile flung him aside.

'Mm! Muh!' Kammler howled. 'Wuh! W-w-w—!'

His eyebrows came together, his lower lip slid up almost to the base of his nose. It was a frown of sorrow, a scowl of concentration, an expression of impotent rage.

Something rippled around Kammler. The air crackled. But not with electricity . . . it was the sound of countless little somethings locking into place. The explosion of Willenskräfte would have ripped Marsh to shreds if he'd still been in front of Kammler when the large man finally unleashed his power.

Marsh couldn't see the barrier that sped out from Kammler's body, only the way it refracted starlight and the torch-shine from Reinhardt, but he knew it was harder than diamond. Its passage threatened to suck the air from Marsh's lungs; his ears popped. The earth heaved underfoot. The expanding barrier dug a yard-deep furrow in the earth, plowing aside tons of soil and stone without slowing.

It raced toward the front of ash and glazed earth.

Marsh ducked. Gretel stood to watch the battle of wills unfolding upon the devastated grounds of her home.

Churned-up soil raced ahead of Kammler's Willenskräfte like water before the prow of a vast ship. It breached Reinhardt's fire line. In an instant, the cold, moist earth flash-baked to brittle clay and shattered against Kammler's implacable wall. A thousand dinner plates tumbled down a thousand stairwells, all at once. Marsh clapped his hands over his ears.

Soldiers unleashed a volley from rifles and machine guns. The rounds tinkled harmlessly in midair.

And still Kammler's barrier moved on. Unperturbed. Undaunted. Untouched by preternatural heat. The heat shimmer became a kaleidoscopic swirl as Kammler forced it back toward its creator. Reinhardt raged within an incandescent halo. The air turned violet from Reinhardt's efforts to scorch a hole through Kammler's willpower. Marsh caught a faint whiff of ozone.

Reinhardt flared again and blazed brighter still. It seared green and purple afterimages into Marsh's vision.

There was nothing the Aryan salamander could do to halt or even slow the relentless advance of the imbecile's barrier. But Reinhardt would never accept that. No. He'd never back down against a *retard*. Not with witnesses around. Marsh prayed for Reinhardt's pride to overwhelm his common sense. Just a little longer . . .

He realized that while Kammler may have been mentally deficient, his simplicity of mind was a virtue. He suffered no stray thoughts to confuse him or distract his concentration. He knew only a handful of concepts, and through the power of the Götterelektron, he brought them into being. Kammler was utterly focused, as only a simpleton could be, on the concept of 'wall.'

Reinhardt's fury lashed against it like the impotent fists of a child's tantrum. The barrier slowed. Wavered.

'Wall!' Marsh's scream tore something. Bitter saltiness trickled down his throat.

Kammler broke through. Rippling streamers of superheated air splashed across the grounds of the farm. Gouts of flame erupted from everything they touched.

Men screamed. The training field stank of charred pork.

Agnes cried. Liv said, 'What are you—'

I grabbed her wrist, dragging her toward the door. 'We have to go.'

'Sir,' said the vicar, 'this is madness. It isn't safe!'

To Liv, I said, 'You're safer with me.' I pulled harder.

'There's room for you here,' said Liv. She leaned against my pull, having overcome the initial confusion enough to realize I intended to take her out of the shelter and into the middle of one of the worst bombing raids Britain had yet suffered. I put my free arm around her waist and chivvied her toward the door.

'Charles! Do something,' said the old lady. She sat on a camp stool beside a cot. They'd folded blankets and pillows into a makeshift crib for my daughter. Good people. Their Anderson lacked the mildew stink of the one I'd built.

The vicar blocked our egress. He swallowed. 'I can't let you take the lady. She's here as our guest.'

I looked him in the eye. 'I can't let you stop me.' I'd gladly beat a man of the cloth, and whistle a merry tune while I left him and his wife to die, if it meant saving my wife and daughter. Perhaps he saw that in my eyes. He stepped aside.

Agnes screamed in our ears. Liv tried to wriggle out of my grasp. But she couldn't put up a real fight while she held our baby. She trembled against me. I hoped she couldn't feel the tightness in my trousers. Even now, in the midst of destruction, she aroused me.

'Commander, please!'

I leaned close, like I used to do when I came home from work and kissed the freckles on her neck, and whispered in her ear. 'Trust me. I'm here to save your life. And I think you know that.'

I'd thought I could read every nuance of her face, every twitch of emotion, every thought that flitted behind her eyes. But when she turned, she studied me with an expression I'd never known of her. Don't know what she saw, but the tension in her hips and back melted away as she leaned into my touch.

'We must hurry.' I guided her toward the door. We left the vicar and his wife without another word. They watched us go. He closed the Anderson behind us, and then it was just me, my family, and the Luftwaffe. The bombing was the equal of anything I'd seen in the original history. Gretel wasn't one for half measures.

Liv let me take Agnes. 'I have a car outside. Run!'

She kicked off her shoes and sprinted for the house. I jogged after her, making *shush* noises to Agnes as I went. A silly thing, I know, but she was my daughter and the sound of her cries hurt me more than all the death and devastation around me.

Liv held the kitchen door for me. Then we were through the house – 'No time!' I yelled when she stopped for the bassinet – and out the front. Liv started across the brick walkway, then stopped. I skidded into her. She wavered like a willow tree in March winds.

'My feet,' she said. Far above us, the sky opened up with a high-pitched whistle.

Shards of glass littered the walk. The nearest blast, the one that had knocked the vicar and me to our arses, had blown out the windows. I transferred Agnes to her. She nestled our baby in the crook of her arm.

'Here,' I said. I took Liv's free arm, pulled it over my shoulders, and wrapped one arm around her back. Like I used to do, when we danced to the music on the wireless. She crouched a bit, bending her knees because she understood what I intended before I said it. My other arm went under her knees. I ignored the flaring pain in my own knee when I took her weight. I tried, but failed, to also ignore the way the hem of her dress exposed her milky legs.

Glass crunched underfoot as I carried my family to the car. I'd carried Liv into the house in Walworth on the day we'd been married. Just like this, though we weren't also balancing a baby at the time. I know we made Agnes that night. Liv's hair tickled my face. She sniffed, as though trying to identify a scent.

I wasn't as strong as I had been in my youth. But there was Liv in my arms, and in that moment I felt as though I could have walked a mile if it meant holding her that much longer. The whistle grew louder but lower in pitch. I winced at the growing agony in my knee.

With shuffling footsteps I cleared the worst of the debris from a small spot on the pavement, then set Liv back on her bare feet beside the car.

Absently, Liv said, 'I think I know this car.'

The whistle became a hum, then three separate hums.

I put Liv and Agnes inside, jumped behind the wheel, slammed the engine into gear.

Hadn't even made it to second when three flashes in the rearview strobed my eyes in quick succession. The bombs fell across the road behind us like a string of pearls. The impacts merged into a single earthquake, rippling the road beneath us and sending the Rolls into a skid. Liv hunched over Agnes, sheltering our baby with her own body. Agnes howled. The car spun.

It gave us a glimpse of the devastation behind us. The first bomb had clipped the edge of the road a few hundred yards away. The second cratered the center of the street, halfway to where I'd parked the car. The third landed in the vicar's garden. Hot rubble, the remnants of the house and shelter, rained down on us.

Liv gasped. 'Oh my Lord,' she whispered. 'Deidre. Mr. Murray.'

Don't think about it, I ordered myself. *You aren't finished. Concentrate on the job.*

I laid my hand on the gearshift, but couldn't get the car into gear. My hand shook too violently.

Five minutes later and they'd be dead now.

'How?' Liv whispered. She was crying.

I shook my head. 'We're not safe yet.' I'm sure she heard how the curling edge of hysteria fluted my voice. No number of steady-ing breaths could dispel the chilly hollow in my chest. What man wouldn't piss himself after a bullet parted his hair?

Drive, I told myself. *You haven't beat Gretel yet.*

Yet my trembling hand still refused to work the gearshift. Liv saw my struggle. She laid her hand on mine. Together, we got the Rolls into gear.

We drove north, out of the city. The cacophony of destruction followed us through the night.

A firestorm engulfed the shattered ruins of the farm.

Good boy, thought Marsh. He put an arm around Kammler, who sobbed helplessly to himself. *To hell with the commander*, he thought. *We'll cut off his wires. Bring him to England. Find him a home.*

He turned to ask Gretel if she had any peppermint sticks. Something soft tickled Marsh's face. It reminded him of lying in bed with Liv, and the way her hair fell across his face and neck when he nuzzled her ear. The tickle was followed by a metallic whisper, like a knife blade winging through the night to carve apart moonbeams, and ended with a quick wet tearing sound. From Kammler's direction, something moist pattered against Marsh's neck.

He turned, thinking the mentally deficient man had spat on him. But a gash had opened in Kammler's throat. It glistened in the commingled light of moon and fire, like a second mouth vomiting blood. From the corner of his eye, Marsh saw the wound still stretching toward the hinge of Kammler's jaw. Another spurt.

Blood curtained down Kammler's throat like a waterfall. Wide, fearful eyes rolled back in his head. Marsh danced aside to avoid getting pinned under the burly man.

From beginning to end, the assassination lasted a few seconds. Marsh aimed a kick at the spot where Kammler's killer must have been standing to slash his throat, but Heike had already moved away.

Shit, shit, shit. Where is she?

Marsh crouched, spun. He searched the ground for signs of movement, signs of footsteps. But the flickering firelight cast irregular shadows across the ground. Heike landed a kick to his temple. He sprawled in the pool of Kammler's blood. Rolled. Jumped back to his feet.

Blood spatter. She couldn't possibly have sliced Kammler as she had without being subjected to blood spray. Had that, too, turned invisible when it came into contact with her? Her knife hadn't become visible when Kammler bled on it.

To his left, a scuffle, like the sound of a boot heel sliding on gravel. Marsh dove aside. A phantom blade nicked his shoulder. He spun, aimed another kick at empty air. The toe of his boot encountered faint resistance, as though he'd brushed Heike, but only just. If he'd hurt her, she didn't make a sound. He doubted it.

He jumped aside again, and did so every few seconds. An exhausting way to stay alive. Gretel was doing likewise. They moved like marionettes with tangled strings. A chaotic dance intended to confound their assailant.

It didn't prevent Heike from landing gashes on Marsh's arms, chest, face. Some shallow, some deep, all painful.

Marsh swung the sack containing von Westarp's journals in a wild arc. It didn't connect, but the scuffling of footsteps told him Heike had dodged. He ducked to one side and felt the breeze of a blade passing close to his face. Ducked again and collided with an invisible barrier.

'Ooof,' he said. Heike said nothing.

Gretel came up from behind and kicked at his invisible assailant. Marsh couldn't tell if the blow connected or not. Gretel dove aside.

He reached for Heike, tried to grapple with her, to pin her arms, but she had already danced away. She'd been trained too well. Her steaming breath should have given her away, but she held it, and only seemed to breathe when Marsh wasn't looking in her direction. He got a good slash across the forearms for his trouble.

The skin along his gashes pulled apart when he swung the sack again. Rivulets of blood ran down his arms, joining into tributaries that coated his hands. The neck of the cloth sack slid through his fingers, widening the arc of the journals and pulling him off balance. Heike rammed the toe of her boot into the small of Marsh's bad knee. The explosion of agony blew out his ability to stand. He hit the ground, and tried to roll away from the inevitable kicks. He failed. His ribs, already sore from Kammler, flared with new pain. Breathing became difficult.

But as long as Heike kicked him, he knew where she was. He slowed, gritting his teeth against the pain but hoping to present an irresistible target. Heike knew better than to attack from the same spot for more than a few seconds. But he was defenseless, bleeding from half a dozen wounds, on the ground ... *Thud. Thud. Thud.*

But Marsh grabbed the phantom boot with one hand and flung the sack at Heike with the other. A knife appeared in midair, where it tumbled into the brush. Marsh yanked on her foot with as much strength as he could muster. The strength that hadn't trickled away through his open flesh.

'Oof.' Heike's breath sparkled in the moonlight.

He half scrabbled, half leapt on the spot where she'd fallen. His blood disappeared when it touched her. Heike jammed stiffened fingers into his throat, his gashes, his eye. He saw stars; the pain loosened his grip. She wriggled out from beneath him.

Concentrating on the ground, eyes searching for any signs of movement, he said, 'Gretel, we ha—'

Something snapped tight against his throat, cutting off his windpipe. Heike was taller than Marsh. His feet left the ground when she heaved. Her muscular forearms pressed against his shoulders, her breasts against his back. Her belt dug into the soft flesh around his throat. He kicked at nothing, tried to slam his head against Heike's face, but the belt was too tight. Cartilage creaked in his trachea.

'I'm homeless because of you,' said Heike.

Her hot breath steamed against the back of his neck. It smelled of the sauerbraten she had eaten for dinner. The burning farm receded down a long, dark tunnel.

Heike shrieked. The belt slackened. Marsh fell to the ground, wheezing.

The invisible woman had released her Willenskräfte. No – her wires had been severed. And a dark stain spread across the back of her shirt, just above her waist, near the kidney. Gretel had recovered the knife.

Agony twisted Heike's face into a parody of itself. Falling to her knees, she managed to land a fist square on Gretel's face. The blow snapped Gretel's head back and bloodied her nose.

Gretel touched a fingertip to the blood streaming from her nose, then licked it.

'No,' she said. 'That won't be sufficient.'

She stepped behind Heike. The other woman tried to pivot on her knees, but with one hand pressed against her stab wound, she lost her balance. Gretel unplugged her own wires and flipped them around Heike's neck. She pulled. Heike arched her back.

Gretel whispered in the other woman's ear.

Heike jammed an elbow into Gretel. The *crack* carried to Marsh's ears and made him wince. But the smaller woman didn't lose her grip.

Heike's eyes, wider and bluer than a summer sky, followed Marsh as he staggered to his feet. He pulled von Westarp's Luger from his belt. But no fear shone through the look on her face, only hatred, as he pressed the gun to her temple. Whether it was for him, or Gretel, or both, he couldn't say.

Bullet to the brain. The commander had been very specific about that. Something about autopsies, and not leaving their brain matter intact.

Gretel released Heike's body. It slumped to the ground. Marsh put a second round into the dead woman's forehead for good measure. Then he crossed over to Kammler, and emptied von Westarp's gun with two more shots.

Every breath became a white-hot marlinespike prizing his ribs apart. Heike had broken at least one. Maybe more. His cuts opened and closed like little mouths when he moved.

They headed into the forest, toward the car he'd stashed that morning. He had to lean on Gretel. She was limping, too.

She said, 'I'll drive.' Marsh slumped into the passenger seat, already succumbing to pain and exhaustion.

'That could have gone better,' he mumbled.

The cacophony of destruction followed us far into the country. We ran out of petrol an hour before sunrise.

I coasted the Mulliner to the side of a country lane, then fetched the spare canister and dumped its contents into the tank.

Spilled petrol all over myself. My hands hadn't stopped shaking after the close call in Stoke Aldermoor.

Liv stepped out of the car. She stretched, yawned. The harrowing night had left her shaken, too. We hadn't spoken for the entire drive. Neither of us could come to terms with the situation. I couldn't believe my girls were truly safe. Hadn't Gretel foreseen this, too? Had she stationed a sniper up the road? What surprises awaited us back in London? And as for Liv . . .

'Thank you,' she said. 'I know I'll never fully understand what happened tonight, but thank you.' She wiped her eyes. 'I feel like you were sent here to protect us.'

I was. And I started to tell her so, but she laid a hand on my lips. I tasted salt.

'Thank you. For everything.'

She put her arms around me. I held her. She whispered, 'I feel safe with you, Jonathan. I want my daughter to grow up feeling that way.'

And there it was: the lifeline I'd prayed for. The second chance I'd strived for. All it took was traveling decades into the past, sending her husband on a suicidal errand, and facing down the Luftwaffe. I'd have done it all over without hesitation, just to hear again the offer implicit in Liv's simple words. My heart felt too big for my chest.

Liv looked up at me. Her lips parted. My knees sagged under the weight of my swollen heart.

How could it be infidelity to kiss my wife?

Her husband didn't deserve her. I knew her better. I'd learned from my mistakes. He never would. I leaned into her.

But what if our places were reversed, and I learned of this moment between Liv and another man? Learned that she had held up her heart, offered it to another? It would shatter me.

Her husband might still be alive. It wasn't fair to saddle him with mistakes he'd never made. Maybe he didn't deserve Liv, but he did deserve the chance to be a better man than I. Liv deserved a good man. A great man. It was too late for me to become that person. The fact I stood there, trembling with desire and crumbling resolve, proved it. But it wasn't too late for him.

I turned away. She kissed my cheek.

It was the one and only thing I'd ever done right in my life. And it left me wanting to die.

You'd better get it right this time, I told my younger self.

THIRTEEN

1 December 1940
Admiralty Citadel, London, England

Will's footsteps echoed through a long concrete passageway. The odor of drying paint cascaded down the stairwells, where it lay like a fog at the lowest level of the bunker. Every breath stung the back of his throat with fumes. The ventilation system hadn't been activated yet; Will had overheard a couple of men from the Royal Engineers discussing some problem with the charcoal filters. A metal conduit ran along the walls and ceiling. The conduit contained telephone and telegraph lines. Every fifteen feet, an olive-drab stencil mark read: CoG. This stood for 'Continuity of Government.' Will supposed a similar conduit ran through the PM's war rooms, which were situated nearby, at the southeast corner of St. James'.

Webber handed his identification papers to a Royal Marine sentry. Will did likewise. The sentry checked their names against an access list. The photographs of both men received careful scrutiny before the sentry permitted them to pass the checkpoint. Will followed the other warlock through a sequence of interlocked doors, like the airlock on a submersible or the sally port in a medieval fortress. Behind him, an iron-banded door clanged shut with enough force to rattle the conduits. The air here had been touched by the Eidolons, whose most recent visit had imbued it with a greasy texture akin to rancid butter. The rubber bladder taped to Will's arm, under his shirt, sloshed against the crook of his elbow. Pretending to scratch an itch, he double-checked the stopcock hidden just above his wrist.

As far as the public knew, the Admiralty Citadel – with its loopholed firing positions and reinforced, twenty-foot-thick walls – was intended as an impregnable bastion in case of Jerry invasion. It could, supposedly, withstand a direct hit from the Luftwaffe. This had yet to be tested.

The elaborate security meant Marsh had no chance of sabotaging another negotiation. It also meant Will had no chance of escape if the other warlocks detected his subterfuge. Pig's blood did not wash out easily; Will had thus far ruined two shirts in the course of practicing his sleight of hand. Marsh was a demanding taskmaster.

The machine-gun chatter of a Teletype machine led Will and his escort into a chamber thirty feet belowground. There they joined Grafton and Hargreaves. The Teletype received real-time updates from RAF sector command stations and the Chain Home RDF observation posts. Grafton read the terse situation report spooling from the Teletype and adjusted the position of pins dotting an immense map of southeastern England, the Channel, and northern France.

The pins represented the RAF's best guess as to the location and disposition of incoming bomber groups. Innocent Britons would die tonight. Fewer, if Milkweed succeeded in giving the defenders a supernatural advantage. More, if Will managed to scuttle the negotiation.

'Hurry,' said Hargreaves. He took a mercury thermometer from the table beside the Teletype. If they were to contribute to the night's defense, they had to achieve an agreement with the Eidolons *and* see it paid.

The summoning fell to Grafton and Webber. Will reflected upon the situation while they drew their knives.

Two weeks ago, after Marsh safely retrieved Liv and Agnes, Will had delivered the first piece of encouraging news since the inception of Milkweed. According to Stephenson, who was hooked into the Y-station listening post network, the forty-eight hours beginning with the Coventry Blitz saw a massive increase in enemy radio traffic pertaining to the REGP. Something big had happened.

Marsh the Younger had carried out his mission. Or, at the very least, he'd made a game attempt.

But, in the short term, the new development allowed Marsh the Elder to pursue more freely the second part of his mission from 1963. Until they knew more about the situation in Germany he still wouldn't attack the warlocks in full. The man wanted to have it both ways. But now he was willing to move more aggressively against the warlocks. He had already eliminated Pendennis, Milkweed's oldest warlock, so for his second target he chose Shapley.

The entire situation was steeped in a nauseating moral ambiguity. The elder Marsh had come back with tales of atrocities and murders and yet, to prevent them, he made himself a murderer. And Will his accomplice. The mathematics of salvation said it was a necessary evil for the greater good. But how did the scales weigh cold-blooded murder against sins that existed only in some phantom version of the future?

Something went wrong the night Marsh slipped into Shapley's room at the Savoy. He moved gingerly for days after the botched assault. The young warlock didn't die quietly in his sleep.

After Shapley was found dead in his hotel room, surrounded by signs of a struggle, Stephenson had demanded the warlocks move out of the Savoy and into the citadel. Will barely avoided the spartan accommodations through vociferous arguments that his brother's position in the Lords might draw undue attention to the citadel if it became known his younger brother had taken up residence there. Stephenson had relented, but only just.

As always, the warlocks drew the attention of something *other* through the use of Enochian, filtered through frail human biology and spilled blood, which carried the promise of eradication. Soon, the small chamber reverberated with a malignance vast as the cosmos. A century passed between each click of the Teletype. The sound burbled to Will's ears, distorted by its passage through thick, greasy air.

Hargreaves tackled the negotiation. Will followed the Enochian call-and-response. Once a price was reached, he would have to join in, to supply the blood that sealed their pact, and to later mark their payment of the blood price.

Salt stung Will's eyes. He wiped a hand across his forehead. It came away damp with sweat. But the effort to speak Enochian provided a natural cover for his anxiety.

Hargreaves donned a pair of leather gloves and snapped the thermometer. Quicksilver skittered across the floor.

Another update bubbled from the Teletype. The Luftwaffe was drawing closer. Hargreaves didn't have time to stand his ground against the Eidolons' demands, didn't have the luxury of carefully worded counteroffers.

The Eidolons demanded the blood of six new people. Six dead souls. In return, they would create a bank of clouds that just happened to contain trace amounts of mercury. Together, the commingled liquids would dust the enemy airplanes with moisture and metal. At which point the mercury would wreak destructive alchemy upon the aluminum airframes in the Junkers and Messerschmitts approaching Britain.

Or so the boffins said. Will didn't understand the details, even after he'd asked Lorimer to explain it. Something about 'oxide layers' and 'amalgams.' But he gathered that mercury could do terrible things to aluminum. The end result being a rain of German aero-scrap over southern England. Not enough to completely wipe out the bomber groups, but enough to give the RAF an edge.

A bit baroque, perhaps, but the important thing was the Eidolons merely provided the mercury. They didn't kill the attackers. Gravity would do that. The mercury would eventually fall as rain, and woe to the farmlands and streams below. But that wasn't the most harrowing sacrifice demanded by this plan.

Six souls. Hargreaves accepted.

Webber lifted the telephone alongside the Teletype machine. It had a direct line to Stephenson, who would have a Milkweed escort waiting for the warlocks when they emerged from the citadel to pay the Eidolons' price.

All that remained was to seal the pact. In the altered reality of the citadel sub-basement, the glow of the incandescent bulbs had become a celestial corpse light, the fading embers of dead stars. It glinted from Hargreaves's blade. The elder warlock flicked his hand to dust the concrete floor with his own blood.

Will produced his grandfather's knife, the one with the handle fashioned from a piece of deer antler, and followed suit with a similar gesture. He added a modest flourish that just happened to swipe the knife handle across his wrist, and thus opened the stopcock. By bending his elbow, he squeezed a good cut's worth of pig blood into the palm of his hand. The folding pocketknife closed the stopcock again when he snapped it closed.

Will flicked the contents of his palm onto the floor. And diluted Hargreaves's offering with useless dross.

The Eidolon sensed the substitution. Its irritation sent ripples through the reinforced concrete walls. It growled something too quick and harsh for Will to discern. Hargreaves glanced at Grafton and Webber, who returned equally blank looks. Nobody understood it. Everybody looked at Will. He made a mental note to ensure he didn't go last the next time around. Will shrugged, then made a show of flicking more blood from his fake wound.

The Eidolon withdrew in a deafening burst of silent malice that knocked the humans to the floor. The concrete walls became fractured glass. The room stank of fossilized bone and newborn starlight.

The deal, it seemed, had been canceled.

Will emerged from the citadel around sunrise. He suppressed the urge to sigh with relief as he passed the sentries and stepped onto the frost-slick cobbles of Horse Guards Parade. The failed negotiation had led to hours of postmortem analysis, including several futile attempts to translate the Eidolon's final declaration. However, by the end of the night, nobody had accused Will of subterfuge.

Stephenson would hit the roof, but Will had become accustomed to that. Better to endure a bit of the old man's temper than to be caught. They executed traitors. Will remembered poor Lieutenant Cattermole.

Will cut through the park on his walk home. St. James' at dawn. The rising sun hung below a layer of ashen clouds that looked destined to hide the sun for most of the day. The first rays of sunrise glinted on the lake and from the thin layer of ice along the shore that had coalesced during a recent cold snap. A raven watched Will from the bare boughs of a scarlet oak.

Will paused on the footbridge that straddled the lake. His breath formed a fog in the still morning air. The pelicans, he noted, were nowhere in sight. Smart beasts. It was chillier by the water. Numbness claimed his cheeks and nose. The sting of pins and needles enveloped his finger stump, as it often did in cold weather.

But the gentle rise in the center of the bridge afforded him a decent view of the surrounding city. Plumes of smoke rose from the northeast, southeast, and west. They reached all the way to the sky, and brushed the clouds with soot. The smoke cast long shadows over London. Somewhere, a lone siren bemoaned the night's horrors.

He wondered how many people had died in the bombing raid. More than six, certainly. He had replaced one atrocity with a greater one. It was a perverse way to go about saving the world. For how long would the war rage, and how many people would it consume in the course of averting Marsh's ghostly future? His certainty could be unnerving when he spoke so matter-of-factly about a future that was barely hypothetical to Will. The man had seen things no human should see.

Will opted to walk home rather than try to hail a taxi so early in the morning. He'd played a part in London's suffering. To follow it up by isolating himself from the city's woes felt immoral. Evil.

Soon the sun disappeared behind the sky's winter gray shroud. Few people were about. Will tipped his bowler to an ARP warden on his way home from his nightly rounds. A newspaperman heaved stacks of fresh papers from the back of a cart to the pavement alongside his stand. Will chose to avoid the morning headlines.

By the time he reached the door of his flat in Kensington, the winter chill had seeped through his clothing into the blood sloshing against his elbow. His arm felt as though he'd dunked it in the North Atlantic. It hurt. Numb fingertips fumbled the key, but he managed to get it into the lock after a few attempts.

He emptied the bladder into the jar of pig's blood in the refrigerator. Weskit and shirt hit the floor on the way to the bedroom. The leather straps left perfect impressions in his forearm when he undid the buckles. The empty bladder went into the chest at the foot of his bed, beneath several layers of books and papers.

Will had just washed up, and was pulling back the sheets in preparation to slide into bed, when somebody knocked at the door. Somebody insistent.

He knew that knock. Only one person was sufficiently brazen to call at such an indecent hour and be demanding while he did it. The 'commander' wanted a report.

Can't you give me a few hours' rest?

Will pulled on his dressing gown, and tied the sash around his waist as he returned to the front door. The knocking grew more insistent.

'Yes, yes,' Will called. 'Not one for social niceties, are you? Can't you let me—'

He opened the door. His caller was indeed Marsh. But not the Elder.

Long thin scabs crisscrossed his gaunt face. He'd been in a fight and taken a few slashes. His hair, poorly trimmed and lank, stuck out in uneven tufts. What on earth had happened to this man?

'Hi, Will, long time no see. I need a favor,' said Marsh. He bulled his way inside with somebody in tow.

Will stood in the doorway, incapable of anything but gaping. His mind had seized up.

'You're alive,' he managed.

'Yes. Now please shut the damn door,' said Marsh.

Will managed this, too, but only just. He embraced Marsh. Marsh winced. 'Welcome home, Pip! Welcome home.'

Marsh's companion tossed back the hood of her overcoat. Gretel said, 'Hello, William. How is your hand?'

Marsh's adventures during the long months of his disappearance had done nothing to lessen his intensity and focus. The man actually had the gall to believe he would visit just long enough to suborn Will into minding Gretel for a few days. The impudence, expecting he could swan right back out again without a word of explanation or even a cursory catching up. But Will was having none of that. He refused to cooperate unless Marsh filled him in.

It seemed he was making a habit of sitting stupefied in his own parlor while listening to a long, improbable tale from Raybould Marsh. If a *third* Marsh appeared on his doorstep, brimming with news of the distant past, Will decided he'd have to turn the fellow away. Two were more than enough, thank you.

Gretel sat in a satin striped armchair that matched the chaise longue. It was almost too big for her; her toes barely reached the floor. She listened impassively to the exchange. The expression on her face lay somewhere between boredom and tolerant amusement. It never changed. Not even when Will feigned ignorance regarding one Commander Liddell-Stewart, though of course she knew the truth.

Marsh had flitted off to Germany before Will undertook his warlock recruitment drive. He knew nothing of the current status of Milkweed, or its efforts during the past half year. Will summarized the situation. But he omitted the part where the commander turned him into a double agent, and how together they were working to undermine and destroy the warlocks.

Will told his visitors about the increased radio traffic. 'It's truly done? Von Westarp's farm is no more?'

Gretel yawned. She hopped to her feet and shuffled into the kitchen. Marsh followed her with his eyes.

'Yes,' he said. He nodded toward the kitchen. 'She's among the last. There are two others. A pair of twins.'

His movements were stiff and awkward. Will could see the bulges of bandages under Marsh's shirt.

Marsh said, 'I assume it was you who sent the Eidolon to find me.'

'Yes.' Will hoped Marsh wouldn't dig deeper. This was another topic skirting the thorny issue of the commander.

'Thank you, Will. I'd still be rotting in a Schutzstaffel dungeon if you hadn't done that.'

Will grinned. 'I'm delighted to know it worked.'

China rattled in the kitchen while Gretel rummaged through Will's cabinets. Will lowered his voice to a whisper. 'Why did you bring her back with you?'

'It wasn't easy getting here, you know. There are flights from Berlin to London these days, but they don't take passengers.' Marsh shook his head. 'Even with her help, it still took a fair bit of doing.'

'Ah.' Another series of clinks and rattles came from the kitchen. Will raised his voice. 'Do be careful, won't you? Those dishes are expensive, and difficult to replace.'

'I'm hungry,' Gretel said in her throaty German accent. Will flinched, imagining the uproar if his neighbors heard her. She held the teakettle under the faucet.

Over the *click-click-whoosh* of the gas fob, Will asked, 'How will you explain this to Stephenson?'

A terrible weariness settled over Marsh. He sat, silent,

unmoving, deep in thought. When he cracked his knuckles against his jaw, his sleeve slid down to reveal terrible gashes on his arm. At last, he admitted, 'I don't know. The old man's going to lose his nut when I turn up. I need to confer with the commander before I do that. But until I see Liv, they can both hang.'

He slapped his knees, then stood. He slung his haversack over his shoulder. 'I can't stay any longer. I need to go home.'

Oh dear. This was going to become very complicated and rather quickly.

Gretel found Will's toaster and set it on the counter. Marsh said, 'Keep an eye on her for a few days, won't you?'

'I don't like this. What happens when they call me for another negotiation? I can't bring her along.'

'A few days. That's all I'm asking.'

Will sighed. 'Very well.'

'Cheers, Will.' Marsh turned for the door. Gretel rattled the kitchen drawers in search of a spoon. The teakettle whistled.

Without thinking, Will blurted, 'There's something you need to know about Liv.'

Oh, sodding. What am I to say? She's being seduced by your older self? She has developed an emotional connection with another man? Another version of you?

'The thing of it is,' said Will, 'she's, that is . . .'

You nearly broke her when you disappeared, and then she had a terribly close call. You weren't there when her life needed saving. I don't know how she'll receive you.

I don't know which of you deserves her more.

'Well, she went to Coventry, you see . . .'

In the kitchen, Gretel fell silent.

Marsh's gaunt face turned ashen. He took Will's arm in a grip of banded iron. His fingers dug painfully at the strap imprints. 'What are you saying? What happened?'

This had been a mistake. Now the poor fellow was terrified. 'Never mind,' said Will. 'I've kept you long enough. Go home to your wife and daughter. They've missed you terribly.'

In the kitchen, a teacup shattered. Then came the bong and splash of a teakettle crashing to the floor, and the gurgle of boiling water.

Gretel screamed.

2 December 1940
Walworth, London, England

Despair worse than anything he'd ever felt in the SS prison turned Marsh's blood to ice water as his taxi approached Walworth. From Will's flat in Kensington, the route took him east, across the Thames. Bomb damage became increasingly prevalent the farther toward the East End they went. The Luftwaffe had been busy.

I've finally solved a long-standing problem.

She went to Coventry, you see . . .

Coventry was already on their list . . .

Was Liv your long-standing problem, Gretel?

Just three streets from his home, Marsh watched a milkman climb over a pile of rubble, the bottles clanking in his wire basket. Bloody close, that one. Liv and little Agnes must have felt it, all alone in their shelter.

Alone.

Dear God, was he frightened. He had abandoned his family. The why of it didn't matter, here in the Blitz-ravaged ruins of the city. The grand strategies of covert warfare meant nothing to widows and fatherless babes. He may have been a decent soldier, a faithful defender of the realm, but he was a failure of a man.

What would Liv do when she saw him? Was their relationship dead? How big was Agnes? Restless tendrils of anxiety squirmed through his gut like a nest of asps. Sweat soaked the underarms of his shirt.

Had Liv moved on? Had she assumed the worst?

Will had wanted to deliver a warning. Anything he might have said was delayed indefinitely by the rush to apply first aid to Gretel. They couldn't risk taking her to the hospital, but the girl was damn lucky. If there was one thing any warlock always had on hand, it was a supply of clean bandages. She'd recover, though she'd carry the scars for the rest of her life.

Marsh had noticed the cracks in Gretel's imperturbable façade as soon as he returned from Berlin. The woman no longer affected her air of perfect sangfroid. She was edgy.

The scene in Will's kitchen was no mere crack. It was complete disintegration.

But then his house came into view, and all he could think about was holding his baby daughter again. He paid the driver with cash borrowed from Will. It emptied his pockets of everything but a few shillings and a bloody rag. No ID, no billfold, no house key. Nothing to anchor him in his home country; no means of walking in and surprising Liv. He'd have to knock on the door like a common salesman. And hope to hell she didn't slam the door in his face.

Flowers. Should he have brought flowers? No. Not if he didn't want to be insulting. No gesture could atone for his absence. To suggest it might would only make things worse.

The house sat proud and silent, outwardly untouched by the surrounding devastation. He knocked. Waited. Knocked again, harder. Marsh tried to peer through the front windows, but it was still morning and Liv hadn't yet pulled the blackout curtains aside. No answer.

He went up the street, cut through an alley, and came around behind the house. The garden gate creaked; for once, he welcomed the racket, in hopes that Liv might be feeding Agnes in the kitchen, where she could hear it. Though if that were the case she'd have heard him knocking, too.

Surely Liv wasn't ... sleeping elsewhere. Surely there was a simple explanation. Perhaps Agnes had been crying, crying for her morning feeding, and Liv hadn't heard the door. Or couldn't get to it.

He'd expected to find the garden in a shambles: untended, choked with winter-brown weeds. But Liv had done a fine job with it. The plot was neat, the soil clear of weeds and ready for next spring. It appeared she'd even grown things atop the Anderson. Clever. She'd done quite well without him. Marsh tried not to take that as an omen.

The kitchen door rattled under the blows from his fist.

'She isn't home,' said a gravel-and-whiskey rasp.

Liddell-Stewart emerged from the garden shed, looking just as wretched as he had on the night he'd spun the lie that convinced Marsh to undergo his mission in Germany. He carried a bundle wrapped in a handkerchief. They shook hands. Strong grip, the commander.

'Welcome back.' He handed the bundle to Marsh.

It contained Marsh's National Registration Identity Card, bill-fold, and keys. He hoped the relief wasn't too evident as he filled his pockets. He went to unlock the kitchen door.

'First things first,' said the commander, nodding toward the shed. 'Let's have a chat.'

Marsh said, 'I haven't been home in over six months, mate. Just try to stop me.'

The scents of home washed over him when he opened the door. A dusting of Agnes's baby powder, on the table. The last slivers from a cake of hand soap at the kitchen sink. Watery tea, long steeped in a pot beside the stove.

The commander waited at the kitchen table. Marsh went through each room, pulling back the blackout curtains as he went. Agnes's baby blanket lay on the floor of the den, alongside her bassinet. Upstairs, he found the bed unmade on Liv's side. She had taken a wedding photograph from the mantel downstairs and set it on the bedside table. It faced her side of the bed, so she could stare at it while she lay on her side. Stephenson's wife had taken it on the day of their wedding. House dust coated the wooden frame.

But where was Liv?

Back in the kitchen, Marsh laid a hand on the teapot alongside the stove. It was cool to the touch. She'd boiled the water at least a couple of hours ago.

Had they evacuated? Relief and disappointment tore through him like shrapnel. Knee-sagging relief at the thought that his wife and daughter were safely away from the bombing. Heart-pinching disappointment, after waiting so damn long to be with his family again to miss them by just a few hours.

No note, though. That wasn't like Liv.

Liddell-Stewart said, 'Are you quite finished?'

'Where—'

'She's safe. We debrief before we play.'

'I haven't seen my family in half a year, mate. Where do you get off telling me to wait longer?'

'Where do you get off putting your personal issues before the safety of the country?'

Christ, what a bastard. But Marsh joined him at the kitchen table.

'It's done,' he said.

'Tell me everything. Omit nothing.'

'I've a better idea,' said Marsh. Maybe it was better Liv wasn't here for this. 'Let's start with your tale about the mole in Milkweed. Spun from whole cloth, wasn't it?'

The commander looked ready to burst. 'What did Gretel tell you?'

'Nothing. But once I got on that wretched U-boat it became clear she'd arranged the rescue herself.'

The commander sighed. 'Yes. It was a lie.'

'You fucking unbelievable bastard.'

'We had a narrow window. I had to get you on that boat. Believe me, this was the best way. I know you better than you think. You would have argued all night long.'

'The best way? Your lie put me in a Schutzstaffel prison cell for months! You've no idea what it was like. I spent months savoring thoughts of how I'd mess you about.'

The commander matched Marsh's fury. 'I'm not sorry. You have no idea how terrible things might be right now if you hadn't gone to Germany. So stop acting a bloody martyr and tell me what happened.'

It took two hours. Marsh started his story at the moment he drove off with Gretel and Klaus. He detailed their voyage in the U-boat, his arrival at the farm, his interactions with members of the Götterelektrongruppe. He described the menial work of cleaning and feeding Kammler. He explained how Gretel arranged the long detour in Berlin. Spoke of the long, dark months in prison. Described his interactions with Himmler. Related the Eidolons' role in his escape and the destruction of the files. (The commander picked through this part of the story with exasperating diligence.) He drank two glasses of water before moving on to his reunion with Gretel, the death of von Westarp, their use of Kammler, and finally the battle at the farm.

Marsh said, 'Got some souvenirs for you. Bit early, but Merry Christmas.' He reached into his pocket, then tossed the blood-stained rag to the commander. 'Menstrual blood, from one of the Twins.'

Liddell-Stewart tucked it away. 'Well done.'

'That's just part of it.' Marsh opened the haversack and set von Westarp's journals on the kitchen table. 'Voilà.'

The commander flipped through the top journal. 'What the hell are these?'

'The personal journals of Herr Doktor von Westarp. His every secret and discovery. Decades of his brilliance. All rendered in the master's own hand.'

'I didn't say anything about bringing these back.'

'I improvised.'

'You went off mission.'

'The mission was spectacularly flawed.'

'Your instructions were—' The commander drew a deep breath. With visible effort, he reined back his temper. 'Very well. I'll see these are properly cared for.'

He truly was a bastard, the commander. Demanding. Rude. Impertinent. Marsh tried to look past it. 'The rag is for the Eidolons, isn't it? You intend to use them as bloodhounds, to track down the Twins.'

'They're the last loose end. They're all that's left of the Reichsbehörde.'

'Not quite. Those two, plus Gretel.'

'You let her *live*?' The commander slammed a fist on the table. The veneer broke apart in a long, jagged crack. An empty salt-cellar bounced across the table. He stood. 'That's the worst bloody thing you could have done!'

'Perhaps you missed the part of my story where the SS had every goose-stepper and hausfrau in the Thousand-Year Reich watching for me. Without her help, I'd never have made it off the Continent. And have you forgotten her little quirk? How on earth do you kill a woman who knows the future? It's impossible, which you'd know if you ever tried.'

The commander squeezed his eyes tight, pinched the bridge of his nose. He rasped, 'And where is she now?'

His wreck of a voice trembled with such hatred that he reminded Marsh of an Eidolon. It brought flashbacks to the archives of Prinz-Albrecht-Strasse, where shadows slithered and men screamed away their sanity. He shook his head, but the waking nightmare clung to him like dusty cobwebs.

'Will's flat,' Marsh said. 'He agreed to watch her for a few days.'

'Are you mad? Beauclerk can't handle Gretel.'

'I'm not so sure. She's … changed. And besides which, she won't be walking anywhere soon.'

The commander fixed him with a narrow gaze. He crossed his arms across his chest. 'Tell me.'

'The change was subtle at first, and you know she's fucking inscrutable at the best of times. But I'd swear she's … less confident. Tentative. We had a miserable time getting off the Continent. It should've been easy for her.'

This sparked something in the commander. His eyes took on a predatory gleam.

Marsh continued, 'But that's not the interesting part. On the night I returned to the farm, Gretel was in consultation with, get this, none other than Hermann Göring. They were discussing—'

'Coventry.' The commander didn't make it a question.

Marsh blinked. 'Yes. That's right. But when I pressed her about it Gretel said she had "finally solved a long-standing problem." That's a quote, by the way.'

'How did you interpret that?'

'I couldn't. Not at the time. But I think I have a good idea now.' Marsh related the incident with the teakettle at Will's flat. 'It's only a guess, but I suspect—'

'—Gretel is losing her ability.' The scars and beard couldn't diminish the glee, the sheer naked malice in the commander's expression. It made Marsh shudder.

The commander said, 'It's almost too much to hope for.'

The clock on the mantel in the den chimed noon. Marsh frowned. Liv still hadn't returned. This wasn't right.

'Right. We're done here.' Marsh went to the vestibule. He lifted the telephone. 'Now if you'll kindly sod off, I'm going to find my wife and daughter.'

The commander coughed. 'That might be a bit of a job.'

Marsh dropped the phone. 'Out with it.'

'Li— Olivia was taken by SIS several days ago.' He raised a hand, quickly, as though fending off an attack. Which he was. 'She's safe. Agnes, too. But they're holding her for questioning.'

'What? Why on God's earth would they do that?'

'Because,' said the commander, 'they're looking for me.'

Marsh jumped him.

FOURTEEN

'You want Liddell-Stewart? I'll give him to you, right now, trussed up like a goose on a Christmas platter.'

The man sitting across the desk from Marsh made a note in his ledger. The nib of his fountain pen skritched across the paper. His haste kicked out errant droplets of ink to stain his fingertips. 'I see. Now, is that Stewart spelled with a *w*, or Stuart spelled with a *u*?'

'Ask him yourself, what?'

The reedy man from MI6 adjusted his reading glasses. The placard on his office door said HARRISON. 'And you say he's a commissioned naval officer?'

'I said he calls himself a lieutenant-commander.'

They sat in an office overlooking Broadway. Stephenson had had an office in this building, in the days before Milkweed. Marsh had delivered the Tarragona filmstrip here.

But this was his first visit to SIS HQ since the move to the Old Admiralty building. It hadn't taken long after he announced himself at the Secret Intelligence Service to get whisked into the office of a man familiar with the case. They had, after all, been watching his house for seven months. And at Marsh's own request, more or less.

After France, when Gretel had flaunted detailed knowledge of Marsh's home life, he'd asked Stephenson to put watchers on the house. But that had been when Milkweed was an obscure group with four members. So the old man, acting in his capacity as a section leader, had arranged the surveillance through other channels in SIS.

Marsh had forgotten all this. He'd had other things on his mind since then.

He'd extracted the rest of the story from Liddell-Stewart, who'd filled in the gaps with educated guesswork. Somewhere along the line, the crew running the observation on Marsh's house had learned that the Security Service, MI5, sought a man who matched the description of a fellow who'd been seen visiting Liv since early summer.

Naturally, they were curious. So they took her.

By the time Marsh made it to the Broadway Buildings, his anger had cooled just enough that he could converse coherently. The fight with Liddell-Stewart had been short and savage. A rib had given way under the bandage. He'd have to see a proper quack after this was sorted.

'And you subdued him when you found him in your home?' *Skritch, skritch*. Harrison leaned forward, smudging his weskit with ink. 'Is that how you received the ... ' He gestured at his own face.

'Oh, Jesus sodding Christ on a sodding camel. Look! These cuts aren't fresh, mate. Brilliant observational powers here in the rest of SIS. We ought to pack it in, you lot have it all sussed out, don't you.'

Skrtich. Skritch. Skritch.

The file folder sitting alongside the blotter contained a summary of the observation team's findings since May. With forced nonchalance, Harrison said, 'I understand that you've been away from home for some time. Just for the sake of completeness then, where exactly have you been?'

Nice try, mate.

Marsh leaned forward. Harrison flinched. 'Milkweed reports directly to the PM. So short of a directive from Churchill himself, or a proclamation from the King, what I do is none of your bloody business.'

Harrison set aside the fountain pen. He pulled a handkerchief from his breast pocket and set about cleaning the spittle from his eyeglasses. 'Mr. Marsh. I understand your frustration. Truly I do. This is a trying time for every Briton. Please understand we're not doing this arbitrarily. We believe that this commander fellow is mixed up in something grim.' He set the glasses back on his nose, then picked up the file. 'When the police nabbed him in St. James', he was carrying a passel of documents supposedly belonging to the brother of a member of the House of Lords.' He squinted at something, then chuckled. 'Rather sloppy work, though. Gibberish, all of it.' Harrison read further. 'That same brother, by the way, later hinted at being involved with secret work for HMG.'

Marsh ran a hand over his face. Under his breath, he said, 'Damnit, Will.'

'I understand you know Lord William. Do you work together?'

'I know him from Oxford.'

'Ah! Very good. Balliol College, '36.'

'Bully for you.'

Harrison frowned, sighed, turned his attention back to the file.

'Well then. Getting back to the police. When asked, this mystery fellow claimed to be John Stephenson. I've spoken with the constables in question. They remember that night clearly. Unusual circumstances, you see.' He tapped his temple. 'Anyway, the name raised a few flags. Seems there had been a Stephenson here in SIS, before he created his own section and toddled off to the Admiralty.'

'You don't say.'

'Now here's where it gets rather interesting indeed.' Harrison set the file open on the desk, then leaned over it with fingers locked together. 'Once set loose, our mystery man shows a remarkable skill at evading trails and escaping detection. Almost as if he'd been trained. MI5 loses him immediately. And he might have been lost forever at that point,' he said. 'But he reappears when our own watchers observe him spending quite a large amount of time with the wife of a fellow agent of the Secret Intelligence Service. An agent who works for John Stephenson. The same Stephenson, it should be noted, who requested the surveillance in the first place.'

He closed the file, and plied Marsh with a we're-all-just-doing-our-jobs-here-surely-you-see-that type of smile.

'So. Do try to see it from our point of view, won't you? Whoever this Liddell-Stewart fellow might be, he's intimately connected to the SIS. And, it appears, your wife. So while you fellows have been having a jolly time running your own little fiefdom in the Admiralty, we've—'

Marsh cut him off by jumping to his feet and wrenching Harrison out of his chair by the necktie. Marsh grabbed the fountain pen. He leaned over the desk, and pulled Harrison closer until their noses touched.

'Stop wasting my time with your internecine bun fight. I

haven't seen my wife and daughter in seven months. Take me to them, now, and in return I'll give you Liddell-Stewart. Or, keep wasting my time, and I'll put the nib of this pen into your carotid before you can call for help.'

A trickle of ink stained his fingers. He shoved Harrison away. The bureaucrat fell backwards over his chair. A man barged into the office. Tall fellow, bit soft around the middle, hair shorn close to the scalp and gone gray at the temples. Ex-army? He gave Marsh a hard look.

'Everything all right, sir?'

Harrison climbed out from under his overturned chair. He'd gone scarlet. He coughed, loosened his tie, and waved the other man away. 'Yes. It's under control,' he managed. 'Thank you.'

Once they were alone again, and Harrison had composed himself, he said, 'They're at a safe house in Croydon. I'll take you myself.'

His experience in Germany had Marsh dreading the worst. He expected to find Liv and Agnes stuck in a lightless oubliette. But the Croydon safe house was, outwardly at least, a perfectly ordinary corner lot on a perfectly ordinary set of dingy brick terraced houses. Harrison stayed in the car while Marsh went inside.

The safe house parlor doubled as a reading room. A pair of windows with quarreled windowpanes overlooked the street. They were flanked by floor-to-ceiling bookcases of leather journals and black binders that Marsh knew, from his experience in MI6, held newspapers. The glass panes had been removed from the bookshelves, as a precaution against Jerry bombs. Battered armchairs with torn upholstery were scattered about the room and around a long table that might have dated from Cromwell, judging from its nicks and gouges. A blanket and two sofa cushions had been turned into a makeshift bassinet.

Liv was in the kitchen. A saucepan and two teakettles adorned the stove. The room smelled of warm milk on the stove and a soiled nappy.

Marsh's breath hitched in his chest. A single glance was enough to quench the furnace heat of his rage, like a campfire buried beneath a glacier. It left him hollow and windblown, uncertain and more than a bit afraid. He swallowed. His mouth tasted sour.

She sat at the table with her back to the door. The crook of her arm cradled Agnes in a pink elephant blanket; she fed the baby from a bottle.

Her hair was longer than when he'd last seen her. Several wisps of auburn had escaped from her hairpins, to dance about her head like a halo. She'd lost the last bit of roundness from the final stages of her pregnancy.

Liv sighed at the sound of his footsteps. Without turning her attention from Agnes, she said, 'We've been over this quite enough. I can't tell you what I don't know. So I do hope you've come to take me home.'

He knew that tone in her voice. The last threads of her patience had come undone, leaving no buffer on her irritation.

Not upset. Not afraid. But bloody angry. Woe to SIS.

'I have,' said Marsh.

Liv froze. From his vantage in the doorway, he saw the subtle tightening of skin along her neck and jaw. He knew she was steeling herself to look. Hoping her mind hadn't played a cruel joke on her. Hoping her husband's voice hadn't been a hallucination. Because her hope for reunion had withered. But now, suddenly, the moment was upon her, bringing with it a surfeit of contradictory emotions. She knew not what to do, nor what to say.

She stood. With great care, she set Agnes's bottle on the table. Next, she straightened her dress. Then she secured Agnes in the crook of her arm, drew a deep breath, and turned.

Liv's eyes were red and watery. Agnes was twice as big as he remembered. Marsh's heart was a snowball. He felt a hollow shell of a person.

'Raybould?' Liv's voice came out thready.

He found his voice. 'Hi, Liv.'

Wife and husband stared at each other. An unbridgeable chasm, each ticktock between heartbeats.

'I thought you were dead—'

'I'm so sorry—'

'—and that I'd never know how or why or where. I never heard from you. Not one word.'

'I'm so sorry,' he repeated. 'I thought about you every single day. Every hour. It kept me alive.'

Not gently, she said, 'I grieved for you, Raybould. I had to come to terms with never seeing you again, and we couldn't even hold a funeral to say good-bye ...' She sobbed. 'I didn't know what to tell Agnes when she grew older.'

Agnes sneezed. Absently, Liv dabbed their daughter's face with a corner of the baby blanket. Their daughter.

'My God, she's so big.' Marsh found he was crying. He held his arms out. 'Please?'

Later, he wouldn't remember how the gulf was bridged, but somehow Liv was in his arms while they cradled the baby between them. Soft lips. Hot tears. Liv's hair smelled of old sweat. Agnes was still tiny, still an infant, yet so large he wanted to rage at the world. He'd lost so much of her life.

'I couldn't tell you where I was. I couldn't tell anybody. I wanted to. Dear Lord, I thought the loneliness would crush me to death.' The words came tumbling past his lips, riding his breath into her ear.

Liv said, 'Just don't insult me by pretending it was work for the Foreign Office.' Her fingertips traced the cuts on his face. 'What did they do to you?'

'I can't . . .'

'I know.' She said, 'When?'

'This morning. Just now. Have they been asking about Liddell-Stewart?' She nodded. 'Don't worry. I caught him sneaking around the house. They'll let you go now. They can question him to their heart's content.'

She pressed her lips to his ear. 'Raybould, no! You mustn't,' she hissed.

'Liv, he—'

'No, you don't understand. He's a friend. You've no idea what he's done for us.'

Marsh tensed. How had that wretched, plug-ugly excuse for a man won his wife's devotion? What had taken place while he was away? Seven months . . . So much could happen in that time. An entire chapter in the life of his family. 'They told me he came to the house.'

Liv hesitated. 'He watched over us while you were away. It was as though he knew, Raybould. I can't explain it, but I'd swear he knew something terrible was coming and he was sent to protect us.'

Marsh asked, 'Protect you from what?' But he knew the answer: *I've finally solved a long-standing problem.*

'He saved us, Raybould. He saved our lives. I tried to stay in London, truly I did, I wanted to be here when you returned, but the bombing was so terrible, every night the airplanes came, and I started to believe you were gone forever. I couldn't take it any longer. Will convinced me to leave London. I wanted to go to Margaret's house in Williton but the commander was dead set against it, and he'd been such a good friend I didn't want to betray his trust. Aunt Margaret called around and scraped up a billet for the two of us, so I took Agnes to Coventry. I thought anywhere had to be better than London.'

'Liv. What happened in Coventry?'

She started to shake. 'It was terrible. You've no idea. The bombs fell like rain. I thought the Jerries wouldn't stop until there wasn't a single house left standing. But then the commander arrived.' Her whispering tickled his ear and cheek. She hadn't brushed her teeth today. 'In the midst of that hell, he came for us. He found us in the middle of this terrible attack, insisted we come with him. Almost dragged me out of the shelter. But then we were in his car and had barely moved and then the house . . .'

Liv trailed off. She pressed her forehead against the crook of his neck. A tear dripped under his collar. Marsh tightened his arms around her, careful not to squeeze Agnes.

Dear Lord: Liddell-Stewart had saved his wife and daughter. And not from a run-of-the-mill raid, either, but saved them from something that Gretel had orchestrated. He'd known what she intended. He'd known the bint would move against Marsh's family. And he intervened. Marsh remembered that night in the garden shed, remembered the passion, the sheer hatred, that entered the broken ruin of the commander's voice whenever he spoke of Gretel.

Never trust Gretel. Never.

A wide-eyed fervor like that, such enmity, didn't arise easily. It was the fanaticism of a man who'd been cut down to the bone.

Of a man who'd seen his life destroyed. And he'd known Gretel would try to do the same to Marsh.

He'd deal with her soon. But first things first.

If not for the commander, Marsh wouldn't have had a family with whom to reunite. Marsh owed him an unpayable debt. And he wanted to know more about the man who could thwart Gretel.

It was Marsh's turn to whisper. He leaned down to touch his lips against the soft, cool curve of Liv's ear. 'The commander is trussed up in our Anderson shelter. I stashed him there before coming here.'

Liv started. She looked up. 'Did you hurt him?'

'No. I don't think so. I mean, not permanently.'

'Oh, Raybould.'

Think quickly, now. What would Harrison and company believe? They suspect a connection between the commander and Will. They know I'm connected to Will . . .

Marsh tipped his head toward the door. 'I'll tell them I've tracked the commander to one of the offices for Aubrey's foundation. The one Will uses from time to time, above the Hart and Hearth. I'll lead them there, in exchange for one of his men driving you and Agnes home.'

That would keep Harrison well away from Liv and the commander for a few hours.

2 December 1940
Walworth, London, England

I came around on the frigid floor of the Anderson shelter. My younger self hadn't lit a lamp for me, but dreary daylight snuck through cracks around the door. Enough to illuminate my situation, once my eyes adjusted.

My wrists ached where my younger self had tied them to the corners of the cot. He'd used lengths of rough, scratchy hemp rope from the garden shed. It didn't take much struggling to abrade the skin on my wrists. He'd pulled my arms as wide apart as the cot would allow. The growing ache between my shoulder blades had woken me. But I couldn't feel a damn thing below my knees. He'd cinched them together with the belt from his trousers; he'd used my own belt to do my ankles, and then more rope to secure my feet to a bolt in the Anderson's steel hull.

He had me stretched out like the Christ figure in a passion play. I wondered if he'd noticed I was wearing his clothes. I ran my tongue along the hard crust at the corner of my mouth. It came away tasting of blood.

By flexing my waist and shoulders, I could lift the cot frame a few inches. Enough to rattle it, but there wasn't enough room in the cramped shelter to work the cot apart. I might have managed if I could have braced my feet against the hull, but my lower legs had all the strength of wet newspaper. I flopped about like a fish, trying to toss my feet into a position with leverage. The Anderson echoed with my exertions. It sounded like a demented Highland drum corps holding a tattoo inside a saucepan.

I'd managed little more than scraping my wrists raw and promoting the pain in my shoulders from a small private ache to a major agony when the door opened. Somebody stood over me, silhouetted in the door. But the sudden light hurt my eyes, and a gust of cold December wind made them water. I couldn't see.

Liv said, 'You made him angry, didn't you?'

'Olivia! I don't know what they've told you—'

'Shush.' She knelt on the floor. Buckles rattled while she undid the belts around my ankles and knees. Renewed circulation flooded through the constrictions. I tried to wiggle my toes. My reward was the sensation of a thousand blue-hot needles piercing my feet.

Liv set to work with the knots at my wrists. I flexed my hands to give her a bit of slack. The wind chilled the sweat from my previous exertions. I shivered.

'I hope you know I never intended—'

'Hush. You needn't explain anything,' she said. 'I don't care what they say.' Her fingers fumbled at the rope. 'You can tell Raybould was a proper sailor at one time,' she muttered. 'But I've always been rubbish with knots.'

Pruning shears would have made short work of the rope. But I refrained from mentioning the pair hanging behind the door in the shed. 'Perhaps a knife.'

Her efforts petered out. Liv was staring at my hand. She took my fingers, gently, and turned my knuckles toward the light. She frowned.

'You have a scar on your ring finger.'

Oh, bugger.

I coughed. 'Do I?'

'Looks like you've had it a long time,' she said.

'Imagine that.' I turned away from her stare, which had suddenly become very intense. Much as it had happened with Will, an extraneous piece of information, some crumb of my carelessness, had kicked into motion the gears of her mind. They spun.

She couldn't possibly piece it together, I told myself. Will's background, his experience with the impossible, had enabled him to make the intuitive leap necessary for sussing out my identity. Liv didn't have that benefit. She lived in a world free of magic and supermen.

I chanced a look at her. Her eyebrows had hunched together, and she was biting her lip. Bad sign. Her gaze locked on to my eyes. I knew this woman. In her mind's eye, she was comparing the color of my eyes with that of her husband's. I looked away too late to stop her.

Liv went back to picking at the knot. 'Where were you raised, Commander? I've never asked.'

Damn it. She had the bone in her teeth now.

'London,' I said.

'Where in London? East Ham? Islington?' She gave the rope a painful tug. Casually: 'St. Pancras?'

'Here and there,' I said.

She wasn't making any headway with the knots. *To hell with it*, I decided. I told her about the shears. She didn't ask how I knew about them.

After that, it was the work of thirty seconds to undo the ropes. I staggered upright on legs that burned as though my blood had turned to acid. I donned my belt again, then gathered the spare along with the severed ropes. Liv watched me all the while, through eyes narrowed in thought.

I didn't know what to say. I didn't need to.

'Go,' she said. 'Before my husband changes his mind.'

I swallowed. Liv was lost to me again. Truly lost. Not just to my feeble attempt at honor. I'd made my choice in Coventry, but she was back with her husband, her real husband, now. And after everything, she still loved him.

'Thanks.'

She touched my shoulder. And when I turned, she laid her

hands on my face and kissed me. She didn't flinch from my beard, didn't recoil from the feel of the leathery scar tissue under her hand. Her lips were still the softest and sweetest things my life had ever known, as soft and sweet as I remembered.

2 December 1940
Kensington, London, England

Will spent the day trying to nurse Gretel. She hadn't yet awoken since her accident in the kitchen, so there was little to do but keep an eye on her. He set a glass of water and a bottle of aspirin on the bedside table, where it would be within easy reach when she came around. Her braids had come undone when Will and Marsh the Younger carried her to the bedroom, so now her raven hair and cranial wires fanned across the pillow like a dark halo. Seepage from her blisters had yellowed the clean bandages on her legs. She'd have scars, though it might have been worse. He felt her forehead. Her skin was cool to the touch; she didn't appear to be running a fever.

Will knew it was only a matter of time before news of her whereabouts reached Marsh the Elder. The sun, hidden behind a bulwark of leaden clouds, hadn't quite begun its descent into the southwest when he arrived. Like his younger self, he carried a haversack slung over his shoulder. Also like his counterpart, he had sunk into one of his particularly serious moods, and thus spared no time for social niceties.

'Let me see her.'

'Good afternoon to you, too. I'm well, thank you so very much for asking.' Will stepped aside to let him in. 'How did you come by those bruises?'

Marsh didn't answer. Will said, 'You made him angry, didn't you?'

They went upstairs. Will leaned in the bedroom doorway while Marsh stood over the unconscious woman. The look upon his friend's face contained raw glee and undiluted malice in equal measure. He wasn't Marsh at that moment, but a leering devil. Will knew, via the Eidolons, how it felt to be the object of complete and perfect hatred. But it wasn't until he saw Marsh gazing upon his own personal bête noire that Will believed such profound contempt could be expressed by mortal flesh. It was frightening to behold. Marsh became a different man when he looked at her.

Marsh's hands quivered. So did his voice when he said, 'I've dreamt about this moment.' He cracked his knuckles. 'How bad are the injuries?'

'As long as we keep her bandages clean, and keep her hydrated, she'll probably recover. She'll have scars, but nothing compared to these.' Will patted his head to indicate the mass of old surgical scars that riddled Gretel's scalp. 'There's no sign of infection yet.'

As Will had done, Marsh felt her forehead. But his hand lingered, and the evil glee returned to his face. The laughter that followed better suited a troll, or goblin – any malign fairy tale beast – than a human being.

Will beckoned Marsh to the hallway. 'What happens now?'

'I'll take her off your hands.'

'I'm sure you will. But what then? Let me guess. A burlap sack, a few bricks, and a long drop into the Thames?'

'She's one of them. A living embodiment of von Westarp's research. As long as any of that work survives—'

'Please don't play the righteous hero with me. We both know your hatred of that girl goes beyond mere duty. You have every reason in the world to want her dead. And I can't blame you for that. Truly, I can't. But look at her now. She's harmless.'

'The woman lying in your bed is the least harmless, least innocent creature you could ever have the misfortune to meet.'

Will said, 'It's difficult enough to turn a blind eye each time one of my colleagues turns up missing or dead. But I accept it as a necessary evil, because I accept that knowledge of Enochian is too dangerous for any nation to hold. Your very existence has convinced me. Meanwhile, I'm doing everything I can to prevent Milkweed from murdering innocent civilians in the name of national defense. So I will *not* be a party to cold-blooded vengeance. And I'm not debating a woman's fate where she may overhear us. A walk would do us both good.'

'If you think I'm going to leave her alone and unsupervised,' said Marsh, 'you're more bent than she is.'

'She isn't moving.'

Marsh unslung the haversack. Kneeling on the floor to open it, he said, 'Forgive me if I don't trust your diagnosis, doctor.' From the sack, he produced several lengths of rope and a leather belt.

Low December clouds spat upon London. Gusts of wind rippled our coats and swirled abortive snowflakes about our legs. The snow pellets were too fine to be snow and too dry to be sleet. They scratched my eyes like frozen grit. The wind came in irritating fits and starts. But it kept our conversation from carrying to unwelcome ears.

'Gretel isn't the last,' I said. 'There are two others. Identical twins. They weren't at the farm.'

'I hope you're not saying your counterpart's ordeal was all for naught.'

Will listened while I explained how the other me had obtained a blood sample from one of the women in question. He knew where this was leading.

'And what do you propose to do with this blood sample?'

'The Eidolons can reunite the Twins and bring them to us. Identical twins, identical blood. I've seen it. It will work.'

'You expect me to carry out a secret negotiation for this purpose, then.'

'We'll do it at the warehouse.'

'Has it occurred to you that I might not know how to perform the negotiation you envision?'

'You'll suss it out. You've done it before.'

'I have?'

'Circumstances were different then,' I admitted.

'Ah.'

We fell silent as we approached the long queue outside a fishmonger's shop. Because fish wasn't on the rationing list, people sometimes queued up outside a shop for hours if they thought it meant a chance for a bit of fish. Will tipped his bowler to a bevy of housewives. The ladies ignored him and stared at my injuries, taken aback by the extent of my wounds. Did they think I was one of the Few? Did they take me for one of the RAF pilots who stuck it out with the Luftwaffe day after day, only to burn when a Jerry ace downed my Spitfire in the soft earth of a Sussex field?

Once safely past the fishmonger's, Will said, 'I take it you'll, ahem, deal with the Twins once they've arrived?'

'This is a war. They're the enemy.'

'Yes, I know. And I haven't begun to doubt your tale of the future. I wouldn't be doing any of this if I had.'

We came to an amber Belisha beacon. London traffic wasn't what it once had been, owing to the petrol ration. Still, the blustery flurries made for poor visibility. We took care on our way across the street, lest a taxi or omnibus blow through the crossing.

'Still,' said Will, 'it's quite another thing to condone the casual murder of the woman sharing my bed. Tied to my bed.' He paused. 'You know what I mean.'

A gust of wind hid my frustration. To myself, I muttered, 'At least you're consistent.'

Will raised his eyebrows. 'Beg pardon?'

I'd seen this part of Will before. This was the same moral quandary that nearly destroyed him the first time around. He'd been eager to serve his country as a warlock. But that changed as the blood prices mounted. Will never objected to turning the Eidolons against the Jerries. They were all we had against an enemy determined to crush us and doing a bang-up job of it. But Will was a good man, and the sacrifices required to secure the Eidolons' cooperation turned him into a drunk and worse. He'd aimed for a slow suicide by morphine addiction. Would have hit the mark, too, if not for Aubrey's intervention.

If he turned Gretel over to me, and I killed her, it would eat at him. Even if we never spoke of it, and that evil bitch quietly disappeared one day, never to be seen again, he'd know. And the guilt would fester inside him. Would it be enough to overcome his aversion to alcohol? Would it be the pebble that started the landslide?

Could I do that to Will? Would the joy of wrapping my hands around Gretel's diminutive throat, feeling the cartilage shift under the pressure of my fingers, watching her eyes bulge as her windpipe pinched off, shaking her like a rag doll just to see the long hair fly and those dark eyes roll back into her skull ... would living that fantasy outweigh the self-hatred that would come with the knowledge I'd destroyed Will again?

Maybe I'd choke her with her own wires. That would be appropriate. Stripped of insulation, the bare copper would cut a fine scarlet necklace into her olive skin when I yanked it tight . . .

My reverie was broken by the bustle of people flowing from the High Street Kensington Tube station. They flowed around us; we had become two pensive stones in a stream of unfamiliar faces. The wind caught the loose end of a man's muffler. It unwrapped itself and snagged in my beard. I flicked it free. He turned to apologize, but blanched at the sight of my face.

When we were alone on the street again, I spoke. 'Coventry wasn't an accident,' I reminded Will.

'But she failed. You weren't there at the flat when she realized Agnes and Olivia survived. I'm telling you, this was the astonishment of a woman who had never known a single surprise in her entire adult life.' Will reached over and touched my elbow. 'You've beaten her, Pip. Let that be your revenge.'

I shrugged him off. I wasn't about to abandon the fantasy I'd entertained for so many years. Not when it was so close. We could go back right now. I could be throttling her right now . . . the weight of my body pressing the air from her lungs . . . But Will had raised another issue that wanted discussion.

'How *did* that happen? Gretel always gets what she wants. Her plan played out exactly as she intended for over twenty years. And now you and my doppelgänger both report something has changed.' I cracked my knuckles against my jaw. 'I've wondered ever since our return from Coventry. The rescue should have been impossible. Gretel should have anticipated it. That's how she works.'

Far to our left, across the Palace Green, no flag fluttered atop Kensington Palace. The Royal Standard wouldn't be seen in Kensington for a while, since the Queen's apartments had been hit by incendiaries almost two months earlier. Extensive fire damage led to haphazard patches to holes in the slate gray roof. Wooden panels covered the missing window glass. No doubt Göring and Hitler slapped each other on the back for that one. Will rubbed his temples as we neared the gardens.

I said, 'You get that look when you're thinking about the Eidolons. Did they do this to Gretel?'

He shook his head. 'Remind me. What exactly did she say just before you embarked on your, ah, journey?'

Illness and the Eidolons' touch had made a hash of my memories of those final moments. Mostly I remembered creeping darkness, a cold wind, and every soul in London screaming in terror while the world came apart. But I recounted the conversation we'd had, he and I and Gretel, during those final moments of history. Those were also the last moments of Will's life, of course, but I saw no reason to emphasize that.

Will asked, 'A new time line. That's what she said?'

'Yes.'

'Interesting.' We walked a bit farther, along the edge of Kensington Gardens, where the wind threaded the boughs of yew trees, and holly swayed under a gray sky. Will chewed his lip.

'Out with it,' I said.

'Her choice of wording suggests she sees all futures as pre-existing entities. Perhaps she chooses between them. But, setting aside the semantics, the important thing is that this time line is different. From her perspective, it didn't exist prior to your arrival. Meaning she couldn't have mapped it out in advance. All of her effort went to exploring and manipulating a time line that, technically, never happened. And now our future has begun to diverge from the one she plotted so carefully. Who knows how long she spent honing her machinations? But the effort left her with detailed knowledge of a future that will never come to pass. My uneducated guess? She's experiencing interference between competing time lines. Like a poorly tuned wireless.'

'She would have foreseen that, Will.'

Will slapped his hands together. The wind muted his clap. 'Ah, but there's the rub. If this *is* a new time line, she *couldn't* have foreseen the problem. To hear you tell it, she was rather proud of herself. Mere mortals such as you and I will probably never fully understand just what it is she achieved. But whatever she did, it was a major accomplishment even to her eyes.' He nodded to himself, warming to his speculation. 'Yes. I think the creation of a new time line was uncharted territory for her. She might have overloaded her own ability.'

Will could be such a foolish toff at times it was often easy to disregard him. But he had rightly been the guilty conscience of Milkweed, and I wondered if perhaps my old friend had seen to the true heart of this matter as well.

A notion long lost in the back of my mind sent up a signal flare in response to something Will had said. I knew it was nothing more than idle speculation, but something told me he was right.

'Interference between time lines.'

Will shrugged. 'Merely thinking aloud. Perhaps best to ignore me. I haven't a clue how she does what she does.'

'I think you're right about the interference. It can happen, and I've seen it. As have you. The other you, from my past.'

Afternoon was sliding into evening, and we swung around the Round Pond to begin our return trip to the flat. Along the way out of the Gardens, I told Will about the Ghost of St. James' Park. In the original history, Will had been the first to see the scarred and bearded figure who appeared and disappeared on the night Gretel escaped from the Admiralty. We had reenacted that encounter, he and I, when I finally caught up with Gretel in *this* history.

'Hmmm,' said Will. 'The two scenarios are quite similar. Same location, same events, same people. Perhaps in rare circumstances it causes cross-talk between the time lines.'

I said, 'It's consistent with your theory about Gretel. But there's a problem with our hypothesis.'

I'd seen the ghost, too, on a cold December night when Milkweed attempted to attack the Reichsbehörde. Didn't realize it was a glimpse of my future self, of course.

Will interrupted my story: 'In the *knee*?'

'I've had the pain all my life.'

And, like the way bad luck supposedly befalls those who speak of Old Scratch, the mention of my knee conjured the ache and twinge of arthritis. I realized I'd been limping slightly but too wrapped up in our conversation to realize. Cold weather stiffened my joints.

'But why would you shoot yourself? I know you two don't get along, but that's beyond the pale. Even for you.'

"You'll thank me for this later." It made no sense at the time, but I understand it now. Nothing short of a kneecapping would have prevented me from going on that raid. But we didn't understand Gretel's ability. She knocked the operation into a cocked hat, and the Eidolons changed the price for our emergency retreat. They brought us back, but in return, they took the soul of my future son.'

Will said, 'John.' I nodded. He said, 'I'm still aghast at that. I am sorry.'

'First, it never happened now. Second, I was wrong to blame you for it. You did it to save my life. There was no way to know.'

Perhaps it was the sting of wind-driven ice that made Will

blink. 'So you were trying to stop yourself from embarking on the course of action that would lead to John and . . . all the rest that came with him.'

'Yes. But do you see the problem? Gretel's escape unfolded identically in both time lines. But if my doppelgänger did as he claimed in Germany, there's no longer any reason to stage an attack on the farm. There is no farm. So what was Milkweed doing that had me so worried?'

'Do you truly believe you experienced a reflection from a parallel future? A future echo?'

'Something is wrong, Will. Very wrong.'

We mulled this in silence during the walk back. The sun had set by the time we returned to the flat. I went straight to Will's bedroom. Gretel hadn't stirred.

3 December 1940
Milkweed Headquarters, London, England

The marine sentries devoted a long, hard stare to the cuts on Marsh's face. Almost seven months had passed since Marsh had been inside the Admiralty building. It felt like seven decades. He'd lived an entire second life between then and now. So had his wife and daughter. But they'd made the first tentative steps toward healing that rift, he and Liv, and compared to that nothing seemed devastating. He'd have things ironed out with the old man right quick. He hoped.

These are the stairs where I chased Klaus, he mused. *This is the wall where he and Gretel escaped into the night.*

Marsh passed an empty pedestal outside the First Lord's office. He wondered where the binnacle compass had gone.

Through Milkweed's west-facing windows he glimpsed a new building that had sprung up between the Admiralty, Horse Guards Parade, and St. James'. Near the entrance, a crew of laborers received instructions from a member of the Royal Engineers; the structure wasn't yet finished. The enormous, ghastly thing squatted upon the parade ground like a toad spawned not from mud but from concrete and iron. It wasn't difficult to imagine a purpose for the bunker, given the current state of London.

This world of walnut paneling and matelots no longer felt like home. He kept expecting officers clothed in gray and black, but instead they wore blue, and it jarred like a jolt of ice water to a loose filling. Royal Navy, not Schutzstaffel. *These are your people,* he reminded himself. *You're safe. You're home. You belong here.*

Except he didn't. He didn't recognize these faces in Milkweed's wing of the Admiralty. New recruits. Fallout from Klaus's visit? Like the sentries, several of the newcomers gave Marsh's injuries a second look. He realized, upon reflection, that they weren't the newcomers. To their point of view, Marsh was the stranger.

At the very least, he expected to find Will roaming the corridors. Stephenson had given Will an office, back in the earliest days of Milkweed, but it was closed and secured. Marsh's knock received no answer. Pity. Having Will around would have eased the reunion with Stephenson.

Sod it all, he wanted to say. He wanted to return to Walworth, to his family. *Let these fresh-faced paper pushers deal with Jerry.* The destruction of von Westarp's farm, along with the eradication of the Schutzstaffel's operational records of the REGP, had obviated Milkweed's original raison d'être. *You're welcome. You lot can handle the rest from here out.*

A long night's conversation with Liv had ground his voice down to a nub of its usual self. It had wicked the moisture from his eyeballs, too, leaving behind only desiccated crumbs of sleep that crunched when he rubbed the corners of his eyes.

Marsh was on the verge of wondering whether his memories of the past spring were nothing more than a flight of fancy when he finally encountered one familiar face. He poked his head into a workshop to find Lorimer and a team of boffins assembling a strange device. Coils of copper wire girded the column, which was a bit taller than a man and about as thick through the middle as a postbox pillar. The bearded Scot dropped a spanner when Marsh entered.

'Hi, Lorimer.' Marsh held out his hand. Lorimer kneaded the curls of his thick black beard. The beard wasn't dusted with flakes of ash as it had been in the past. And the odor of cigars didn't waft from Lorimer's clothing. Good tobacco had become a rarity.

Lorimer didn't shake Marsh's hand. 'We'd written you off,' he said.

'Long story,' said Marsh. 'Is the old man in?'

'Aye.'

Marsh stuffed his unshaken hand into the pocket of his trousers. He nodded toward the column. 'What's that?'

Lorimer squinted at him. Marsh sensed he was gauging the cuts on his face. 'Stephenson's going to shit himself when you walk in.'

Then he returned to his work. No 'Welcome home.' No 'Good to see you.' Marsh had expected awkwardness, and of course suspicion, but not outright hostility. But if he could make things right with Liv, of all people, he could turn this around. Marsh didn't blame them for being wary. He would be, too, under the circumstances. But their tune would change when they realized he'd done their job for them.

Lorimer's difficulty in finding tobacco worth smoking didn't affect Stephenson. The scent of Lucky Strikes lingered like a fog in the corridor outside the old man's office. An old friend, that odor. Marsh relaxed, feeling at home for the first time since entering the Admiralty.

Stephenson sat at his desk, paging through a file. His reading glasses were perched at the tip of his nose; a frown had etched itself into the corners of his mouth. A pack of cigarettes lay on the desk, alongside his jeweler's loupe. Sleet pattered against the window glass behind him. He'd donned a pullover to ward off the chill from the drafty window, but hadn't bothered to pin up the empty sleeve. It dangled at his side.

Marsh knocked on the door frame. 'Permission to come aboard, sir?'

Stephenson had been Royal Flying Corps, not navy. But it seemed appropriate given their surroundings. And, Marsh hoped, it would break the ice a bit. Will would have known exactly how to accomplish that.

Stephenson hid his surprise better than Lorimer. He blinked, twice, then waved Marsh to one of the wingback leather chairs fronting his desk.

Stephenson tapped the Lucky Strike pack against the edge of his telephone, deftly shaking out a new cig. He struck a match, puffed until the tip of the cigarette glowed marigold orange, and stared at Marsh through a pearly cloud. He smoked the entire thing down to a smoldering cinder before uttering a word.

Stephenson crushed the butt into a marble ashtray. He said, 'Well, well, well. At long last, the prodigal son returns.' The old man had smoked most of a pack since last emptying the ashtray.

'I wondered when you were going to show your face. Have to admit I was a bit hurt when you decided to check in at the Broadway Buildings first.'

'I had to,' said Marsh. 'They had Liv.'

'I know.' Stephenson shook out another cigarette. He crushed the empty pack and lobbed it into the rubbish bin. His gaze hardened. 'Where the blue pencil have you been? You'd better have a dynamite story, lad.'

The old man was a better listener than Liddell-Stewart. He didn't interrupt. Only once did his reactions betray him. Confusion flashed across the old man's face when Marsh described how an Eidolon had facilitated his escape from the Schutzstaffel.

Marsh's second recounting of his activities since May proceeded more quickly than the first, in spite of the fact that he'd had to start the story earlier, in the immediate aftermath of Gretel's escape. He omitted the part about trussing up the commander, then letting him go after learning about the events in Coventry. Marsh wanted the full story before Milkweed had a chance to trundle the commander away to an internment camp on the Isle of Man. The sleet tapered off while Marsh told his tale.

'Let me see that I've got this,' said Stephenson. 'A stranger swans in, some piker whom you've neither seen nor heard of, feeds you a line about Jerry infiltrators inside Milkweed, and you decide on the spot to hop on a U-boat for Germany. Once there you single-handedly win the war for us. Would you say that's an accurate summary?'

'I said nothing of the sort. And I had help. It would have been impossible without Gretel.'

'Oh, you're too modest, lad. Very well. Perhaps not the war.

But I do think I should get on the horn to the PM, don't you? He can disband Milkweed now that you've been so considerate as to fulfill our mandate for us. I'm sure he'll sleep better knowing the REGP is no longer a threat.'

'I know how it sounds, sir. But I also know you're tapped into communications intercepts. If you've been monitoring Jerry's wireless traffic, surely you know—'

'Don't burden yourself,' said Stephenson. 'We'll take a close look at your story. You can be certain of that.'

'I had to take the opportunity. I have at least as many reservations as you regarding Liddell-Stewart. But I have to give the bastard credit. His information about the Reichsbehörde was bang right. All of it.'

'Lucky for us he's on our side.'

Marsh shook his head. 'I didn't say that, either.'

Smoke jetted from Stephenson's nostrils. 'I notice you're moving a bit stiffly. Feeling well?'

'If you still have a quack on staff, I could do with a visit.' Marsh lifted his shirt to show the bandages around his chest.

'Ah, right. Your tussle with the invisible woman. You did mention that. I presume that's also where you won the cuts to your face?' Marsh nodded. Stephenson said, 'She sounds a bloody dangerous witch. Glad to know she's out of the picture.'

'Me, too, sir.'

'There is one detail that bothers me. Tiny thing, but there it is. One of my men turned up dead recently. Shapley. There's no way you could possibly know him, of course. He came along after your time. He was found dead in his hotel room. There had been a struggle. Messy business. Whoever did it managed to slip in and out while eluding Shapley's protection detail. Quite a professional, from the look of it.' Marsh opened his mouth to object, but Stephenson didn't give him a chance. 'I confess I didn't know Shapley particularly well. They're an unpleasant lot, Beauclerk's contemporaries. One thing I do know about the warlocks, however.' Stephenson crushed out his cigarette, then lifted the handset of his telephone. 'They all carry knives.'

He dialed a single number. An internal line. 'Dickie. John here. Send up a pair of sailors, won't you?'

They tossed Marsh into a cell in the citadel.

5 December 1940
Admiralty Citadel, London, England

The bladder gurgled gently in its hiding place at the crook of Will's elbow. It wasn't audible over the whirr of the ventilation system, the bang of slammed doors, the echo of footsteps, and the clatter of a Teletype. Sound ricocheted along the citadel's bare concrete corridors as easily as shell shrapnel through aspic.

He handed his identification papers to a sentry. The marine was a stocky fellow who, judging from the time he took to study Will and his papers, took his responsibilities seriously. Will feigned boredom and poise, meanwhile wondered which, if any, of the doors he'd seen on the way down held Marsh the Younger.

The marine waved Will along. Will passed through a sally port to the deepest, darkest heart of the citadel. The air here scraped rather than flowed across Will's skin. The Eidolons' displeasure had imbued it with the moist sandpaper texture of a cat's tongue.

Tonight's rotation put White in charge of the negotiation, with Grafton as his second, and Webber on map and Teletype duty. Will and the others were to stand by and join in as necessary, depending on the flow of the negotiation. But Will had volunteered to spell Grafton, who had vomited blood and broken snail shells in the aftermath of the Eidolons' burst of displeasure last time around.

The Teletype clattered. Paper tape spooled from the machine. Webber moved map pins in accordance with what he read on the tape.

Will took his place alongside White. The older warlock launched into Enochian, cutting himself as he did so. Will provided the expected chants at the appropriate times, like a parishioner attending a demonic High Church service.

The vial in White's lap contained several thermometers' worth of mercury. Will had been among those who painstakingly recovered the liquid metal, one tiny silvery bead at a time, from the previous negotiation attempts. It made more sense than continually destroying thermometers and barometers. Otherwise, by springtime, at the rate Will was sabotaging negotiations, the Met Office wouldn't have anything left for forecasting the weather.

Will nudged the stopcock hidden beneath his wristwatch. He feigned the motion of cutting his palm, simultaneously using a gentle squeeze of the elbow to squirt a trace of pig's blood into the cup of his hand. He flicked his tainted contribution into the circle.

A hand clamped on his wrist.

Will tried to pull away, but Hargreaves twisted his arm to expose the rubber tube still dribbling animal blood.

'I knew it,' he said.

Sweat instantly dampened the undersides of Will's arms. His forehead, too. This was the very thing he'd feared. They executed traitors.

Will blurted, 'Listen, this isn't what you think. I'm not a traitor.' But of course it was. And, technically, he was.

Webber abandoned the Teletype and smoothly took Will's place in the circle. The negotiation continued without interruption while Hargreaves forced Will from the room.

Stephenson was waiting in the corridor. He shook his head as though weighing a personal tragedy.

'You were right,' said Hargreaves. He used his own pocket-knife to slice open Will's shirtsleeve. Stephenson grabbed Will's arm to inspect the bladder.

He said, 'Why, Beauclerk?'

Will didn't know what to say. His racing mind couldn't find the magic incantation that would release him. There wasn't one. He repeated, 'This isn't what you think.'

'I believe it's exactly what I think,' said Stephenson.

Together, Stephenson and Hargreaves frog-marched Will away from the negotiation chamber. They brought him to a steel door. Hargreaves tied Will's hands behind his back while Stephenson produced a brass key. He twisted it in the lock; the corridor lights glinted on the lustrous finish of the brass.

Stephenson heaved on the door, using his body weight to lever it open. He beckoned into the shadows. Marsh stepped out, blinking and shielding his eyes from the bright light of the corridor.

'Your story checks out,' said Stephenson.

Marsh stared at him. Then he noticed Hargreaves, looking triumphant, and Will, who stood with shoulders slumped with his hands behind his back. 'Will?'

'Pip! You—'

—*must trust the commander*, he wanted to say. But Stephenson clapped his hand over his mouth.

The old man said, 'Gag him.'

Hargreaves removed his own necktie. The warlock shoved it between Will's teeth and tied the loose ends behind his head. It tasted of the starch in Hargreaves's collar. The salt from stale neck sweat stung the corners of Will's mouth, where the skin had split open. The old warlock tasted of rancid strawberries.

Stephenson shoved him into the cell just vacated by Marsh. Marsh asked, 'What happened?'

'Liddell-Stewart was right after all,' said Stephenson. 'We've found his Jerry infiltrator.'

'Trust the commander,' Will tried to say. But it came out as muffled gibberish. When the reverberating clang of the cell door finally died away, he could hear the rush of blood through his ears and the whisper of his breath through the silk of Hargreaves's necktie.

29 December 1940
Bermondsey, London, England

Central London burned while I paced the ruins of yet another warehouse. Jerry's raids had come less frequently as December weather settled in, but old Göring wouldn't let the year end quietly. Seemed like they'd doubled up on incendiaries this time around. The worst fires were a few miles to my west, near the center of London. They cast an infernal glow on low passing clouds and the smoke smudges of antiaircraft flak.

Smoke wafted from the barrel where I'd started a smaller fire of my own. It rode a cold wind through gaping holes in the ceiling and the jumble of crumpled beams at the far end of the bay. The cold made me shiver; the smoke burned my eyes. I wrapped myself in an army surplus blanket from the Great War. It stank of motor oil. I tossed the last of von Westarp's journals into the flames.

Embers of the burning city spiraled up into the night like departed souls, following the paths slashed into the darkness by the sway of searchlights. I wondered what would be left of the city, come morning. The Blitz had made it damn difficult to find undamaged properties near the docks. My original hiding spot had long ago succumbed to the raids. I'd moved twice since then.

Somewhere, deep beneath the wail and warble of sirens, deeper even than the crump of distant explosions, I imagined the chthonic rumble of Enochian echoing through tonight's conflict. Somewhere, in a citadel near the center of the furnace, the warlocks had convened. Had they succeeded? Would they blunt the sharpest edges of this attack?

'Are they using the Eidolons tonight?'

Gretel didn't answer. During a momentary lull in the wind and the ack-acks, I heard a faint *tink-slap* when she flipped another coin.

'What happens tomorrow?'

Gretel ignored my taunt. She sat a few feet away, behind the glass partition of the foreman's office. The braids were gone, replaced with wild, tangled snarls. Sometimes she woke up screaming.

Her battery had to be dead by now. Couldn't get her to part with it, though. I tried to remove it while she napped, but the crazy bint looked ready to scratch my eyes out when she caught me.

I didn't bother with her bandages. They were her problem. Will couldn't fault me if she died writhing in pain from an infection. It was better than she deserved.

Tink. Slap. She never looked at the coins. Just flipped them.

I could have watched her for hours. Sometimes I did. It was perfectly delicious, her slide into ruin. I savored it as another man might savor fine red wine and the darkest Belgian chocolate.

And therein lay my mistake. I'd been so busy gloating over Gretel's disintegration that I hadn't paid much mind for the first couple of days after Will disappeared. Only after I started watching his flat did I realize he hadn't been home in days. And he wouldn't have toddled off to Bestwood without alerting me. Which left one conclusion.

Will's capture changed things. I had no access to the warlocks. They were safe and snug in their armored citadel. Where, if I knew Stephenson, they'd also be keeping Will. If they'd kept him in the Admiralty cellar, as in the old days, I might have had a chance. But I didn't. I couldn't get near them. And without Will spiking their efforts, the warlocks were now free to wreak their unnatural influence on the war. How long before they became permanently entrenched in my country's defense?

All my efforts would amount to nothing if I couldn't get to the warlocks.

I spent weeks pacing the warehouse like a caged animal, my repeated thoughts eroding channels in the pathways of my mind. There had to be something I could do. I twined a bloody cloth around my fingers, wondering if I'd ever have a chance to use it.

Another brace of explosions rattled joists in the warehouse roof. I paused, listening for the grating moan of tortured metal on metal. But the roof didn't collapse on us. The thrum of wind through the loose rafters matched the tension vibrating through my aching muscles.

After everything I'd done, everything I'd endured, I'd come so close to fulfilling my mission only to have it all fall apart. But I knew better than to blame Will. This had happened because I'd laid too much responsibility on him. He wasn't trained for subterfuge. Wasn't built for it. Thanks to me, he was now in great danger, but I couldn't help him.

I thought long and hard about approaching my younger self. My advice had steered him right; von Westarp's farm was no more. Surely I might parlay that into a bit of trust? How would he take it if I revealed my true name and purpose to him?

But it was moot. For by now Stephenson hadn't merely confirmed my doppelgänger's tale about the devastation of the REGP. He'd also verified there was no Liddell-Stewart associated with the service – nobody who matched my description, however remotely. 'Lieutenant-Commander Liddell-Stewart' was, doubtless, a person of extremely high interest to MI6. Already twice I'd barely escaped their net. Just as with the warlocks, I couldn't get anywhere near my younger self. Or Liv. And while my younger self might have entertained my warning about the danger posed by the warlocks, his superiors wouldn't. If they caught me, it was all over.

So now I was stuck in the cold, with no foreseeable end, a fugitive from my own government, harboring a useless Nazi ex-precog who could barely bathe herself. The woman I loved had been reunited with her husband; my long-lost daughter reunited with her father. Yet I couldn't even take solace in the belief my little girl would have a long happy life, because every day Milkweed's warlocks pushed the world a little bit closer to that screaming oblivion I still heard in my dreams. And there was nothing I could do about it except hide and watch all my efforts crumble.

God forgive me, but I found myself wishing Gretel would weigh in with her advice. Perhaps she sensed it. She looked at me, and started weeping again.

INTERLUDE: GRETEL

Olivia cannot be alive. She can't be alive. She can't be alive. She can't be alive. Can't be alive. Can't be can't be can't be can't be can't why is Raybould's tart whore still alive when it's impossible? Impossible things don't happen therefore it didn't because William is lying yes he's lying because she saw William say ~~I don't know how to tell you this~~ I've kept you ~~I'm sorry, Pip, so very sorry~~ long enough ~~to have to tell you~~ go home ~~they went to Coventry~~ to your wife ~~where they thought they'd be safe, we all did~~ and daughter ~~but we were terribly wrong~~ no no no that's not what he said she had it all planned and then he didn't say what she saw him say she saw him deliver the news and Raybould ~~screamed and~~ said are you sure everything is all right ~~crumpled with grief there on the floor of William's flat~~ yes of course now go home and say hello to Olivia ~~and she held him while he cried and he tried to knock her away~~ thanks for this Will ~~but she forgave him because he was overcome with sorrow and~~ I'll see you soon ~~she's been hit before and knows how to shrug it aside~~.

She sent the planes to ~~Williton~~ Coventry that happened because she remembers it.

Why wasn't that tart whore killed in Coventry? Why isn't Olivia dead with her freckles and her forehead and her hair and her smell and baby and nose that ran in the cipher future in the corridor outside Raybould's hospital room where she wept over lost opportunities and the death of love and they talked about the wedding in a garden and Olivia still carried the evacuation tag but why isn't she dead like her future love for Raybould and she is impolite and selfish and she should be dead and its very very rude that she's not.

Her legs hurt under the bandages and and she can't remember how the blisters got there and they hurt very much but she never hurt before even when they tried to control her with the hurt did the doctor and Pabst and others in the cipher future at a place called Arzamas but she went somewhere else somewhere else in her head where they couldn't follow and they failed always they failed.

Raybould tries to take her battery she doesn't let him she needs it needs it to see the coin shining ~~heads tails~~ spinning ~~tails~~ up ~~heads~~ up ~~tails~~ up ~~heads~~ spinning ~~heads tails~~ shining ~~heads~~ down ~~tails~~ down ~~heads~~ down ~~tails heads tails~~ she will not look no she's not wrong she just won't look and then she won't be wrong and everything will be the way she planned it once Olivia is dead the coins will be right and everything will be back to the proper path but the fog hides the coins hides both sides and makes them blurry.

There is fog only fog no shimmering gossamer of unconsummated possibilities no golden threads to pluck and make the universe dance because everything is shrouded and gray it kept drawing closer closer closer but always she could see a thread a path a way forward not very far but she could see far enough to guide Raybould even though they ~~were caught in the kitchen caught in the woods caught in Kammler's room~~ were caught in the doctor's study she saw how to distract the doctor ~~and make the doctor shoot Raybould in the eye the heart the throat~~ and save Raybould's life and then he kills the doctor and brother and Reinhardt and ~~Kammler~~ Heike kills Kammler ~~and Raybould~~

and Raybould kills her too and then they made it back to England ~~got caught in Weimar caught in Lauterbach executed in Frankfurt~~ recognized in Frankfurt ~~shot dead in Cologne captured in Belgium~~ because she could see ahead not very far but it was enough and then the fog was supposed to envelop her and she'd be through it to the other side to a brand-new virgin universe awaiting her touch waiting for her to make the decisions that would push the universe on its proper path but the fog is endless and there is no other side and her bandages itch.

How did this happen when did this start it isn't her fault it isn't her fault she did everything perfectly and it worked and she tricked the Eidolons she tricked them into letting Raybould create a new time line for her where she lives and they're together and she doesn't cease to exist because the Eidolons hate her with such intensity and oh God what if the Eidolons are in the fog OH GOD what if they are there on the other side what if they are all around her now and what if they did this to her whatifthisistheir-revenge*ohGodohGodOHGOD*—

Raybould comes in looking very angry and he is wearing a blanket and suddenly it is dark outside. She doesn't remember screaming but he said she was screaming and maybe she was because her throat is sore and Raybould says she's out of her bloody mind if she thinks he's going to scrounge up a cup of hot tea to soothe her nerves she can bloody well forget it because she can fucking die screaming for all he cares but she doesn't like tea because it means kettles and a teakettle hurt her legs and it was William's fault for telling lies about Olivia and that was very ungrateful of him because he's living in the time line she created even though she made it for herself she lets other people live here and they are ungrateful and they don't even know the horror that might have been.

everything is broken because of Olivia. alive when she shouldn't be. nothing will be right. the coins won't behave until she fixes this

the eidolons didn't send the fog couldn't have because they haven't found her here no but when did it first appear she glimpsed it on the gossamer horizon on the day raybould arrived it wasn't there and then it was there and so was he because it worked everything she planned had worked and then the fog

appeared oh god

she did

no no

did this

no no no

to

herself

FIFTEEN

Marsh studied the maps on the wall of Stephenson's office while waiting for the old man to return from his meeting with the Prime Minister. It must have gone long.

The pins arrayed across the maps told the story of a secret war. Black pins marked the places in southeastern England where a corrupted rain had fallen, cloud water salted with traces of mercury. It had drizzled on the Channel, too, but of that they could do nothing except perhaps survive the war and wait for long-term consequences. Milkweed had done what it could to monitor the areas where the poison fell on farmland, in some cases even requisitioning properties and tracts of land 'for the war effort.' It did the same when rumors circulated of a new Messerschmitt or Heinkel down in the countryside, its fuselage riddled with corrosion. Milkweed ran off the books; it didn't have to give answers.

The first black pins had appeared in December, immediately after Will's imprisonment. Milkweed's saboteur had been caught quite literally red-handed.

There had been no black pins during January and February, when winter weather had curtailed Luftwaffe operations. The warlocks had pitched in when the raids started up again in March. Gauging the extent of their contribution was difficult. Two months free of alerts had done the RAF well.

Red pins on the map of Egypt showed places where the warlocks had attempted to exert their influence. The results here were more sporadic. The action in North Africa moved too quickly, and the local conditions were too varied, for the warlocks to devise an approach. Not that the Italians had offered much of a fight to the Western Desert Force. Africa had been a relatively reliable source of good news, until Rommel had arrived.

A smattering of blue pins dusted the Balkans. The warlocks had enjoyed more success there.

Two days earlier, the Führer had opened a new front in the east. Nobody was surprised when he turned round and stabbed Uncle Joe in the back. No pins on the Russian front yet; the situation there was too fluid.

Marsh opened the window. Dust from the window sash clung to his fingers with a damp grittiness. Warm spring rains had put the green back into St. James', and now a light breeze wafted through the office, carrying with it the scent of victory gardens and ozone. It gave Marsh a brief respite from the smell of tobacco, for which he was grateful. He wiped his hands on his trousers.

He yawned. Another long night, entwined in hushed conversation with Liv. His long absence had scarred them both. They had to get to know each other again. He'd been back in England, back in Liv's house, her bed, barely longer than he'd been on the Continent. Their relationship had survived, so far, but like a fractured rib, the trust and love knit back together slowly. The scar tissue was there, invisible to the eye but undeniable to the heart, much as the thin welt of pale skin where an assassin's knife had nicked his jaw felt like an immense disfigurement to his fingertips when he shaved, yet shied from the mirror when he looked for it.

It was still a fragile thing, this rediscovered intimacy between them. Thoughts of Liv, her loneliness and her long-empty bed, invariably caused Marsh to wonder about Liddell-Stewart. How much time had they spent alone together? He didn't dare ask. Open it again, and the scar might never heal.

The commander had gone to ground after Marsh's return from Germany. Will was their only lead on Liddell-Stewart but he wasn't cooperating. Marsh had had to work on Stephenson for two months before the old man agreed to let them take the gag out of Will's mouth. They stationed a sentry outside his door, who would enter the cell and knock Will about if he launched into Enochian. Weary duty for the sentries, and a silly use of manpower in time of war, but more humane than leaving a man gagged twenty-three hours a day.

'Trust the commander.' That's all Will would say.

Stephenson entered. He carried a brown dossier under his arm and an umbrella in his hand. When he turned, his empty sleeve kicked up like the skirt of a dancing girl. With his hip he shoved the door closed, while at the same time tossing the umbrella handle over a coat hook beside the door. Rainwater spattered across the wainscoting. Water stains stippled the wood polish beneath the hooks where this had happened with some frequency. The old man had eased into his seat behind the desk and already held a sterling letter opener to the ribbon that sealed the dossier before the umbrella pendulumed to a rest.

Marsh eyed the ribbon. Black. Not good.

'Your meeting with the PM went long,' he said.

'Not just the PM,' said Stephenson. He cursed under his breath; the ribbon was giving him trouble. It slid away from the dulled blade of his letter opener. He needed another hand to hold down the dossier while he hacked the ribbon apart. Marsh knew better than to offer. 'Menzies was there. Ellis, too. We had to speak circles around them.'

'Ellis?'

'Army intelligence.'

Lieutenant-Colonel Menzies ran the Secret Intelligence Service. Stephenson's post, if he hadn't given it up in exchange for a free hand to run Milkweed. Not even C knew Milkweed's true purpose. So what brought him, and a bloke from army intelligence, into a meeting between Stephenson and Churchill?

The ribbon snapped apart. Stephenson flipped open the dossier. A fine dusting of sand sprinkled out. Fishing around in a desk drawer for his jeweler's loupe, he said, 'This package arrived via special courier late last night.'

Stephenson fell silent while he studied the photographs. Marsh fidgeted, though it did nothing to ward off the icy apprehension trickling through his veins. Stephenson slid a quartet of photographs across the desk, along with the magnifier. 'These were taken in Egypt, three days ago.'

The first photo was a wide aerial view of stony, wrinkled terrain. With the use of Stephenson's magnifier, Marsh could see tents and other structures scattered within the labyrinth of ravines.

The second photo was also from aerial recon, but gave a clearer and closer view of a subsection of the previous photograph. Now the tents were clearly visible, as were armored vehicles and embedded artillery positions. Two of the tents were circled in red. Marsh knew he was seeing an Afrika Korps forward position.

He glanced at the terrain in the first photo. Ravines.

A bit over a week earlier, Britain's Western Desert Force had suffered a demoralizing defeat near the border between Egypt and Libya. 'Operation Battleaxe' intended to evict Rommel's forces from a strategically important position known as Halfaya Pass, as part of a larger push to relieve the besieged port of Tobruk. The first day of Battleaxe saw an entire British tank squadron obliterated.

The third photograph was terribly grainy. It had been taken from a great distance, through a fog of heat shimmer, and then enlarged. The photographer had hid in the shadows of a ravine to get the shot. It showed a narrow slice of an Afrika Korps position, tents and half-track transports. In the background, a man held the entrance flap to a tent as though just stepping out. The dark leather bands of a harness ruined the clean lines of his pale uniform. Sunlight glinted from something at his waist.

So extreme was the devastation at Halfaya that the few surviving Tommies had given it a new nickname. They called it 'Hellfire Pass.'

Marsh ran the lens over the man in the photo. The enlargement had washed out his facial features. But the coloration fit. And the man wore dark goggles to protect his eyes from the desert glare. As though he had very pale eyes . . .

The fourth photo had, like the third, been taken from a great distance. Its subject was a shirtless man with his back to the camera. He stood alongside an antiaircraft gun, hands laid upon it and head bowed as though in prayer. Something dark trailed from his head to his waist. The gun was halfway submerged into the sand.

The Desert Fox had taken to burying his eighty-eights, large antiaircraft guns, up to their muzzles. When positioned like that, they melted into the heat shimmer and became invisible. A gun designed to knock bombers from the sky could shoot through the heavy armor of a Matilda tank at over half a mile. He'd killed a lot of Tommies that way.

Big job, burying an eighty-eight. Unless you happened to have a fellow who could render its base insubstantial.

Marsh slid the photos back to Stephenson. The old man said, 'Well?'

'Too blurry to say for certain. The fellow in the tent might be Reinhardt. It would fit. He trained extensively for a deployment to Africa. The fellow with the gun could be Klaus.'

'Might be? Could be? You told me you'd splashed both of them.'

'Thought I had.'

'You told me you'd leveled the place. You and your crackerjack team. The girl and the retard.'

'We did!'

First thing Stephenson had done after tossing Marsh into the clink was report to the PM. Churchill, in turn, had ordered the RAF to perform a risky aerial reconnaissance mission over the farm. Within a day, Milkweed had a parcel of photos consistent with Marsh's story. The complex had been destroyed in the manner he described: smashed to flinders, then burned to ash.

'Batteries.' Stephenson indicated the first photo with an unlit cigarette. 'Have they resurrected the research?'

Marsh shook his head. 'Come on, sir. You saw the photos. There was nothing left to resurrect.'

But . . . He squinted at the window while Stephenson struck a match, remembering a conversation he'd overheard on the day he arrived in Germany. At Bremerhaven. He hadn't thought anything of it at the time. *Shit.*

'Unterseeboot-115,' he said. 'Gretel made certain it was stocked with spare batteries.'

'Her again. Well, she's long gone now.' Smoke jetted from Stephenson's nose, like a dragon warning off would-be thieves who ventured too close to its hoard. 'You were soft. You ought to have killed her.'

'I thought I could trust Will.'

'We all did.'

Marsh shook his head. 'I just don't understand why—'

Stephenson snapped his fingers twice. 'Focus! This is our current problem.' He jabbed a fingertip on the photos. 'These bastards are more persistent than a wart. Especially the ghostly fellow. Hansel.'

'Klaus.'

Marsh thought about what he knew of Klaus, what he knew of the Willenskräfte. 'I suppose that if he can become insubstantial to a brick wall, he could also make himself impervious to a blow from Kammler's Willenskräfte.'

'Pity you didn't think of that at the time.'

'I was just the tiniest bit preoccupied at the time.'

'This is damn troubling.'

'They're only men, sir. What about Lorimer's gadget? That would bugger them nicely, to hear him tell it.' The Scot had been more than a little annoyed when he learned that Marsh's efforts had obviated the pixies before they ever saw use in the field. He was proud of his creation, and he wanted to stick one to the Führer. 'And I think it would cheer him a bit.'

Stephenson said, 'Perhaps it would, if we could get one in range. But our two friends are hunkered in quite effectively. Rommel controls Halfaya. Bit difficult to swan into those ravines with a commando team. They'd see us coming from twenty miles away.'

Marsh stood. 'We'll have to find a way.'

'Are you off to give the good news to Lorimer?'

'I'll leave that for you. I want to try Will again.'

'Waste of time.'

24 June 1941
Admiralty Citadel, London, England

Will perched on the edge of the cot, long legs folded under him like a carpenter's rule. He scratched the itchy beard he'd grown during his incarceration; Stephenson wasn't about to let him near a blade. His fingers massaged thick curls. He hadn't expected to have time to grow a beard. After a few days he realized they couldn't execute the brother of a duke without making a show of it. Which would have drawn attention to Milkweed.

So he was bored, but otherwise well rested. Things had been a little better since Marsh the Younger convinced Stephenson to let Will have reading materials. Newspapers were still off-limits.

There was no stool. Marsh crouched beside a stack of novels, mostly Kipling and Hammett. Close enough that the sentry wouldn't hear the conversation that unfolded below the thrum and whisper of ventilation stirring the stale air.

Marsh got straight to the point. 'Gretel's brother is alive,' he said. Will cocked an eyebrow. 'So is another one of von Westarp's brood. They're in North Africa.'

A sharp inhalation whistled through Will's teeth. He saw it all in a flash. *The second future echo. They plan to magic a team into Africa.* 'I take it your paterfamilias doesn't know you're sharing this news.'

'The commander needs to know. How do I contact him?'

Will frowned, but didn't say anything. Marsh ran a hand over his face. 'I hope you realize that whatever you're not telling me about the commander, whatever the two of you are hiding, events are passing you both by. I don't understand how he talked you into doing what you did because you won't tell me. But he protected my family while I was away, and that's earned him some consideration in my eyes. Still don't trust him, but I'm willing to hear him out. This isn't a trick, Will. Where is he?'

Will prodded the curls beneath his chin with his finger stump. 'You're certain her brother is alive?'

'Yes.'

'And you think she planned that.'

'I don't know. But the commander should be aware of the possibility.'

'Yet you say you don't trust him.'

'He isn't who he claims to be. There is no Liddell-Stewart. Of course I'm wary.'

'He isn't your enemy.'

'Damn it, Will! Why won't you tell me what you know?'

'Because it's complicated. Better if you suss it out for yourself.'

'Then tell me how to contact him. Please.'

Will sighed. 'It's been too long. I wouldn't know where to find him now because he moves about. He has to, because of the raids. He was camping out in a warehouse on the Bermondsey docks, but as you know, the Luftwaffe took a special interest in the East End.'

'He's hiding in the ruins. Clever.'

Will couldn't help but smile at that. *Let me guess. It's what you would have done?*

Marsh stood. 'Is there anything you need? Anything I can try to get for you?'

Will gestured at the pile of books with a languid wave of his long fingers. The spiderweb of scars arrayed across his palm flashed in the actinic light of his cell. 'I could do with something fresh. I find Kipling grows a bit stale on the third read.'

'Consider it done.'

Will asked, offhandedly as he could manage, 'Has Stephenson decided what's to be done with me?'

'Afraid not. He has other things on his mind.'

'Ah. Well. I suppose he would.'

Marsh turned to go. Before he knocked for the sentry, Will said, 'It might be wise to sit this one out, Pip. The transit will be far worse than my colleagues let on.'

The look that settled over Marsh's face indicated that gears had been set into motion. It was the same look he got when chewing on a new puzzle, or when confronted with a new set of facts. He sat again. 'What transit?'

Will cradled his head in his hands. 'Oh, sodding.'

25 June 1941
Bermondsey, London, England

'He's coming,' said Gretel.

She stood before a cracked and grimy window, bare feet black with soot. Her weight shifted side to side as she curled and uncurled her toes. Pucker marks of old, broken blisters stippled her skin. Her hair was a ravel too matted for braids.

So confident was her announcement, so matter of fact, I thought perhaps she had recovered some measure of her prescience. Which left me conflicted. I needed access to her ability, to the things only she could know. But I wanted her suffering to know no solace. Wanted the yearning for her lost godhood to be endless. Eternal.

Her wires hung free. The window-glow of sunlight gleamed on the copper connector.

I stood. Followed her gaze. I glimpsed my doppelgänger ambling up the wide street, skirting uncleared debris. He carried a haversack over his shoulder. I couldn't read the look on his face.

Gretel spun, putting her back to the window. Wires and greasy hair cartwheeled around her head, tickling my arm. I wanted to flay my skin and scour away the stain of that incidental contact.

'I knew,' she said. The edges of her voice curled under the razor edge of rising panic. 'I knew before I looked. I did. Knew he'd come for me. He comes for me. He always does.'

His hands were empty. Didn't mean he wasn't carrying an Enfield, however. I considered my chances of vacating the warehouse with a stumbling madwoman in tow before he arrived. Slim indeed. And he'd find us again, the mule-headed bastard.

I quit the foreman's office and descended the swaying stairs. Fire damage had warped some of the supports, causing them to curl away from weld seams popped wide by Luftwaffe bombs. I stood just inside the entrance, watching as he assessed the cavernous warehouse. A whistle blew somewhere on the Thames to our east.

He paused before entering. As I would have done, had our roles been reversed. I stepped into the light.

'You here to shut me down?'

'You intend to give me a reason?'

He unslung the haversack, opened it, and produced a bottle of brandy. Pinched, no doubt, from the bottom drawer of Stephenson's desk. Though I pretended not to know that.

Instead, I said, 'That's a rare find these days.'

'I know a good source. But it's a vein I can tap only once.' He uncorked it. He held it to his lips for the duration of one loud swallow. 'I think I've visited half the ruins along the river. Thirsty work, that.'

I took the bottle. Ever since I had swallowed fire, liquor and my throat went together like feral cats in a wet sack. But I managed to not cough, then gestured him inside.

'One at a time is best,' I said. 'Stairs are dodgy.'

My younger self didn't know what to make of Gretel's long fall since she'd brought him home from Germany. He'd seen the beginning of that descent, but I'd been there for the hard landing. She flinched as though seeing the two of us together caused her pain. Perhaps it did. She bowed her head, hiding unfocused eyes behind ash-streaked tresses. My doppelgänger and I crossed the warehouse mezzanine to blunt the sharpest edges from her keening.

He said, after another swig of the old man's brandy, 'What have you done to her?'

'Nothing she hasn't done to herself.'

'It's gone now, isn't it?' He pointed at his head, pantomiming wires. 'All of it.'

'Your unannounced visit would've sent her sobbing if she hadn't glimpsed you through the window.' I pulled a wooden crate closer to the panes. It creaked under my weight. 'But you're not here out of concern for Gretel.'

The look he gave me was hard, calculated, wary. But not unfriendly. 'After Coventry? No.'

Ah. Liv had told him about our narrow escape. The catch in his voice told me everything I didn't want to know about the state of their relationship. Everything I couldn't help but picture when I imagined the two of them together. She'd taken him back.

I said, 'I'd like to know what became of Will Beauclerk.'

He said, 'I'd like to know what sent you to Coventry.'

We stared at each other. Then he sighed, leaned forward, and took the bottle from me. 'He's safe and unhurt. And adamant I should trust you. He certainly did, given what you had him doing.'

'I'm not your enemy,' I said. Another swig from the bottle had me coughing brandy into my sinuses.

'Yet you're hiding from SIS and the security service. And,' he said, 'you had Will undermining Milkweed.'

Yes I did. 'It's complicated.'

'Like your relationship with Gretel,' he said. 'Whatever that is.'

'Yes.'

'I could take you in right now.'

'You could.'

He cracked his knuckles against his jaw. Thinking hard, my young counterpart: he did both hands. He reached a decision, and it didn't involve dragging me to the Admiralty. For which I was grateful. I wasn't up for fighting him, and losing, a second time.

He said, 'Stephenson received a parcel of photos.' I waited. 'Couriered from Egypt,' he added.

And then I knew why he'd tracked me down. This was an addendum. A professional courtesy. A postscript to the secret mission we'd run together. The mission we'd thought a success.

'Hellfire Pass.'

'Apparently.'

'Anybody else?'

He jerked a thumb over his shoulder, in the direction from which came Gretel's moans. 'Big brother.'

'Damn,' I said. Because I also knew, in the next instant, why Will had decided to help him find me. This was a message from him, too: beware the future echo. I didn't need the old Gretel to tell me how this would unfold. Sooner or later, some clever boy at Milkweed would gin up a cockeyed scheme for using the Eidolons to teleport a team to Halfaya. The smart wager was on the very clever boy sitting across from me.

He said, 'I think she arranged this.'

I wondered about that. She might have, once upon a time. 'I don't know,' I admitted.

'She prepared a cache of batteries separate from the farm.' He told me about U-115 and its unusual cargo.

'Does Milkweed have a plan?' I asked.

'Not yet,' he said. 'You going to spike it when we do?'

I remembered the night the Ghost of St. James' Park tried to shoot me in the knee. I finally knew what he'd been trying to do. And what I was soon to do.

'I want those bastards dead just as you do.'

My younger self frowned, sensing the evasion. I changed the subject.

'Why'd you come here?'

'Figured that after everything—' His gesture took in Gretel, the warehouse, Liv, Agnes, Coventry. He twisted the cork back into the bottle, packed it with the heel of his palm. '—you deserved to know.'

'Stephenson will cut your bollocks off if he gets an inkling of this.'

'I've known the old man a long time,' he said. 'He'd give me a fair listen before he stretched my neck.'

'That he would.'

He frowned at that, too. Wondering, no doubt, how I knew the old man. But he gave me a pass on that as well. His consideration of me had risen considerably since last we met. All it took was saving the lives of his wife and daughter. But I knew myself, and knew he still didn't trust me without reservation. What fool would?

He returned the remainder of the brandy to the haversack. I could hear it sloshing, faintly, when he slung it over his shoulder. He caught my eye, jerked his head toward the far corner of the mezzanine. Gretel was watching us again.

'She's changed, but I don't think she's quite finished yet. Watch yourself. That's what I came here to say.'

Through a window coated with years of industrial grime, I watched my younger self recede on his way past the docks. His demeanor had changed in the months since I'd last seen him. Still every bit the abrasive lot he'd always been ... I'd always been. But he was more relaxed now.

I wondered how long it had been before Liv took him back into her bed. It could have been me beside her.

As he disappeared into the distance, I wondered if I had made a grave error by not telling him the full truth. But my identity was my trump card, and the fact he'd sought me out meant my doppelgänger accepted that I was on his side. Though wary, he accepted me as an ally. So I'd chosen to keep that card in reserve.

For months, I'd thought that if I could get to him without MI6 nabbing me, I'd explain everything to him, thus securing his cooperation in eliminating the warlocks. But that was when we believed all vestiges of the REGP destroyed, all of von Westarp's children dead.

But they weren't. He hadn't completed his mission to the farm as we'd originally believed, meaning we still hung between Scylla and Charybdis.

My younger self thought Klaus's reappearance meant Gretel had played us. Thus he'd come to warn me. Good of him to do so. But he'd been misled by the extra cache of batteries hidden away on U-115.

He still didn't know Gretel as I did. Didn't understand the full context of her manipulations.

True to form, she'd prepared a soft landing for herself. After the dust settled, when all was said and done and we'd averted the threat of the Eidolons, why on earth would she forsake her ability? Gretel sure as hell wouldn't. So U-115 carried enough batteries to last her through all the years of a long life spent gazing down on us mortals with faint amusement. Perhaps she'd kick the anthill from time to time, just for jollies.

But the creation of a new time line had overwhelmed her precognition with the psychic equivalent of radio hash jamming a navigation beacon. She hadn't intended the batteries to find use in North Africa. Reinhardt and Klaus were supposed to be dead, not deployed with the Afrika Korps.

I knew how things would progress. I felt like Gretel.

Even now, my younger self was formulating the idea of mounting a surprise attack via the Eidolons. Just as I'd had the same idea, long long ago, to send teams to the farm. No amount of reasoning would dissuade Raybould Marsh from going on the raid. The mule-headed prig would insist on seeing things through to the end. Nothing short of a crippling injury would stop him.

Which, of course, I would deliver. Because if he went and the raid went pear-shaped all over again, the Eidolons would demand the soul of his next child in exchange for rescue. Thereby consigning Liv and he to life with a soulless monstrosity. It would destroy them. And, eventually, the world.

Future echoes. Will's phrase was quite apt.

But none of this brought me any closer to destroying the warlocks. It brought to a high boil the anxiety I'd wrestled with for months on end. So I decided to do what I always did when my frustration became unbearable. Taunting Gretel never failed to lift my spirits.

She huddled in the corner, as she did most days, surrounded by little stacks of coins. Uneven strands of greasy hair hid her eyes. She'd taken to chewing on it. Eddies of soot licked at my footsteps when I approached her. Our current accommodations had become available after the Fire Watch had failed to keep Jerry incendiaries from claiming a good portion of the warehouse. The building would have to be demolished one day, if the war ever let up.

Like a monk reciting the rosary, she murmured to herself for hours on end. The steady drone had put a rasp into her throaty voice.

'... shecan'tbealiveshecan'tbealiveshecan'tbe ...'

On and on it went. She was too deep in her thoughts to notice me, so I kicked a stack. Ha'pennies went bounding and clicking across the warehouse floor. That got her attention. She looked up at me through a fringe of hair. Her lips still moved, but at least she shut up.

'Thought you might want some good news,' I said. The words felt like rose petals on my lips. 'Your darling brother Klaus is alive and well.'

A shimmer in her red eyes joined the tremble of her lips and chin. Her face contorted, and for a moment I thought she might start weeping again. I particularly enjoyed it when she did.

Gretel said, 'Why must you ...' She inhaled sharply. Her eyes widened. 'Duck!'

I hit the floor, arms crossed over my head.

Nothing happened.

I counted sixty beats of my palpitating heart before climbing to my feet. Gretel convulsed with laughter.

It wasn't the gentle laughter of the faintly amused, nor was it the self-assured and carefully calibrated gaiety of times past. It came out of her in a wild confusion between gulping breaths, a stunted hybrid of joy and despair. She shook with hysterical glee and chest-heaving sobs.

I stood. 'Very funny,' I said. *Evil bitch.*

'See? You still trust me. We have a connection.'

Something fell out of my pocket as I brushed away the worst of the soot. I plucked a bloody rag from the floor. I'd been carrying it for months, clutching it like a talisman while I climbed the walls with frustration for my inability to access the warlocks.

My plan for the Twins had been so simple. But everything had gone straight out the window with Will's capture. I didn't have a warlock ally to negotiate the Twins' reunion. And all the surviving warlocks were hidden away in their citadel, safe and snug and slowly destroying the world. I couldn't get near—

And then I had it.

I had the solution.

The heavens didn't crack apart. Epiphany didn't come to me on the wings of angels blasting golden trumpets. But it damn well should have.

If I timed things right, I could solve virtually all of my problems and wrap up the mission that had sent me twenty-three years into the past with just a few hours' work.

It was so goddamned obvious.

Joy rose within me, like a golden bubble escaping stygian depths. It melted the despair that had settled on my soul like a sheen of hoarfrost. My fingers tingled.

I joined Gretel in her laughter. A pair of cackling maniacs, us.

*

Took quite a while to fall asleep that night. Epiphanies are like that, I suppose.

I'd been dreaming of Liv when something jerked me into consciousness. Her smell, her laugh, the tickle of her hair across my chest, it all evaporated, leaving me disoriented and aroused. In spite of the river-scented breezes that gusted through the scars of bomb and fire damage, summer heat left the warehouse stuffy and close. I slept without a shirt or a blanket. But when I tried to sit up, something held me back.

Gretel's arm. Draped across my stomach. Her leg, across my knees. Her wires across my chest. The odor of her unwashed hair in my nose.

She'd wormed into my cot and pressed her naked body against me. Moonlight shone on the curve of an olive-colored thigh. A tangle of raven-black hair concealed the swell of a breast. Her skin was cool to the touch, but sweat-soaked canvas squelched beneath the small of my back.

Her skin glided across mine where our bodies touched. She was smooth and soft and slick. And so much younger than me.

It had been so long since I'd lain beside a naked woman. An eternity had passed since I stopped thinking of Gretel as human. But she was, and in her body's prime. I could smell her arousal.

'We have a connection,' she whispered.

Her breath stirred the hairs on my neck. Her fingers left a trail of gooseflesh down my stomach. My body betrayed me. I cursed my traitorous flesh. How long had it been since a woman touched me?

'Olivia isn't your wife,' said Gretel. The tickle of her lips against my earlobe sent unwelcome tremors down my spine. I involuntarily arched my back. Her breast rubbed against my shoulder. Her fingers plucked at my trousers.

She shifted against me, laid her other hand across my open mouth when I tried to speak. Her fingers tasted of a thousand coin tosses. They were moist. I spat out the sour tang of her own excitement.

Gretel straddled me. I belted her.

She toppled from the cot with enough force to rattle the floorboards. I jumped to my feet and gave her a barefooted kick for good measure. My heel thudded against her sternum, knocking her down again.

'You're sicker than I ever thought possible. I'd sooner bed the Devil herself than you.' I knelt, and grabbed her by the throat. 'Never touch me again.'

'Olivia will never touch you as I do,' she croaked.

'She's lost to me because of you!'

With fistfuls of hair and wire, I dragged her across the warehouse and flung her into the corner. I hoped the floorboards riddled her arse with splinters. Though nothing could have been rough enough to scour away the disgust I felt at my own body's betrayal.

Gretel kept her hands and thoughts to herself the next morning. I packed up my few belongings and prepared to move us out. We went west, across the river. There I kept an eye on St. James', and waited for history to repeat itself.

SIXTEEN

2–3 July 1941
Westminster, London, England
Halfaya Pass, Egypt

The promise of sunrise coaxed the songbirds of St. James' into a serenade for Marsh. The blackout retreated to the western reaches of the city like a fugitive cutpurse seeking refuge in grim alleyways, while the eastern sky faded from black to wet wool gray to a chalky blue like the veins beneath Liv's skin.

He'd left Walworth in the middle of the night, taking care not to wake Liv as he slipped out of bed. If he could manage it, he'd catch a nap in the Admiralty later. But for now, the prospect of finally seeing an end to the work that had begun with Krasnopolsky made sleep impossible. So did the collywobbles that came from knowing there were a dozen ways for the plan to go wrong.

Once this was over – well and truly over – he could look into a change of profession. Something that didn't take him away from home for six months at a time. Something that didn't involve lightless dungeons. Something that didn't require lying to Liv.

Marsh recited a two-part password to a pair of sentries. The larger one, a blotchy-faced fellow a thumb under six foot tall, opened the gate for Marsh. This was the only portal through the ten-foot privacy fence, barricades, and coils of concertina wire that had enveloped a good portion of St. James'. A raven eyed Marsh's passage through the checkpoint. It fluttered away with the whoosh of wide black wings when the gate banged shut.

Pain flared in his knee. He stumbled. Marsh put his back to a mulberry tree and massaged the razor-edged ache. The pain was rarely this acute. Not even during physical training for the Navy, and later at Fort Monckton.

Not now, he prayed. *Just one more day. Then I'll happily live out my days as Liv's dot-and-carry-one.*

Wispy ankle-high mist clung to the dewy grass. It swirled around Marsh's legs and sloshed across the walkways trodden into the grass between the tents. The mist was thickest over the lake. But it was shot through with the first light of day, so it dissipated quickly. In its place, a humid scent arose from the lake. Warm day ahead.

Not as warm as a summer day in Egypt. And yet warmer than the desert night, where Marsh's plan would unfold.

Marsh scratched at the sticking plaster affixed to his hand. Yesterday, the warlocks had taken a few drops of blood from him and all the others slated to go on the mission. Stephenson had made certain they didn't prick fingers or cut palms, anything that might interfere with the use of a weapon. So now Marsh had a nick on the back of his left hand. It itched.

Mud squelched beneath his boots. The ground near the tents had been churned up by frantic activity as Milkweed turned the park into a staging ground. Marsh lifted a tent flap and ducked inside. One of the sniper teams would receive its final briefing here. In one corner of the tent stood a plaster mannequin. It wore a mock-up of a Reichsbehörde battery harness. A second battery model, sculpted from wood and Bakelite, sat on the table. They looked sufficiently close to the real thing that they'd be indistinguishable from a distance. And that was the only thing that mattered. The mock-ups had been used for training the snipers. Anybody wearing a battery was a prime target.

Four photographs hung on the blackboard: the same set that had come to Stephenson via special courier. Arrows in several colors of chalk indicated various tents in the Afrika Korps encampment, including most prominently the one Milkweed's analysts believed to contain the battery stores. KLAUS had been written in block letters beneath the blurry photo of the man with the eighty-eight. A terse summary of his known characteristics followed, drawn heavily from Marsh's recollections. A similar list accompanied Reinhardt's photograph.

Marsh went back outside and checked one of the Nissen huts closer to the lake. Milkweed had built three such huts. One team would depart from each. The huts were arranged in St. James' Park in a very precise geographic relationship. If the warlocks did their jobs correctly, the distribution would be retained when the teams and their equipment arrived in Egypt. And if Milkweed's read of the recon photos was accurate, it meant they'd place their teams at strategic locations within the maze of ravines that formed Halfaya Pass.

The huts were necessary for concealing the Dingos: fast four-wheel-drive armored recon vehicles. The Dingos were necessary for two reasons:

First, the warlocks hedged quite a bit when Stephenson pressed them on how accurately they'd be able to land the strike teams. A bit of driving might be necessary, which unfortunately meant reducing their element of surprise.

Second, Lorimer's gadgets – he called them 'pixies' – were too

large to be carried by hand. Somebody had cleaned out the
Milkweed vault around the time of Gretel's escape (Marsh reckoned he knew the culprit), meaning Lorimer hadn't had enough
time to study Gretel's battery to back out an accurate circuit
model. Thus, the pixies compensated for a lack of finesse with
what the Scot called 'real nadger-crushing power.' He claimed
that more portable versions were possible, but such would have
required tuning the inner workings of the pixies specifically to
details of the Reichsbehörde battery design.

This Nissen hut also contained a workbench, sledgehammer,
chisel, and a stone dredged from the lake. A lacquered box alongside the stone contained dozens of bloodstained handkerchiefs.

The echo of boot steps reverberated through the corridor and
into Will's cell, rousing him from a nap. Napping was the cen-
terpiece of his life in the citadel. He spent his days napping,
reading, and quietly going mad.

It sounded as though an entire phalanx of marines had come
down. A surge of panic launched him to his feet. He coughed,
twice, the second time bringing up something hot and bitter. Why
would Stephenson send an entire squad of marines to Will's cell?
Had the old man overcome his reluctance to execute the brother
of a peer?

Will stood at the door. He watched through the tiny square of
wire-reinforced glass. But the squad of marines tromped past in
pairs. They formed a bodyguard troop around the remaining
warlocks: a pair of marines, then Grafton and White, four more
marines, followed by Webber and Hargreaves, and two more
marines to round out the bunch. Four men to guard each pair of
warlocks.

They were only allowed to leave the citadel when it came time to pay another blood price. Even then only two warlocks were permitted outside at any time. And always in the presence of bodyguards.

But now the lot were moving out. That meant one thing: a very large blood price. Larger than two men could pay on their own. It meant that tonight they would put in motion Marsh the Younger's plan for ambushing and eradicating the last vestiges of the Götterelektrongruppe.

The Eidolons would take him apart. Study him. And steal the soul of a child yet to be born.

He pounded on his door. One of the sentries shot him a look. Will pressed his face to the glass. 'You don't know what you're doing!' he cried. His voice echoed in the cell, but the steel and glass surely filtered out all emotion.

Grafton paused. The line bunched up behind him. He turned, frowned at Will. Stark electric light glistened in the pockmarks that riddled his skin.

Will continued, 'Listen to me. Please, don't try this. The consequences will be far worse than you imagine.'

The lead sentries came back. Now the other warlocks stared at him, too.

'I know whereof I speak,' said Will.

'You know nothing,' said Grafton. He turned. The marines formed up again.

Will remembered what Marsh the Elder had told him about the time line he'd barely escaped. The Britons of that world had had a term for the hundreds of civilians who had died mysteriously, or disappeared, during the war. The Missing. Victims of a network of fifth columnists. A vast network, said the prevailing wisdom, yet it somehow evaporated without the tiniest bit of residue at war's end.

Because nobody credible suspected Whitehall in the atrocities. Who could believe that?

'How many?' shouted Will. 'How many must bleed to satisfy your masters?'

These marines guarded men who, they were told, held the survival of the country in their hands. But doing so would make them accessories to tonight's atrocities. Young men who had joined up to serve their country, to protect it from all ills, would have to stand idly by while their charges merrily derailed trains, sank barges, set buildings afire.

Did they know what the evening held in store? It was blood magic. It was war. It was murder.

Will pounded on the door. 'Marines! Listen to me! You don't know what these men are planning!'

Hargreaves unbuttoned his collar. The burn scars twisted his flesh into grotesque shapes when he removed his necktie. He handed it to a marine.

'We shall wait while you gag Lord William,' he said.

The sentry posted beside Will's cell unlocked the door. Two marines entered. Will backed away, saying, 'Gentlemen, if you carry out tonight's assignment, you will be guilty of treacheries that far outstrip my own. I promise you.'

They subdued him in seconds. They weren't interested in what he had to say.

I am an Englishman.

At rest, my heart beats to the drip-drop patter of a gentle drizzle. Other times, it hammers in my chest with the relentless thrum of a summer thunderstorm. In dry weather, my heartbeat measures the interval between rain showers. I am intimate with rain. As are we all.

But also, in my time, I have been a gardener. I know down to the dirt beneath my nails that rain is alchemical. It coaxes seeds to life, blossoms to bursting. And, like the greenery for which our verdant island is famous, I am nourished by a good English rain.

That is how I felt when a dozen men emerged from the Admiralty Citadel. They stepped into bright daylight that shone in the midst of a bone-soaking shower. Clouds hovered above our piece of London like the Lord's own barrage balloon. But they did not block the lowering sun, and so the rain that sheeted on Horse Guards Parade became a golden mist that enveloped the procession.

I'd been at my vigil so long that I gave out a little cry of relief at the sight of the warlocks and their marine escort. Even Gretel fell silent. I adjusted my binoculars, focusing over rooftops, past a forest of chimney pots, beyond the tents and Nissen huts that infested St. James' like a profusion of toadstools. I could barely make the men out, so brilliantly did the rain shimmer in the sunlight.

Four older men in various states of decrepitude and ruin, surrounded by a bloody honor guard. Warlocks. Who else would these fellows be?

I'd spent day after miserable day cramped in the stuffy garret of a theater building on Regent Street. Thanks to the cordon around St. James', it was the only perch from which I could watch the Citadel. Each day my spirits sunk in equal measure with the rising heat. It was enough to drive a man mad. More so, when forced to share his confinement with Gretel. I didn't mind the rats.

How appropriate, this sunlit rain. A beginning and an ending, alpha and omega. My mission – that one that began in a Spanish hotel a quarter century ago, by the reckoning of my drip-drop heart – was coming to an end. With just a bit more work, and a touch of luck, I could have my rest.

The warlocks' departure to commit their government-sanctioned blood prices opened my window of opportunity. I reviewed my plan while changing, for what I hoped would be the last time, into the uniform of Lieutenant-Commander Liddell-Stewart. First stop, the Admiralty. Then, off with the uniform, and with carpetbag in hand, I'd become a warlock again and infiltrate St. James'.

I could deal with the Twins and the warlocks in one go. I'd even devised a means of excluding my younger self from the mission to Africa. It was dead simple. No need to hobble him. To hell with Will's theory of future echoes. I was forging my own history. And without Gretel to warn them of the impending attack, Klaus and Reinhardt didn't stand much chance if Lorimer's pixies worked.

But all of this had to come, of course, after I subdued Gretel. That evil, barmy bitch would never again be the mistress of her own destiny. Much less the world's. From my carpetbag I produced the ropes and belts with which we'd tied her to Will's bed. She might have enjoyed it, the twisted bint, if she hadn't been passed out from pain. I glanced into the corner but, like me, she'd vacated her nest. I sought her among painted flats and costume racks. My footsteps sent coins bouncing between the floorboards.

'We don't have time to mess about,' I said. 'So be a good little Nazi while I finish the task you brought me here to do.'

But she wasn't sleeping on the pile of theatrical costumes she used for a mattress. And she hadn't taken station at one of the dormer windows, as she often did, to watch the inscrutable world spin along without her guidance. The door to the rear stairwell hung open.

Bloody fuck.

How long ago had she fallen silent? I dashed back to the

window and cranked it open as wide as possible. Leaning out, I used the binoculars to scan the street below.

There she was. Striding up Regent toward Piccadilly. Gretel set a brisk pace, but even in the rain her steps were light and purposeful: she glided through London as though she owned the place. She'd found a purpose. And, just like the old Gretel, she knew exactly what she was doing.

The Tube stop at Piccadilly was in the opposite direction from my destination. Catching her, if I could even get to her before she boarded the Underground, meant a long delay. She had seized this moment to scamper off, knowing damn well I couldn't afford to chase after her. The fucking demon.

Should have let the younger me strangle her during his visit to the warehouse. God knows he'd wanted to.

I had to leave. My window of opportunity was good only as long as the warlocks were occupied elsewhere.

I'd just emerged onto Regent, fuming and cursing and probably scarlet with rage, when intuition struck me like a mortar shell. I knew what Gretel intended.

Somehow, even after all this time, I still underestimated her.

I went numb. And then I broke into a dead run.

Silence had enveloped Milkweed's wing of the Admiralty. Almost everybody was in the park, or resting up for the evening's adventure. I had to step carefully; my younger self would be taking a nap somewhere nearby. Similarly for the other troops slated for the mission. Lorimer would be in St. James', putting the final touches on his pixies.

That left Stephenson. But if I knew my mentor, he'd be chasing down updates about the Halfaya encampment. Where Klaus and Reinhardt were.

The old man had locked his office. But I'd long ago made a copy of my doppelgänger's keys; he'd handed them over on the night he departed for Germany. I slipped inside, closed the door, and went straight to his desk. The items I sought wouldn't be in the vault. Stephenson would have collected them quietly. Surreptitiously.

My quarry was something I'd never known about at the time. But the Will of 1963 had deduced its existence long after the fact. John Stephenson had carefully laid the groundwork for Milkweed's role in postwar foreign policy.

My sprint from Regent Street had left me sodden, shaky, and breathless. Fucking Gretel. I rummaged through Stephenson's desk, doing my best not to drip on anything important. If I'd had the time I would have looked for anything that might have been a veiled reference to children, orphanages, anything of the sort. But I didn't have time. And if I read my altered history correctly, Stephenson wouldn't have progressed that far into his planning. These were early days.

I found what I sought in the bottom drawer where he kept his brandy. The old man had stashed a cigar box inside a false backing at the rear of the drawer.

At first glance, the box contained nothing but flotsam. Shavings from a wooden floorboard. The corner torn from a map. A stiff leather tourniquet.

Each stained with blood. Each labeled with a name: Webber. Grafton. Beauclerk. Shapley . . .

Every negotiation with the Eidolons began when the warlocks cut themselves. Bloodshed was the lubricant that made the process work. The warlocks' blood, in particular, was part of the process for contacting the Eidolons. So of course Stephenson would have collected it. Carefully, when nobody was looking, he'd tear the corner from a bloodstained map, or perhaps he snuck back later and scraped up a piece of flooring with his letter opener.

I removed Will's tourniquet, then tossed the cigar box into my carpetbag. After locking Stephenson's office behind me, I ducked into the loo. There I changed out of my uniform, and flushed the tourniquet.

Gretel had a good twenty minutes on me. And I had to get into St. James' Park before the warlocks returned and the place became a circus. I had one hope of intercepting her. But I'd made no preparations to enter the Citadel. Many of my current problems sprang from my inability to do just that. So now I had to wing it.

'Back already, sir?'

The sentry took me for Hargreaves. I saw the look of consternation cross his face a second later. He'd focused on the burns and nothing else, but now he realized a second late that Hargreaves was a hideous but *clean-shaven* man. At least he caught his mistake.

His eyes slid away from mine. 'Sorry, sir. Thought you were somebody else.'

'Have my colleagues already departed?'

This I asked in my normal speaking voice. The fire damage to my throat could easily be mistaken for Enochian tissue damage. I looked the part. I sounded the part. I even carried a carpetbag. My only hope was that the sentries not directly attached to Milkweed found the others like me too unpleasant to watch closely. But if they knew the mysterious old men from SIS numbered four and only four ... well, then I was truly buggered.

'Yes, sir. 'Bout half an hour ago.'

'Damnation,' I said. Inwardly, I screamed at myself to hurry, screamed at this mental deficient to get out of my goddamned way, screamed with inchoate rage at the entire world. But I held it in check, just barely, and kept to my script. 'Did they ask after me?'

He frowned. Shook his head. 'No. No, sir.'

'Bloody typical, isn't it.'

'If you say so, sir.'

'Didn't bother to leave a message, I expect.'

'No, sir.'

I handed him my forged Identity Card. He spent a good moment on it. Had another Raybould Marsh come through recently? Apparently not, because he waved me through.

Finding Will was another delay I couldn't afford. I reckoned they'd have thrown him into the deepest, darkest hole they had, and I was right. They'd posted a guard outside his cell, thank the Lord. The sentry didn't move, but turned his head at the sound of my footsteps. My impatience got the better of me.

'I need to talk to the prisoner. Now,' I said.

'Sir?'

Will's face appeared in the window of the cell. His eyes widened in surprise.

'Why is he gagged?'

'Mr. Hargreaves's orders, sir.'

'Well, that won't do at all. How can he answer my questions with a necktie stuffed in his mouth?'

Overplayed my hand with that. The touch of confusion tugging the sentry's eyebrows together turned into outright suspicion. He held out a hand. 'Papers, sir.'

His other hand went to the revolver at his belt. I took out my Identity Card. He unsnapped the holster. 'Your other papers, sir.'

So I jumped him. Managed to tackle him before he brought the Enfield to bear. The shot ricocheted from the concrete and went pinging through a Continuity-of-Government conduit. Will yelped.

The boy was younger and stronger. But by now the frustration and anxiety had my rage going at a good simmer. Landing atop him, I slammed my forehead against his nose. Hurt like hell. He responded with a knee to the groin and a fierce jab to my jaw when I reared back again. He tried to bring the gun up. I slammed his arm down. His thumb sought my eye socket. I twisted away. His stiffened fingers glanced off the ridge between the orbit and bridge of my nose. Kept my eye, but lost my grip on his forearm. He lifted the revolver. I laid my left hand over his right, as though trying to wrest the gun out of his grip, but instead used my leverage to push his hand back and expose his wrist. His free fist snapped my mouth shut with enough force to crack a molar. Pain like a white-hot needle shot through my jaw. I put most of my weight into a punch at his overextended wrist. Something clicked inside his forearm. He grunted through clenched teeth. The gun hung limply in his fingers. His hand flopped around like a beached fish. My next punch slammed his head against the floor.

When I was a younger man, I probably wouldn't have stopped until I'd pulped the sentry's skull. But he was out of commission now, so I reined in my rage just enough to fish out his keys, unlock the cell, and untie Will.

Will looked faintly ill as he eyed the fellow on the floor. 'Relax,' I said. 'He isn't dead.'

I didn't like doing it. Poor lad was just doing his job. But so was I. And mine was far more important.

'Help me get him inside.' We dragged the half-conscious

sentry into the cell. There was nothing we could do about the blood smears. I pushed Will into the corridor, then slammed and locked the cell behind us.

'You shouldn't have done this, Pip. They—'

But I was already headed for the exit. 'Get to my house, as quickly as you can,' I said. We jogged up a flight of stairs.

Will panted along behind me. 'What's happened?'

'Gretel's gone. Slipped away the instant I couldn't spare the time to stop her.' We reached the top. I slowed to a rapid walk, lest our haste draw undue attention from the sentry posted outside.

'And you think she's headed to Walworth?'

'Try to think like Gretel for a moment. Who would she blame for the failure of her power?'

Will inhaled. 'Oh, no.'

We emerged from the citadel. Sunset shimmered on recent puddles scattered around Horse Guards Parade. I drew fresh rain-scrubbed air into my lungs. The sentry nodded at me. I ignored him.

I laid a hand on Will's shoulder, as though I could physically propel him across the river. 'Don't let Liv out of your sight. Go!'

And off he went. Gretel had been to our house just once, in the dark. But twenty years from now, in a future that didn't exist, Liv had shown her Agnes's evacuation tag. It had our home address on it. I knew how Gretel worked; that was all she needed. But her ghastly wires and German accent would raise suspicions. She would have to traverse the city with care, while Will could go directly to the house. I hoped it was enough.

The puddles splashed the cuffs of my trousers. I crossed the road toward the checkpoint at St. James'. Two sentries manned the gate. They eyed my scars and carpetbag.

One of the men stepped into my path, rifle held across his chest. 'Can't let you through, sir. Password?'

'Habakkuk,' I told him. And to his companion: 'Rookery.' They stepped aside.

Funny how the big things change, yet the little things stay the same.

Once through the checkpoint, I had the run of the place. The warlocks hadn't returned from their deadly errands, and my younger self still napped in the Admiralty. The others wouldn't start filing in until evening.

Milkweed's staging area differed from what I remembered of a cold December night in a nonexistent history. I had to search around a bit before I found the hut from which the warlocks would carry out the negotiation. The Dingo came as a surprise. So, too, did the bulkiness of the pixies. I remembered them being light enough for two men to carry.

A workbench sat in the middle of the hut. The bench held a piece of Portland limestone. Just as I remembered, an iron chisel had been driven into the stone, at the center of a bloody hand-print. A sledgehammer rested on the bench, ready to finish the job of cleaving the stone.

But I didn't care about any of that. The object I sought was hidden under the bench: a box of blood samples. The Eidolons had to perceive the men to move them. The box contained a sample from each of the soldiers, plus one for the unlucky war-lock who had to initiate the return trip.

Everything I'd worked for boiled down to the contents of this box. A few additions, one subtraction, and then I'd have to sit and wait for the aftermath.

To the box of blood samples I added the rag my doppelgänger had lifted from Germany, and the contents of the cigar box from

Stephenson's office. The warlocks would get a bloody great surprise when they teleported the strike teams to Africa. That had been my epiphany: rather than agonize over how to breach the warlocks' protection, the solution was to get them to do my work for me.

Next, I sifted through the soldiers' samples. One of these belonged to my younger self. I could exclude him from the transit to Africa simply by removing his sample from the group. No need to shoot him in the knee . . .

Or so I thought. But the soldiers' samples weren't labeled.

I shook with the effort not to bellow with rage.

I'd already known I couldn't leave the park. Couldn't race to Liv's side, couldn't join up with Will to intercept Gretel. Because I had to stay here, prepared to ambush any surviving warlocks who returned from the accidental jaunt to North Africa.

But I also couldn't remove my counterpart's blood sample from the roster of travelers. Stephenson could, but the old man would do so only if his protégé were incapacitated. Raybould Marsh had to be badly wounded, and Stephenson had to see it.

All of which meant I had no choice but to hobble him if I wanted to prevent the birth of another soulless child. Little things stay the same . . . God damn it. Because I also wanted to send my younger self to Walworth, to protect our wife. The anxiety had me grinding my teeth and flinching when pain lanced from my broken molar.

But I had to trust Will. He'd once confessed to me the depths of his affection for Liv. He wouldn't let Gretel near her.

So I had no choice but to retreat to a mulberry grove in a distant corner of the enclosed parkland. There I massaged my aching knee and waited for my doppelgänger to arrive.

*

The staging ground came to life as evening fell. Three teams converged on three separate Nissen huts. A pair of snipers passed Marsh's tent, Enfield rifles slung over the shoulders of their ghillie suits. The spotters carried submachine guns. Every man had rubbed his face with burnt cork, even the drivers for the Dingos. Every man wore a sticking plaster over a small scratch on the back of his left hand.

Marsh couldn't make out the snipers' banter as they receded into the shadows – the balaclavas muffled their voices – but he recognized the tone of false bravado. Each man banished the collywobbles in his own way. Most sought camaraderie. Marsh had chosen to be alone in the final minutes before the negotiation began.

Ding. A bell chimed. The five minute mark, calling teams into their final positions.

He double-checked his kit. The ritual enabled him to overcome the growing pain in his bad knee. He chewed another aspirin tablet and focused on counting his gear: One combat knife, six-inch blade. Six Mills bombs. Four white phosphorus grenades. One Enfield double-action revolver (No. 2, Mk. I). Five six-round cylinders for same. One Lee-Enfield bolt-action rifle (No. 4, Mk. I). Five ten-round magazines for same. One electric torch. One garrote. One Very pistol with three magnesium flares. One compass. One medkit. One canteen.

Marsh shrugged into the shoulder straps of the haversack. Then he stuffed a few extra cylinders and magazines into the webbing pockets of his belt, slung the rifle over his shoulder, and stepped from the tent into shadows and humidity. Blackout on a summer night.

Ding. Ding. Three minutes.

Footsteps whispered through grass nearby as other team

members scrambled for their final positions. A breeze rustled the cat-tails along the water's edge. Ripples lapped gently against the shoreline. The cloy of spilled petrol from a fueling mishap involving one of the Dingos overlaid the earthier scents of mud and water.

Marsh turned for the Nissen hut where Stephenson, Lorimer, and the warlocks had converged. A figure emerged from the shadows behind the tent. The newcomer blocked Marsh's path.

Marsh said, 'It's starting. Get to your team.'

The silhouette replied, in a familiar rasp, 'We need to talk.'

'How the hell did you get in here?'

'You should talk to the old man about changing his password protocols.'

'Your sense of timing is one for the books, mate. Have you any idea what's about to happen?'

'Better than you.' Starlight glinted on the barrel of a pistol in the commander's hand. 'You mustn't go.'

Marsh froze in the act of reaching for his own sidearm. 'You're barmier than Gretel if you think I'll sit this out. After everything I went through? After what you and she *put* me through? We're within a hair's breadth of finishing this. And now you want me to step aside?'

A door creaked. A brief flash of light tore the darkness. The shrieks and rumbles of Enochian leaked out with the light. The old man's voice bellowed across the park. 'Raybould! For God's sake, get your arse in here!'

Liddell-Stewart cocked the revolver. 'Cry out. Stephenson must believe you're injured. He has to eject you from the team.'

Marsh said, 'You wouldn't dare.' He raised his voice. 'On my way, sir!'

'Damn it,' said the commander. 'There's no time for explanation. But I'm trying to help you, you stubborn git.'

Stephenson again called into the darkness. 'We can't wait any longer. We have to do it now. Hurry!'

Then the door creaked again, and yellow light fell briefly upon the trampled grass of St. James' as Stephenson went inside. The Enochian call-and-response hit a crescendo. The door slammed. Darkness rippled.

Marsh prepared to dash around the commander, but Liddell-Stewart raised the revolver. He aimed at Marsh's knee. 'You'll thank me for this later,' he said.

The hairs on Marsh's arms crackled with ghostly static. The air turned icy cold, bubbling with greasy unreality and malign disdain. The Eidolons had seen him.

The commander's eyes widened in surprise. He felt it, too. 'No! Blood—'

He pulled the trigger at the same instant the Eidolons sheared the here-and-now from Marsh's body. He was a hole in space, an impossible bifurcation slithering through the mortar of the universe. He tried to brace himself, but he was—

Will sprinted along the Mall, away from the Citadel and toward the strongpoint erected in Admiralty Arch. Trafalgar Square, just a few seconds beyond the arch for a man running full tilt, was his best bet of finding a taxi.

He wouldn't let Marsh down. He couldn't fail Liv – she'd called him her champion. After everything they'd been through, together and separately, fates intertwined through the bonds of braided fate and historical paradox . . . *Just one more time*, thought Will, *let me be her champion again*.

Rain puddles splashed his trousers. Every stride squelched

water from the sodden leather of his shoes. He hadn't run since university; the stitch in his side felt like a nail in his kidney. Or was that his appendix?

He couldn't bear the thought of harm befalling Olivia. Just once, he wanted her to look on him not with bemusement and sisterly affection, but something else.

Will drew odd glances from the bored Home Guard volunteers manning the strongpoint's machine gun. The Führer had indefinitely postponed preparations for Sea Lion last autumn, but most of London's invasion preparations remained in place. So the HG men had nothing better to do than to lounge on the sandbag revetments and watch the gangly fellow in the mud-splashed bespoke suit.

One called, 'Where's the fire, guv?'

The last rays of sunset illuminated Nelson's Column. Will panted up to the first taxi he saw, opened the suicide door, collapsed into the rear seat. He had to catch his breath before he could recite Liv's address for the driver. His throat felt like sandpaper. 'I'll pay double if you get me there in ten.'

'You're on.' The driver wheeled his taxi around Trafalgar, boomeranging back toward the river.

Will sank back, closed his eyes. He felt for his billfold. But, of course, his pockets were empty. They'd been empty since the night Hargreaves had caught him out.

'Ah,' said Will. 'Ha. Oh, my. Hi, hi, driver. This is embarrassing. I'm afraid I've misplaced my billfold.'

The car skidded to a crooked halt on the pavement just short of Waterloo. The screech of tires drew an angry glance from a bobby standing on Victoria Embankment.

'Sorry,' said the driver. He killed the engine. 'Can't help you.'

'I assure you I'm good for it.'

'Not right now you isn't.'

'This is a matter of life and death, man!'

'That's life in wartime, mate.'

'Look, I'll give you my name and my address—'

'Oh, I know your type. Too rich to pay for a taxi ride. The war makes a good excuse for shorting the help, don't it? I'm surprised you're in the city at all. Probably got a nice funk hole out in the country.'

Will said, 'Sir, I understand your frustration. I promise you that my brother—'

'Out,' said the driver. 'Out now, or I call that copper over here.'

'Did I say double? Triple! Please.'

The driver rolled down his window. He waved at the bobby. 'Oy! Over here.'

Will sighed. Not only was he without his billfold, he didn't have his Identity Card on him, either. He'd never get to Liv's house in time if the police questioned him.

'Very well, very well. I'm off. See? I'm stepping out now.'

The taxi pulled away, probably to return to the taxi stand at Trafalgar. Will approached the iron girders of the temporary replacement for the demolished Waterloo Bridge. 'Temporary' being a relative term; the original Waterloo had been closed for years before Will entered university.

He'd find another taxi. He hated to do it, but he'd have to wait to discover his billfold missing until after he'd already arrived at Liv's.

Somebody tapped him on the shoulder. Will turned.

The bobby said, 'Sir. A moment, please.'

*

—too late, I was real again.

That made the fourth time I'd been disassembled and then reassembled by the Eidolons, but the first time it had happened by accident. The journey from '63 still topped the list in terms of residual misery, but accidental teleportation came damn close.

I stumbled. The ground crunched underfoot. The soft grass of St. James' Park had become a precarious scree of sandy gravel mixed with large jagged stones. I scraped my hand open when I reached out to catch myself. My tumble kicked up plumes of dust that coated my eyeballs with grit. I exhaled the last traces of humid, verdant parkland, and inhaled the smell of dry desolation. The air was cool, but the stony earth reradiated the day's surplus of sunlight.

The Eidolons had deposited us into the talus at the base of a towering escarpment. Dim starlight and the setting half moon showed the craggy cliffs to be riddled with narrow ravines. The mouth of Halfaya Pass leered at us like a gap-toothed hag. The escarpment formed a natural border, and barrier, between the Egyptian coastal lowlands – where the roads were – and the Libyan plateau, which stood hundreds of feet higher. Halfaya was the only means near the coast of driving heavy armor from Egypt to Libya. Other routes meant long diversions to the south.

The Mediterranean Sea was several miles behind us, too far to hear or smell it in this arid expanse. The sandy lowlands on the north end of Halfaya, where we now stood, offered little in the way of cover. Similarly the rocky highlands atop the pass. But the pass itself was a labyrinth easily defended against intruders.

Looking like the trunk of a felled tree, the barrel of an anti-aircraft gun loomed at us from the mouth of the widest ravine. It resided in a trench deep enough to hide everything but the barrel and breech, which stuck out just a couple of feet above the ground. Up close, it wasn't hard to see how these things could shoot through a Matilda.

The pain in my knee was gone. The lingering ache I'd had for as long as I could remember, the arthritic twinges that had plagued me since my youth, had disappeared. Not receded, but disappeared. As though they had never existed.

I glanced at my younger counterpart. He had hunkered down among the talus, taking stock. He wasn't bleeding, he wasn't screaming in pain, so I knew at once my shot had missed. The Eidolons had yanked us away in the instant while the bullet was in transit. He massaged his knee. Yes, he felt the change, too.

Then he noticed me. He whispered, 'What on God's earth are you doing here?' He glanced at my hands, to see if I wore a sticking plaster like all the other participants. I didn't, of course.

'Bloody great oversight,' I admitted.

I'd never intended to come along. But I'd been so focused on tampering with the blood samples – the Twins', the warlocks', my younger counterpart's – that I'd overlooked the simple fact he and I shared the same blood. To the Eidolons, we were two aspects of the same person. And thus, where he went, I went. First, I overlooked Gretel's capacity for treachery, then this ... Twice over, I was a fool.

Could have been even worse. At least the Eidolons' special interest in us, our blood map of circles and broken spirals, managed to keep our bodies distinct.

He unslung his Enfield, worked the bolt. The sound ricocheted through the windswept ravines that confronted us. 'I can't let you interfere.'

I rasped, quietly as I could, 'I'm on your side, you damn fool.'

'Moment ago you didn't want us here,' he said.

'I didn't want *you* here. I want the mission to succeed.' As if I needed a reminder why people call me stubborn. Here we were, deposited by demons into the outskirts of a secret Reichsbehörde camp in the middle of Egypt, and he wanted to have a bun fight. 'But there's bugger all I can do about it now.'

My counterpart dashed across the scree, squeezed around the trench holding the eighty-eight, and disappeared into the deeper shadows. I followed, bitterly aware that I had no spare cartridges for my revolver. The shingle made for unsteady footing and a racket that funneled straight down the twisting ravine.

We hadn't been far from the Nissen when I'd accosted him in St. James', and that distance held here in Halfaya. We joined the commotion surrounding my counterpart's team just inside the first bend of the ravine. I tripped over a man curled into the fetal position, who rocked in the sand while crying and sucking his thumb. Not everybody weathered the transit with sanity intact.

I could make out the Dingo, loaded with one of the pixies. The moonlight barely penetrated to the depths of our canyon, so I couldn't make out more detail than that. But one thing I noticed immediately: the team was too big, and it was too loud. Somebody, a whole group of somebodies, was having a very urgent conversation.

I knew the first part of my plan had worked.

A forced whisper in Lorimer's voice: 'Everybody shut your sodding holes right fucking now.' He'd been a sergeant in the Great War. Decorated.

That quieted most of the discussion. But somewhere in a dark canyon spur to my left, somebody mumbled to himself, 'I can't exist. I can't exist. I can't exist.' Ritter. He'd had the same reaction on the original raid.

Lorimer directed the surviving commandos into three groups. Four men stayed to guard the warlocks, two scouted a retreat path toward the Egyptian side of the pass where my counterpart and I had landed, and two scouted the path forward through the ravine. It led to the camp, if the recon could be believed. My counterpart pushed through the commotion to confer with Lorimer. That left four extra men – five, counting myself – who weren't meant to be here.

Gravel pattered down the sheer sandstone cliffs. I looked up and caught a brief glimpse of a dark figure eclipsing the moon. The high, fingerlike tables made excellent positions for the snipers, as well as their spotters, who carried Sten submachine guns. Milkweed had positioned them well.

The warlocks huddled behind the Dingo. Keeping to the deepest shadows, I sidled closer. They were arguing. Two or three of the bastards wanted to make the return trip immediately. It was too dangerous for them here. Four old men in the middle of a battle with superhuman monsters? They were vulnerable as newborn kittens. Which is why I'd gone to such pains to get them here.

But if the warlocks sent themselves home . . .

Lorimer scuttled over from his conference with my counterpart. He didn't see me. 'Oy! You lot! I hear one more word about leaving and I'll cut your tongues out. Nobody's going home until this is finished.'

. . . they'd drag everybody else back to England, too.

My oversight in getting pulled along meant I had no way to join Will in protecting Liv, but it meant I could take a more direct hand in the warlocks' demise. Once the shooting started, any second now, the fog of combat would make it impossible to discern an unfortunate ricochet from a deliberate execution.

I focused on the task before me. I tried to put thoughts of Liv aside, and inched closer to the old men.

And tripped over something elastic. Another clatter accompanied my sprawl on the talus. This time I landed in something wet. The mélange of vomit and offal assaulted my nose. I hastened to my feet. And found myself standing over the ruptured body of a young woman.

Rather, two young women. One head gazed at me through lifeless eyes, one pale and the other dark in the moonlight. The suggestion of a second head protruded from the crook between neck and shoulder; it, too, had mismatched eyes, but the mirror reverse of the first.

The Eidolons had done as they were bid. They read the blood map that described this person's life, and sent the person described by that blood to this spot. Except, in this case, that blood was shared by two separate bodies. The Eidolons brought both women to the identical location. But that was too much person for one body to contain. I counted three and a half arms. One leg forked into two shins below the knee. The instantaneous spike in pressure had found release in the soft tissues by forcing out the viscera.

I coughed. Struggled to fight down the gorge.

That explained the vomit. Somebody had tripped over her and had the same reaction.

My God. This was my doing. It was exactly what I'd planned. Never thought it would be this messy. I closed her eyes, all four of them, and wondered if they'd ever had names. I hoped it was quick and painless. Quick, probably, but not painless.

I'd met them. They weren't bad girls. But they were the product of a technology that couldn't be allowed to exist. This had to be done. I ripped out the wires and rummaged through flesh and muscle and spurs of bone for the dead Twins' batteries.

'You sick ... You planned this.' My counterpart had found us, me and my victims. His lip curled in disgust at the squelching sounds my hand made. 'You knew their blood was …' He trailed off again. 'Identical.'

The tone in his voice made me uncomfortable. His eyes narrowed, as they sometimes did when I was deep in thought. Any moment now he'd crack his knuckles.

And in fact his hand was moving in that direction when a scrape, a shout, and a clatter echoed through the defile. A man tumbled into our staging ground from above. His head clanged against the Dingo, hard enough to knock him backwards for a heavy thud on the gravel. He came to rest with his head flopped over his shoulder. Broken neck.

One of the snipers had slipped from his perch. Loudly.

His Enfield landed amidst the warlocks. Didn't go off and kill any of them, though, damn the luck. I leapt on it, then looted the spare magazines from his corpse.

The short, sharp chatter of a machine pistol ricocheted through the canyon. Echoes made it impossible to know the source. The glow of a klieg light panned across our ravine, killing my night vision and evoking shouts in both German and English.

I fired twice into what remained of the Twins' heads, smashed the batteries to flinders, and ran to join the fray.

The bobby pointed at the taxi. 'What was that about?'

'That? Nothing.' Will tried to laugh. 'Bit of a disagreement over the fare, I'm afraid. Silly thing.' Then he realized he'd been given a blessing in disguise. 'Actually, officer, I'm glad to have found you—'

'You asked him to drop you on Waterloo?'

'Ah. No. Not exactly. We had a difference of opinion regarding the matter of my destination. But that's water under the bridge now, isn't it, ha ha. But as I was—'

'Difference of opinion?'

Will sighed. 'Look, officer. I've left my billfold behind. I haven't a penny on me. And I'm desperate to reach a friend in Walworth. She's in terrible danger.'

The bobby's demeanor changed. 'What sort of danger?'

'I believe somebody is on the way to her house this very moment, intent on doing her harm.'

'How do you know this?'

'For heaven's sake, man! I'll give you my entire life history. But won't you please send somebody around?' Will recited Liv's address. 'It's life and death!'

'I'll call it in. Follow me.'

The bobby headed for a police box up the street.

'Thank you,' said Will. And then he sprinted across the replacement bridge, footsteps slapping heavily against the girders. The bobby's whistle was shrill against the gurgling of the Thames.

Marsh kept low, hugging the contours of the ravine on his way toward the camp. Another burst of gunfire raked the striated cliffs behind him. Flakes of hot stone pelted him like a rain of fléchettes. He hit the sand.

They couldn't afford to get pinned in the ravines. They had to push forward, gain ground toward the camp, so the Dingos could come forward and deploy the pixies.

And they were already down several men because of the detail guarding the unexpected party of warlocks. No mystery how *that* had happened. Liddell-Stewart's handiwork again. But why?

Marsh pressed himself behind a rib of sandstone. More gunfire swept the ravine. He popped off a covering shot with his revolver, then dashed a few yards to a wider spot behind a boulder. Heavy footfalls crunched through the ravine. He glanced over his shoulder. The commander had taken position behind him.

Lieutenant-Commander. We even share the same rank.

The boulder gave him decent cover and a view of the south end of the ravine. It opened on a relatively flat clearing that housed a dozen tents or more. The clearing was a natural break in Halfaya Pass, surrounded by escarpments and knife-narrow ravines. The pass continued beyond the clearing, for miles and miles.

One of the forward scouts lay on the ground amidst a scarlet puddle. His partner was pinned behind a narrow lip of granite. He had no room to draw his weapon without getting plugged, much less run for more suitable cover. Marsh lobbed a Mills bomb toward the pair of Afrika Korps gunners trying to flush him out. Neither wore a battery.

The blast scattered the Jerries and took down a tent. It gained the scout precious seconds to dash across the ravine and take position behind a waist-high shelf of stone. The canyon amplified the noise and stretched it out, turning a single blast into a long, continuous thunder. Marsh's ears rang.

He popped up, sighted on another Afrika Korps uniform, pulled the trigger, dropped into cover again. Still no sign of a harness. Where were they? They could play pheasant hunt with Rommel's men all night long, but it wouldn't do a damn bit of good if they didn't get Klaus and Reinhardt.

The commander – that name would have to do, for now – motioned at him. It was easy to divine his intent, because Marsh was having the same thought. He nodded. Then he held his hand where the commander could see it. Counted backwards on his fingers: three, two, one. And charged forward under the commander's covering fire.

Marsh joined the scout. 'We have to hold this spot until they get the Dingo up,' he said. Somewhere nearby, an engine roared to life.

'I know!' said the scout. He looked to be in his early twenties. Blood trickled from gashes on his temple, probably from shards of stone. 'What the hell are they waiting for?'

'They need a signal.'

An explosion shook the earth, followed by a lightning crackle that tore the air and ripped through the sounds of combat. The concussion loosened a rain of stones. Marsh ducked, arms wrapped over his head. To his left, an electric-blue glow strobed the clearing and illuminated the dusty air above the neighboring ravine. All around the camp, the klieg lights died. Darkness reclaimed the battleground. The metallic odor of ozone wafted through the night air, strong enough to sting the eyes. One of the teams had fired its pixie.

Its effort was rewarded with another glow. The haze above the ravine blazed brighter than daylight. The chatter of gunfire intensified, as the spotters atop the ravine walls sighted on the source of the light. The glow became a blinding flash that ignited every speck of grit kicked up by the battle. A fireball enveloped the neighboring ravine. Men screamed. Superheated air smelled like house dust caught in a radiator on the first cool day of autumn.

Marsh knew that glow. He'd seen it before. The ravine would have acted as a funnel, a mirror, for the searing heat of Reinhardt's body. Their pixie hadn't worked, and now the men in that ravine were dead.

The other team was having better luck pushing into the camp. The blast from a Mills bomb cratered the nest where two Afrika Korps men had taken position behind a machine gun. Up top, the spotters laid down suppressing fire, while the remaining snipers picked off the men who tried to scuttle between tents for a better position.

And now they knew where Reinhardt was. They needed another pixie. Marsh pulled out his flare pistol.

High over our heads, the magnesium flare shone like a star pulled from the firmament. It washed out the moon and scoured shadows from the deepest corners of the ravine. If the moonlight was silvery, this light was pure platinum and stark enough to bleach the color from the world.

We had to keep the path clear for Lorimer's pixie. I worked the bolt on my pilfered rifle, popped up from behind my boulder, and let off another shot. Desultory return fire knocked chips from the escarpment behind me and *pinged* from the boulder. Though we'd lost the element of surprise at the last minute, we'd still caught Jerry with his pants down. The spotters and snipers up top were taking a toll on the mundane soldiers of this Afrika Korps outpost. This time around, Gretel (Where was she now? Had Will reached Liv first?) hadn't dissected the entire plan of our attack days before we knew it ourselves. I tried, and failed, to keep one eye on my younger self and the other open for Lorimer's advance with the Dingo.

Speaking of which, what kept him?

My counterpart looked at me. His thoughts exactly.

Another concussion reverberated from the sheer cliffs. The ravine behind me erupted in shooting and yelling. My hiding spot beside the boulder didn't provide a clear view of the staging ground, which was a few dozen yards around the bend. My counterpart and the scout covered my retreat. I worked the bolt on my rifle along the way.

My knee didn't protest the running. And I felt a strange exhilaration, almost a sense of peace. There was only one person in the entire outpost who could have snuck around behind us. It would have meant holding his breath and navigating through solid rock, but, of course, he'd been trained for that.

The warlocks wouldn't have a chance against him. It was tempting to take my time, but Lorimer was a good man, as were the poor sods trying to guard the warlocks. They needed help.

Shadows grew as the flare descended. They slithered from their hiding spots among the defile's fissures and gullies. When a gust of dry desert wind nudged the flare, the lengthening shadows capered in response. I crouched amidst their dance to peer around the corner.

Lorimer had set four men to guarding the warlocks. Three lay dead at Klaus's feet. From the condition of their scattered bodies, I reckoned he'd emerged through the talus and dropped a grenade into their midst. A man disfigured by pockmarks lay on the sand nearby, hands pressed to his stomach, shuddering. Shrapnel in the gut. His gaze was glassy, unfocused. Grafton wasn't long for this world.

Lorimer yelled, 'Use the pixie!'

But blind panic made the surviving warlocks stupid. They piled into the Dingo. Webber took the driver's seat, Hargreaves sat beside him, and White climbed atop with the pixie. The engine screamed. Webber flailed at the controls. His panicked attempts to get the Dingo in gear brought the tooth-rattling grind of metal shearing against tortured metal.

'The pixie! Hit it *now!*'

The pair of men assigned to guarding our retreat path charged into the fight, summoned like me by the commotion. Klaus dropped one with a shot from his sidearm. The bullet became substantial as soon as it left the barrel of his pistol. Lorimer and the surviving soldiers concentrated their fire on Klaus. The bullets passed through him more easily than sunlight through window glass. But he couldn't hold his breath forever, and the fusillade forced him to remain insubstantial. Timed right, a person could sneak up and cut his battery wires at the moment he rematerialized to take a breath. But the hail of gunfire passing through his body made it impossible to get close.

Klaus used this to great effect. He kept himself between the men while he advanced, so they risked shooting each other. He strolled through the Dingo, trying to draw the soldiers' fire into the panicked warlocks. He shot another soldier while standing between unarmed Hargreaves and White. Leaving the easiest for last, I realized. Hargreaves flailed at the ghostly man with his knife. Klaus aimed his next shot at Lorimer, who rolled aside at the last second. I glimpsed an attachment to Klaus's battery harness. I'd never seen it before.

Webber slammed the Dingo into gear. It lurched backwards. Klaus whirled. His outstretched arm swept through the engine block. Chunks of metal flew through the armor plating to clatter against the escarpment. The gutted Dingo rolled to a stop, spewing petrol and motor oil.

Klaus had gone scarlet with the effort to hold his breath. He sprinted into the cliff face. I realized the attachment was a breathing tube. Sneaky bastard was going to catch his breath while safely ensconced in sandstone.

That was new. Even the older, more experienced Klaus had never developed that trick. But the breathing tube was still a weakness. I charged forward, eyes fixed on the patch of cliff where Klaus had disappeared.

'Lorimer!' I screamed. 'Phosporus grenade, now!'

But he didn't hear me. He slammed his fist on a red Bakelite panel at the waist of the pixie. The device emitted a high-pitched whine. Clever fellow. He was trying to time the detonation for Klaus's reemergence. The three remaining warlocks leapt from the dead vehicle. Lorimer and the last surviving soldier retreated deeper into the ravine. They screamed at the warlocks to evacuate the blast radius.

They did. But they came in my direction instead.

'Not into the camp, you fools!'

The whine from the pixie grew in intensity and pitch, rocketing through registers that vibrated my eyeballs and loosened my fillings. Lorimer and his companion had no choice but to retreat. They dove for cover behind the eighty-eight.

My right hand went to the pistol at my waist while my left beckoned to the fleeing warlocks. 'This way! Quickly! Take cover!'

They couldn't see my face in the moonlight. They couldn't tell I wasn't supposed to be there. All they saw was a man directing them to safety.

I shot White in the chest. His momentum sent him tumbling face-first in the gravel. Webber didn't have time to react. My second shot hit him just below the heart. Hargreaves skidded to a halt. He stared at me.

'I know what you are,' he said. Then he turned and fled the way he'd come.

Which took him straight into the blast from the pixie.

Will waited until the driver turned onto Liv's street before confessing a certain awkwardness to his pecuniary situation. He did try to give the driver his name and address, but the fellow was too busy hurling abuse to listen. The driver shoved Will from the car while unleashing a stream of blue-pencil epithets, some of which might have made even Stephenson blush.

Will ran to the door. He knocked. The door swung open. *Oh, no.*

Light spilled across the pavement, piercing the darkness that had fallen during Will's journey to Walworth. He scooted inside and closed the door, an automatic reflex born from enduring nearly two years of blackout regulations.

'Olivia? Hello?'

A scuffling sound came from the direction of the kitchen. *I'm too late.* He bolted through the vestibule.

And plowed into the telephone stand. He went down in a tangle of wires and table legs. The water bowl splashed him. He kicked free of the table. The telephone clattered into the den.

Will entered the kitchen just in time to see Liv's fist smack into Gretel's hatchet nose. Liv had a height advantage. The German woman staggered back, fell against the oven, and slid to the floor, legs splayed before her.

'Ouch.' Liv shook her hand. Then she finally noticed him. 'Will? What are you doing here?'

'I came to rescue you. From ... ah ... her.' He pointed at Gretel on the floor. 'You see.'

'Oh. Well done, then.'

'How did you ... ' He made a fist. Shrugged.

'My husband. He insisted I know how to defend myself.' She sucked on her knuckles. Frowned. 'You're drenched.'

'I'm afraid I made a mess of your foyer.'

'These things happen,' she mumbled. 'Where have you been for the past six months? And how did you know to come here now? Who is this woman? And what are those things in her *head*?'

Sloe-eyed Gretel glared at her, woozily. The hem of her skirt had slid up to reveal the mottled skin of her lower legs. The burns had healed, but not without scars.

Will looked away before she could turn her gaze at him. She frightened him. The shadows behind her eyes frightened him even more. But instead of turning her glare on Will – or Liv – Gretel started to sob.

'That's a rather long story.'

'Did Raybould send you?'

'Yes. I mean, no. Well, he and the commander did. Both of them. Together.'

'You wouldn't believe the terrible things she said about Raybould.'

'Oh, indeed I would. But I shouldn't take them to heart, were I you.'

'She's German.'

'As I said, it's a long story.'

'I think I ought to call the police.'

'Ah.' Will tugged on an earlobe. 'Your telephone may be a bit, um, wet.'

'Oh, Will.'

The flare sank lower and lower, yet still the Dingo didn't come. They couldn't have missed the signal. Instead, the noise of combat filled the ravine behind Marsh.

A solitary figure emerged from the leftmost ravine, keeping to cover as he headed for the camp. Marsh couldn't see him clearly. But if there was only one survivor of that massacre, he reckoned he knew who that would be.

Reinhardt's silhouette sprinted another few yards, then dove behind a half-track. He wasn't glowing, wasn't armored in his own corona of searing Willenskräfte. But this wasn't a retreat, Marsh realized. Reinhardt would never do that. No. He was going for another battery.

Marsh tapped the scout's shoulder. 'Cover me.'

Then he was over the shelf and sprinting for the tents. Hoping, belatedly, that any remaining spotters and snipers wouldn't mistake him for an Afrika Korps trooper. He jumped into the dugout of the toppled machine-gun nest. Marsh unslung his rifle, but wasn't fast enough. Reinhardt dashed across open ground to another hiding spot. Marsh missed.

Reinhardt passed the gap between two tents, then disappeared again into the shadows. Small camp. He couldn't be far from the batteries. Marsh scrambled over the body of an Afrika Korps machine gunner and followed. The camp smelled like cordite and ozone. The odor of charred pork wafted from the ravine Reinhardt had just vacated. A burst of automatic fire perforated a tent to Marsh's left. He ducked around the corner.

He found himself alone in the center of the camp. Behind him, canvas rippled against canvas. Marsh spun. He caught movement in the periphery of his eye, where night vision was strongest. The sound he'd heard was the susurration of a tent flap falling closed.

Reinhardt. The battery stores from U-115.

Marsh plucked a Mills bomb from his belt. Sprinting for the tent, he pulled the pin, yanked the flap aside, tossed the Mills, and dove for cover. He hunkered in the gravel, arms over his head, tensed for a detonation that never came. Instead, a surge of heat ignited the tent and crisped the hairs on his arms.

God damn it. Reinhardt must have swapped out his battery in time to knock out the grenade. But he'd reacted on reflex. And the bubble of Willenskräfte that fried the grenade had engulfed everything else in the close confines of the tent. Crackling flames fanned the cat-piss stink of ammonia into the camp. Marsh remembered a similar stench when Kammler smashed the farm's battery store.

Reinhardt emerged from the burning tent, wreathed in blue fire. Heat shimmer rippled his silhouette.

Marsh fired his revolver, twice. Both shots flared a dark purple when they touched Reinhardt's corona. The salamander steadied himself against the momentum of the vaporized rounds, then turned. He saw Marsh.

'Ah! Englishman.' Heat shimmer warbled his voice. 'How I'd hoped to find you here.'

Marsh made to fire again, but the Enfield's octagonal barrel sagged. He dropped the gun before it scorched his hand. He said, 'I'm surprised you're willing to show your face after the debacle at the farm. Can't imagine the shame, being beaten by Kammler.'

Reinhardt's corona flared from blue to violet and then to incandescent white. Gravel skittered toward his boots, pulled along by the updraft from his furnace heat.

Marsh scooted backwards. The gravel turned tacky beneath his boots. Firelight from the burning tent illuminated something he'd missed in the photographs in Stephenson's office. The salamander wore a double harness. Two batteries. That explained how he'd weathered the pixie blast. He must have switched to the spare after the pulse knocked out his first.

Reinhardt said, 'I knew I'd be the one to avenge the doctor. My partner's mongrel blood makes him weak and unreliable. Like his sister.'

The bubble of heat expanded. Marsh ran. All around him,

tents flared into ash. Gravel turned to molten slag, gripping the soles of his boots like thick molasses. He staggered, tripped over a tent stake. He rolled, trying to bring his rifle to bear on the blazing figure who loomed like an avenging angel.

Thunder shook the camp. The lightning crackle of a pixie detonation echoed through Halfaya Pass.

The blast that engulfed Hargreaves flung me like a scrap of newspaper in a gale. Don't know how far it tossed me, but I remember flopping to a halt in the bend of the ravine. Took me a moment to regain myself. I came to atop the jagged scree at the base of the escarpment that formed the western wall of the canyon. I had too many cuts and bruises to count. But I slid to my feet, gingerly, and found I hadn't broken my legs.

The Afrika Korps outpost burned to my right, past the knife-narrow opening in the canyon. To my left, behind the bodies of the warlocks I'd shot, a wall of flame blocked off the northern egress. The pixie blast had ignited the spilled petrol from the Dingo.

Thinking of the pixie roused me to action. Where was Klaus? After checking my revolver, I crept toward the charred hulk of the Dingo. I paused to check Webber and White for signs of life. No heartbeat. They'd bled out. The blast hadn't left much of Hargreaves, nor Grafton.

I scoured the ravine for signs of Klaus. A rock bounced down from one of the high tables. I spun. But I was alone. Had Klaus moved elsewhere? Had he ghosted into another ravine, to cut down more of our men?

But then I found him. Well, part of him.

Flames licked at a hand protruding from the stone cliff. Klaus's olive skin turned a shriveled black. As I neared the stone, I could

see part of his face: the curve of a cheekbone, an eyebrow ridge
and part of his forehead, the tip of his nose. The smooth fabric
of a trouser leg, from waist to knee, broke the gnarled surface of
the escarpment. The rest of his body was permanently embedded into the rock. I wrestled the battery from the remains of his
harness. I checked the gauge. It was dead.

The pixie had gone off just as he emerged. He was frozen in
the act, like a diver perpetually gasping for air.

An autopsy would be impossible. Even if the Jerries found
him and decided to chisel him free, his brain was fused with
sandstone. Klaus's corpse would be useless to anybody seeking
to reverse-engineer von Westarp's work. Before long, scavengers
would clean away any flesh the fire didn't consume. In time there
would be nothing but a scattering of finger bones among the
talus, and a few smooth protuberances that happened to look,
just a bit, like bone. And the dusty desert wind would take care
of those.

A pang of emotion caught me off guard. It wasn't regret – this
man was an enemy of my country, and his destruction had been
necessary for the greater good. Instead, I felt pity. This Klaus
would never learn to paint. He'd never learn what sort of person
he could be when not yoked to the ideologies of twisted madmen.
When he wasn't a test subject. When free of his sister.

I'd known that version of Klaus briefly, and even worked
alongside him. Through Gretel, our lives had been tied together.
Our fates spun in related orbits. He could have been a good man,
if life had let him.

The pop of gunfire broke my reverie. Reinhardt was still out
there. I raised one hand in respectful farewell to Klaus, and broke
into a tired run.

*

The pixie's electric-blue flash swept over the camp. It snuffed Reinhardt's Willenskräfte like a candle. His corona blinked out.

'*Scheisse!*'

He fumbled at his waist. The inrushing superheated air ignited his uniform. Without the protection of the Götterelektron, his human body couldn't withstand the heat he'd willed into his surroundings. Reinhardt burned like a Hindu widow.

Marsh fired. The shot clipped Reinhardt's shoulder and spun him around. He dropped to the ground, blazing, writhing, and grasping for his battery.

Marsh leapt to his feet and charged across the smoldering sand. It was like running across a sticky frying pan. He had to reach Reinhardt before the bastard switched batteries. Sand jammed the bolt of his rifle. He flipped it around and gripped the barrel like a club.

Reinhardt's right arm hung uselessly at his side. His flesh sizzled against the bubbling sand. He tried to scream in agony, but it came out as a desiccated gurgle. The furnace heat had scorched his throat and lungs.

Yet still his left hand clawed at the battery latch. Indomitable willpower, to the very end.

Marsh rammed the butt of his rifle into Reinhardt's temple. 'Just!' *Slam.* 'Bloody!' *Slam.* 'Die!' *Slam.* The salamander's head yielded with a mushy crunch.

It hurt to breathe. The air scalded Marsh's nose and mouth. He retreated from the slag. He staggered to where a dead Afrika Korpsman clutched an MP 38. Wrestling the machine pistol from the dead solder, he realized he recognized the man's face. He'd been one of the LSSAH troops assigned to the farm.

The magazine was almost empty. But not quite. Though he'd already pulped Reinhardt's skull with the Enfield, Marsh finished the job by unloading a half-dozen rounds into the Overman's brain.

Around him, the sounds of combat had dwindled to a few desultory pops scattered through the remains of the camp. The commander trotted from the ravine. In the firelight, he looked even worse than normal. He looked like Marsh felt. Marsh beckoned to him.

The older man pointed back toward the ravine with his thumb. Marsh pointed at Reinhardt's body.

'Klaus is dead,' said the commander, at the same moment Marsh said, 'Reinhardt is dead.'

They fell into an awkward silence.

'I feel a bit silly,' said Will, 'barging in as I did.'

Liv touched his hand. She said, 'Nonsense. You were brilliant, Will.'

She looked so lovely, with her freckles and her disheveled auburn hair. Will forced himself to look away. He drained the last of his tea.

'Forgive me for saying so, but the beard doesn't suit you.'

'Agreed. I had little choice in the matter, I'm afraid.'

They were seated at the kitchen table. Gretel hadn't moved. Will kept an eye on her, just in case. Long snarls of raven-black hair hid her eyes, but that was probably for the better. She rocked back and forth, murmuring to herself and fingering the copper connecter at the end of her wires.

He hadn't yet decided what to tell Liv. Marsh hadn't left instructions for this scenario. Will didn't know how to approach the subject. Liv was running out of patience with his evasions.

'Let's start at the beginning,' said Liv. 'Who is this Jerry bint, and how does she know my husband?'

'Ah. Well. That's a bit of a story, you see. Perhaps it would be best to let him explain.'

'Raybould isn't here at the moment. So I'll have to make do with your explanation.'

'Right. Of course. Well . . .'

Outside, on the street, a car screeched to a halt. It was followed by heavy footsteps and a persistent knocking on the front door.

'Mrs. Marsh?' said a muffled voice.

Liv glanced at the clock over the stove. 'Who would call at this hour?'

'Ah,' said Will. 'I suspect that's the police. I took a detour to warn them of your plight.'

Liv smiled. 'You really are a champion.' She kissed him on the cheek, soft as a feather. He blushed.

The door rattled again. 'Mrs. Marsh, are you home?'

'Well,' said Liv, 'I'd better let them in before they break down the door.' She stood, turned, and walked into the den.

Gretel leapt to her feet. She held her cranial wires taut between her fists.

'Olivia!'

Will lunged from his seat. His hands caught Liv in the small of the back and pushed her out of Gretel's reach. Liv stumbled over Agnes's bassinet. She turned, scowling.

Will wanted to apologize, to warn her, to ask if she were hurt, but the wires snapped tight around his throat. His fingers fumbled at the wire, but it dug so deeply he could find no purchase.

The scowl on Liv's face became pale wide-eyed alarm. 'Will!'

Will fell on Gretel but it didn't loosen her grip. Liv stood over them, yanking on Gretel's fists, but the wire only cut deeper. A dark tunnel contracted around Will's vision, framing Liv's face and tears and disheveled auburn hair. Distantly, he remembered a freckled coquette he'd once met in a pub. Somewhere very far away, somebody pounded on a door.

Liv ran for help as the world faded to black.

Lorimer gathered the other Milkweed survivors. They swept through the encampment, flushing out the last of the Jerries and finishing off the battery tent. They had it under control. My counterpart and I watched.

He said, 'Rommel will reoccupy this camp within a day or two. Not much of a victory.'

'Perhaps,' I said. 'But he no longer has Klaus and Reinhardt. We've destroyed the last of von Westarp's technology. *That* was our war. And it's over now.'

The eastern sky, far across the Egyptian coastal plain, blushed at the approach of sunrise. Desert heat would follow the rising sun. It was a long way to Sidi Barrâni.

I was glad to see that the battle had spared the tall mast of an antenna. The camp had a radio, of course. We'd use it to contact the Western Desert Force. England was still many days away, though my thoughts were firmly in Walworth with Liv and Will and Gretel.

I said, 'The warlocks are dead. We'll have to take the long way home.'

'I suppose so,' said my counterpart. 'But perhaps it's for the best. I imagine you have a long story to tell.'

We sat in silence for a while. Flames crackled in the canyon. Lorimer barked orders to his men. The sun rose. We retreated to the cooler shadows of Halfaya. My counterpart took a long draw from his canteen. He handed it to me. I washed from my throat the taste of smoke and grit, of battles lost and won.

'It started in Spain,' I said.

SEVENTEEN

1 September 1941
Shetland Islands, Scotland

The fisherman kept his distance from the strange trio who had hired his services just after sunrise. That suited the government men perfectly well. They kept to themselves. But quiet errands like this weren't unusual in the Shetlands. If the fisherman had bothered to ask, the men would have carefully given him the impression they were connected to the group of Norwegians hiding out at Lunna and Scalloway.

The third member of their party, the small one wrapped in the long cloak, never made a sound.

The fisherman cut the engine. His boat glided through the last few yards of foamy gray sea. The prow crunched gently over the shingle.

The older one, the one who looked and sounded like he'd lost a tussle with Old Scratch, flipped a coin to the fisherman. 'Sit tight,' he rasped. Then he tossed his carpetbag to the shingle beach, lifted the person in the cloak, and handed him over the gunwale to the one named Marsh. If he had watched the handoff carefully, the fisherman might have glimpsed a flash of bony ankle under scarred olive skin.

This particular island didn't have a name. Many maps ignored it entirely. One needed local knowledge to find it. Windswept, low to the sea, measuring less than twenty yards at its widest point, it offered nothing to reward anybody who did make the trek. Even lichenologists gave it a pass.

The island was a rocky shelf, kept barren by sea winds constantly scrabbling across the thin soil. (Far too thin for a flower garden.) Tufts of grass here and there provided bits of green to relieve the monotonous zigzag cross-bedding of the Old Red Sandstone, but the sheep kept the grass trimmed short. Blotches of moss and lichen ranged in color from ash white to bruise purple.

Until today its only occupants were the occasional passing seabirds, such as puffins and petrels, and a few sheep. The hut was a recent addition.

The men tromped across the beach with the prisoner held between them. The smooth round stones tinkled like glass beads beneath their boots. The tintinnabulation stood out amongst the constant *thrum* and *whoosh* of ocean waves, the hiss of wind, the screech of seabirds.

Once inside the hut, Marsh checked the cabinets. The supplies had arrived. Sacks of flour and rice. Several dozen packages of dehydrated egg. Potatoes, onions, root vegetables that would keep. Somebody had thoughtfully provided a fishing rod. Several cords of firewood for the stove had been stacked outside. Installing the rain catchers and water cisterns had been the most difficult job. There was one cot, one chair, and a table. The wind made an eerie keening sound in the stovepipe.

Used judiciously, the supplies would last one person six months. Until the next delivery.

Gretel whimpered when Marsh removed her cloak. She took one look at her surroundings, and started to cry again. 'Please, Raybould. Please don't do this.'

The commander sighed.

Commander. They'd made a tacit agreement to adhere to this fiction. It kept things simple.

'Why are you so cruel? After all we've endured together. You still don't understand what I did for you. For us! We're connected, you and I.'

He set his carpetbag on the table. Then he jerked a thumb in the general direction of the boat, their only means off the island. 'She's likely to scream. Think he'll hear us?'

Marsh glanced out the window. It was hard to hear anything over the cacophonous static of wind and sea. But the island was damn small. 'Better not risk it.'

Gretel didn't struggle when they gagged her. She did try to squirm free of Marsh's arms when the commander approached with the razor. Long black tresses fluttered to the floor like raven feathers as he shaved her scalp. Marsh released her. She fell to her knees, gathered handfuls of her hair, and pressed them to her tears.

'You should keep those,' said the commander. 'Maybe you can learn to weave. Winters here are long, cold, dark, and damp.'

Her façade of docility disappeared when the commander produced the garden shears. Marsh had to pin her to the floor. He straddled her waist, facing her feet, and clamped his hands around her ankles. Her skin was cold to the touch. The commander knelt on her wrists.

He was right. She screamed bloody murder.

Seizures racked her body when the blades bit into her wires. They resulted from stray electrical currents induced by the contact between dissimilar metals; Lorimer had warned Marsh to expect this. Behind him, the shears clicked together. Gretel's body went limp.

Marsh continued to hold her down while the commander dealt with the rivets in her skull. Removing them would require a surgeon's skill, but mangling the stubs beyond usefulness required only strong hands and good pliers.

They removed the gag and prepared to leave.

She lurched to her feet when the commander opened the door. She addressed them both, but focused on the commander. Marsh supposed that made sense. He didn't feel particularly jealous.

'Raybould! Please! Don't leave me here.'

'It's better than you deserve,' said Marsh.

'You killed my daughter,' said the commander. 'You killed—' But a sob bubbled up through the ruin of his voice, choking off his words. His head hung low.

'If you endure a thousand years on this godforsaken rock,' Marsh finished for him, 'it will still be too good after what you did.'

She said, 'We have a connection, you and I. Don't you remember? I found you before we ever met; you were there in so many time lines, again and again, and sometimes we're lovers and sometimes enemies, but I knew you were special, so special they named you, because you were meant to come to me, and you did, you came back and you saved me and together we fixed the world and, and, and I remember things, I still remember things, things about the future, things I'll share with you, dreadful wonderful ugly beautiful things, things I'll share if you take me with you.' They stared at her. She moaned, fingers scrabbling across the stubble of her scalp. Her next words alternated with chest-heaving sobs: 'Please ... don't ... leave ... me ... Raybould. Please.'

The commander said, 'Isn't this what you wanted? This is the future you sought. The future you worked so hard to create. The only time line where the Eidolons never find you.' He took one last look around. 'A girl can't have everything.'

'Let's leave,' said Marsh.

They stepped outside.

Gretel's voice was weak and small. Smaller even than her tiny island. She asked, 'Where is Klaus?'

'Your brother is dead,' they said in unison.

Marsh shut the door before her wailing could scare away the fisherman.

They arrived on the mainland in late afternoon. They retrieved their car in Thurso, and drove south. Miles of heather moorland passed without either man saying a word. Each was lost deep in his own thoughts.

Apropos of nothing but a need to break the silence, Marsh said, 'I think we'll move. After the war.'

'Oh?'

'Liv doesn't want to stay in the Walworth house. Not after Will . . .'

'No. I suppose she wouldn't. Neither would I.'

The men sighed in unison. First the commander, then Marsh, wiped his eyes.

'I wish I could have been there,' said the commander, referring to the funeral service. It had been a high-profile affair, given Will's station and the grisly manner of his death. He had served the Crown; they gave him a hero's burial. 'I was a wretched excuse for a friend. I failed him at every turn straight to the accursed end.'

'No, you didn't,' said Marsh, even though he felt much the same about himself. 'Most of that never happened.'

'It happened in my memories.' The commander gave a rueful chuckle. 'In the other … From where I came, he actually read his own obituaries at one point. I think he rather enjoyed that.'

Marsh said, 'That sounds like Will.' They shared a laugh in memory of their friend.

The commander changed the subject. 'The war could go for years yet,' he said. 'Probably will. Nobody knows how it will turn out. Not any longer.'

'That's as it should be.'

'Yes.'

'Still think we ought to have killed her,' said Marsh. 'She was a monster, right down the line.'

'Trust me,' said the commander. 'I've known her longer.' Marsh shrugged aside the frisson of discomfort that arose whenever the commander talked like this. He hadn't fully come to terms with the situation. Never would.

'I can't begin to count the number of times I've imagined killing her with my bare hands. I spent decades on those revenge fantasies. But this is better. She suffers the most this way.'

'In that case,' said Marsh, 'I hope she lives a very long time.'

'This is the worst possible punishment for Gretel.' The commander cracked his knuckles against his jaw; Marsh tried not to flinch. 'Forced to live out her years like a regular human being? Merely mortal? She used to be a goddess. Gretel will never stop pining for the power she lost. Meanwhile, she's forced to live from one day to the next like the rest of us. Will it be cold tomorrow? Will the sun come out? Will it rain?'

Marsh said, 'It's the bloody Shetlands. Of course it'll rain.'

'Even so.'

'Yes.' Now it was Marsh's turn to crack his knuckles.

'Stephenson won't pass up the chance to question her every so often. He holds out hope we might shake loose a few useful crumbs of information about the future.'

The commander shook his head. 'You won't. Not about the real future.'

'I know.'

'She might remember bits and pieces of the other, but even those are likely growing hazy.'

Now Marsh changed the subject. 'How's the knee?'

'Never better. I should have tried to shoot you a long time ago. Yours?'

'The same. Still don't understand it.'

'Will could have ventured a decent guess.'

They lapsed into thoughtful silence again. Later, after Marsh turned west, the commander said, 'You've missed the turn. This isn't the road to Edinburgh.'

'We aren't headed to Edinburgh. Well, I am. But not you. Look in the glove box.'

The commander reached inside the fascia. He found a slim leather valise. It was similar to one he'd retrieved from Spain long, long ago. Marsh knew, because he'd been there.

The commander caught the resemblance. He frowned.

'Look inside.'

He did. He pulled out a fake passport, a train ticket to Dublin, a voucher for a berth on an Irish ferry, and one thousand pounds sterling.

'Oh, very droll,' said the commander.

'Thought you'd get a laugh out of it.' Marsh paused, checking his blind spot before passing a slow-moving truck. 'No joke, though. The travel documents are real,' he said.

'I sussed that out, thanks.'

'You can't stay in England,' said Marsh. 'You're wanted for the deaths of Shapley and Pendennis, and the assault of a marine sentry in the citadel.'

The commander shook his head, sadly. 'Necessary evils.'

'Stephenson won't stop looking for you. Likewise SIS and the Security Service.'

The commander yawned, pinched the bridge of his nose. The boredom was an act, of course. Marsh knew he couldn't bear the thought of leaving. He wouldn't have been able to, had their roles been reversed.

The commander tucked the documents inside his jacket. 'Speaking of the old man, what are you lot going to do? I've a feeling Milkweed isn't long for this world.'

Marsh said, 'Stephenson is casting about for a new mission. But I think we'll ride out the war, probably stick around in one form or another for a while after that. We'll be watching, in case somebody tries to revive von Westarp's program. Red Orchestra has agents all over Germany.'

'They won't find anything,' said the commander.

Marsh agreed. 'Von Westarp's work is no longer a threat to us. And with all the warlocks dead' – his voice hitched when he said this; he saw the commander swallow a lump in his own throat – 'the Eidolons are closed off.'

The commander asked, 'You've burned the lexicons?'

Marsh rolled his eyes. It wasn't the first time the commander had asked. 'Yes. They're destroyed.'

'You'll watch for interest in children. Newborns and orphans.'

'Yes.'

They topped a rise. The Firth of Clyde lay spread before them, and beyond that, the gray shimmer of the North Channel and Irish Sea. The commander started to fidget as they approached Port Glasgow. Still, there was little that remained to be said.

Poor old codger. He'd been through so damn much for the sake of Britain. But now he had to leave it behind.

Marsh walked the commander to the pier. He pretended not to notice how the older man kept rubbing at his eyes.

When he did speak, the commander's voice was rougher than usual. 'Give my love to Liv and Agnes?'

'Every day of my life.'

They shook hands. Marsh said, 'I never thanked you properly for saving them. Doubt I ever could.'

'Yes you can. Be a good husband and father. Be the man I never had a chance to be.' The ferry blew two short, impatient bursts of its air horn.

'Well. That's mine,' the commander said. He paused at the base of the gangplank. 'If you do hear rumors of the Reichsbehörde technology, you'll contact me?'

'You know I can't.'

The commander sighed again. 'Right.'

He climbed the gangplank. At the top he gave Marsh a little wave and salute. Marsh returned it.

Marsh stayed at the port until the late dusk of the northern latitudes, watching the ferry until it disappeared in the darkness. Then he started the car, and drove to Edinburgh. From there, he caught a night train to London. To home. To his family.

That December, America entered the war.

EPILOGUE

The cricket ball nicked a fence post. It bounced up, still spinning, and landed on the pavement beyond the garden. The gate creaked open a few seconds later. A boy ran out to retrieve the ball. He looked about ten years old. He tossed the ball back into the garden, and then, after studying the gate for a moment, decided it would be more fun to shimmy over the fence.

He never noticed the old man, who watched from the car across the road.

The man had been there for several hours. He'd have to leave soon. His ship to Buenos Aires departed Liverpool in the morning. It wasn't safe for him to stay. But he'd gone to a bit of trouble to find this house, and now that he was here, he wanted to see what he could see.

There had been another house, years ago. But this was larger than the place in Walworth. It had to be. It needed room for a family of four.

He'd come to London for a funeral. But it would have been too risky to stand at the graveside while they buried the one-armed man; he'd attended the ceremony with the aid of binoculars. After the burial, he'd discreetly followed a pair of mourners to their home on the outskirts of London. And he'd been parked outside ever since. Just to see what he could see. To hear what he could hear.

He listened while the boy reenacted Denis Compton's recent career highlights. Great cricketers like Compton had come to be seen as a source of hope and inspiration for a country still emerging from a war eight years past.

The ball whistled over the fence again. It bounced on the pavement, skipped across the asphalt, and banged against the driver's side door. It rolled to a stop in the middle of the road.

A girl's voice said, 'Now you've done it.'

The boy dashed through the gate again. But when he saw the dent, and the man in the car, he hesitated. The old man stepped out of the car to retrieve the ball. It was almost new. The shiny red leather had taken a few scuffs from the fence, and rain puddles had stained the bright stitches. The boy retreated into the garden. He looked ready to run for the house.

The old man called out. 'Wait! Not so fast.'

He struggled to speak clearly, so the boy wouldn't be alarmed by the gravely rasp of his voice. The cold, damp leather evoked an arthritic twinge from his fingers. He wasn't ancient, a few years short of seventy, but he looked a fair bit older than that. He crossed the street.

'I believe this is yours,' he said, lobbing the ball over the fence. The boy caught it one-handed.

Like the house itself, the garden was a bit bigger than it had been in Walworth. There was a shed, of course. Furrows in the dirt marked the places where beets and carrots had recently been planted for the winter garden. Rye provided a bit of ground cover for keeping out winter-hardy weeds. The remains of a few mushy tomatoes, rejects from the autumn crop, dotted the garden. A girl sat on a stool beside the shed. She had turned thirteen in May.

The boy glanced at the dent in the car door. 'What will you do to me?'

The man shrugged. 'Nothing. It's not my car.'

The boy stared at him. 'What happened to your face?'

'Don't be horrid,' said the girl.

She had long, dishwater blond hair. It had pulled free of the hair-slides holding it back, so the curls brushed her shoulder when she frowned at the boy. A handful of freckles dusted the pale skin of her face. She held a book in her lap. The title on the canary-yellow cover said, *Wisden Cricketers' Almanack*.

The boy said, glumly, 'That's my sister. She's supposed to read the scores, but she does it wrong.'

'Hello, Agnes,' said the old man. 'It's wonderful to meet you. You're growing into a lovely young woman.'

He stared at her so intensely that the girl blushed. She shrugged, frowned, and went inside. The man looked stricken. A snippet of music escaped the kitchen when she opened the door. A woman with a fine voice sang along to the wireless. The girl closed the door behind her. The music disappeared. The man made a funny sound and rubbed his eyes.

'Hey,' said the boy, tugging on the old man's sleeve. 'I didn't tell you her name. How'd you know that?'

The old man pulled his gaze away from the kitchen door where the girl had disappeared. He looked at the boy. His eyes shimmered with tears, but the corner of his mouth quirked up in a half smile.

'What's your name, lad?'

The boy's gaze flickered from the old man's eyes to the tangle of beard and scar tissue along the side of his face. He considered the question for a long moment, as though weighing consequences.

He stuck his chin out. 'William Marsh, sir.'

'You're quite a clever lad, aren't you, Master Marsh?'

'That's what my dad says, sir.'

At that, the old man smiled. 'I suppose he would.'

'You know my dad?'

'A bit.'

Movement caught the corner of the man's eye. Somebody pulled the kitchen curtains aside. He glimpsed auburn hair.

'I have to be off.' He raised a hand, tentatively reaching to tousle the boy's hair, which was the color of wet sand. The boy tensed. The man lowered his arm. 'Say hello to your mum and dad for me.'

He had just reached the car when the kitchen door opened behind him. A woman's voice, the same voice that had been singing a few moments earlier, said, 'William? Who were you talking to?'

'I dunno. Some codger. Said he knew you and dad.'

Footsteps scraped lightly on the garden gravel. The old man opened his car door. The dent screeched along the running board.

'Hello? Sir, may I help you?'

The man stopped. He drew a deep breath, then turned.

The woman gasped. She touched a hand to her lips.

The man said, 'You have a lovely family, Mrs. Marsh.'

She swallowed. 'Yes. I know.' Her voice was barely more than a whisper. 'Thank you.'

He sat in the car. She gestured at the house. 'Would you like . . .'

He hadn't meant to speak to anybody. Hadn't meant to be seen. It was dangerous to be seen with him; he was a wanted man. She knew this. He shook his head. 'I have to be off.'

'Oh,' she said. 'Do you have a family?'

He thought about that. 'Yes. But they live far away from me.'

'I'm sorry to hear it.'

He started the engine.

'Wait, please.' She crossed the garden. Leaning over the fence, she said, 'Are you well?'

'Yes. Well as can be.'

'Are you lonely?'

The old man looked down. He couldn't meet her eyes.

'Sometimes,' he lied. Then he added, 'This helped.' Which was somehow true, although the hurt was worse now than it had been in years.

'I wish you could stay.'

'Me, too. More than anything.'

She looked like she might cry. She looked like he felt. 'I'd begun to wonder if I had imagined you.' She hugged herself. 'Thank you,' she said. 'For everything.'

'You're welcome, Liv. Always.'

Then he put the car in gear and drove away. He didn't have the strength to look back.

AUTHOR'S NOTE

The Milkweed books have always been, at heart, an attempt to tell an entertaining adventure tale. But no fiction could ever equal the true-life heroism, evil, and intrigue of the Second World War. Thus the story borrows heavily from real historical events and details, not only to lend (one hopes) a sense of verisimilitude, but also to identify the nooks and crannies of history where this story might have unfolded.

The following isn't a complete list of research sources, but it does include the material consulted most frequently during the writing of this trilogy. Regardless of research, the speculative nature of the story required perpetrating a fair bit of violence to history. That lies at my feet and mine alone.

Churchill, Winston S. *The Second World War*. 6 vols. Boston: Houghton Mifflin, [1948–1953] 1985.

Dallas, Gregor. *1945: The War That Never Ended*. New Haven: Yale University Press, 2005.

Dorril, Stephen. *MI6: Inside the Covert World of Her Majesty's Secret Intelligence Service*. New York: Simon & Schuster, 2002.

Gilbert, Martin. *The Second World War: A Complete History*. New York: Owl Books, [1989] 2004.

Höhne, Heinz. *The Order of the Death's Head: The Story of Hitler's SS*. New York: Penguin, [1969] 2000.

Keegan, John. *The Second World War*. New York: Penguin, [1990] 2005.

Kynaston, David. *Austerity Britain: 1945–1951*. New York: Walker & Company, 2008.

Liddell Hart, B. H. *History of the Second World War*. New York: Da Capo Press, [1971] 1999.

Longmate, Norman. *How We Lived Then: A History of Everyday Life During the Second World War*. London: Pimlico, [1971] 2002.

Reitlinger, Gerald. *The SS: Alibi of a Nation, 1922–1945*. New York: Da Capo Press, 1957.

Shirer, William L. *The Rise and Fall of the Third Reich: A History of Nazi Germany*. New York: Simon & Schuster, [1959] 1990.

Trustees of the Imperial War Museum. *The Home Front: Documents relating to life in Britain, 1939–1945*. London: Imperial War Museum, 1987.

Trustees of the Imperial War Museum. *The Battle of Britain: Documents May to September 1940*. London: Imperial War Museum, 1990.

Weinberg, Gerhard L. *A World At Arms: A Global History of World War II*. New York: Cambridge University Press, [1994] 2006.

BBC WW2 People's War Archive:
http://www.bbc.co.uk/ww2peopleswar/

ACKNOWLEDGMENTS

Once again, I am indebted to my friends, colleagues, and mentors in Critical Mass, who helped me shepherd this story from a rough idea to a finished trilogy. This year it was Terry England, Ty Franck, Emily Mah, Vic Milán, John Miller, Melinda M. Snodgrass, S. M. Stirling, and Walter Jon Williams who braved the first drafts. Thanks to everybody who stuck with me on this project.

Thanks also to S. C. Butler and Char Peery, Ph.D., for critical reading; Michael Prevett for smart questions; Edwin Chapman for copyediting; and Kay McCauley for her faith in me.

Finally, heartfelt thanks to my editor, Claire Eddy.

extras

www.orbitbooks.net

about the author

Ian Tregillis is the son of a bearded mounte-bank and a discredited tarot card reader. He was born and raised in Minnesota, where his parents had landed after fleeing the wrath of a Flemish prince. (The full story, he's told, involves a Dutch tramp steamer and a stolen horse.) Nowadays he lives in New Mexico, where he consorts with writers, scientists and other unsavoury types.

Find out more about Ian Tregillis and other Orbit authors by registering for the free monthly newsletter at www.orbitbooks.net

if you enjoyed

NECESSARY EVIL

look out for

HOUNDED

by

Kevin Hearne

Chapter 1

There are many perks to living for twenty-one centuries, and foremost among them is bearing witness to the rare birth of genius. It invariably goes like this: Someone shrugs off the weight of his cultural traditions, ignores the baleful stares of authority, and does something his countrymen think to be completely batshit insane. Of those, Galileo was my personal favorite. Van Gogh comes in second, but he really was batshit insane.

Thank the Goddess I don't look like a guy who met Galileo – or who saw Shakespeare's plays when they first debuted or rode with the hordes of Genghis Khan. When people ask how old I am, I just tell them twenty-one, and if they assume I mean years instead of decades or centuries, then that can't be my fault, can it? I still get carded, in fact, which any senior citizen will tell you is immensely flattering.

The young-Irish-lad façade does not stand me in good stead when I'm trying to appear scholarly at my place of business – I run an occult bookshop with an apothecary's counter squeezed in the corner – but it has one outstanding advantage. When I go to the grocery store, for example, and people see my curly red hair, fair skin, and long goatee, they suspect that I play soccer and drink lots of Guinness. If I'm going sleeveless and they see the tattoos all up and down my right arm, they assume I'm in a rock band and smoke lots of weed. It never enters their mind for a moment that I could be an ancient Druid – and that's the main reason why I like this look. If I grew a white beard and got myself a pointy hat, oozed dignity and sagacity and glowed with beatitude, people might start to get the wrong – or the right – idea.

Sometimes I forget what I look like and I do something out of character, such as sing shepherd tunes in Aramaic while I'm waiting in line at Starbucks, but the nice bit about living in urban America is that people tend to either ignore eccentrics or move to the suburbs to escape them.

That never would have happened in the old days. People who were different back then got burned at the stake or stoned to death. There is still a downside to being different today, of course, which is why I put so much effort into blending in, but the downside is usually just harassment and discrimination, and that is a vast improvement over dying for the common man's entertainment.

Living in the modern world contains quite a few vast improvements like that. Most old souls I know think the attraction of modernity rests on clever ideas like indoor plumbing and sunglasses. But for me, the true attraction of America is that it's practically godless. When I was younger and dodging the Romans, I could hardly walk a mile in Europe without stepping on a stone sacred to some god or other. But out here in Arizona, all I have to worry about is the occasional encounter with Coyote, and I actually rather like him. (He's nothing like Thor, for one thing, and that right there means we're going to get along fine. The local college kids would describe Thor as a "major asshat" if they ever had the misfortune to meet him.)

Even better than the low god density in Arizona is the near total absence of faeries. I don't mean those cute winged creatures that Disney calls "faeries"; I mean the Fae, the *Sidhe*, the actual descendants of the Tuatha Dé Danann, born in Tír na nÓg, the land of eternal youth, each one of them as likely to gut you as hug you. They don't dig me all that much, so I try to settle in places they can't reach very easily. They have all sorts of gateways to Earth in the Old World, but in the New World they need oak, ash, and thorn to make the journey, and those trees don't grow together too often in Arizona. I have found a couple of likely places, like the White Mountains near the border with New Mexico and a riparian area near Tucson, but those are both over a hundred miles away from my well-paved neighborhood near the university in Tempe. I figured the chances of the Fae entering the world there and then crossing a treeless desert to look for a rogue Druid were extremely small, so when I found this place in the late nineties, I decided to stay until the locals grew suspicious.

It was a great decision for more than a decade. I set up a new identity, leased some shop space, hung out a sign that said THIRD EYE BOOKS AND HERBS (an allusion to Vedic and Buddhist beliefs, because I thought a Celtic name would bring up a red flag to those searching for me), and bought a small house within easy biking distance.

I sold crystals and Tarot cards to college kids who wanted to shock their Protestant parents, scores of ridiculous tomes with "spells" in them for lovey-dovey Wiccans, and some herbal remedies for people looking to make an end run around the doctor's office. I even stocked extensive works on Druid magic, all of them based on Victorian revivals, all of them utter rubbish, and all vastly entertaining to me whenever I sold any of them. Maybe once a month I had a serious magical customer looking for a genuine grimoire, stuff you don't mess with or even know about until you're fairly accomplished. I did much more of my rare book business via the Internet – another vast improvement of modern times.

But when I set up my identity and my place of business, I did not realize how easy it would be for someone else to find me by doing a public-records search on the Internet. The idea that any of the Old Ones would even try it never occurred to me – I thought they'd try to scry me or use other methods of divination, but never the Internet – so I was not as careful in choosing my name as I should have been. I should have called myself John Smith or something utterly sad and plain like that, but my pride would not let me wear a Christian name. So I used O'Sullivan, the Anglicized version of my real surname, and for everyday usage I employed the decidedly Greek name of Atticus. A supposedly twenty-one-year-old O'Sullivan who owned an occult bookstore and sold extremely rare books he had no business knowing about was enough information for the Fae to find me, though.

On a Friday three weeks before Samhain, they jumped me in front of my shop when I walked outside to take a lunch break. A sword swished below my knees without so much as a "Have at thee!" and the arm swinging it pulled its owner off balance when I jumped over it. I crunched a quick left elbow into his face as he tried to recover, and that was one faery down, four to go.

Thank the Gods Below for paranoia. I classified it as a survival skill rather than a neurotic condition; it was a keen knife's edge, sharpened for centuries against the grindstone of People Who Want to Kill Me. It was what made me wear an amulet of cold iron around my neck, and cloak my shop not only with iron bars, but also with magical wards designed to keep out the Fae and other undesirables. It was what made me train in unarmed combat and test my speed against vampires, and what had saved me countless times from thugs like these.

Perhaps *thug* is too heavy a word for them; it connotes an abundance of muscle tissue and a profound want of intellect. These lads didn't look as if they had ever hit the gym or heard of anabolic steroids. They were lean, ropy types who had chosen to disguise themselves as cross-country runners, bare-chested and wearing nothing but maroon shorts and expensive running shoes. To any passerby it would look as if they were trying to beat me up with brooms, but that was just a glamour they had cast on their weapons. The pointy parts were in the twigs, so if I was unable to see through their illusions, I would have been fatally surprised when the nice broom stabbed my vitals. Since I could see through faerie glamours, I noticed that two of my remaining four assailants carried spears, and one of them was circling around to my right. Underneath their human guises, they looked like the typical faery – that is, no wings, scantily clad, and kind of man-pretty like Orlando Bloom's Legolas, the sort of people you see in salon product advertisements. The ones with spears stabbed at me simultaneously from the sides, but I slapped the tips away with either wrist so that they thrust past me to the front and back. Then I lunged inside the guard of the one to the right and clotheslined him with a forearm to his throat. Tough to breathe through a crushed windpipe. Two down now; but they were quick and deft, and their dark eyes held no gleam of mercy.

I had left my back open to attack by lunging to the right, so I spun and raised my left forearm high to block the blow I knew was coming. Sure enough, there was a sword about to arc down into my skull, and I caught it on my arm at the top of the swing. It bit down to the bone, and that hurt a *lot,* but not nearly as much as it would have if I had let it fall. I grimaced at the pain and stepped forward to deliver a punishing open-hand blow to the faery's solar plexus, and he flew back into the wall of my shop – the wall ribbed with bars of iron. Three down, and I smiled at the remaining two, who were not so zealous as before to take a shot at me. Three of their buddies had not only been physically beaten but also magically poisoned by physical contact with me. My cold iron amulet was bound to my aura, and by now they could no doubt see it: I was some sort of Iron Druid, their worst nightmare made flesh. My first victim was already disintegrating into ash, and the other two were close to realizing that all we are is dust in the wind.

I was wearing sandals, and I kicked them off and stepped back a bit toward the street so that the faeries had a wall full of iron at their backs. Besides being a good idea strategically, it put me closer to a thin strip of landscaping between the street and the sidewalk, where I could draw power from the earth to close up my wound and kill the pain. Knitting the muscle tissue I could worry about later; my immediate concern was stopping the bleeding, because there were too many scary things an unfriendly magician could do with my blood.

As I sank my feet into the grass and drew power from it for healing, I also sent out a call – sort of an instant message through the earth – to an iron elemental I knew, informing him that I had two faeries standing in front of me if he wanted a snack. He would answer quickly, because the earth is bound to me as I am bound to it, but it might take him a few moments. To give him time, I asked my assailants a question.

"Out of curiosity, were you guys trying to capture me or kill me?"

The one to my left, hefting a short sword in his right hand, decided to snarl at me rather than answer. "Tell us where the sword is!"

"Which sword? The one in your hand? It's still in your hand, big guy."

"You know which sword! Fragarach, the Answerer!"

"Don't know what you're talking about." I shook my head. "Who sent you guys? Are you sure you have the right fella?"

"We're sure," Spear Guy sneered. "You have Druidic tattoos and you can see through our glamour."

"But lots of magical folk can do that. And you don't have to be a Druid to appreciate Celtic knotwork. Think about it, fellas. You've come to ask me about some sword, but clearly I don't have one or I would have whipped it out by now. All I'm asking you to consider is that maybe you've been sent here to get killed. Are you sure the motives of the person who sent you are entirely pure?"

"Us get killed?" Sword Guy spluttered at me for being so ridiculous. "When it's five against one?"

"It's two against one now, just in case you missed the part where I killed three of you. Maybe the person who sent you knew it would happen like that."

"Aenghus Óg would never do that to us!" Spear Guy exclaimed, and my suspicions were confirmed. I had a name now, and that name had been chasing me for two millennia. "We're his own blood!"

"Aenghus Óg tricked his own father out of his home. What does your kinship matter to the likes of him? Look, I've been here before, guys, and you haven't. The Celtic god of love loves nothing so much as himself. He'd never waste his time or risk his magnificent person on a scouting trip, so he sends a tiny little band of disposable offspring every time he thinks he's found me. If they ever come back, he knows it wasn't really me, see?"

Understanding began to dawn on their faces and they crouched into defensive stances, but it was much too late for them and they weren't looking in the right direction.

The bars along the wall of my shop had melted silently apart behind them and morphed into jaws of sharp iron teeth. The giant black maw reached out for them and snapped closed, scissoring through the faeries' flesh as if it were cottage cheese, and then they were inhaled like Jell-O, with time only for a startled, aborted scream. Their weapons clattered to the ground, all glamour gone, and then the iron mouth melted back into its wonted shape as a series of bars, after gracing me with a brief, satisfied grin.

I got a message from the iron elemental before it faded away, in the short bursts of emotions and imagery that they use for language: //Druid calls / Faeries await / Delicious / Gratitude//